...mayne was fascinated with Greek ... that ... ...
... and adventure. That p... ... ... orical
...nture, weaving fictional characters into real-life
...istory dramas, is the driving force behind her writing.
Her childhood holidays were spent in Cornwall and she
still makes regular pilgrimages to the land whose beauty
and atmospheric moods have always haunted her.
Married with two children, Kate now lives in Sussex.

To find out more about Kate Tremayne's Loveday novels,
see her website www.katetremayne.com or read her blog
at http://thelovedaybooks.blogspot.com

LIBRARIES NI
WITHDRAWN FROM STOCK

By Kate Tremayne

Adam Loveday
The Loveday Fortunes
The Loveday Trials
The Loveday Scandals
The Loveday Honour
The Loveday Pride
The Loveday Loyalty
The Loveday Revenge
The Loveday Secrets
The Loveday Conspiracy

Kate Tremayne

The LOVEDAY CONSPIRACY

HEADLINE PUBLISHING GROUP
An Hachette UK Company
338 Euston Road
London NW1 3BH

www.headline.co.uk
www.hachette.co.uk

headline

Copyright © 2009 Kate Tremayne

The right of Kate Tremayne to be identified as the Author of
the Work has been asserted by her in accordance with the
Copyright, Designs and Patents Act 1988.

First published in 2009 by
HEADLINE PUBLISHING GROUP

First published in paperback in 2009 by
HEADLINE PUBLISHING GROUP

1

Apart from any use permitted under UK copyright law,
this publication may only be reproduced, stored, or transmitted,
in any form, or by any means, with prior permission in writing
of the publishers or, in the case of reprographic production,
in accordance with the terms of licences issued by the
Copyright Licensing Agency.

All characters in this publication are fictitious and any resemblance
to real persons, living or dead, is purely coincidental.

Cataloguing in Publication Data is available from the British Library

ISBN 978 0 7553 4767 4

Typeset in Bembo by Avon DataSet Ltd,
Bidford-on-Avon, Warwickshire

Printed in the UK by CPI Mackays, Chatham, ME5 8TD

Headline's policy is to use papers that are natural, renewable and recyclable
products and made from wood grown in sustainable forests. The logging and
manufacturing processes are expected to conform to the environmental
regulations of the country of origin.

HEADLINE PUBLISHING GROUP

LIBRARIES NI	
C700998601	
RONDO	08/03/2012
F	£ 5.99
CLL	

Moving home has many joys, challenges and the chance to meet new friends. We were especially blessed in our neighbours and fellow novice twitchers Paula and Rob for all the help and laughter.

To my amazing and talented artist husband Chris who makes all things possible and is my constant inspiration.

Acknowledgements

As ever I am indebted to my wonderful agent Teresa Chris and to the dedicated team at Headline: Jane Morpeth, Sherise Hobbs, Jo Stansall, Jane Selley.

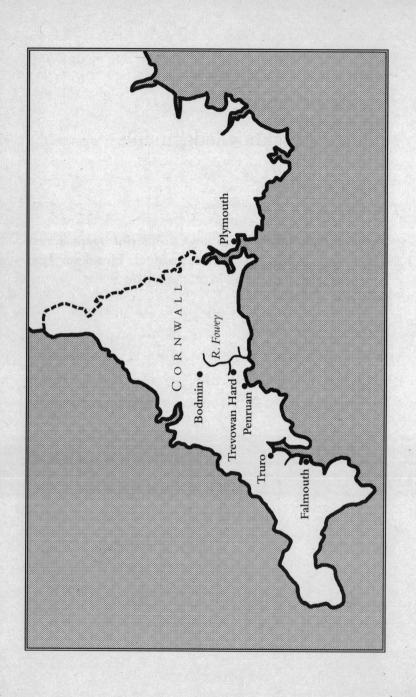

THE LOVEDAY FAMILY

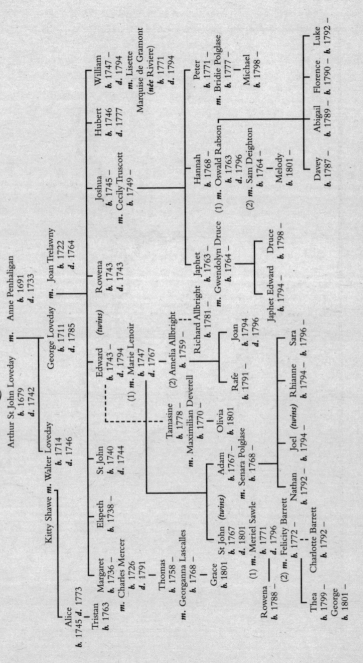

Prologue

A flame snaked across the cracked flagstones, and as it
sizzled along the fuse to the top of the powder keg, the
captain and four of his crew covered their faces with their
arms. Each gulped a lungful of air, their bodies braced.
There was a blast of heat. Then orange flames momentarily lit the dungeon. The impact of the explosion flung
the men back against the wall, scalding the breath from
their bodies. A shower of debris and dust billowed around
them, stinging their throats and nostrils. With hearts
pounding louder than a blacksmith's anvil, they waited,
peering through the clearing smoke. The thick oak door
hung crookedly on its hinges. Behind it in the black pit
that was the prisoners' cell, cries of terror and coughing
were silenced by a shout.

'We are friends. You have been freed. There is little
time to get away before the garrison will be called out.
Follow us!'

Men staggered out, their features hidden beneath
matted beards and sores. Most wore some degree of naval
attire, which had been reduced to rags. Despite the cold,
all had been stripped of their jackets and boots, the
officers as dishevelled as the deckhands. A few civilians
also emerged, their silk or fine cambric shirts in tatters

around bruised and whip-lashed bodies; the colour of their torn breeches indistinguishable after months of lying on filthy straw and rats' droppings. They were a motley group, weakened by dysentery and starvation rations.

'There is no time to lose,' the captain ordered. He was shocked at their condition. Some seemed barely able to walk. He could not tell if any were wounded or incapacitated by infirmity or age. There were more prisoners than he expected, and it was his duty to save not only the English prisoners of war, but also any Frenchman who faced the guillotine because of his birth. From his hasty inspection some could barely stand and were unlikely to be able to make the short dash through the port to the longboat.

'God praise you!' Voices greeted them.

'Save your breath for what lies ahead,' the captain warned. 'The greatest danger is still to be faced before you are aboard my ship.'

The strongest had pushed their way to the front, and these were given the spare daggers and cudgels the captain's men had been able to carry.

'Help the wounded where you can, but once the fighting starts, it will be every man for himself.' It was not a decision the captain wanted to make, but too much depended on them getting quickly away. If he lost his ship, many more lives would be in peril.

Two of his men helped to support the wounded. The captain, seeing the terrified face of a youth not much older than his own eldest son who was clinging to the wall for support, hooked the lad over his shoulder. With his sword raised, he stepped over the bodies of the two guards, each with his throat cut. Their greatest danger was the steps to the entrance of the lockup. If the sentries came hurtling down them, both prisoners and rescuers would be trapped. They could all die.

The captain breathed easier that no alarm had so far been raised, but the explosion would have alerted the guards on the city walls. They would have only a few minutes to escape, unless his accomplice Monsieur Grande had created a diversion in the town.

Halfway up the steps he smelled the first taint of smoke in the air. As he flung open the door to the courtyard, an orange glow lit the sky behind the quay. The thud of running feet and the sound of voices raised in panic were headed away from them. The fire that had been set was next to the grain store, and if that burned down, the citizens would endure a winter facing starvation.

'Keep to the shadows!' the captain warned the prisoners. He stood at the doorway urging those lagging behind to catch up with the others. He also glanced anxiously along the quay. Lord Grande must not be far behind them. There were only two longboats to row out to their brigantine, and he could not afford to wait long for his accomplice to board. Yet without him the rescue would have failed.

'Hurry, my friend,' he groaned as he sped after the prisoners.

The outcry and frenzy in the town had drawn many of the sailors from the quayside taverns, but there would still be some placed on watch on each vessel. In times of war, every furtive move was regarded as suspicious.

'Halt. Who goes there?' A command was barked out in French. 'Halt or I shoot!'

Up ahead there was the sound of a scuffle and of a shot being fired. The captain could just make out the first of the prisoners climbing down the stone steps of the quay to a longboat. Others were fighting.

This could be disastrous. The captain felt his blood freeze. From out of a tavern a dozen soldiers appeared, half of them carrying muskets. Their officer had raised his sword aloft and was rallying more men to his side.

The captain drew his own pistol and fired at the officer, who went down, shot through an eye socket.

'At them, men! For England and King George!' the captain shouted. He was now in the thick of the skirmish and laying about him with his sword. He was slowed by the weight of the youth, who also hampered his movements.

A volley of musket fire brought down more prisoners, but it would take the soldiers more than a minute to reload, and some of the prisoners charged them, wielding cudgels against muskets now used as clubs.

There was little moonlight, but the glow from the fire not only lit up the sky but was reflected in the water of the harbour. Only fifty yards separated them from the longboat.

'Give me the boy.' A white-haired prisoner took the youth from the captain.

No longer restricted, he was now able to defend the backs of the stragglers. The fight was frantic and those left on the quay were outnumbered. Desperation reignited their failing energy when the stamp of booted feet from the direction of the town signalled reinforcements. But for which side? Had Lord Grande made it to the quay, or was it more French?

There was no way of telling. It was difficult to discern friend from foe, except for those soldiers in French uniform, who made easy targets. Several figures writhed or lay prone on the ground. Two more fell, slain by the captain's sword. The cries of the wounded mixed with the pungent smell of sweat and blood.

One of the prisoners had fallen near the captain, a bayonet having laid open his cheek. A ragged companion hauled the injured man to his feet and half dragged, half supported him to the steps. Still the captain defended their backs, fighting off two men at once. The French had been gaining ground, but fortune held in that no alarm bell had been rung. That would have alerted the fort on the headland and they would have been bombarded by cannon fire when their ship sailed out of the harbour.

There was a splash of oars, warning that the first of the longboats was pulling away. They had only moments to stop the French raising the alarm. 'Show these French dogs how an Englishman fights!' The welcome rallying cry of Lord Grande sounded further along the quay, firing the captain's blood. He defended the top of the steps as his men fled to the longboat. Lord Grande was finally at his side, but he was breathing hard, his face streaked with blood and smoke.

'Go, my friend,' the captain ordered.

There was sweat in his eyes and his sword dripped with blood as he ran through the last of the enemy and followed Lord Grande into the longboat.

There was no time to recover their breath, the oarsmen pulling hard to reach the shelter of the first hull, which would shield them from further fire from the quay. But the muskets had fallen quiet.

A glance back at the town showed several of the storehouses on fire. All available men were needed to fight the blaze. The white shape of Pegasus, the ship's figurehead, reared above their heads and the dark hull of the brigantine rose out of the water. Whilst the men climbed up the rope ladders thrown over the side, the flap of unfurling canvas and the creak of the anchor being raised resounded about them. The ship was already moving by the time the captain swung his long legs on to the deck.

He raised his eyes to the headland, where the dark silhouette of the fort was another danger between them and the open sea . . .

There was a deathly hush.

'And did they escape?' a young voice demanded.

'Of course they did, numbskull,' Nathan Loveday taunted. 'Otherwise Papa would not be telling the story.'

'I knew the captain was you, Papa,' Joel shouted and gave his older brother an indignant shove.

'And Lord Grande? Was that Long Tom, Papa?' Nathan asked.

'Lord Gregory Kilmarthen to you,' laughed Captain Adam Loveday. 'We could not have rescued the English sailors without him.'

'But did the fort fire on *Pegasus*?' Joel persisted. 'How many battles have you fought in her?'

'Those stories are for another night.'

'One more story, Papa. How many times did you fight the French and how many émigrés did you rescue?'

'No more questions, Joel.' His mother stood by the bedroom door. 'You should be asleep by now.'

'Now you heed your mama,' Adam warned. 'Or she might order me to walk the plank for keeping you up so late. Good night.'

When Senara joined him in the drawing room shortly afterwards, he broke through another moment of reverie to smile at her.

'You miss those days, do you not, my love?' Senara always knew what he had been thinking.

'I am older now and have more responsibilities at home.'

'And if this truce with France does not hold, where would your heart lie then?'

He drew her down on to his lap and kissed her. 'My heart is always with you and my family here at Boscabel.'

'Until Long Tom or government duty calls,' she returned, unconvinced but surrendering herself to her husband's fierce embrace.

Chapter One

January 1802

'Dry your tears. Head up, shoulders back and do not look behind you.' Amelia Loveday addressed the occupants of the carriage and squared her own shoulders. As the coach rolled away from the house that had been their family home, she bit the inside of her lip to control its quivering at the uncertainty that lay ahead of them. Her pallor showed her pain and shame at this latest scandal to strike their family. She had vowed that she would be the mainstay of the refugees and now made her voice firm. 'Trevowan is lost to us. But we have a new life and a new future awaiting us. And we will hold up our heads with pride.'

The sunlight shafting through the window deepened the lines around her eyes and she swallowed against the rush of memories: not least her arrival here fifteen years ago as the bride of her second husband, Edward Loveday. She would not give in to the fear that churned in her stomach. Beneath a black bonnet sporting a curling black plume, the shock of recent events had leached the last of the autumn tints from hair that was now snowy white.

She studied her stepdaughter-in-law, the youngest and

latest mistress of Trevowan. Although Felicity was locked in her own silent grief, she sat ramrod straight and was braced against whatever challenge fate now threw at them. Her blond hair and delicate features were hidden behind the veil of her widow's weeds and in her arms she cradled her dispossessed baby son, once heir to the family estate. Felicity had been mistress of Trevowan for only four years, and in that time not only had she produced a son, but also a daughter, born eighteen months earlier. With her ten-year-old daughter, Charlotte Barrett, by her first marriage, and a rebellious and wilful fourteen-year-old stepdaughter, Rowena, as her responsibility, she was the more financially insecure of the two women in the coach. And upon her fell the greatest shame, that her husband St John Loveday had gambled away his inheritance and family home, then shot himself.

Amelia's chin creaked a notch higher. She would not allow her own shame to crush her spirit. Since her marriage to Edward, she had learned to weather scandal and speculation. It had been a shock to learn how unconventionally the Loveday men acted in their role as gentlemen. Outwardly they appeared perfectly respectable as the owners of a large estate and profitable shipyard. Yet beneath this veneer they consorted with smugglers, rogues and privateers. Edward had always held himself above common gossip. Neighbours could tittle-tattle until their voices failed, but he believed in family loyalty, and that had carried him through any adversity.

Such challenges made the weak weaker and the strong stronger, Amelia reminded herself. Dear God, let her remain strong!

The coach turned a bend in the drive and Trevowan was in view through the window. A cloud had passed over the sun, and the natural stonework of the house looked grey and mournful. The tall chimneys and gables stood protective as a citadel on top of the cliff, an edifice to the fierce Loveday pride. Amelia blinked rapidly to dispel a wayward tear. What was done was done. There had been recriminations enough against St John in the last weeks. They solved nothing. He was dead, and if there was eternal life, he was facing the judgement of three generations of men who had been master here before him. In the hundred years since the house had been built, each of his forebears would have laid down his life and withstood any sacrifice to ensure the financial stability of Trevowan. In pursuit of his own selfish pleasure, St John had brought the estate to ruin in less than a decade.

'It is so unjust,' Rowena pouted, her blond brows drawn down in a rebellious scowl. 'I do not want to leave Trevowan. Cousin Tristan said it could remain our home.'

'Where is your loyalty to your father, child?' Amelia rounded on the girl verging on the brink of womanhood. 'Tristan Loveday deliberately set out to ruin him. We will not live on his charity.'

'Aunt Elspeth is,' Rowena glowered, too self-centred to see beyond her own deprivations. 'I do not understand why we have to live in a cottage instead of the comfort and splendour of Trevowan.'

'It is different for Elspeth.' Amelia refused to be drawn further. She did not comprehend her sister-in-law's motives, but Elspeth was too formidable a woman to be swayed in her decision, and was also a law unto herself.

'Amelia, to be fair, Tristan only bought up St John's debts from others.' Felicity's loyalty to her late husband had been sorely tested during the last year of their marriage and she could not conceal her bitterness. 'St

John squandered his inheritance in his own self-gratification. At least Trevowan has remained in the family and not been taken over by strangers.'

'I cannot see the merit in that.' Amelia could no longer contain her anger. 'There was malice behind Tristan's motives. He wanted Trevowan for himself. He never forgave the family for his childhood of poverty and squalor. Yet his grandfather turned his back on Trevowan and took to a life of crime. Walter Loveday was disowned for his misdeeds and was the family's darkest secret. And his ghost has come back to haunt us with a vengeance in the shape of his misbegotten grandson.'

Felicity flinched at the violence of Amelia's outburst, and unable to halt her condemnation, the older woman struck her clenched fists on her knees as her anger continued to burst forth. 'Tristan was born a guttersnipe and now, despite his gentleman's airs, he retains the morality of a ne'er-do-well. I will not be beholden to such a cur. Our circumstances may be greatly straitened, but we will live with dignity and pride.'

'And the price of your moral high ground is to live little better than peasants in a cottage.' Rowena voiced her own hostility. 'Why can I not go and live with Uncle Adam at Boscabel? He said I could.'

A shuddering sigh emerged from beneath Felicity's widow's weeds and she placed a hand to her brow. 'Like your parents, you have no thought for anyone but yourself. Adam has his own family to provide for and a busy shipyard to run.'

'He would not have offered if he had not meant it,' Rowena retaliated.

'Is this move not difficult enough?' Amelia interceded, having regained control of her outrage. 'Let us not quarrel. It would not be right to expect Adam to support us. We will live comfortably enough with only two servants. And you, young miss, think too much of yourself and not enough of others. Your place is with your sister and brother.'

'They are babies!' Rowena remained mutinous. 'I do not want to live with babies and old women.'

The fine cord that girdled Amelia's patience again snapped. 'You will learn respect for your elders and your family and mend your selfish ways. Or do you intend to end up like your mother?'

There was a shocked gasp from Felicity. 'You are too harsh, Amelia.'

'I speak the truth. The woman was selfish and self-seeking. She married St John for his money and encouraged her husband in his extravagance and wastrel ways. She brought humiliation and shame to us all. Is that what you want for Rowena? The girl must learn to curb her wild blood.'

Rowena tossed back the blond curls that tumbled over her shoulders, her eyes flashing with fury. 'I am not Mama. I am a Loveday. I know what that means.'

Felicity held her baby son closer to her chest in a defensive gesture. 'Mayhap Rowena would be better served in Adam's household. She needs a strong man to control her.'

Rowena grinned smugly, sensing triumph. The smirk was quickly wiped from her face as Amelia retaliated. 'The minx can wind any man around her scheming finger, including Adam. Her place is with her sister and baby brother.'

The heated exchange set Felicity's daughter Charlotte crying, and she sat huddled beside Rowena sobbing uncontrollably. Her weeping also set the toddler, Thea, wailing in distress, which added to the tension in the coach. Amelia drew the youngest girl on to her lap and attempted to distract her from her tears.

Felicity battled to stem her own fears as she tried to calm her daughters, and her voice shook. 'Amelia, I think you have said enough. Accepting a new life is not going to be easy for any of us.'

She stifled the tears threatening behind her veil. She was frightened that she had little financial security for herself and the children. It was different for Amelia, who had an income from the rental of London properties that were in trust to her son Richard from her first marriage. With her marriage settlement to Edward she had also safeguarded the money she had inherited from her parents. This money had enabled her to purchase Reskelly Cottage, which was large enough for all the dispossessed women. Amelia had also sold to Adam this coach they were travelling in and the four horses, and had purchased a pony and trap, which was awaiting them at the cottage for their use in the future.

Realising that in her anger towards her husband she was being ungrateful when Amelia had been so generous, Felicity rallied her spirit. Her shoulders straightened and her lips set in a determined line. She had known before her marriage that St John had a reputation for gambling, and a shrewd lawyer had set up a trust fund to provide for Charlotte from the estate of Felicity's first husband. It would provide a modest annual income of one hundred pounds.

Despite her resolve to be strong, a shiver gripped her body, and to regain control of her emotions she kissed the brow of her son. They were not penniless, for fortunately it was only the house and grounds that had been lost in payment of the debts; the family had kept the contents. The furniture that was not required had been sold and the money would ensure that they could live in modest comfort. It would not be easy but it would be bearable. At least they could continue to hold their heads high amongst their own society.

The journey continued in an uneasy silence for the two miles to Reskelly Cottage, which was set on the side of a low hill overlooking Trewenna village. The January sun had disappeared behind Trewenna church and the air carried the chill of winter. As they made their approach, Felicity lifted her veil to view their new home. Half of the front of the limewashed cottage was covered with ivy. It was larger than she had expected, with several windows facing them. Above the slate roof, smoke rose from its three chimneys, proclaiming a welcoming warmth within. Once the building had been two cottages, but the last family who lived there had knocked the two into one larger residence, which, with its five bedrooms, dining room, parlour, kitchen and morning room, made it more than adequate to house the Loveday women and children.

Although their circumstances were much reduced, Jenna Biddick had come with them from Trevowan as their general and nursery maid. There was also another female servant, Edna, who did the cooking and cleaning, and her husband, Mo Merrin, who acted as groom, gardener and general manservant for all the heavier work.

As the family alighted from the carriage, the servants assembled to welcome them. Jenna, in immaculately starched mobcap and apron, dipped a curtsy, not a single dark hair out of place. Mo whipped off his red woollen cap with work-grimed hands and tugged his greasy forelock. He was thickset, with fox-coloured hair and whiskers and a ruddy complexion. He wore a creased smock and breeches. His slouching manner was graceless, though he seemed eager to please. Edna was slight of build, her narrow cheeks spangled with pockmarks, and her thick dark brows joined on the bridge of her beaked nose. Her mobcap was askew and tufts of frizzy hair straggled around her temple and neck. At the approach of the women she wrung her hands in nervous anticipation, as though some calamity was about to befall her. Both the Merrins were in their thirties. They had married last year, but had fallen on hard times when Mo's fishing sloop had capsized and sunk during a November gale. Fortunately he had been rescued, but with the loss of the sloop he had been deprived of his livelihood. Edna, who had always had a fear of the sea, had pleaded with him to take work on the land. Before her marriage she had worked in the kitchen of a tavern in Fowey and was an accomplished cook. The Merrins had a room behind the stables, and Jenna shared a room with Thea and baby George in the attic of the house.

Jenna, plump and hearty, who had served the family for twenty years, came forward to take the sleeping baby from Felicity. 'The furniture has been arranged as you instructed and the bedrooms made ready for you. Edna has prepared a pie and pottage that will restore your spirits and can be served when you are ready to dine.'

'I will examine the rooms first,' Amelia insisted. 'Rowena and Charlotte should go and explore the garden. Through the trees over there it leads down to a stone ford over a stream. That is how the cottage got its name. Reskelly means "ford by the grove".'

'I have no wish to explore a boring garden.' Rowena tilted her nose in the air. 'It is so childish. I shall walk down to the village.'

'Then take Charlotte with you,' Felicity instructed.

Rowena flounced away in the direction of the church.

Her great-uncle Joshua was vicar at Trewenna church and lived in the rectory with his wife Cecily. She was hoping to win her great-aunt and uncle to her side so they would support her wish to live with Uncle Adam at Boscabel. His estate and also the shipyard at Trevowan Hard were only a mile from the village. It was not as though she would never see her half-brother and sister again. Amelia could be so unreasonable at times. Rowena's stride was long and purposeful, forcing Charlotte to run to catch her up.

Amelia linked her arm through that of her daughter-in-law and paused a moment on the threshold to survey the village and its dozen cottages, the whole dominated by the church. 'It will be pleasant to be so close to Joshua and Cecily. I daresay my husband's brother will find us some good works to perform within his parish.'

Felicity watched Jasper Fraddon turn the coach. He tipped his hat in salute to her as he flicked the whip for the two pairs of matched bays to proceed. 'Will you miss your carriage, Amelia? You were never one to ride out.'

'Adam paid me a good price and was insistent that we can use it whenever we wish. However, we have the pony and trap to visit neighbours. What do you think of the cottage?' She forced more enthusiasm than she was feeling into her voice.

'It seems very pleasant. I lived simply in a small house in Falmouth before I married St John. But then there were but the two of us. Now we are six, and that is without your youngest son Rafe, who is away at school. Richard, your eldest, is a man now in the navy; how will he regard the change in our circumstances?'

'Naval life will keep him for long periods of time from our new home. He is of marriageable age and will want his own establishment one day.'

'He is indeed fortunate. But when we are all gathered under one roof, we must take care that we do not step on each other's toes.'

Amelia frowned at any hint of dissension that could lie ahead. 'A home is where the family lives. It is not the bricks and slate and it would be foolish to judge it by its size or style. This will suit us very well, and we have the furnishings, household goods and ornaments from Trevowan.'

The younger woman gasped and put her hand to her mouth. 'My dear Amelia, I did not mean to sound ungrateful. I am indeed moved by your generosity in providing us with a home and independence. I thought you would prefer the comfort of a London house. You still have friends there from your first marriage.'

'I have no love for the noise of the city now. Cornwall is convenient for when Richard docks at Plymouth when he is home from the navy. And Edward would have wanted Rafe to grow up in Cornwall with his half-brother and cousins. But it will be some months before either of my sons joins us. And in the meantime we have our own future to build. No doubt there will be challenging times ahead – but when did a Loveday ever fail to conquer a challenge?'

Chapter Two

A week later, when the new owner arrived to claim Trevowan, he came alone on horseback and without baggage. The day was overcast and traces of the morning mist still lingered to bring a chill dampness to the air and veil the surrounding hills and trees. Even the thin trail of smoke rising from one of the tall chimneys was sluggish and unwelcoming. No housemaids appeared to greet their new master and there was no groom to tend to his horse. The fields were bare of livestock. Obviously the beef herd had been sold, and he could discern no sheep on the far ridge beyond the house where they would normally be grazing.

It was as Tristan Loveday had expected, but it still left a hollow feeling in his gut. Trevowan had become a mausoleum to his forebears and the vibrancy that had pulsated here had fled its proud heritage. It was over a quarter of a century since he had last regarded this as his home, when he had run away in disgrace at the age of fourteen.

He tethered his horse to an iron ring by an old stone mounting-block and noted that in a distant field he could hear men at work. At least the labourers from the tied cottages were about their duties. He saw two men digging out a ditch and a youth driving a pregnant sow back to her sty after foraging in a wood. Behind the cow byre on the top field another two men were loading the soiled straw on to a handcart to spread on the nearest fields. A rhythmic thud proclaimed that another unseen workman was chopping wood.

The estate workers depended on their jobs here to keep a roof over their families' heads and Tristan knew he could rely on their co-operation if not their loyalty. But would he still have the senior servants who would efficiently continue to run the estate? He would not put it past Adam to lure them away to make life more difficult here. Tristan had no experience of land and farm management. Most of his life he had lived in cities and made his money in trade. He did know that a profitable estate needed a bailiff as manager who knew how to get the best from the soil and the men working under him. He had sent word that all tenants and servants would be kept on, but realised that some would prefer to take work from an original family member if it were offered to them. The Lovedays had always treated their workers well and earned their loyalty.

His sharp stare turned upon the house, where the front door was closed but not locked. The sound of his top boots resounded loudly on the black and white marble of the entrance hall and the wooden floors, now bare of carpets, as he walked through the empty house. There was no smell of cooking drifting from the kitchen or any sign of domestic life. The walls showed the marks of mirrors, paintings and placement of furniture, all of which he remembered clearly. Their absence was a shock. Without the furnishings that had given the house so much of its character, the place now felt more like a corpse, the life's blood sapped from its arteries.

Tristan shrugged at such a fanciful notion. An infusion of new blood was about to resurrect it. The furniture had not been part of the debt and held no sentimental value to him. The house and estate that George Loveday, his great-uncle, had been so proud of were what mattered. He did not want to be reminded of his two years spent here as the outcast poor relation, reclaimed from the gutter and barely tolerated. They had not been happy years.

The echo of ghostly laughter, of boys' voices raised in rivalry, memories of men brash in their comfort and sense of place were embedded in these walls. The whispers in his mind continued to mock him. *Interloper! Outcast!*

His chin jutted forward and his head tilted to regard the carved plasterwork of the ceiling. 'No interloper,' he proclaimed. 'No outcast. I am master now!'

'You can call yourself master, but it takes a special man to follow in the footsteps of those who ruled here before you.' A spate of scornful laughter spun him round and he regarded the black-clad figure of an elderly woman standing on the curve of the stairs.

He swept his high-domed beaver hat from his short dark curls and bowed with extravagant mockery. 'Dearest Aunt Elspeth, so you did not fly the nest with the rest of my kin?'

'Apart from the children, they were incomers. I was born here. I always thought it would be where I took my dying breath.' The skin of her face was moulded so finely to her skull that few wrinkles blemished her coun-tenance. There was no spare flesh either upon the slender form, which was clad in a severe mourning gown, and her grey hair was pulled tight in an uncompromising bun. She had never married, and Trevowan had been her home for over six decades. For more than twenty of those years she had ruled the household with a rod of iron, until her widowed brother Edward had married Amelia Allbright.

'I vowed to turn no member of my family from their home,' Tristan replied stiffly.

'And why would they wish to live upon the benevolence of the man who as good as murdered the true master of Trevowan?' Aunt Elspeth never pulled her verbal punches, and those words struck his solar plexus as forcefully as a hammer blow.

He held her accusing stare and shrugged off the insult. It was no less than he expected. 'And God speed to you, dear aunt. You never give quarter in any jousting of words or contest of wills. Our conversations will certain not lack vibrancy.' There was an ironic lift to his brow as he stretched his lips into an insincere smile.

'I am glad you have not lost your caustic repartee.' There was a gleam of appreciation in her stern eyes.

'Since you are here, you clearly do not feel that I am an unworthy wretch who has brought shame and ruin to our kin. Should I be grateful?' he challenged.

'I know you for what you are.'

The old woman's capacity for a tongue-lashing had not diminished since he had last faced her wrath. Despite all his wealth and success, it was still within her power to mentally reduce him to the wayward child who was tolerated upon sufferance.

She leaned heavily upon a silver-topped ebony walking cane as she slowly descended the stairs. Over the top of her pince-nez her stare swept across his caped greatcoat, pausing a moment upon the large emerald stock pin, the cost of which would have kept her horses in feed for several years; then travelled over his moleskin breeches and the Italian leather of his boots, all made in the very latest mode and of the finest quality by his London tailor and bootmaker.

'Fine clothes do not always a gentleman make,' she clipped out.

Her cool gaze lifted to his face, noting the ebony eyes under fine arched brows, the Roman nose and firm cleft chin. 'Except for that chin, you have the Loveday looks and now sport fine feathers. You repaid our kindness with deceit and treachery. Your parents, not us, were responsible for you being born in the gutter. You showed your cowardice by running away instead of defending yourself. No man of honour would have so struck the hand that fed him by seeking our ruin.'

Anger heated his blood, but he had long ago learned the peril of losing his temper. He was no longer the child to be criticised and condemned.

'I more than repaid my debts to the Lovedays,' he returned with a patronising smile. 'The merchant ship I commissioned to be built saved the family yard from ruin.'

'And your vengeance brought my nephew to take his own life when you used deceit and trickery to steal our home.'

The smile did not waver as he parried the barbs of her censure. 'If that is what you believe, why are you still here, old woman? Or did they abandon you to my charity so you could be their spy?'

Elspeth drew herself to her full height, and over the top of her pince-nez her forthright glare fixed him with her scorn. 'You have a twisted view of the world. St John is dead because of your vengeance. Did you hate us so much?'

His full lips parted as he unleashed his mockery. 'A weak man who was a wastrel took his own life rather than face the consequences of his failings. I have nothing to answer to any man for. Had I not bought up his debts, the banks and his creditors would have foreclosed on his loans months ago.'

Their gazes locked, assessing and accusing. To his surprise, his aunt gave a slight nod of acceptance.

'St John was all that and more,' she commented. 'But your conduct will be judged by many as profiting from your family's misfortune. Not a good way to establish your reputation in the county.' Her expression softened and her tone changed to resignation. 'In truth you have little to thank us for. We all should have been more understanding. You were judged on the circumstances in which you were found – an orphan surviving in the gutter in the most squalid part of the city. You were as wild as a moorland colt and should have been brought more gently to the saddle. We expected too much from you and I did not have the maternal instincts that you deserved.'

With a start, Tristan realised that this was Elspeth's way of apologising, but he continued to be suspicious of her motives.

Her manner remained uncompromising as she proceeded. 'If, as St John confessed, you were innocent of the crimes of which my father believed you guilty – consorting with wreckers, who are the scourge of our coast - you should have stood up for yourself. I thought you would have fought tooth and nail for your right to be accepted.'

'I knew when I was beaten.' His obsidian eyes hardened. 'Your father made it clear that he expected me to go the same way as my grandfather – a rogue and a thief. He assumed I must be guilty of working with the wreckers that night, when in truth it was his precious heir. My protestations of innocence would have fallen on already condemning ears.'

The old woman had the grace to look shamefaced. 'My father did not want reminders of the wild blood that could be a curse in our family.'

Tristan still had come no closer to learning why his aunt was here. His stare was belligerent. 'Have you alone chosen to continue to live at Trevowan?'

'I am too old to wish to be cast from my home.'

Tristan inclined his head. 'Where are the other estimable ladies and their brood residing? At Boscabel?'

'Adam offered them a home, but they have taken a cottage on the edge of Trewenna village.'

'And you did not wish to accompany them?' he repeated with cold calculation.

'I do not relinquish my right without a fight.' The gauntlet was thrown down.

He gave a slow, lopsided smile. 'I have no intention of fighting you, Aunt Elspeth. Yet what does my illustrious cousin Adam say about your defection, or is it as I speculated earlier: would they use you as their spy in my camp?'

When she limped down the remaining stairs, Tristan noted that the knuckles gripping her cane were white from her inner turmoil and pain. Even so, her tone lost none of its scorn. 'I weary of the rivalry that for too long has threatened to tear my family apart. Whilst I live at Trevowan there is a means to build bridges. A family feud is the last thing we need.'

'Noble sentiments, but Adam has made it clear he regards me as the cuckoo in the nest. He will never rest whilst I am master here.'

She limped towards the winter parlour, looking back over her shoulder to ensure that he followed her. 'Are you staying to dine? The servants were allowed to make their own choice as to the master they served. Sarah Nance has cooked my meals, and her daughter Kitty acts as maid. My bedchamber and adjoining parlour are furnished, as is the winter parlour for my comfort. Adam is proud and he is angry at his twin's death. I take no sides. I want this as my home and place my trust in you that you will allow me to keep at least two of my mares.'

He followed his aunt and saw that a fire had been lit in the winter parlour and that it was furnished with a sofa, two armchairs, a table and four dining chairs. The Chinese wallpaper with its peacocks was as he remembered, but the blue window hangings and red and blue carpet were more recent. A decanter and glasses sat on a side cupboard.

'You are welcome to keep all your mares. Though I notice that your leg seems to pain you. Are you still able to ride?'

'It is an old hunting accident.' She dismissed her injury as unimportant. 'The day I give up my horses is the day they nail down my coffin.'

Tristan admired her courage, for the lines of years of pain were etched around her mouth and eyes. She would never admit to any frailty or weakness. He asked, 'Are there grooms to tend them? The place looks deserted.'

'The elder Tonkin boy is acting as stable-lad. Jasper Fraddon trained him well.' She sat by the fire and gestured for Tristan to be seated opposite her.

He continued to stand. Her information was not unexpected. 'New servants will be engaged and a housekeeper employed. I will not be taking up residence here for some time.'

Elspeth raised a questioning brow, and when he did not elaborate further, she added, 'Then all the better that a Loveday remains in residence. The work on the estate must continue if you wish for a harvest next summer. I will act as housekeeper for as long as you have need of my services.' At his nod of acceptance, she went on, 'It would also be more practical and less of a burden upon your finances if my possessions were moved to the Dower House.'

He paced the room, head bent and his hands clasped behind his back. When he next regarded her, he was frowning. 'If you live here, you are my responsibility. It disturbs me that you will be alone apart from the servants. You are used to your family around you.'

'They have always been a boisterous brood, which can be wearisome at times. I am content to keep my own company and I will have my mares.' She guarded her expression. Just as she thought she had won her place here, his change of manner filled her with apprehension.

The rigid set of his body was uncompromising. During his time here as a child, Elspeth had certainly shown more love and tenderness towards her horses than to her young charges. Curtly he informed her, 'I would be failing in my duty, as I am sure my cousin would be the first to remind me, if your safety was in question.'

Her head shot up and she leaned on her cane, pushing herself upright to regard him. 'It is inconceivable that I would be at any risk within my own family home.' Anger blazed from her eyes and her frail figure trembled with outrage. 'A maid of all work will be ample for my needs at the Dower House and she will live in. I assume Dick Nance, the present gamekeeper, will continue to patrol the grounds of a night as a safeguard against poachers. I had also intended to keep a dog both as a companion and to deter intruders. Squire Penwithick has a two-year-old deerhound bitch that injured her leg and is no longer able to hunt. She will suit me very well. Does that satisfy you?'

He considered her words for a long moment and with each second her heart raced faster, fearing his rejection. It made her more defensive, and in a burst of indignation she brandished her walking cane.

'The estate workers are loyal to me. They would defend me with their lives, and I am no cowering nincompoop to lie shaking in my bed at the first sound of a floorboard creaking. My father taught me how to shoot a pistol. I am not afraid to use it on anyone so reckless as to attempt to break into my home.'

A reluctant grin lifted the corner of his mouth. 'I do not doubt that you are a formidable adversary, but with respect, Aunt, you are no longer young, and that makes you vulnerable. Are you sure you would not be happier living with Adam? I will not be residing here for many months, as I have several business interests to attend upon before I make my home in Cornwall.'

Her stare was forthright and unwavering. 'As an old woman, I demand the right to die in my family home.'

'Very well. I would be happier if you lived in the Dower House until I take up residence. I will inform you of any work to be carried out to the house and when the new furniture and furnishings are to arrive. Also a new gardener will be employed who will landscape the grounds. I expect no interference with any of the work I instruct to be carried out.'

Her lips clamped shut. She had not expected changes to be made. Trevowan was a comfortable home set in pleasant surroundings.

'I daresay you will wish to put your own seal upon the property,' she snapped. 'Though in my opinion, restrained elegance shows a man's breeding more potently than the lavish extravagance of a parvenu.'

His eyes narrowed. She had clearly hit a nerve. He flung back with venom, 'I will endeavour not to let the guttersnipe indulge in a gaudy and crass display of wealth and bad taste.'

She permitted her lips to stretch into a smile. She had won her battle to stay, and though praise was not something she lavished lightly, she knew when it was due. 'Despite all that has happened, I am pleased that you have prospered over the years. For what it is worth, my father died regretting that he had driven you away. We last heard after St John's funeral that you were staying in Truro. Will you join me to dine? And do you wish a bed made up?'

'I will dine with you after I have spent an hour or so with the servants and tenants. And I shall inspect the house before I leave to ascertain its requirements. But I have taken a room at an inn for this evening in Launceston and will take the post-chaise to London tomorrow to attend to business matters.' He bowed curtly and marched from the room.

Elspeth sat back in her chair and let out a shaky breath. The encounter had taken more out of her than she had expected. She believed that a grudging respect had formed between herself and the new master of Trevowan.

Tristan walked through the upstairs rooms, where an occasional bed or heavy chest or table had been left and some of the faded hangings remained at windows of little-used chambers. The master bedroom still contained the ornate canopied bed, a new addition since his great-uncle's day. He doubted it was to Adam's taste, and neither was it to his, and it was too large to be of use to the women in a cottage. He would have it moved to a guest room.

As he descended the sweeping staircase to the hall, a man appeared from the servants' quarters at the rear of the house. From his sturdy brown breeches and jacket Tristan guessed he was the overseer or manager. A pimply youth hung back behind him.

'Mr Loveday.' The thickset, ruddy-faced man bowed respectfully. 'Isaac Nance at your service, sir. We did not know when to expect you. Winnie Fraddon, who was the cook, and her husband Jasper, the head groom, have left to work at Boscabel for Captain Loveday, and one of the maids went with the womenfolk to Trewenna.' He turned to the youth. 'This is my youngest lad, Jeb. My eldest, Dick, be gamekeeper but he be helping out in the turnip field, which they be harvesting. We'll need an old hack purchased, though, if you want the crop taken to market.'

'All that will be dealt with. As will other necessary purchases and procurement of servants. You would serve me well by writing a list. My visit is short, Nance. Send your lad to summon what servants there are to the stables. We will talk as I inspect the grounds. Miss Elspeth will be my eyes and voice in my absence.'

As soon as they set foot outside, Tristan said without preamble, 'How do the tenants and families in the tied cottages view the present changes? I want honesty, Nance, not some polite answer you think I want to hear.'

The bailiff cleared his throat, obviously uncomfortable at being so forthright. 'The truth be they were shocked at first, especially with the master dying so tragically. The tenant farmers are the same families as when you visited here as a youth, and of course my family, the Tonkins and the Holmans are in the tied cottages and work on the estate. Cap'n Loveday gave instructions for work to continue as normal until we received instructions from you.'

Tristan studied the man who had been newly employed as manager when he was here as a child. Isaac Nance coloured under Tristan's scrutiny and scratched the two days' growth of stubble on his chin. George Loveday in his time would never have countenanced his overseer being unshaven.

Tristan was sharp in his warning. 'I do not expect any standards of work to fall, even though there is mourning for my late cousin. The estate fell heavily into debt under his management. I expect it to prosper, and that will mean changes. But I have a large purse where necessary expenditure is needed. I also demand high standards. There is a certain amount of refurbishment needed to the house, and during this time I trust your good wife will provide cooked meals for the workmen, who will sleep in the grooms' quarters in the stables. I will not be in residence for some time.'

They had walked to the nearest paddock, and Tristan stopped and surveyed the fields. The mist had disappeared but the clouds were low and oppressive; a light drizzle formed droplets in his hair and settled on the fine wool of his greatcoat. 'My great-uncle always said that this was good soil, and I expect high yields. The land was wasted on a beef herd. My cousin was too indolent. Employ more labourers; there are enough men out of work from the closure of the mines. I want six fields put to the plough this year. The price of corn is high, since the war with France. Where the ground is less productive on the high slopes, we will graze it with sheep. How many do you suggest?'

Nance rubbed his chin, taking time to weigh up his answer. Too many suggestions he had made in the past to

St John had been disregarded. 'In the old days we had as many as two hundred. I'd say eighty to a hundred would be a good number to start with, and of course a full-time shepherd.'

'We will start with a hundred. There was a time in my great-grandfather's day when the flock at Trevowan yielded good-quality fleeces. That will happen again. The old shepherd's hut will need repairing, and I leave you to employ a hard-working man.'

Since the men and families were coming in from the cottages and the fields, Tristan returned to the stables. An hour later he departed Trevowan leaving a stunned group of tenants under no illusion as to what was expected of them and the estate in the future.

Dick Nance whistled under his breath. 'Don't know what Cap'n Loveday will say about all these changes.'

His father shot him a warning glare. 'What Cap'n Loveday says is none of our concern. I doubt they will dare call the new master guttersnipe to his face once he be in charge here. And unless I miss my guess, Cap'n Adam Loveday has met his match in that cousin of his.'

Chapter Three

The next morning, a few miles from Trevowan, the golden shards of the rising sun burned brightly in the sky as the giant orb appeared above the eastern tor. The wind-bent trees were stunted and twisted silhouettes on the horizon as the first skylark rose from its nest, its pure notes interspersed by the ring of steel pounding relentlessly upon steel. An early mist continued to swirl around the top boots of the two men facing each other in a macabre ritual that would lead to a momentary lowering of a guard and the delivery of a death thrust.

Neither opponent felt the chill breeze that blew in from the coast; their linen shirts were damp from the sweat of their exertion and clung to their shoulders and arms. Their muscles were honed from hours of practice and an uncompromising need to succeed, whether within their work or during combat. They were evenly matched, neither prepared to give ground or cede mercy. The next frenzied clash of blades sent curious rabbits scurrying back into their burrows, and two pairs of boxing hares broke apart to speed towards the safety of their forms.

The mournful coo of a wood pigeon carried on the wind. The sound of laboured breathing and the breath misting before the duellists' set features were testimony to the rigours of their battle. Their hair was streaked in dark tendrils to their temples, and eyes sharp as machetes were riveted upon their adversary. They broke apart and circled, teeth clenched as they drew respite breaths. The lull was momentary and the air crackled with menace and lethal intent. Each stood with his knees bent and his free hand resting upon his hip, weapon poised with perfect balance as he assessed his opponent and his next jab and counterattack. Then, with the speed of striking hawks, both men lunged, parried and riposted with deadly precision. When steel sliced through the linen of a full sleeve, a drop of scarlet blood smeared the blade.

'Concede, blood is drawn!' the older of the two declared.

'A paltry graze of no significance.'

'Would you rather I skewered your gizzard?'

''Twas but a lucky strike!' the younger, slightly leaner man rapped out with scorn. 'Your strength fails. Your prime is past. You are as blown as a quarry nag.'

The piercing intensity of the hazel gaze narrowed, a warning many a lesser adversary had not heeded before he received a mortal blow. Fashionably shorn straight hair framed the swarthy complexion, and despite the deep breaths being drawn into his lungs, he remained as dangerous as a cobra rearing up from its coils. 'Not so blown that you will leave this field to brag of your success.'

His antagonist merely laughed, and with the litheness of a panther leapt aside, his own blade arcing to skim past the guard and slice through the folds of a stock. A gold pin fell to the ground to be trampled underfoot and lost.

'You are fast, but not fast enough.' The swarthy complexion was cast into shadow as the older man circled, placing his back to the sun. His white teeth flashed in a crooked smile, whilst his eyes remained predatory, preparing for the deft flick of the wrist that had disarmed many an adversary. Then his palm jarred from the impact of the basket-weave sword hilts locking together. As both men disengaged and sidestepped, the edge of his sword nicked his opponent's ear lobe and a dark lock of hair fluttered to the grass.

Blood mingled with the sweat that ran down the tendons of the younger man's neck as he taunted, 'You'll pay for that, old man. I've spared you until now.'

'And you will eat your words, insolent whelp.'

Sweat streaked both their faces but neither man was prepared to give any quarter. From the height of the sun and the growing weariness in his aching muscles, the older man guessed that they had been fighting for the best part of a quarter-hour without pause. He must indeed be turning into a greybeard, for not so many years ago his sword would have been pressed against an opponent's heart within the pace of a half-dozen parries. A duel fought on rough ground was a far cry from an hour's sword practice in the comfort of a long gallery. His lungs, which were struggling to regain their breath, now felt that they had been scalded by hot pitch. His survival instincts kicked in at the intensity of the next cut, thrust and parry and briefly he regained supremacy. Then, as he sidestepped, his foot caught in a tussock. The glint of sun bouncing off steel momentarily blinded him, and he stumbled. Before he could recover, the cold edge of his opponent's sword point pricked the skin of his throat.

'Do you now concede, or will your blood run upon this ancient moor?' There was no mercy in the avenging gaze that glinted along the metal of the blade.

For a long moment, whilst every muscle strained with

the tension of the battle, each man assessed the other for signs of weakness, then in an instant the atmosphere changed. One combatant winked and the other grinned.

'I concede, but I was careless to stumble. It showed my lack of practice. But do not let this triumph go to your head, cousin. I will have my revenge upon you next time.' Japhet Loveday held his hands up in supplication. 'And I will have the devil's own work explaining this gouge on my neck to my dear wife. Gwen will suspect I have succumbed to a fit of palsy whilst shaving.'

Adam Loveday lowered his sword and rubbed his own ear lobe below a gold earring. His long hair was tied back in a black ribbon and the fine linen of his shirt clung uncomfortably to his skin. 'Heavens knows what Senara will make of yet another cut. There are only so many accidents I can blame on work in the shipyard.'

'Yet we are agreed they must be shielded from knowledge of our practice, cousin?' Japhet insisted.

'We both have sworn enemies who we have vowed to call to account for their treachery against us.'

Japhet nodded. 'When the time is right, they will both pay. Until then, let our wives believe that we are industrious about our work when we leave our beds at such untimely hours for sword practice.'

Adam straightened his waistcoat and shrugged into his jacket before picking up the pint flagon of cider that he had brought with him. He removed the stopper and drank deeply before passing it to his cousin.

Japhet pulled on his own jacket and greatcoat and wiped the sweat from his face with a kerchief before taking the flagon. 'I have waited many years to bring to justice the man who laid false evidence against me so that I was banished from this land and my reputation destroyed.'

'Do you plan to kill Sir Pettigrew Osgood?' Adam asked, although he believed the answer was a foregone conclusion. The Loveday pride would never countenance such treachery without demanding retribution.

'That would be too easy. Society and custom has sadly moved on from such barbaric revenge. But Osgood will pay for his treachery.' Japhet took a long drink of cider before he returned the challenge. 'And what of our cousin, who has so grievously wronged you?'

Adam ran a kerchief over his sword, then placed the blade in his scabbard and tied it behind his saddle. It was some moments before he replied, for the subject was one he had considered for many weeks. 'Although I hold Tristan Loveday responsible for my twin's death, I will not avenge St John by killing our cousin. His actions were devious and underhand, but he acted within the law. I will show the world the blackguard for what he is. A life for a life destroys the killer as well as the victim, but I do not intend that Tristan will enjoy the fruit of his treachery.'

The two men's eyes locked in silent conspiracy. They had made their vows to stand side by side to overcome their enemies. The Lovedays were again united, loyalty to their own their greatest strength. In the past it had made them invincible. Yet this time their enemy was also one of their kin.

Adam mounted his horse and waited until Japhet swung into the saddle of the three-year-old colt. The horse was impatient to continue its morning gallop and exercise. Adam studied the bay appreciatively. Like all the horses from his cousin's stable, it was a fine thoroughbred.

'When is your first race?'

'Next month at a local meeting. I've entered three races, with two three-year-old mares and a two-year-old colt. I need at least two of them to be placed, if not actually to win, to make my mark as a breeder. Too many in the sport will be expecting me to fail.'

'And it will give you great pleasure to prove them wrong.' Adam grinned. 'How is the new trainer's performance at Tor Farm? Is he all you had hoped?'

'He's something of a rough diamond but he seems to have a way with the horses that gets the best from them. Though his reputation is not untarnished from some dealings he had in his past, and the horse world is a tight fraternity.' Japhet gave an ironic laugh. 'Not that I would condemn a man whose reputation is not all it should be. I judge by results. We will need to produce some spectacular finishes to overcome the prejudices that both our reputations bring to the sport. There must be no hint of any scandal or underhand exploits, or that will be the end of my future as a horse breeder of any note.'

'Your Arab stallion Emir Hassan will produce top-class foals. They will not be able to ignore you.'

Japhet shrugged. 'That is some years in the future. I have my own reputation to redeem first. Many will remember that I was transported for highway robbery before they recall that I was pardoned after the convict ship sailed for Sydney Cove. But that is what makes the challenge all the more interesting. I will breed a future Derby winner and they will all choke on their prejudice.'

Adam frowned. 'And we both have to live with the scandal surrounding St John's death and our loss of Trevowan. Many will see all our kin as tarred with the same wastrel's brush. I have already had one customer asking to look at the shipyard's books to confirm that it is free of debt before they agree to pay the first instalment on their ship.'

'It is not the scandal that troubles you,' Japhet said

heavily. 'We have weathered many such in the past. It is losing Trevowan, is it not? I fear that was inevitable once St John allowed his fever for gaming to control his life. At least it is not entirely lost whilst a member of our family is still its master. Whatever you think of Tristan, he is still a Loveday. He shares our great-grandfather's blood. And if the stories are true, Arthur St John Loveday was by far the greatest and most ruthless rogue of us all. As children we revelled in tales of his exploits.'

Adam remained tense, his voice edgy. 'Yet many people today would consider that Great-Grandfather lived in a less civilised age, when buccaneers ruled the waves and the gentry still governed their land like medieval barons. They expect more from today's generation.'

Japhet snorted. 'Ah, those were the days, dear boy. Society and custom have sadly moved on. But beneath its prim and proper air, every family has its skeletons and dark secrets.'

As Adam Loveday rode to the shipyard, he was a man mentally at war with himself. He prided himself on his fairness and lack of hypocrisy and lived by the family code of loyalty. But loyalty, as he had recently found to his cost, could be a two-headed coin.

A cold and deadly rage consumed him. He could not sleep and neither could he concentrate on his work. Every hour of every day his anger was relentless, grinding like millstones in a remorseless ache. He was angry with his twin for gambling away his inheritance. He was furious that St John had been too proud and stubborn to come to him for help, and he was outraged that his brother had then taken his own life. For as long as Adam could remember, he had been at loggerheads with his twin. Their childhood fights had turned to youthful rivalries that had continued throughout their adulthood. Too often St John had goaded him with his gloating that he was the heir, until Adam lost control of his temper. How could his brother have been so reckless and foolish – so self-centred? Adam did not see his death as taking the only honourable course. It was the coward's way, leaving his family to bear the shame of his disgrace. Even so, St John's life had been tragically short.

Adam closed his eyes against a rush of pain. His twin may have been the bane of his life, and on countless occasions he could cheerfully have throttled him for his selfishness. Yet now he was dead there was a void that could not be filled. Strangely, Adam felt incomplete, and his grief was sharper than when he had mourned his father.

All that anger was now channelled upon the man he believed responsible for his twin's death. And that was the problem. For over twenty years he had been led to believe that Tristan had betrayed his family's trust. Yet on his brother's death Tristan had been vindicated by St John's confession. His twin, not Tristan, had been the one who had brought dishonour to their name. St John had lied and deliberately turned the family against their kin rather than face the consequences of his own wicked actions on the night of the shipwreck.

Undeniably, Tristan had been wronged. Was it any wonder that he had carried a grievous hatred against his family, and sworn to return and prove that he was not only their equal but also the better man?

But the boy brought up in the gutter had reverted to type in his revenge. He was as slippery as a nest of serpents and as cunning as a pack of wild dogs. Adam could not regard him as kin. He was the enemy. The interloper. The outcast who had stolen by foul treachery the family home and as good as murdered St John.

That Tristan had probably saved St John from public disgrace by buying up all his debts, Adam refused to accept. The fact that he had also commissioned a merchant ship to be built in the shipyard, which had saved the family business from ruin, also added to Adam's anger. He should be grateful, but how could he feel gratitude when Tristan had caused so much pain and suffering to those Adam loved, and now lorded it as master of Trevowan?

Chapter Four

Japhet was also deep in thought as he returned to Tor Farm. He never did anything without a purpose, and the sword practice was necessary if he was to bring to account the blackguard who had used bribery and treachery to ensure he was transported before he could receive his pardon. Following his return to England, after six years away from its shores, Japhet had expected to feel more at peace with himself. The years of transportation, though served not without their scars, had provided him with a far greater fortune than he could have achieved in England within the same time. He was now independently wealthy, and no one could say that he had achieved his success built upon his wife's fortune. He had a home and property to enable him to obtain his dream of breeding thoroughbred racehorses. He had a wife he adored and two fine sons.

He shifted in the saddle as the familiar frustration blazed through him. The sense of fulfilment and peace he had expected on his homecoming continued to evade him. His past could not so easily be put to rest. He cared not about his reputation as a womaniser and rakehell, for those ways were behind him and could no longer give him pleasure or satisfaction. What gnawed at him was that he had spent a year in Newgate and been transported not because of a crime he had committed, but because of the jealousy of one man who had laid false witness against him. That betrayal had been compounded when on the brink of Japhet receiving his pardon that knave had bribed the turnkeys to drug him and take him on board a ship bound for New South Wales an hour before it sailed.

At the memory of those black days, Japhet's eyes crinkled against the glare of the sun now high above the trees. It was the cowardice of Osgood's revenge that enraged Japhet, and his fury was blistering in its intensity. The need to call the other man to account for his treachery almost destroyed his resolution to bide his time.

In a burst of outrage, his hands tightened over the reins, causing the colt to prance sideways. Japhet brought it quickly under control and forced his body to relax, but a growing need to confront Osgood continued to flay him. If he had not promised Gwendolyn that his priority on his return was to establish the stud farm and secure the financial future of his family, he would have pursued Osgood to the ends of the earth if necessary.

But he would never break his word to Gwendolyn. With thoughts of revenge burning through his mind, he knew his mood would not escape the notice of his wife. To delay his return he turned his horse toward Polruggan. Since his return, he had spent more time with Adam than with Peter. Throughout his exile he had regretted the rift between himself and his younger brother. The eight-year gap in their ages and the difference in their personalities had not made them close in his youth and early manhood. He had also found it hard to stomach his brother's piety and sermons. To be fair to Peter, Japhet had seen the change in him since his marriage, and with a twinge of guilt that he had spent an hour of this day with Adam, he was determined to build more bridges with his sibling.

As he neared the parsonage he was surprised to hear childish squeals of delight. He dismounted and tethered his mare to a fence post before walking towards the garden at the side of the house. A maid was startled in sweeping the path and bobbed a hasty curtsy. Japhet put his finger to his lips to stop her announcing his arrival to her master. He grinned as he came upon Peter, demurely dressed in clerical black and Geneva bands, chasing his son round a mulberry tree. Michael was laughing and running as fast as his short legs would allow him. Bridie, the boy's mother, was also joining in the game, though she was holding a red muffler in her hands, clearly intent upon putting it around her son's neck against the chill of the morning.

Both parents swooped down on their son, but Michael giggled hard as he ducked through his father's legs and escaped. The boy's cheeks were red from his exertions. Bridie and Peter collided. Unaware of Japhet's presence. Peter grabbed his wife and started to tickle her. She was laughing hard and slapping at his hands to stop his teasing whilst Michael ran excitedly around his parents.

Japhet grinned at the happy family scene. This was a glimpse of the youth Peter, before piety and religious fervour had stripped him of his sense of humour and adventure.

Enjoying the merriment, he frowned when Michael tripped and started coughing.

Immediately the loving family atmosphere was broken and the couple drew apart. Peter scooped Michael into his arms.

'Take him inside, my love.' Bridie was fussing and anxious. The coughing had turned to a rasping in the boy's chest. 'We should not have got him so excited.'

'Children are tougher than you think,' Japhet said, from his experience of two strong, rough-and-tumble sons.

Bridie took Michael from her husband. She smiled a greeting at Japhet, saying, 'Michael has a weak chest. We cannot be too careful.'

He thought she fussed too much, but then supposed that as the boy was an only child that was natural for a woman. Michael continued to cough as he was taken inside, and Peter looked worried. 'He has had that cough all winter. It seems worse today.' He turned his attention to Japhet. 'What brings you to Polruggan, brother?'

'With my work at the stud, I feel I have neglected you of late. I had hoped that an early visit would catch you before you were consumed by your parochial duties.'

'You are welcome, brother.' Peter grinned. Another bout of coughing from within the parsonage brought a return of his troubled look. 'I should send for Dr Yeo. It will put Bridie's mind at rest. I have to leave for Truro in an hour for a visit to the bishop. I will be away a couple of nights.'

'I will not keep you. Gwen will wish to visit Bridie while you are away.'

The short visit had brought a return to Japhet's good humour. It amused him how Peter and Bridie cosseted Michael, though the boy was a delightful child. His own sons had been toughened by their years in Australia and had loved the wild and often hard existence they had lived. England now provided them with a life of ease compared to those days.

As he approached Tor Farm, he contemplated the changes he had already effected here. He noted that the doors to the newly built stables stood open and the mares and colts were grazing in the paddocks. One horse held his attention more than the others. The proud black head of Emir Hassan sniffed the air at Japhet's approach. His flowing tail flicked up and his muscles rippled as he set off across the field at a canter towards his master. Japhet dismounted to stroke the stallion's head. The Arab snickered, his eyes showing white at the corners. Blue and purple lights glinted along his sleek coat as he snorted and reared before turning to gallop around the perimeter of the fence.

The encounter filled Japhet with pride. The magnificent stallion was the future of his breeding stable. He walked his mount towards the yard and flung the reins at a young groom. Gwendolyn came out of the house and stood waiting for him. There was a look on her lovely face that warned him she had seen through his ruse. He should have known that nothing missed his wife's concerned eye.

'Another dawn ride, husband? The fifth in three weeks.'

'I could not sleep. The horses need their exercise.'

'With a sword strapped to your saddle?' Her colour was high as she voiced her anger. Her features were striking rather than beautiful, but Japhet had known many beautiful women who had left his heart cold. Gwen had won his love by her courage and her faith that the character of a rogue and reprobate he showed to the world masked more noble sentiments beneath. That faith had saved him in his darkest hours and given him the strength to prove that she was right. Though there were times when he wished his wife did not know him so well. There was resignation in her eyes as she continued. 'Are these meetings with Adam? I can guess their purpose.'

He shrugged and gave a reassuring grin. 'Adam and I always practised our swordplay in the old days. It is a sport we both enjoy.'

'And I doubt either of you is doing this for old times' sake. You promised me you would not pursue Osgood.' She was trembling in her distress.

Japhet took his wife into his arms. 'I would not break my word to you, Gwen.'

She pulled back from him, her eyes accusing and her skin pale against the rich chestnut of her hair. 'But this swordplay is not innocent. Adam is capable of calling out Tristan. And you . . . you will not let Osgood escape your justice, will you? But we have been home for just a few months.' Her voice rose in alarm.

'A gentleman should never neglect his fencing skills.' Japhet was deliberately flippant.

She struck his chest with her fist. 'Do not humour me. I know what you plan. If not this week, this month, this year, or the foreseeable future, but you will not let this matter rest. Forget Osgood. He is a cowardly knave.'

'I am not the only one of our family whom Osgood planned to ruin. Adam said that his lecherous eye also singled out my cousin's half-sister, Tamasine, during a visit she made to London. When she refused his advances, Osgood tried to abduct her. Fortunately, Tamasine was rescued by Maximillian Deverell – the man she later married.'

'But that was years ago, when you were still on the ship to the penal colony.' She breathed heavily in her exasperation. 'Tamasine was staying in London with

Cousin Thomas. He called Osgood out. Family honour is satisfied. He even scarred the knave's face in the duel. Since then, little has been heard of the baronet. He has retired to his country seat to hide his disfigurement.'

'And he was there until last year,' Japhet announced. 'He has since disappeared – rumoured to have gone abroad. So you see, your fears are in vain. He is out of reach.'

Her stare searched his and showed no sign of being reassured. 'Promise me that you will not seek him out.'

He took her into his arms again and his voice was husky and seductive. 'Have I not promised that I will live quietly and concentrate on establishing a racing stables and stud? That is my intention.' His hand stroked her cheek and his gaze lingered upon her lips before capturing them with his own. There was the briefest resistance before she surrendered to his kiss and he felt her body melt against him.

Then with a sigh she pulled away. 'I will not be sidetracked by sweet words and caresses, my love. Say you will not go after Osgood?' When he did not immediately answer, she gripped the front of his greatcoat, her eyes beseeching. 'Promise me, Japhet.'

He cupped her lovely face gently in his hands. 'I certainly have no intention of going off on a wild goose chase hunting him down. But I will make you no false promises, Gwen. If Osgood crosses my path then that is a different matter. But he is not likely to search me out. He has proved himself too craven for that.'

He kissed her until he felt her anger melt and the tension leave her body. 'Do you think that I would risk all that we have for that knave? I am no longer the hothead, the reckless rakehell. You and our sons and this stud farm are what is important.' His arms held her tight, but over the top of her head his stare was uncompromising.

When the time was right, Osgood would face retribution and pay for his treachery.

Chapter Five

A strategic retreat was sometimes necessary to regain the upper ground. It was not Tristan's wish to alienate his cousins to such an extent that all of their acquaintances in the county took against him. And it would be tactful that the rawness of their grief and their hot blood was given time to cool. Therefore it was both diplomatic and of benefit to himself if he spent some months in London. He had many pressing business matters to take care of now that he intended to end his wanderings and make his home in England.

He usually preferred to travel to the capital by sea rather than road. A ship from Fowey to Tilbury could complete the voyage in two or three days with comparative case if the sea was not rough. The recent weather, however, had been stormy and he had no wish to endure the rigours of rough seas, for it often took him several days to get his sea legs and overcome the sickness that assaulted him whenever he sailed. The bone-shaking land route by post-chaise involved five or more nightly stops at inns until they crossed the Thames at either Vauxhall or London Bridge.

Unfortunately, this meant being confined in the cramped conveyance with a varied though usually unpleasant assortment of passengers. There was the bombastic Member of Parliament returning to London after an eight-month absence; the prim and pompous deacon who squinted at everyone through a monocle; the doughty major with the buxom, monosyllabic wife; and the sour-faced middle-aged governess who glared at anyone who presumed to engage her in conversation. At Okehampton they were joined by a businessman and his overdressed wife who continually boasted of the month they had recently spent in Paris.

'It is quite the gayest place now that the war has ended,' the woman proclaimed. 'Why, you would hardly think there had been a revolution there were so many balls to attend, and the playhouses were full.'

'I doubt the murdered aristocrats would agree with your sentiments,' Tristan said caustically, hoping to stop her chattering.

'The First Consul has brought the country to good order. It prospers,' the deacon informed them. When he drew a long breath to expand further, Major Quigley barked his disgust.

'That upstart Corsican has broken the Treaty of Amiens, and it is barely a year old.' There was an abundance of gold braid on his scarlet uniform, and his wide greying side whiskers were speckled from his frequent taking of snuff. The puckered scar of an old battle wound disfigured one ruddy cheek. 'There are embargoes on British goods that will cripple our country. Bonaparte is using this time of peace to replenish his coffers at our expense. We may have beaten his army in Egypt and Turkey, but he still has his eye on expanding his borders. The peace is temporary, you mark my words. What do you say, Mr Hayle, our worthy member in the house?' He glowered at the Member of Parliament.

'I fear you may be right.' Hayle was slight of form, with sallow sunken cheeks and the obsequious manner of a man who served the interests of the patron who had paid for his seat in his borough, rather than the greater good of his country. 'At least the trouncing we gave Boney has stopped his plans to invade England. We have shown we are more than a match for the Little Corporal.'

'Deride Bonaparte all you will,' Tristan snapped. 'Only a fool would underestimate him. He has risen fast and he has risen high. A nation that so short a time ago crushed its nobility and sovereign has much to justify. The French are not beaten, they are only resting, and when they next rise up, the whole of Europe had better be prepared to fight them or be conquered.'

'You sound like a damned republican,' Mr Hayle retorted. 'Any decent Englishman is a royalist in support of our monarchy. Or would you again see civil war tear our country apart, sir?'

Tristan fixed the Member of Parliament with a piercing stare. 'You mistook my meaning, Mr Hayle. Like any loyal Englishman I am a staunch royalist. But I am also a realist.'

The deacon adjusted his monocle and looked down his long nose at his companions. His voice rang sharply with all the resonance of a hellfire-and-brimstone sermon. 'Gentlemen, your discussion is too heated when there are ladies present. We should all pray that the peace is a lasting one.'

'Amen to that,' the governess complied. 'Talk of politics, war or religion is best left to your gentlemen's clubs.'

The atmosphere in the coach became strained for the rest of the afternoon. Tristan maintained the pleasantries, but he was seldom interested enough in their mundane conversations to join in. He preferred from his seat by the window to assume an interest in the changing countryside. Inevitably this led to hours of introspection and reflection.

Tristan had decided long ago that there was no room in his life for regret. He regarded it as a weakness. Any form of vulnerability allowed one's enemies to gain the upper hand. Ever since he could remember, he had lived on his wits just to survive. It had stood him in good stead. The only time he had lowered his guard and permitted circumstances to over-rule his usual mistrust and suspicion had been during his time at Trevowan, after the death of his mother. Then his desperation to fit in as a member of the family had been his undoing. He had been scared of rejection and was determined never to return to his old life of a guttersnipe. Throughout his early childhood he had lived from hand to mouth and was never more than a few steps away from being nabbed by the constables for stealing. That was the only way he could keep both himself and his mother alive. Inevitably, drink and poverty had taken his mother's life and he had spent weeks surviving on his wits amongst the worst of the criminal fraternity in the slums of Bristol. That was when George Loveday had given in to a twinge of conscience and decided to discover what had happened to his brother's family.

Walter Loveday, Tristan's grandfather, had run away from Trevowan as a youth after quarrelling with his father and refusing to follow the family tradition of life in the navy. Respectability had been a thin veneer covering Walter's hunger for adventure that his wild blood dictated. Whether Walter Loveday had achieved the adventure and fame he had sought Tristan thought debatable. He had certainly earned notoriety as the leader of a gang of villains who terrorised the decent citizens of Bristol, and had ended his days mortally wounded from a knife wound. Before death claimed him, Walter had written to his father pleading with him to help his family. There had been no response, and Kitty, his wife, had drunk herself into an early grave by the time Tristan's mother Alice was fourteen.

Life had not treated Alice much better. She had been easy prey to any handsome rascal and within a month had been seduced and introduced to a life of crime. Tristan had been born in a hovel; his first memory of his mother was of her falling down the rickety steps and passing out in the gutter. Of his father she never spoke or mentioned his name. He had never married her and abandoned her a month before Tristan was born. In her maudlin moments Alice had often related to him the tales her mother had told her of their wealthy kin in Cornwall living on a grand estate at Trevowan.

When his mother was too drunk to work, which was most days, Tristan had been used as a lookout by local gangs and given a few pence, money that kept him and his mother alive. When sober, there was only one trade Alice could now turn to: that of a whore. It provided her with gin and often a savage beating. By the time Tristan was six, he had been taught to cut a purse and dip his fingers undetected into a gentleman's pocket or a lady's reticule.

He closed his eyes against those painful memories and for a moment was plunged back in time. Vividly he recalled the stench of musty ragged clothes, unwashed bodies, disease, decay, drunkenness and despair – the noisome aroma of poverty. He could hear the cries of starving babies and children, the whine of beggars, the brutality of beatings and abuse. Again he felt his stomach raw and aching with hunger, his flesh itching and crawling from sores, bedbugs, lice and fleas. Sights of untold deprivation flashed behind his eyes: people a dozen to a room fighting over a few scraps of food, rape, murder, feral gangs of orphans living an existence no better than animals, cursed, kicked and unwanted.

Then he heard his mother's voice, cracked with pain and regret. 'It be wrong for you to live like this, son. You should be a gentleman like those cousins of yours. You should have a fine carriage, dress in velvet and be tended by servants. That be your birthright. Your Grandpa Walter should've done right by me ma. He should have made his peace with his kin. You gotta do that.' Her impassioned speech was cut short by a coughing fit. They had become more virulent in recent months and this one went on all night. 'You gotta promise me, son. You seek out your kin.'

'I've got you, Ma. I don't need no kin looking down their noses at me,' he had protested. The thought of their ridicule had chilled him even then. The Loveday pride ran thickly in his veins. If he met his kin, he wanted to do so as their equal so that they would be proud of him.

Alice's pleading became more insistent with every week that passed, as he watched her grow thinner and thinner, her face covered with sores and her rotting teeth falling out. He took greater risks with his thieving to buy not only food but also coal or wood for a fire to keep her warm.

One evening he came home to find her bodice streaked with blood and a trickle of it running from her mouth. 'I bain't long for this world, son. But I've done right by you. I've paid a scribe to write a letter to your Great-Uncle George. You be his kin. You deserve what be yours by right.'

When his mother died two weeks later there was no

money for a coffin and she was thrown into a lime pit with the other paupers. That was the first time Tristan had felt real hatred for his wealthy kin. His great-uncle should have done right by his niece when written to all those years ago. They had ignored her existence and heartlessly condemned her to a life of degradation and poverty. He hoped his Cornish kin would all rot in hell.

And Tristan learned all about hell in the following weeks. It had rained persistently, and with few people on the streets, pickings were scant. His starved body succumbed to a fever, his ragged clothing falling apart as its thin fabric rotted on his body, and he shivered, weak with delirium, in any rat-infested hole that provided some measure of shelter. That was where George Loveday's agents found him.

Having suffered all the horrors of poverty, he was slow to give his trust. He mourned his mother and there was a deep anger in him for the pitiful waste of her life and all she had endured. She should have had the chance to enjoy this luxury. It had been her birthright, with a far closer bloodline than Tristan's. So he took the fine clothes and education they offered and found he enjoyed the comforts of a soft bed and plentiful food. He learned their refined way of speaking and manners, for he had suffered the prejudices of the underclass too long not to appreciate the advantages of being accepted amongst gentlefolk as an equal. He also tolerated the boisterous antics of his new-found cousins whilst secretly despising them. Scorn was a more acceptable weapon than owning that he was jealous and resentful of their privileged childhood. Of all of them he was closest to Japhet, who had the streak of a rogue ready to break through without thought of the consequences. Adam could be equally daring but was more concerned as to the rights and wrongs of a matter, and Tristan disliked such caution. As to St John, Tristan trusted him least of his new companions. In that he had been proved right. St John's lies had been his undoing. No one believed the guttersnipe over the heir, and George Loveday declared that he had reverted to type.

Tristan had run away, persecuting himself with his insecurities at being an interloper and an outsider, convinced that he would never be accepted as good enough by the Lovedays. In the following years he had cursed that one moment of weakness, when anger and a sense of betrayal by his cousin had made him act in the manner that was expected of him instead of following his instincts and fighting to prove the old man wrong.

Now he stamped down the painful memories of the years when he had been driven by obsession. He had travelled half the world and built a small empire with business enterprises by both scrupulous and less savoury means.

Without the hardships of the past, would he have been driven to achieve the success both in position and fortune that was his today? He doubted it. He was not bound to answer to any man, but he hoped that his grandfather Walter would have found it fitting that he was master of Trevowan. Tristan had no wish for further contention. Adam could fester in his rage and grief if he chose. If Tristan had not taken Trevowan for St John's debts, another would have done, and the Lovedays would no longer claim it as their ancestral home.

His eyes narrowed and he could not contain a glow of satisfaction. The Loveday name was something to be reckoned with in Cornwall. Many might speculate that his blood was tainted, but he doubted that the first Loveday to live at Trevowan would have achieved his mastery there if he had been any less of a rogue in his time.

It was Trevowan that gave Tristan the status he craved. That won, he must think of the future. What use Trevowan without an heir? For that he must take a wife.

Chapter Six

So far Senara had kept silent about her husband's early-morning meetings with his cousin. Occasionally he returned with some minor wound and a ready excuse to explain it as an accident in the yard. She knew better. She was too skilled at tending the cuts and abrasions of the shipyard workers, and she knew a sword nick when she saw one. It was also obvious to her why he was practising his swordplay. Adam would never let his twin's death go unavenged, or the loss of his family home.

For a rational and compassionate man, Adam could be intractable upon matters of family pride and honour. His wild blood rebelled at the shame his twin had brought to his family. With St John dead, Adam could not take his fury out on the culprit, and his anger had become focused upon the new owner of Trevowan. Old prejudices, even if later vindicated and proved wrong, had festered too long to be so easily dismissed. He was also consumed with grief and guilt over his twin's death. And that grief fed his anger.

Senara hoped that time would heal his need for revenge. She doubted it would ever cure the loathing he felt towards the new master of Trevowan. Much of the rivalry between Adam and his twin had been due to

Adam's passion for his family home and the knowledge that he would never be its heir.

That knowledge filled Senara with sadness. Adam had achieved so much. The shipyard was now free of debt, and more prosperous than it had ever been during his father's lifetime.

Through a window overlooking the stable yard, she watched Adam at work. The late February air was damp from a persistent drizzle of rain. A cartload of timber had arrived from the shipyard and had been stacked outside the old coach house. The carpenter who had driven the cart was now listening to Adam's instructions. Now that they had acquired Amelia's coach, the old coach house roof needed to be watertight. Half the original shingles were rotten or had blown away in gales, and many of the crossbeams also needed replacing. A lock of hair kept falling over Adam's brow, and he brushed it impatiently away.

Senara's pale face, framed by hair the colour of freshly tilled earth, was reflected back in the diamond panes. The green of her muslin gown and her white fichu showed the rounded curves of her figure, which had borne four children, two of whom were twins. Her features with their high cheekbones and wide, generous mouth had remained free of lines except for a few at the corners of her green eyes, where she crinkled them against the sun. Her complexion had a healthy glow from hours spent working in her herb garden. Her pose was serene from a deep inner contentment in her marriage and home. Yet now the way her teeth caught at her lower lip showed that despite her outward calm on this occasion, she had a nagging unease that her husband would allow his actions to be coloured by his grief. He could be proud, honourable, loyal and courageous in so many matters and events, yet over this he had remained stubbornly resolute.

She fingered the diamond and gold cross at her throat, seeking reassurance. A year ago she would never have worn such an emblem of faith, for her religion had been steeped in the ancient ways of her gypsy forebears. But that was now behind her, for fearing that she had inadvertently called upon the wrath of the old gods when a man who was their enemy had been killed, she had recanted and asked Uncle Joshua to baptise her. Since then she had been true to the teachings of the Christian faith. She could not, however, ignore the prickling of premonition that nudged the corners of her mind. Such insights had never failed her in the past. Yet these feelings now were indistinct, a sense of warning that danger to her loved ones was near – but its source remained elusive.

Did the threat lie within her husband's antagonism towards Tristan Loveday? She could think of no other reason. Pride had been wounded, and that was always dangerous in a Loveday confrontation. Unless reconciliation could be reached, she feared that turbulent times lay ahead for the family, which could truly rend it asunder.

Her troubled eyes continued to watch her husband. The buildings protected him from the biting wind that carried inland from the sea and he had removed his jacket, the light rain gradually making his shirt stick to his broad shoulders as he ignored the elements and sawed through a length of wood. He always resorted to physical work to keep his emotions at bay. He was still a handsome man, and after ten years of marriage he could still make her heart race faster. She would not be the only woman so affected by his presence if others were to meet him in a ballroom or salon. He was upwards of two yards tall, and slim of hip. When his mood was light and beguiling, his intelligent eyes were the compelling blue-green of the Cornish sea on a bright summer's day, or they could change to the colour of storm-tossed waters when his emotions darkened. His chiselled features were browned from his time spent outdoors at the shipyard or on the estate. His strong jaw showed great strength of purpose and his long-fingered hands were those of both craftsman and artist – all the ships now built in the yard had been designed by himself.

Every sweep of his arm was precise and controlled, but Senara could almost feel the tension coiled within her husband's lithe figure. There was no need for him to use the skill he had perfected in his childhood working in the Loveday shipyard; he had over a score of carpenters in his employ to perform so menial a task. The taut line of his full lips and the tension in his shoulders revealed the anger that he was channelling through his exertion.

She went to the kitchen and nodded to Carrie Jensen and Gilly Brown, who were plucking a brace of pheasants and a chicken for the evening meal. She entered the deep stone larder, poured cider into a pottery tankard and took it outside to her husband.

Adam was squinting along the alignment of his length of sawn wood and put it aside as she approached.

'I thought you could do with this.' She offered him the drink.

He downed half its contents, a trickle of the amber juice glistening on his jaw. He wiped it away with his palm.

'That was good. It must be almost the last of Uncle Joshua's cider. I hope this year our own orchard will yield enough apples so that we can make our own. The trees should be mature enough for a sizeable harvest.'

He finished the tankard and handed it back to her. 'I

thought you were visiting your mother and sister today at Polruggan.'

'I was sorting through some of Joel's clothes I had packed away that may now fit Michael. I shall also take some goose fat for his chest; he still had his cold when I saw him yesterday. It has dragged on and his chest has always been weak. I shall go shortly.' She made an arc with the toe of her shoe in the wood shavings. 'I thought you were going over the estate accounts today.'

'My mind was too restless.'

She put a hand on his shoulder. 'You push yourself too hard, my love. You must not punish yourself because of St John. He was the instrument of his own downfall. I pray you, do not allow your anger to—'

'I have much to do,' he cut in abruptly, and kissed her cheek in apology for his curtness. 'I will leave young Wakely to continue the work here. I need to check that adequate rope was ordered for the damaged rigging of the Falmouth packet at the yard. This is only the second ship the mail has sent to us for repairs. I cannot allow anything to delay her completion. Other orders may rest on the speed of our work.'

Billy Brown, Gilly's husband, ran up to him with several questions about the estate's livestock, and Senara returned to the house. Nothing she could say could ease Adam's pain. For the present, only work seemed to keep the demons from his mind. Pride had often proved the family's undoing in the past. It had also been its strength.

The Tudor house at Boscabel had been a ruin when Adam had bought it, and the estate badly run down. His skill at renovation had restored the house to its Elizabethan splendour, keeping the old hammer-beamed roof of the great hall, the oriel window and minstrels' gallery, whilst modernising other rooms to make it a spacious family home. Over the years, all the profits from the yard had been used on the estate to rebuild the dilapidated outbuildings, replenish the livestock and put the fields to the plough for their best advantage. Boscabel had risen from a ruin to be free of debt and in recent years had become far more profitable than Trevowan.

Manor houses in Cornwall were generally more compact than the grand residences of the nobility and gentry in other parts of the country. Boscabel, with its eight bedchambers, family dining room, music room, salon, library, morning room and long gallery the length of the upper floor, was a substantial family home any wife would be proud to live in. But it still retained its intimate atmosphere, as most of the rooms were used daily. Even the three guest bedchambers were frequently occupied; since the weather could change drastically from one hour to the next, often a visitor who had come to dine would discover that either fog or a downpour prevented them returning even a few miles to their home.

Senara had become an accomplished hostess, although in the first years of her marriage, the prospect of entertaining Adam's friends and family had terrified her. Her elevated status as Adam's wife had changed her from a reclusive gypsy girl to a sophisticated woman. Adam had been born a gentleman, and though the adventurous side of his nature often caused the family to break with convention, he was still regarded as a pillar of society.

As a child, Senara had run barefoot and half wild, living a nomadic existence in a barrel-roofed caravan with her older brother Caleph and her grandmother. After her father died, her mother, Leah, decided to leave the tribe, taking ten-year-old Senara with her. Caleph had refused to go with them, and Senara had seen him only infrequently in the intervening years.

There were times when she stared in a looking-glass or regarded the wealth and splendour of her marriage to Adam and did not recognise the young gypsy waif. If she had changed so much, it had also been obvious on her meeting with Tristan that his manners were as polished as those of his cousins. All traces of the guttersnipe had been ruthlessly erased. Surely, in the intervening years of Tristan's exile, much would also have changed in his character.

Senara entered her herb room, which led off from the kitchen and had once been a storeroom. A fresh pitcher of water and an empty hand basin were on a bench ready for her use. On shelves around the room were small pottery jars of prepared unguents and phials of tincture for common ailments. Locked in a wall cupboard was a bottle of laudanum obtained from an apothecary in Fowey and a flagon of brandy that was used in restoratives or as a preservative in some of her remedies. Bunches of dried herbs hung from the roof beams, and the room was sweetened by the predominant perfume of dried lavender, rosemary, camomile and calendula leaves and flowers. A small fireplace and chimney had been built into the corner, and in an iron cauldron hanging on a hook over the fire, the herbs Senara had been simmering in boiling water for an hour added their pungent aroma to the room.

She picked up a wooden ladle and stirred the pot, satisfied that the liquid had reduced to a thick consistency. Using a cloth to lift the cauldron on to the scrubbed oak table, she laid a piece of muslin over a bowl and strained the mixture. Once it had cooled, she added several spoonfuls of honey and poured it into a stoppered jug. Michael had coughed a few times yesterday, and she would take the tincture with her in case it had got worse.

If he did not need it, Bridie would pass it on to a sick child of a parishioner. There had been a worrying outbreak of the morbid sore throat and ague in several of the villages this winter.

Senara collected the stone jar of goose fat from the cool larder and placed the remedies in a straw basket. Then she added four oranges from their dwindling supply, bought last month at Launceston market; they were a luxury that a parson's stipend did not stretch to. The bag was soon filled with a rabbit snared by Eli Rudge, a dozen ginger and spice fairings, some saffron cakes baked this morning, a quarter-pound of tea, a leg from a freshly killed lamb and a bottle of Madeira, to which her mother Leah had become very partial. There was also a Sunday-best suit that her youngest son Joel had outgrown four years ago and which would soon fit Michael.

Despite all her commitments as mistress of Boscabel and her visits most days to tend any sick needing her services at Trevowan Hard, she rode the four miles to the parsonage at Polruggan at least twice a week to visit Leah. Most days during term-time she saw her sister at the shipyard, where Bridie was the schoolmistress. But this week the school was closed. Most of the children and their mothers would be helping with the spring sowing and clearing the ploughed fields of stones.

The morning was mild and dry, with a patchwork of clouds trailing across the sky from an offshore wind. The sun was breaking through the thinning clouds, but it would no doubt rain by mid-afternoon.

While Senara waited for her mare to be brought out of the stable, she heard her daughters, eight-year-old Rhianne, who was Joel's twin, and six-year-old Sara, laughing as they ran through the meadow with the three family dogs chasing them. By rights the girls should be at their lessons, but the teacher who had been employed at Trevowan had taken another post after St John's death. Now that Charlotte and Rowena had moved to Reskelly Cottage, once a governess was engaged at Boscabel, Amelia would bring the girls here each morning to study. Amelia had already interviewed a woman, who would join them at the end of the month. Senara would welcome the daily visits of the children. She missed her sons, who were boarding at their schools. Bryn, their young ward, had also joined the older boys at school this term.

She hoped that Bryn was settling in, for his young life had been traumatic. Last year he had been rescued from a coach accident, and was left with no memory of his identity. The driver of the coach had been killed and so had a young woman whose identity also remained a mystery. Bryn had no knowledge of her or of why they had been travelling in such a desperate hurry, as though fleeing some danger. Adam had posted reports of him in the local and London news-sheets, but no member of his family had come forward. It was all very puzzling, for Bryn, as he had been named by Joel, was well spoken and clearly from a good family. Adam had promised him a home until his parents were found or his memory returned. Senara had come to love him as one of her own.

As she rode under the entrance arch of the wall surrounding her home, a glance back at the sundial, which was now in sunlight, showed her that the morning had progressed more than she had intended. The remedy preparations rattled in the straw basket hanging from the pommel of her saddle. Bridie would be anxious at her lateness; her sister fretted too much, particularly over her son, who was often sickly. Although born prematurely and tiny, Michael had grown stronger with each year. Yet it was a mother's way to fuss, especially since after Michael's birth, Bridie had been warned that to conceive another child could kill her.

Chapter Seven

Polruggan was a small village not much larger than a hamlet, its cottages scattered along a rutted track and its church, with its tall square tower, surrounded by yew trees. The village green with its pump and communal stone washing tub also had a set of rusty-hinged stocks to punish miscreants. A more pleasant scene was the duck pond, surrounded by rushes and overhanging willows, beneath which was a stone seat that provided rest and shade during a hot summer. The cottages were mostly the homes of farm labourers, but there was also a thatcher, a carter and a farrier living here. The village had its own kiddley on the outskirts, and all the women earned extra money by making lace; an industry Bridie had set up when she first married Peter.

The parsonage was a long, sprawling two-storey building built of local stone covered in yellow spots of lichen. Senara frowned at seeing a horse tied to the gatepost. It was Dr Yeo's bay mare. It was rare that a parishioner could afford his fees and summon him from Fowey. With a racing heart Senara leapt to the ground and tethered her mount. She prayed that Michael had not taken a turn for the worse and that his chesty cough had not developed into something more ominous.

As she hurried into the parsonage, the stocky figure of Dr Yeo was standing in the hall, clutching his bag and clearly on the point of leaving. Even in the poor light of the dark-panelled passage his expression was drawn with concern. Bridie had a hand to her elfin face, which was streaked with tears. Her dark hair was twisted into a simple chignon and held in place with a tortoiseshell comb. She was shorter than Senara; her slender body slightly stooped, showing her weariness, which made the twist to her spine more pronounced.

'Good morning, Dr Yeo. Bridie. Is it Michael who is ill?' Senara dipped a polite curtsy but her voice cracked with growing dread.

'Thank God you are here.' Bridie looked pale and close to collapse, though Senara knew her sister was far more resilient than she appeared. 'I sent a boy to Boscabel not long since, but you must have missed him if he cut across the fields.'

Dr Yeo bowed to her. 'Good morning, Mrs Loveday. You have no need to fear for Michael. He has a slight cough but is none the worse for it. He was chasing chickens round the garden when I arrived. I regret it is your mother who is my patient. Your sister summoned me to attend upon Mrs Polglase. She had a fall outside when feeding the chickens and knocked her head. She was found unconscious. I fear it was not a matter of tripping but that she had suffered an apoplexy. Fortunately I was on my way to visit a patient at the next farm when Mrs Loveday saw me passing.'

'Fortunate indeed, Dr Yeo. Has my mother recovered consciousness?' Senara was frightened. It was not the first time Leah had suffered such an attack, and she knew such seizures could be fatal. Of all the physicians in the district,

Dr Yeo had never derided her remedies and had frequently praised her skills.

'I am pleased to say that she has,' he said encouragingly. 'However, she cannot speak or move her left arm or leg. There is little that can be done for such cases, as I am sure you are aware. If she does not have another seizure in the next day or so, she may recover some of the use of her limbs and speech in time. I bled her to help restore the humours of the body. I would prefer that she is given nothing of an opiate nature at this stage so that I can judge her progress when I call on the morrow.'

At Senara's nod of agreement, he continued in a serious tone, 'Mrs Polglase must be kept calm. I am reassured that you are here. She will need all your care and attention for the next few days. I will call upon her tomorrow.'

'Is my mother in pain?' Senara asked.

'She will be in some discomfort but mostly she will be confused. Do not let her become upset.'

Senara walked with him to the door. At that moment there was a squeal of laughter and Michael came running round the corner of the parsonage clutching a ginger kitten. He also held a squashed bunch of primroses. 'Look, Aunt Senara. This is Snuff. Uncle Japhet gave him to me.' His short dark hair was a riot of curls about his face and his cheeks were flagged with high colour. The exertion of his run made him start to cough.

'Michael!' Bridie wailed. 'Why is your coat undone, and where is your scarf?'

'I lost it chasing Snuff and I was hot from running.' He smiled disarmingly and held out the primroses to his mother. 'These are for you.' Then he coughed again and the kitten wriggled free of his arms and ran off to chase a dead leaf tumbling along the ground in the breeze.

When Michael made to chase after it, Senara said, 'Does your aunt get no greeting?'

Michael beamed at her and held out his arms for her to lift him up. She could not resist the invitation and hugged him and kissed his cheek, noting that his face was hot. He gave a squeal of pleasure. 'I think you should go inside,' Senara said. 'Snuff will follow. It is cold for him out here.'

Bridie ushered her son and the kitten towards the door.

'Come play with me and Snuff, Aunt Senara,' Michael giggled as he ran inside.

Although Senara was anxious to see Leah, she walked with Dr Yeo back to his horse. Inside the house, the sound of Michael's coughing continued. The physician frowned towards the parsonage. 'That cough is harsher than when I examined him earlier. The boy has been much stronger this winter than other years. Children often grow out of a weak chest. It is probably the exertion. But there have been some cases of quinsy in Polmasryn, St Winnow and Golant.' He paused significantly. 'Do not hesitate to summon me if my services are needed. Neither Michael nor Mrs Polglase could have a better nurse. Good day, Mrs Loveday.'

He swung into the saddle and, placing his high domed hat on his head, tipped it in salute to her.

Senara hurried into the house. Bridie was in the kitchen and dosing Michael with a cough tincture. The young boy pulled a face. 'Nasty.'

'Then you should have kept your scarf on,' Bridie scolded.

Senara put her straw bag on the table. 'There is some goose fat in here. You could put a warming poultice on his chest that may ease the congestion. I'll go to Ma now.'

She went to the room on the ground floor that had been turned into a bedchamber for Leah. Her mother lay with her eyes closed, her figure frail and scarcely causing a rise under the patchwork quilt. One side of her face was dragged down, twisting her lips into a diagonal line.

'Ma, oh Ma!' Senara murmured in anguish.

Leah looked so old and wrinkled, her skin like bread dough. Senara gasped and drew up a plain wooden chair to sit by the bed and take her mother's purple-veined hand. The room was simply furnished with a bed, table and chair. Two colourful rag rugs lay on the floor and a plain wooden cross hung on the wall. On the mantelshelf was a wooden gypsy caravan that Adam had carved for Leah one Christmas. From two wooden pegs on the wall hung the old woman's cloak, two every-day dresses and her Sunday dress. Under these was a wooden coffer for her petticoats and hose and two pairs of stout buckled shoes. A fire crackled in the grate, and the curtains were pulled back to allow as much light as possible into the room, though it remained dimmed from the shadows cast by the yew trees outside.

Leah opened her eyes; one lid remained pulled down. She blinked twice, looking confused and frightened, and her mouth moved as she tried unsuccessfully to speak.

'Just you rest, Ma. It's me, Senara, your daughter. You are in the parsonage, where you live with your other daughter Bridie and her husband Peter.' She knew that frequently victims of an apoplexy suffered loss of memory at first, and she wanted to reassure her mother.

Leah continued to look at her in bewilderment and managed to raise her right hand to flop it against her head in a tapping movement.

'I know, Ma. You must wonder where you are and what has happened. You had a fall. The doctor has called to examine you. He says you must rest. Sleep now. I will stay with you, and Bridie is also here.'

When Leah closed her eyes, Senara turned to look up at her sister, who was leaning against the wall, tears glistening on her cheeks. Michael had stopped coughing, and Beth, the maidservant, could be heard getting him to ladle some milk into a bowl for his kitten.

Bridie groaned. 'There was no need for Ma to feed the chickens. I've told her so many times that we have a servant for such work. I thought she had just fallen. Her injured knee has given way several times lately but she will not use the crutches Adam had made for her.'

'Ma needs to feel useful. She does not like to be waited on,' Senara said softly.

'I brought her here to look after her, not to have her look after us.' Bridie wrung her hands in her distress. 'I should have kept an eye on her, but I was fussing over Michael, wrapping him up against the cold when he insisted on going outside to help her. Beth had gone to the kiddley to get fresh milk.' She dabbed at her eyes. 'I am so relieved you are here. Peter is away seeking an audience with the bishop for funds to repair the church. Some thieves stole the lead from the roof, and every time it rains, the water gushes into the nave and it floods. He will not be home until tomorrow.'

Senara rose to comfort her sister. 'You must not blame yourself. You have provided a good home for Ma. She is happy here.'

'Is she going to die, Senara?' Bridie whispered. 'She has never been this bad before.'

Senara watched Bridie wipe her eyes with her palm and force a watery smile. She needed to deal with practicalities to calm her own fears. 'I see she is still dressed in her work gown. We will not disturb her until later, when we will put on her nightgown and settle her for the night. How is Michael? His coughing seems to have stopped.'

'I wish I was strong like you.' Bridie sighed. 'I know I fuss over him too much. Ma is always saying I will turn him into a milksop.'

'It is natural to worry. But sometimes children need the opportunity just to be children.'

Bridie forced a tremulous smile. 'Your brood are so healthy and boisterous. Michael is sickly. He is small for his age.'

Senara glanced down at her now sleeping mother. She wanted to keep her sister's mind occupied to stop her from worrying. 'Did Dr Yeo give any other instructions concerning Ma?'

'He said to make sure she takes some liquid and a light broth if possible.'

'I put some oranges in my bag; I know Michael enjoys them. Since Ma looks to be sleeping peacefully, I will make the broth.'

Later that afternoon Adam called at the parsonage to see if Leah was as sick as the messenger had warned. He was saddened that she did not appear to know him and had to be reminded again that the two sisters were her daughters. She was still unable to speak.

'You must stay for as long as you are needed.' He addressed Senara. 'Is there anything you need?'

'I noticed they are running low on wood for the fires. Could Billy Brown bring some over in the cart? Michael has been coughing on and off all day. I think both he and Ma should have a fire in their room tonight. And Ma needs one throughout the day. The parsonage can get so damp in winter.'

'Brown will bring the wood within the hour. Is there anything else?' Adam asked.

She shook her head. 'I am also worried about Bridie. She looks worn out, but she will not rest. Several of the parishioners have called and given their good wishes. It shows how much Leah has been accepted here, which is very comforting.'

'The villagers have great respect for Bridie. You should be proud of her.' He stooped to kiss her cheek. 'As I am proud of you, my love. I hope Leah recovers and regains all her faculties and the use of her limbs. Uncle Joshua will want to take a service here tonight in Peter's absence to pray for her recovery. I will send word to him and get the churchwarden to announce the service.'

Michael was excited that Senara was staying the night and insisted that she read him stories before he went to sleep. Snuff was curled up on his bed and Michael begged that the kitten be allowed to stay.

'Your father has said that no animals are to be allowed in the bedchambers.'

'Papa is away.' Michael was wide eyed in his entreaty. 'Could this one night be our secret, Aunt Senara?'

'That is up to your mama.' Her own children all slept with the family dogs and cats in their rooms.

As she read to him, Michael coughed occasionally and scratched at the red flannel cloth bound tight round his chest, which was smothered in goose fat. The smell of it in the hot bedchamber kept attracting Snuff, who meowed to be lifted on to the bed. Bridie refused to allow Michael to sleep with the kitten, and it was chased back downstairs.

With Michael asleep and Leah also dozing after she had been changed out of her day clothes and fed more of the broth, the sisters were torn between staying close to the sick room and attending the evening service. 'Ma is in good hands. Peter would expect you to attend church,' Senara advised. A candle burned by the side of Leah's bed and the fire was banked up in her room. Beth was instructed to summon them if there was any change in Leah's condition.

In her early thirties, Beth was a competent maid of all work and a woman of sound common sense. She was the widow of a fisherman who had been lost at sea in the first year of her marriage. Until Bridie had employed her at a hiring fair, she had found it difficult to find work. After the loss of her young husband she had taken to drink. One night she had stumbled on the stairs of the cottage she shared with her sister in Tregony and her unbound hair had caught alight from the flame of the candle she had been carrying, scarring her cheek and leaving her bald on one side of her head. Her scalp was always covered with a white headscarf tied under her chin, but this could not hide her disfigurement.

Since her recovery from her accident, Beth had been teetotal, and despite all she had suffered, she remained cheerful and without bitterness. She had also become devoutly religious and was an ideal servant for a parson's family. She was devoted to Michael, but even so Bridie was reluctant to leave her son in her care when he could be coming down with a fever.

When it was time to leave for the service, the wind had stiffened and a splattering of rain ran down the windowpanes as Senara closed the curtains. She had attended her sister as she visited the child's bedchamber to reassure Bridie that Michael could be left. Although two bright pennants of colour stained his cheeks, the tisane appeared to have eased his coughing and he had fallen asleep a half-hour ago.

'He will sleep soundly until we return, as will Ma,' Senara insisted, and linked her arm through her sister's to lead her from the room.

Bridie pulled back. 'Oh, I know I should attend the service, especially with Peter away, but—'

'There will be no buts.' A firm voice was accompanied by a heavy step on the stairs and the diminutive figure of Peter's mother appeared in the doorway, having already removed her cloak and hat. 'Joshua is in the church and expecting you. I've put my head round the door and found Leah sound asleep like this little one here. Beth and I will sit with the patients.'

Aunt Cecily waved the two younger women away. 'Now off with you to your prayers. I knew you would be upset at leaving Michael, my dear. Adam said he had been coughing this afternoon. I have said more than a godly measure of prayers this day for both him and Leah. Allow me the pleasure of watching over my grandson.'

'It was good of you to come, Mama, and on such an inhospitable night,' Bridie said as she kissed her mother-in-law's cheek.

'We all do what we can in times such as these. You must take heart that Leah is a strong woman despite her years.'

Senara bit back a smile, for Leah was probably no more than a half-dozen years older than Peter's mother. Though obviously the harder life she had endured had taken more of a toll on her body.

Cecily was determined to reassure them. 'Peter will be distraught that he was away when Leah has been taken so poorly. We are fortunate that Senara has such healing knowledge. There is no one else I would have tend my family at such a time.'

With Cecily settled by the fire in Michael's room,

Bridie left with Senara for the church service and took her place at the front in her usual pew. Senara took a seat close to the door at the back, where it would be easy for Beth to summon her without causing too much disturbance to the congregation. It was heartening to see so many villagers in attendance.

Senara tried to focus on the Bible reading, but her glance kept straying to the door. She had tended many patients who had been partially paralysed with an apoplexy and she knew that the next hours could be critical for her mother. Unfortunately there was little her skill could do apart from keeping Leah as comfortable as possible.

The Reverend Mr Joshua Loveday knew that a short sermon often had more impact on his flock than a lengthy diatribe. At least fewer fell asleep. He was also conscious of the anxiety of his daughter-in-law and niece by marriage. His prayers were for the sick in all his parishes as well as his family, and also for King George, who was again rumoured to have lost his mind. The Bible reading included the raising of Lazarus and the miracles of the sick healed by Jesus, and in his sermon he beseeched them in time of crisis to have faith in the power of prayer.

They were singing the second verse of the twenty-third psalm when the door clicked open and Beth beckoned urgently to Senara.

'Come quickly, Michael bain't breathing too good.'

She ran down the aisle to Bridie, and the terrified mother hurried after her fleeing sister.

Chapter Eight

There followed the longest night and day that Senara could remember. The sound of Michael rasping to snatch the tiniest portion of breath was heart-rending. Bowls of steaming herbs were placed in the room to try to ease his breathing, but his frail figure was now drenched in sweat. Dr Yeo had called – Joshua had ridden to Fowey after the service – and both grandparents had slept overnight at the parsonage.

Before Joshua and the doctor returned, the earlier rain had developed into a violent storm. Every few minutes the sky was streaked with blue-white lightning and the ground shook from the boom of thunder. The wind gusted at gale force, battering the windows and sending smoke swirling down the chimney to add its choking fumes to the bedchambers. Water had been thrown on the fire in Michael's room, and to keep him warm, extra bedclothes from Bridie's bed were piled on top of him and hot bricks wrapped in towels placed near his feet. In the pale, shuddering candlelight, the women's haggard faces had aged by a dozen years, their eyes hollowed and darkened by fear.

As the young boy's fever climbed, he kept throwing off the blankets and counterpanes. Cecily was wringing out damp cloths to place on his head whilst Bridie attempted to dribble drops of the cough linctus into his mouth. Senara had never felt so powerless. Her last examination of her nephew had shown a membrane forming at the back of his throat that was blocking his breathing passage. It was what she had feared most. Few children recovered once this obstruction formed, for they slowly choked to death. Bridie was doing everything that could be done for her son and Cecily could frequently be heard uttering prayers.

Leah, as though sensing that something was dreadfully amiss, was also awake, her eyes large and staring in her confusion and her inability to speak. Senara left Michael's sickroom to tend her mother. As she stroked Leah's hand, her voice was low and soothing. Death was stalking the narrow rooms of the parsonage and mocking her ancient healing remedies. When nothing else was left to ease the suffering of her two patients, she resorted to prayer and sheer force of will that each thread of life would draw from her own strength and belief.

A thunderclap immediately overhead made Leah cling to her daughter, her eyes wide with horror, her frail body trembling in her terror. It was not the violence of the storm that made her fearful, but the spectre of death that hovered in the shadows.

Senara tried to calm her mother, her eyes misting as she stared at the lightning illuminating the room through the closed shutters. The drumming of the rain now vied with the howling of the wind. A particularly bright flash of lightning was followed almost immediately by another loud explosion of thunder. It was certainly not a night to risk life and limb on the road. Branches and trees would be down – she hoped they would not block the winding tracks between villages – and from the sound of the torrential hammering of rain, there could be localised flooding. But surely Dr Yeo would not desert them, though he and Uncle Joshua would be drenched and exhausted if they ever managed to reach them through the storm.

She prayed with increasing intensity. Whenever there was a break in the noise of the storm, the wheezing cough from upstairs now seemed to reverberate throughout the entire building. When the strain became too much, Senara murmured a hasty reassurance to Leah and called Beth to sit with her mother as she hurried up the stairs to check on Michael. Bridie sat on the narrow bed, holding the boy in her arms, rocking him to soothe his whimpers of pain. At each hoarse snatch at breath his small chest rattled and rose feebly to draw in air.

Bridie stared at her sister, her voice husky with pleading. 'You must be able to do something.'

The child had passed beyond Senara's skill, but her sister needed hope to sustain her. 'I will brew another posset.' She murmured a few more words of encouragement and fled back down the stairs to the kitchen.

As the hours stretched on and the doctor and her uncle had not arrived, it appeared that Michael was holding his own. He was a fighter. If he could last a few more hours, the crisis could pass.

Bridie sang to her son to rally his spirits. Cecily increased the fervour of her prayers. Senara moved from sickroom to sickroom, her ears straining for the sound of horses announcing the arrival of Dr Yeo. Beth busied herself making tea for the women, which was left half drunk to go cold. She also had kettles constantly boiling over the fire, and every so often could be heard the steady thump of dough being vigorously kneaded on the

82

kitchen table as a way for the maidservant to work off her own fears and inability to do more.

Senara knelt on the floor by her mother's bed, her hands clasped in prayer, while the candle burned lower and the heart-rending gasping sound carried through the house from upstairs.

Leah was disorientated and confused, but there were moments when she seemed more lucid, and managed to mumble, 'Mial. Mial.' Which could only mean Michael.

It took all Senara's strength and reasoning to calm her. 'You must not worry about Michael. Rest, Ma.' But her words had little effect and she had to administer a few drops of laudanum before Leah drifted again into sleep.

Then, as the thunder rolled away into the distance and the wind lost its fury, Senara heard the snort of a horse in the road. Ordering Beth to stay with Leah, she ran outside to hold the horses. The expanse of earth that formed the road through the hamlet was running with water, and Joshua and Dr Yeo were splattered with mud.

'Michael is worse,' she shouted above the rustling of the yew trees to Dr Yeo. Water was funnelling off the brim of his hat and running down the oiled skin of his cloak that had given his clothing some protection from the rain. 'I'll put the horses in the stable.'

Uncle Joshua swung down wearily from his mount. 'I will tend to the animals, my dear. Go inside. You will do more good within.'

Dr Yeo apologised for his delay. 'The bridge was washed away in the flood and we had to find a shallow place to ford the river.'

'Thank God you are here and both safe.'

Gratefully Senara took the doctor's cloak, hat and gloves. As the physician wiped his wet face with his kerchief, the single candle burning on a table in the hall showed that his eyes were darkly circled. 'I was tending a patient at Golant when Reverend Mr Loveday arrived. My wife insisted he wait. I came as soon as I could.'

'I feared the storm would delay you. Michael is weak and feverish, his breathing becoming more difficult,' Senara explained. 'Beth will bring you a hot toddy upstairs. You must be half frozen from your ride.'

'That would be most kind. And how is my other patient?'

'My mother seems aware something is wrong. She became fretful and would not settle. I gave her some laudanum, although I know you advised against it.'

'In the circumstances, you did what was right. We must avoid her suffering any further distress.'

Senara handed him the candle from the hall to light his way up the stairs. Joshua came into the house and stamped the mud and straw from the stable off his sodden boots. Senara helped him remove his drenched greatcoat and placed it over the back of a chair by the kitchen fire where steam rose from it, filling the kitchen with the smell of musty wool. He followed her and she motioned to Leah's rocking chair by the fire.

'Uncle Joshua, sit and warm yourself. Let me help you off with those boots. Beth is making a hot toddy. I must soon return to sit with Mama.'

Beth had poured a mix of wine and brandy into two horn cups and plunged into each the glowing poker she had taken from the fire.

'My dear, go to Mrs Polglase now,' Cecily said as she came into the kitchen. Her eyes were red rimmed from crying. 'I will help my husband.'

Senara nodded. 'Then Beth will build up the fire in the parlour, and now that the storm has passed, another should be lit in Michael's room. If Mama is sleeping soundly I shall join you. Dr Yeo will call if he has need of me. Michael needs the comfort of his mother's presence more than anyone.'

The early-morning hours dragged out interminably. Joshua and Cecily dozed lightly but jerked awake at any sound from upstairs. Senara had sent Beth to get some sleep and took her place by her mother's bed. In the first brightening of the morning sky, Leah opened her eyes, but there was no recognition shown towards her daughter. She had suffered a second seizure while she slept. Senara bent her head and prayed. She had done everything that she could for Leah; whatever happened now was God's will.

An hour after dawn, Dr Yeo came down the stairs, the dark shadow of stubble on his jaw accentuating his haggard expression. Outside, the rain had finally stopped and a watery sun was breaking through the cloud. There was the sharp warning cry of a blackbird and the cawing of distant crows.

Senara, Cecily and Joshua met him in the hall passage. 'The fever continues and the membrane has not broken. I am sorry. I am surprised he has lasted so long. But while he continues to fight, there is always a chance.'

'Are you leaving, Dr Yeo?' Cecily voiced her shock. 'Surely Michael needs you.'

'As do my other patients that I promised to attend this morning. There are several cases of quinsy.'

'Your pardon, Dr Yeo.' Cecily dabbed at her eyes.

Dr Yeo bowed. 'I will call again this evening.' He turned to Senara. 'I will examine Mrs Polglase before I leave.'

Senara stood by the door of her mother's chamber as he made his examination. His voice was sombre as he said,

'You are aware that Mrs Polglase has suffered another seizure and is now unconscious.'

'Yes,' Senara answered, fighting the prickle of tears in her eyes.

'I could bleed her again but she is very weak. If you can, coax her to swallow a few drops of an infusion to thin the blood. This is a very sad day for you.'

He bade them farewell, his step heavy as he entered the stable to saddle his horse. Senara left one sickroom to visit the other. Cecily was trying in vain to get Bridie to rest on her bed. 'You will make yourself ill if you do not sleep. There are enough of us who can tend Michael.'

'I will not leave him. I wish Peter were here. Michael has been calling for his papa.'

'And Peter will not thank us if he returns to find you exhausted,' Cecily pleaded. 'Try and sleep, even if it is just for an hour.'

Bridie was pale as tallow, her eyes red rimmed from tears and exhaustion. 'Michael needs his mother,' she said fiercely.

'He needs his mama to be strong and healthy,' Cecily said more sharply. 'You look about to collapse.'

'Aunt Cecily is right, sister. Lie down just for an hour,' Senara urged.

'You also have not slept.' Bridie's face suddenly crumpled. 'And what kind of a daughter am I? I have not even asked after Ma. How is she?'

Senara shook her head. 'Her life is in God's hands now.'

'I must see her.' Bridie limped to the door.

'Then promise me you will rest,' Senara insisted. 'I could not cope with another invalid on my hands.'

Bridie agreed.

They called her two hours later, and she was with

Senara at their mother's side when Leah passed peacefully away. She simply ceased to breathe in her sleep. Blinded by her tears, Bridie broke away from her sister's embrace and staggered back up the stairs to tend to her son, who showed no sign of improvement.

'Please God, let his fever break,' Cecily groaned. 'Let Michael be saved.'

By midday, Senara had laid Leah out in her chamber. She had dressed her in her best gown, and a white lace cap covered her grey hair. A candle was lit at the foot of her bed. Joshua had gone to arrange with the gravedigger for her final resting place to be prepared in the churchyard for her funeral. As Senara straightened the folds of her mother's dress and smoothed the last wrinkle from the patchwork coverlet beneath her figure, the front door burst open.

'Bridie! I'm home,' shouted Peter, his voice excited. 'Great news. Wife, where are you?'

He halted at seeing his mother come out of the parlour. Senara held back as she watched them from the doorway of Leah's room.

Peter was animated and laughing as he burst out, 'Mama, you will rejoice in my news. Papa will be so proud. Not only did I receive the money for the church roof, but also I have been given a new parish. A much larger one in Launceston, and my stipend has been doubled.'

The misery on his mother's face finally registered through his excitement. His voice sobered. 'Mama, what is amiss?'

Cecily opened her mouth to answer and instead broke into tears. The slow tread of Bridie's feet echoed on the stairs and in bewilderment Peter spun round to gaze up at his wife. The high colour from his morning's ride drained from his face. 'Is it Michael?'

Bridie could not answer at first and clung to the newel post. Painfully she dragged out, 'He has been calling for you.'

Peter took the stairs two at a time, and then his anguished cry resounded through the parsonage. Bridie raised her tear-streaked face to her mother and sister.

'Michael is dead.' She fell in a swoon at their feet.

The funeral was the next day. Bridie could not bear the thought of her precious child lying alone in the cold ground, so the two coffins were placed in the same grave. Peter had refused to take the service and stood in stony-faced silence throughout the ceremony and interment. Adam had stayed up all night crafting Michael's coffin. Joshua's voice cracked several times during his eulogy for his grandson. At the side of the grave Bridie leaned heavily on Peter's arm for support, and there was soft sobbing from all the womenfolk, both family and villagers, for Michael had been greatly loved amongst the congregation. Bridie was stoic, her tears spilling silently down her cheeks.

'May God have mercy on their souls,' Joshua concluded and nodded to his son to throw the first handful of earth into the grave.

For some moments Peter did not move, then abruptly he wrenched himself away from his wife's side and strode off across the cemetery. Senara put her arms around Bridie as she threw down on to her son's tiny coffin a set of six painted wooden soldiers that had been his favourite toy. Then she guided her gently away from the grave, their heads close together in their grief. Bridie's limp was pronounced and her body was bent forward as though trying to shield herself from her inner torment.

'Michael will be watched over by Ma,' Senara comforted.

'Peter cannot accept that he is dead,' Bridie groaned. 'I thought that as a preacher he would be sustained by his faith. He says God has forsaken him.'

'Peter will not turn his back on his vocation. His anger at the moment is understandable. And perhaps the new parish will be a fresh challenge for him, which could be what he needs.'

Bridie halted and picked a primrose flower and held it to her breast. 'I still have the bunch Michael picked for me when he was playing with Snuff in the garden.' Her throat worked in agony. 'They were Ma's favourites too.'

By the time they entered the parsonage, where the freshly baked funeral breads and cakes were laid out awaiting the mourners, Bridie had pulled herself upright and composed her emotions. 'Ma would be the first to say that life goes on. Michael will always be in my heart.'

Chapter Nine

When the mourners returned to the parsonage they were surprised not to find Peter there.

'He'll be wanting some time to himself,' Joshua explained, but he seemed ill at ease.

Beth, who was carrying a large tea tray into the parlour, bobbed a hesitant curtsy to the Reverend Loveday. 'If you please, sir, the parson did not come into the house but went straight to the stable and rode out.'

'Just his way of wanting to clear his thoughts,' Joshua insisted, but when the rest of the mourners were taking their tea, he slipped out to the stable. The village women were gathered around Bridie, giving her their condolences. Bridie was in a grief-locked daze and had not appeared to notice that her husband was not present.

Joshua was concerned. Peter was acting strangely. He would always put others' feelings before his own and be mindful of his duties to his parishioners. The talk they had had that morning had disturbed Joshua. Peter had been distraught, blaming himself that he had not been here when his son needed him.

Joshua had tried to reason by quoting the scriptures, and when that failed had said simply, 'It is not for us to question God's will, my son. Michael was an angel in our midst. We were blessed to have him amongst us even for so short a time. God would want him at his side.'

'But God can have him for eternity.' Peter's dark eyes were glazed with pain. 'He was my son and I loved him. What did I do that was so wrong that he was taken from me?'

'We are all tested in different ways.'

'And have I not faced my demons and given my life to God?' Peter had raged. 'I have always fought temptation and was a born sinner. Not so Michael.'

'Peter, you have taken your vows to serve God, not to question him. Take solace in prayer. The Lord will give you strength. You are a fine preacher. Your flock needs your guidance.'

Peter had backed away, shaking his head, and locked himself in his study until it was time for the coffins to be taken to the church. He had appeared then and pushed his brother and cousin Adam away and lifted Michael's coffin into his arms. 'I alone will carry him.'

Japhet, Adam and two men from the village had taken Leah's coffin on their shoulders and carried it to Polruggan church.

Now, when Joshua entered the stable, his unease increased. There by Peter's mare's stall were his crumpled Geneva bands, the sign of his office. The wide-brimmed cleric's hat was also flung into a corner and the mare had trampled it as she left the stable.

Joshua picked up the soiled bands and clenched his hands over them as he knelt in the straw to pray for his son. Peter had curbed his wild blood for so many years; now that it had been unleashed by his grief, he would be capable of any folly.

When Joshua returned to the parsonage, Cecily immediately accosted him. 'Have you seen Peter? He should be here supporting his wife. Bridie has lost a child and her mother.'

'He has taken his horse. He will come to his senses soon,' Joshua reassured her.

'This is so unlike him.' Cecily was both impatient and con-cerned. 'Peter is always so reliable. What was he thinking, going off like that?'

The voice of Gert Wibbley rose loudly from the parlour. There was no one who could spread gossip or stir up trouble faster. 'Where be the parson? Some say he be out of his mind with grief.'

'I had better speak with her,' Cecily groaned. 'Such talk will not help Bridie.' She went away and picked up a plate of fruited funeral bread to help pacify the villager.

Overhearing his parents' discussion, Japhet detached himself from the men with whom he had been conversing. He addressed his father. 'I fear Peter is not thinking clearly. Should Adam and I go after him?'

Joshua shook his head. 'His faith is being tested. He needs this time alone. Peter will be back soon. He will not forget his duty.'

Amelia was threading her way through the mourners, looking anxious. She sought out Adam and whispered, 'Have you seen Rowena?'

'She was being unusually helpful assisting Beth, but it has been some time since she came in here.'

'She was told to stay in the house.' Amelia sighed. 'She insisted on coming to pay her respects. I wanted her to remain at the cottage with Charlotte, Thea and the baby, but she made a scene, saying we kept treating her like a child, and eventually I gave in.'

Gert Wibbley was quick to scent gossip. 'Did I hear you mention Rowena? She was talking to that Trevanion youth. He could not take his eyes off her during the service. Not fitting conduct for a young gentleman during a funeral, if you ask me.'

'The Trevanions recently moved into Polruggan Manor and have called to pay their respects. They are part of Peter Loveday's congregation.' Amelia tartly attempted to quash any gossip Mrs Wibbley would spread. 'Mr Trevanion is a widower with a young daughter, and his brother lives with them.'

Gert smiled smugly and bobbed a salutary curtsy. 'I'm sure it be of no interest to me how the gentry behave, but if Rowena were my daughter I'd want to know what she be up to, flirting at such a time.' She moved off, making straight for her cronies, pressing her head close to theirs, no doubt revelling in her latest gossip.

Amelia sighed. 'Adam, would you look outside and call your niece to account. This conduct does no good to her reputation. Wilbur Trevanion is seventeen and Rowena is far too susceptible to his attention. She will not listen to me.'

Adam sauntered outside, hoping that Rowena was behaving herself. He could not see the pair but he heard Rowena's laugh from behind the stable.

'Rowena!' he called and moved swiftly, angered that he might find her compromised. He had not met this branch of the Trevanions. They had inherited the manor from their uncle, the old squire, who had died some time ago and lived his last years as a recluse. The house had been shut up for many years, and it was reported that Mr Bruce Trevanion had for most of his marriage lived in Switzerland, where the air was thought to be beneficial to his wife. She had recently died of consumption.

When Adam turned the corner of the stable, he found his niece leaning against the wall, holding the kitten

Snuff. Wilbur Trevanion was a foot away from her, but there was a guilty flush to his cheeks.

'Captain Loveday,' he stammered.

Adam ignored the remark. 'Get back into the house, Rowena. Amelia was worried at your absence.'

The girl cast him a look from under her lashes as she stroked the kitten. 'I saw Snuff being pursued by one of the village dogs and thought he would be hurt. Mr Trevanion chased the cur away.' She held the kitten out to her uncle. 'See, Snuff is perfectly safe. Michael adored him so; I could not have borne it if he had been hurt.'

'You have duties inside, Rowena,' Adam repeated, his stare fierce as it rested upon his niece's companion. Trevanion shifted uneasily.

Rowena remained unruffled and dipped a curtsy to the young man. 'I could not have saved Snuff without your help, Mr Trevanion.'

Wilbur Trevanion watched Rowena walk back to the parsonage and bowed stiffly to Adam as he prepared to follow her.

'Not so fast, young sir.' Adam stopped him in his tracks. 'You are aware that Rowena is only fourteen. She may have recently lost her father, but be assured that her uncles will not tolerate her reputation being compromised.'

'I assure you, nothing untoward has happened, Captain Loveday.'

'Then take care not to seek her company when other members of her family are not present. I will not warn you again.'

'I have only the deepest respect for Miss Loveday.'

'I am pleased to hear it. You will have a regard for her reputation in future or you will answer to me. Your brother has paid his respects and is about to leave. I suggest you join him.'

Trevanion could not get away fast enough. Adam frowned. Rowena was a provocative minx and a beautiful young woman who looked older than her age. A dangerous combination for a young, hot-blooded male. She would need careful watching in the future.

When he returned to the house, he frowned at discovering Felicity being handed a glass of canary by another man he knew only by sight. This was Bruce Trevanion, the new master of Polruggan Manor. Adam was surprised that he was younger than he had expected, of a similar age to himself. His dark hair was cut short and flecked with grey at the temples but his face was unlined by age. The long aquiline nose was the only marring of his otherwise handsome features and his dark eyes were bright with intelligence. However, Adam was not so pleased to notice that his sister-in-law had a flush of excitement in her cheeks, unbecoming in so recent a widow.

He bowed to the new squire. 'Captain Loveday at your service, sir. We have not been introduced, but I believe you recently moved into the manor.'

'Adam, this is Mr Bruce Trevanion.' Felicity was visibly flustered. 'He was acquainted with St John and wished to express his condolences.'

'How were you acquainted with my brother, Mr Trevanion? Your name is Cornish but I do not believe we have met before.'

'Our father was from Redruth and had little contact with his older brother at the manor. I have lived abroad for many years.'

'I understand you have recently been widowed. I offer my condolences.'

He inclined his head in acknowledgement. 'And I on your own recent losses, Captain. My brother Wilbur is here somewhere. We are only slowly getting to know our neighbours.'

'I met him earlier. He was talking to my niece.'

'Ah, the pretty blond girl.' He smiled at Felicity. 'The Lovedays have many beautiful women among their number. After so many years away from my homeland, I find Cornwall has much to recommend it. We cannot deny our roots, can we, Captain Loveday?'

He bowed to them both. 'I have enjoyed many an invigorating sermon delivered by your cousin, Captain.'

Through the window Adam watched him stride away, joining his younger brother, who was still lingering in the lane.

'I trust Mr Trevanion did not importune you, Felicity.'

'He was polite and pleasant. His daughter is five. We were talking of children and of course coming to terms with the loss of loved ones.' The colour remained heightened in her cheeks.

Felicity was still young and attractive. Adam could not envisage her being a widow for long; she was less independent than the other Loveday women and was the type to lean upon a man for guidance and security. But it made him uncomfortable that Trevanion had shown more than neighbourly interest in her. His brother Wilbur was no better, pursuing Rowena. They were a family he would be wise to keep an eye on where his womenfolk were concerned.

Two hours passed and still Peter had not returned to the parsonage. The mead and ale supplied for the wake had all been drunk, and only a few crumbs remained on the plates of food laid out. Most of the villagers had paid their respect and left, but others like Gert Wibbley and two of her cronies were hovering and making comments about the parson's absence. Beth and Gilly Brown, who had come over from Boscabel to help with the extra work, discreetly cleared the plates and Joshua took charge to escort Gert and her friends from the house.

'I thought those gossip carrion would never leave,' he remarked. 'There is peace and quiet at last.'

'Too much silence, that is the trouble,' Amelia said as she and Felicity came forward pulling on their gloves. 'A void that was once filled with the laughter of a child is the hardest of all to bear.' She wiped a tear from her eye.

Felicity linked her arm through the older woman's. 'This day must have brought many painful memories for you. Joan is missed by us all. She would have been six had she lived. She was barely a toddler when she died. And dear brave Michael was just three.'

'You two mothers are blessed that you have other children still living,' Elspeth tartly reminded them. 'Bridie is not so fortunate.' She turned to Adam, who had been chillingly polite to her since she had decided to remain at Trevowan after the other women left. 'I will not disturb Bridie and Senara in their grief. Leah was a good woman. Give your wife and her sister my heartfelt condolences.'

She walked out, calling out a loud goodbye to the others in the house.

Adam followed. 'Despite our recent differences, I would ensure that you are safe, Aunt.'

Her expression mellowed. 'I appreciate your concern. However, I cannot leave the stables at Trevowan without an infernal groom whom Tristan has employed to accompany me upon my rides. He will be outside tending the horses.'

Adam tensed at mentioned of his cousin, and Elspeth narrowed her hooded eyes. 'I may resent being treated like an imbecile by the new master of Trevowan, but he has my welfare at heart. I tolerate the groom because you would blame Tristan if any harm befell me whilst I was under his protection.'

'He does no more than his duty, Aunt.'

Elspeth snorted. 'Stubborn as mules, the pair of you. Whatever the wrongs of the past, you would do well not to forget that you are family. Your father put great faith in loyalty to our own.' Her walking cane resounded on the flagstones as she limped out of the parsonage.

Adam swallowed his anger. Did his aunt think it was so easy to put the wrongs of the past behind them? His father also held great store by family pride. And you could not forgive the unforgivable.

Amelia and Felicity also left, and a strained silence stretched between the men as they heard muffled weeping from upstairs.

'Perhaps we should search for Peter,' Adam suggested to Joshua and Japhet.

'He will be back before dark,' Japhet replied, but he kept glancing towards the lane outside the parsonage, his head cocked as he strained to listen for the sound of hoofbeats.

'And you should get Gwen back to Tor Farm,' Joshua advised. 'The rain has held off so far today, but those clouds look ominous. There will be a downpour later.'

Adam said, 'I'll stay until Peter returns. Senara will not leave Bridie.'

'Cecily and I will stay,' Joshua declared. 'Your little Sara will be missing her mother. Senara has been away two days.'

Adam climbed the stairs to fetch his wife. He and Senara would call again at the parsonage in the morning.

Chapter Ten

'It is my fault that Peter has abandoned his parishioners,' Bridie sobbed the next morning. 'I was not a good enough mother. This is my punishment.'

None of the Loveday family had slept peacefully that night. Peter had not returned to the parsonage. Cecily sat up all night comforting Bridie, and Joshua either paced the rooms or spent the night kneeling in prayer. In the morning, Bridie was so exhausted she could hardly stand, but she refused to go to her bed.

'There will be no more talk like that,' Cecily said firmly. 'No mother could have cared for her child better than you. Several children have died from quinsy this winter. There is no cure. You must accept it as God's will.'

'But Peter has not.' Bridie sat in Leah's chair by the kitchen hearth and locked her arms across her chest, rocking back and forth. 'He blames me or he would be here. He adored Michael. How can he forgive me?'

'There is nothing to forgive,' Cecily said sharply. 'Knowing Peter, he is probably blaming himself for not being here when Michael was taken ill. That is why he cannot face you.'

Cecily was relieved to hear Senara and Adam's voices as Joshua greeted them outside. Senara hurried into the kitchen, and at the sight of her, Bridie burst into a fresh bout of weeping. Adam paused only long enough to say, 'I'll ride to Tor Farm. Japhet and I will find Peter.'

'I'm going with you as well,' Joshua insisted, and glanced anxiously at his wife.

'Three will find him faster than two.' Cecily looked relieved that a decision had been made. 'I'll stay here to keep at bay the likes of Mrs Wibbley, sniffing round for gossip.'

It took three days to track Peter down. On the first two evenings the men returned to the parsonage and reported what they had learned. As Peter had been so emphatic about needing time to himself, they doubted he would have visited a town, and concentrated instead on the vastness of Bodmin Moor.

'Our Lord spent time alone in the desert wrestling with the taunts of the devil.' Joshua understood the religious torment his son would be facing. 'Peter has his own demons to slay.'

'Then he could as likely have sought solace at the hermit's chapel at Roche,' Japhet insisted. 'He liked to visit there as a boy and climb up to the ruin.'

'That is where we will search tomorrow,' Joshua decided.

They left just after first light and rode hard towards St Austell and across the moorland waste, out of which rose a prominent granite tor. On top of this were the ruins of a hermitage cell and small chapel dedicated to St Michael. Roche had been a favourite haunt of Peter's in the days before his marriage when he had roamed the villages of Cornwall as a lay preacher.

There was no sign of Peter's mare cropping the grass beneath the great rock. They stared up at the steep sides of the tor to the ruined chapel with its arched window. It had been built in the early fifteenth century and inhabited by a hermit.

'My days of clambering across rocks like a mountain goat are long past,' Joshua sighed. 'I'll hold the horses.'

Laboriously Adam and Japhet climbed the treacherous steps, made more dangerous by the morning drizzle. Entering the ruined two-storey chapel, they saw a figure lying on the stones, protected from the elements. Japhet ran forward, but stopped short of the body. Up close, it was heavily bearded with long matted hair, and was clearly a vagabond using the place as shelter.

'Wake up, man!' Japhet demanded. 'Has anyone else been on the rock today or yesterday?'

A spate of curses came from the ragged figure, which rolled into a sitting position. 'What be it to you?'

Japhet stood over the surly man, his hands itching to drag him to his feet and shake the information out of him. 'I am looking for my brother, a well-dressed gentleman in black with dark hair. Was he here?'

'Happen he were. Happen he weren't.'

Japhet dug a silver coin out of his pocket and allowed it to glint in the sun. 'Will this help your memory?'

The vagrant licked his lips, his gaze fixed on the coin. 'Happen he were here late yesterday. He was sitting on the edge of the rocks staring out across the moor. Sat for hours like a statue. Didna move. Didna speak. Didna even seem to hear. Walked past me like a man whose wits had gone begging.'

Japhet flipped him the coin and the vagrant's hand snaked out, snatching it in mid-air.

'God bless you, sir.' The coin was bitten between blackened stumps to check it was pure metal.

'What direction did the man take?'

'How much that be worth?' He grinned artlessly.

Japhet's hand shot out and grabbed the filthy muffler at the vagabond's throat. He hauled him up into a crouched position. 'You've had your money. You can either tell me, or I'll beat it out of you. And do not think to send us on a wild goose chase, or I'll come back and find you.'

The man's eyes rolled with terror. 'No need to take on so,' he spluttered.

Japhet loosened his throttling hold and the ragged figure gasped for air.

'The gentleman left just afore dark, heading to the village.'

Japhet released him and tossed a few copper coins on the ground, then nodded to Adam to follow him.

They climbed back down and made enquiries at the village inns. They had success at the second tavern, the Rock. The burly, bewhiskered landlord said that a man of Peter's description had passed out drunk and spent the night slumped over a table.

'If he had not been a gentleman by his speech and dress,' he added, 'I'd have thrown him out into the gutter. He left as soon as the inn was astir.'

'Which way did he go?' Joshua asked.

The innkeeper shrugged. 'Ask the ostler. He would have saddled his horse.'

The ostler was more helpful, running an appreciative eye over Japhet's mare. 'Bain't you Japhet Loveday? Heard tell you'd returned to these parts and set up a stud farm. That be a fine horse you be riding. I thought the gentleman in question had the look of the preacher fellow Loveday. He used to sermonise around here some years back. Used to threaten hell and damnation to sinners. He didn't look like a holy life had done him many favours.'

'Did you see in which direction he rode?' Japhet asked, ignoring the ostler's prying.

'If it were Preacher Loveday, he looked like he had the world on his shoulders. He took the Bodmin road.'

Convinced that Peter would not go to the town, Japhet was all for continuing their search, as there were two more hours before dark. Adam disagreed.

'We should stay at the inn for tonight. I do not like the look of that lowering sky across the moor, and already there is a mist rising. It is too dangerous.' The memory of the smuggler Harry Sawle being sucked into the bog was still too fresh in Adam's mind for him to risk such a danger for themselves. Peter had also been with the party that hunted Sawle and arrested him. He too knew the risks. He would take shelter.

When they awoke the next morning, however, it was to a thick mist obscuring the moorland tracks, and they had to wait a frustrating two hours before it began to clear. They headed for Brown Willy, the highest peak on Bodmin Moor, but the mist lingered and their pace was slow until midday, when it suddenly disappeared.

Unfortunately none of the moor folk they questioned had seen Peter. It was not until the middle of the afternoon that their luck changed and a shepherd said he'd seen a rider that morning heading Warleggan way.

'Didn't Peter often stop at Golitha Falls when he was this way preaching?' Joshua said, his flagging energy reviving. 'I took him there once myself.'

The falls were in a wooded valley on the upper reaches of the River Fowey. At this time of year the river had swelled from the winter rains and the water tumbled over boulders through lichen-covered trees. They rode accompanied by the roar of the water, and rounded a bend in the river to discover Peter's mare tethered to a tree. Within moments they discovered Peter sitting on a boulder completely motionless, looking down into the cascading water. He seemed unaware of the sound of their approach.

They dismounted and Joshua called his son's name. Peter did not move. Japhet and Adam held back and allowed Joshua to approach him. His father talked to him for some minutes before Peter flung himself into Joshua's arms and sobbed.

The two cousins withdrew and sat on a boulder some yards upstream. It was a long time before Peter regained control of his emotions. His brother and cousin waited patiently, each thinking of their own children and the devastation they would feel if one of them died and they never saw them grow to adulthood.

Eventually Joshua spoke softly to Peter. 'Come, my son, it is time to return to your wife. She has need of your strength.'

Peter allowed his father to guide him to the horses. As he drew level with Adam and Japhet, they were shocked at how haggard he had become. His unshaven cheeks and ebony hair added to the dark cloud that seemed to have settled over him. His eyes were dull and he gave only the briefest of nods to acknowledge their presence.

Chapter Eleven

Whilst most of the Loveday family were in deep mourning, Amelia's elder son, Richard Allbright, was making the most of having recently docked in Plymouth. He had accepted an invitation to spend a month in Bath with the family of his friend and fellow officer Lieutenant James Chandler. They were then to travel to Chandler's father's estate in Somerset.

Before Richard could leave for Bath, a letter was delivered to him that had been held by the Admiralty. It was from Amelia, informing him of his stepbrother's death and the change in her circumstances.

There had been a momentary twinge of guilt when he realised that his mother would expect him home, for the alteration in their living circumstances did not exactly fill him with pleasure. And during his last visit to Trevowan, he had resented Amelia's lectures on morality when rumours reached her that he had shown an interest in some of the village wenches. His mother wanted him married, but at twenty-two, nailing himself to one woman was not in his plans for some years in the future. And being confined to a cottage with several women and children was not his choice of entertaining shore leave.

He quickly justified his excuses to himself. He had

been away at sea for almost two years, enduring cramped quarters and sparse rations: first in the Mediterranean and then, after the Treaty of Amiens, in the Caribbean. He had not set foot on land in three months, and during his recent voyages had encountered enemy action twice. He had escaped injury, but one of his closest friends had been killed. After so much hardship and danger, he felt he deserved to experience the pleasures life could bring. He considered that he had earned it by serving his country. He never had been close to St John, who had mocked him for following Adam's example by going into the navy. Although he was saddened that his stepbrother had taken his life, he was also resentful and angry that his dissolute lifestyle had brought such devastation to the family.

He wrote a letter to his mother expressing his condolences and stating that he would visit her as soon as he was released from his naval duties. He hoped that would satisfy her and allow him a few weeks' grace to enjoy himself with his friends. He was looking forward to the entertainments Bath offered.

The house close to the Royal Crescent, with its elegant façade, was much more to his liking. Chandler's parents were an amiable couple, popular amongst the gentry, and every night there was an invitation to a musical soiree, dinner or card session. The Assembly and Pump Rooms were also to be visited on every possible occasion, when the most fair of women could be selected.

Tonight the splendour of the Assembly Rooms scarcely registered with Richard. He had spent the first half-hour noting the women with the trimmest ankles or the boldest glances. Under the light of the huge chandeliers, jewels sparkled in the ladies' hair and upon their throats. The scarlet of military finery dominated the darker hues of naval uniforms or the cutaway coat and breeches of gentlemen. On the dance floor, long lines of dancers performed a cotillion to the strains of a stringed sextet, the edges of the room packed with conversing groups. Normally his eye passed quickly over the younger, obviously unattached women, but a particular blond-haired, blue-eyed maid kept appearing in his range of vision, her stare bold as it held his appraisal.

'That one certainly cannot take her eyes off you,' Chandler encouraged. 'There's no chaperone that I can see, or at least no one who would question your interest. The woman at her side could be an older sister or cousin, and she is flirting with every man who notices them.'

Richard studied the woman with more interest. Both ladies were regarding him, though the fairer one was more nervous, constantly touching an earring or bracelet. It pricked his interest. Perhaps she was not as innocent as he had first believed.

'Do you know them, James?' Richard asked. It would be impossible to approach them without a formal introduction.

'Sadly not. Though I did see Gus Frobisher talking to them earlier. He's a family friend and we were at Winchester together. He would introduce you if you wish. The younger filly looks somewhat out of sorts and in need of cheering.'

'She is too young,' Richard protested. In addition, he had detected an air of melancholy in her demeanour. He had also taken an interest in a dark-haired woman across the room, dressed in a glittering array of diamonds, who had danced with several partners and was as vivacious as she was curvaceous.

'Nonsense, she must be twenty.' James was undeterred.

He dived through the press of people to return within minutes with the affable Gus Frobisher, a gentleman in his thirties with a broad Somerset drawl to his vowels.

'So you wish an introduction with Miss Emma Madison.' Frobisher grinned. 'She is a sweet little thing. One of four daughters of Major Henry Madison. Her mother died five years ago and the major is serving in India. Miss Madison is the third eldest. None of her sisters have married. The two eldest are dowds and look after their younger siblings. Her companion, Mrs Kellerman, is a widowed cousin who has invited Miss Madison to Bath for the Season.'

Across the room, Lydia Kellerman was chiding her companion. 'Smile sweetly, my dear. The young man is handsome and most eligible. He is already a lieutenant in the navy, and I gather he owns several properties in the most prestigious areas of London.'

Emma averted his gaze from the naval officer. She was not interested in him, and inwardly her heart was breaking. 'How do you know so much? This is the first time I have set eyes on him.'

'I make it my business to learn all I can about eligible bachelors. I am quite determined to see you settled this Season. I owe it to your late mama.' Lydia scanned the room assessingly. 'He is most presentable, and has been at sea for two years. That can make a man more eager for the comforts a wife can offer.'

Emma was aware of curious glances in her direction. Did they pity her that she had been spurned by a beau who had ardently pursued her these last three months? There had been speculation that an announcement was about to be made between them. Emma had been no less expectant, and then it had all gone horribly wrong. The shame was almost too much to bear. The curious glances were too humiliating and the room with its press of people was becoming intolerably hot.

'I am faint. Let us go home, Lydia. I can feel people watching me.'

'Nonsense, my dear. Take deep breaths. We are here to show these gossipmongers that you care not a whit that the despicable Captain Jevington played you so false. It but proved you had a lucky escape from the attentions of such a knave.'

Emma closed her eyes against another wave of mortification. Her cousin's voice drummed in her ears.

'My dear, keep your stare upon the lieutenant, if you want to win his interest. No man can resist such attention from a pretty woman. And do not dare look towards that knave Jevington, who as good as jilted you.'

'Please, Lydia, take me home. I cannot do this.' Her companion had forced her to remain in the ballroom when Captain Theodore Jevington entered. One glance had almost sent Emma into a swoon, and her legs still felt they would give way at any moment. Theo, with his dark side-whiskers and imperious figure, had looked so handsome and dashing in his cavalry dress uniform of scarlet and gold. You could not sweep love away when it consumed you to the depths of your soul.

Lydia rapped her sharply on the arm with her fan. 'We shall not leave. It is your duty to show that knave that his perfidy has not touched you. Poise and disdain are powerful weapons in a woman's armoury. Show him what he is missing by bestowing your beauty, wit and charm upon another. You may even bring the cur to heel, if you are still foolish enough to want him. And if you wish to regain his interest, then what better way than for him to see another fawning over you.' Lydia gripped her cousin's wrist. 'Do not turn round, Emma. Jevington is behind you. The Claythorpe girl is not here tonight. I heard she was suffering with a cold from her carriage ride with your beau; they were caught in a downpour. Jevington must see that you have not a care in the world.'

Her cousin's words were well intentioned, but Emma was crushed. It took every particle of her willpower not to glance in the direction of her former swain. She had believed that Theodore Jevington was the most honourable of men when he had paid court to her. Not a week had passed when he had not sought her company, and she had fallen in love with him, expecting his proposal any day. Then the Claythorpes had arrived in the spa with their beautiful niece Elizabeth, who was heiress to a vast fortune. Theodore had been escorting Lydia to a musical evening when the Claythorpes had first appeared. Emma had been shocked at the immediate change in her beau, who had all but ignored her, unable to take his gaze from Elizabeth. Within half an hour he had abandoned Emma into the custody of the two couples who had accompanied them, and joined the Claythorpes' party.

For an hour refusing to believe she had been so cruelly deserted, Emma sat through the music recital certain that Jevington would return to her side. He did not, and burning with humiliation and heartbreak at his neglect, she had left during the interval. Jevington's conduct was an unforgivable breach of etiquette and an insult to Emma. She had locked herself in her bedchamber, refusing food and sobbing uncontrollably. There had not been a single word, not even an apology from Jevington. That was three weeks ago, and this was her first outing in public since his brutal rejection.

A sharp jab to her ribs by her cousin's finger jolted

Emma from her bleak reflections. The magnificent chandeliers of the ballroom were blurred by the tears that had formed in her eyes. Lydia's voice was sharp.

'This is not a time for moping. Head up. I swear Jevington is glowering at your handsome naval officer. He's noted the man's interest. Give us your brightest smile. Show that knave that he is but dust beneath your feet and that others see your beauty and charm. For all her looks, I hear the Claythorpe heiress is a vapid creature, given to much swooning and inane conversation.'

Emma turned large blue eyes upon her cousin. 'I cannot act so at odds to how I feel. Take me home, Lydia.'

'Oh, my dear, that simply cannot be done.' Lydia was growing impatient with Emma's protests. 'Your handsome naval lieutenant advances. You will flutter your eyelashes and dance with him as though you had not a care in the world. And you will take pains to ignore that blackguard Jevington.'

Pride came to Emma's rescue. She knew she had led a sheltered life before coming to Bath. She had just passed her eighteenth birthday. Since the death of her mama, her father's widowed sister Aunt Myrtle had provided the necessary chaperonage for Emma and her sisters, and having failed to marry off the two elder girls had sent Emma to stay with Lydia in the hope that she could succeed in finding at least one of her charges a husband before her younger sister became of marriageable age.

If Emma had one major trait, it was her wish to appease and to please. When her father was at home, his barked orders, which had taken no insubordination from his troops, had her scurrying to obey. It was expected of her to return from Bath with a husband, and to fail would ensure she faced censure and disgrace.

As the tall, blond naval lieutenant approached, she blinked twice to dispel any lingering tears. Her chin tilted up a notch and her lips stretched into a welcoming smile, though it felt as though her face muscles would snap with the strain. He bowed. She curtsied. Augustus Frobisher effected the necessary introductions, and as the musicians struck up the opening chords of the next dance, Emma found herself in the middle of the ballroom floor, lightly holding Richard Allbright's hand as they paraded in stately fashion through the opening steps. Lydia's warning whisper as Emma was led away lingered in her mind: 'Do not forget who is watching. Show him what he is missing.'

'I will not bite, Miss Madison, I do assure you. Pray, do not look so nervous.' Richard smiled to make light of his words. 'I declare, you are the fairest woman here. I hope to make more of our acquaintance.'

The words were a balm after her cruel rejection. They gave her confidence. She would not let Jevington think he had crushed her. Was not her partner handsome and wealthy? She lifted her gaze to meet the lieutenant's persuasive smile and a pretty blush heightened the colour in her cheeks.

'You are very kind, sir. I am not used to such gatherings. Before coming to Bath I lived very quietly in the country with my sisters.'

'Such a glorious English rose should not be kept hidden away.'

When his eyes sparkled in the most disarming manner, she looked up at him through her lashes in the way in which Lydia had schooled her, declaring that men found it captivating. Theo Jevington had never been so flamboyant in his flattery. Whenever the dance permitted she studied her partner anew. He was possibly even more handsome than her captain, and certainly taller and broader in the shoulder. Whereas Theo had a soft boyishness to his looks, Richard Allbright had a more dangerous worldliness about his lean features that you would expect from a man who had risked his life for his country. Disloyalty pierced her heartache. What had Jevington ever done? He was the impoverished third son of a baronet and his regiment had never been further than Brighton.

'You must have met many beautiful women, Lieutenant Allbright. My cousin has warned me about men in uniform. The ladies cannot resist them.'

Richard heard the breathless timbre to her voice and his smile broadened. 'You overestimate our popularity.'

'Oh, I think you have made many conquests.' She glanced sidelong at him in a delightful, unconscious manner. She was a heady mix of innocence and provocation that he found fascinating.

By the end of the ball they had danced three times and it was agreed that he would call upon her on the morrow. During the evening Emma had twice caught Theo frowning in her direction, his gaze assessing her handsome partner. It had given her confidence. Was it possible that he was jealous, that he realised he was still in love with her? The thought had brightened her smile as she studied her partner when they passed Jevington in a dance. She had flirted more coquettishly with her lieutenant while her mind savoured bringing her lost lover back into her arms.

Richard Allbright was not the only member of the Loveday family to have turned his thoughts upon romance. Tristan had spent the Season in London with an eye to finding a wife. So far, no woman he had met had fulfilled his criteria of breeding and position. He was also aware that his own credentials were far from impeccable and would meet disapproval from the most eminent families. He could afford to bide his time. He had spent his days ordering furniture of the finest quality to be made and dispatched to Trevowan. He had also used his time to be seen about town as a man of fashion, means and influence. It would have helped him to establish his reputation if he could have used his family connection with his cousin Thomas Mercer, who until a few months ago had been the owner of Mercer and Lascalles Bank. Thomas had sold his interest and was now embarked upon his plan to build a new playhouse where his own plays, which had for years been highly acclaimed, would be performed. However, that entrée into society had been stopped by Tristan's affair last year with Thomas's neglected wife Georganna. He had learned that Georganna had given birth to a daughter – Tristan's child – who had been accepted by her husband.

His motives in seducing Georganna had been mostly to do with vengeance and getting back at the family who had slighted him. Making a cuckold of Thomas had been an error of judgement. Yet Tristan did not believe in regret. He would have preferred acceptance by his family, but they had showed their true colours when they had united in loyalty over St John's death.

A narrowing of his eyes was the only emotion he showed upon recalling the tragedy of those events. He had not intended his vendetta against St John to end so drastically, but it had added greatly to his wealth and his position in society. If he wanted to prosper by his Loveday connections, he had to uphold the reputation of their family name. In the future, his actions and business dealings must be beyond reproach.

It was, however, impossible for him to change his hunger for power and the need to increase his fortune. Ever the opportunist, he had studied the current political climate. He did not believe that the peace with France would last for long. Bonaparte had risen to be First Consul but Tristan doubted that would be enough for him. In many ways he and the little Corsican were alike. Both had come from obscurity. Both knew the measure of their fellow man and how to manipulate him. Tristan admired Bonaparte for all he had achieved. He saw no reason why their stars would not rise together.

His ship *Good Fortune* would soon return from her first voyage. He would use her to sail to France.

Chapter Twelve

With the death of Michael, all the vibrancy seemed to have been sucked out of the occupants of the parsonage. Beth was constantly red eyed, and although Bridie presented a brave face to the world, she had grown visibly thinner since the funeral. Even when Japhet related his funniest anecdotes they could barely summon a smile, let alone a laugh. Bridie valiantly performed her parochial duties and insisted that the lace-making sessions continue as usual. His parishioners rarely saw Peter unless he was taking a service. If they entered the church at other times they would often find him on his knees by the altar for hours at a stretch. His religious fervour had always been exceptional; in his youth his cousins had called him Pious Peter.

Three weeks after the funeral, Peter attended upon his father in Joshua's study. He had deliberately chosen the afternoon when Cecily called upon Amelia and Felicity.

'Sit down, my son.' Joshua waved towards an old armchair with tufts of horsehair escaping from a split in the seam. The leather was scuffed but he had refused to discard it in favour of a more serviceable one from the furniture taken from Trevowan, though there was a new sofa and two armchairs in the parlour, and hangings from Trevowan at the parlour window and also on the fourposter bed and window in his bedchamber.

Peter appeared not to hear his father as he paced the small study. His haggard eyes refused to meet Joshua's gaze.

'How are you and your good wife?' Joshua asked. 'Bridie has been coping well with her duties. She is a fine woman.'

Peter held up a hand to stop his father speaking. There was a tremor in his fingers, which Joshua assumed was from exhaustion. For a moment his son paused and stared at the carved wooden Celtic cross on the wall. 'You have always preached of a merciful God.' The hollows deepened in his face, his voice taut with despair. 'Where was his mercy when Michael was ill?'

'Faith is also about acceptance,' Joshua began. 'How can we administer and guide our flock if we have not suffered ourselves? You are a good priest or the bishop would not have given you a larger parish in Launceston.' Joshua stroked the side of his cheek with the stem of his empty pipe as he considered his son's words. 'You should rejoice that you were blessed with having Michael even for so short a time. The Lord has other work for you to do, my son, working with the poor in Launceston. Have you discussed with your wife how you feel?'

Peter shook his head. 'I cannot even find the words to console her.'

'Then you must find them. Bridie deserves that you be completely honest with her.'

In the days following the ball, Lydia Kellerman constantly praised Lieutenant Allbright to her companion. 'He is handsome and charming. Such a beau is a feather in any woman's cap. I have seen how the young women flutter their eyes at him in the Assembly Rooms. He is in constant demand at dinner parties and private dances. He has called here four times to pay his compliments and partners you whenever you both attend the same dances. Yet still you remain cool towards him.'

The older woman stood in front of the mirror over the fireplace in the upper salon of her house and carefully tied the silk ribbon of her peak bonnet. The air was mild for March and they could take their promenade through the town for an hour without risk of rain. Emma, in bonnet and pelisse, gripped her gloves in both hands, but did not respond. There was no point in speaking of her heartbreak over her lost love. Every time Jevington's name was mentioned it was like a sword thrust to her breast, and any sighting of him within the town made her ache with longing for a glance or a smile from him. Twice they had come across each other unexpectedly. Lydia's heart had pounded so hard she thought she would faint. He had momentarily frozen, then cruelly looked straight through her as though she was invisible. Each time the Claythorpe woman had been clinging tenaciously to his arm and he had turned to her and whispered in her ear which had her giggling with pleasure. The attentions of Lieutenant Allbright had not brought him to his senses. He had not declared his love, and Emma had made a fool of herself by encouraging another.

During the day she avoided the Pump Room and the popular walks and had learned in company to mask her emotions while inwardly she wept. Night-time was the worst. Then he would invade her dreams and she would relive the joy of his touch and the sweetness of the illicit kisses he had stolen.

But Lieutenant Allbright had proved a persistent beau and gradually she had come to like him well enough. She was conscious that many of her acquaintances regarded her pityingly because of the way Jevington had discarded her, and the naval officer's ardent attentions eased her wounded pride.

Lydia turned from the mirror and regarded Emma with exasperation. 'Are you made of stone that your handsome lieutenant has no power to sway your affection?'

'I cannot force myself to feel a fondness for him beyond that his company is pleasing,' she hedged.

Lydia lost patience. 'He is an extremely eligible bachelor. You need to repair the damage done to your reputation by that knave Jevington.'

'Damage!' Emma squeaked, the room swaying dangerously around her. She gripped the edge of the chair.

Lydia's eyes narrowed. 'Pray do not take me for a halfwit, Emma. Twice he contrived that you were alone with him for some time during the weekend excursion we took out of town.'

'Nothing untoward happened,' Emma insisted and burst into tears. 'I cannot help it if I still care for him.'

'You must accept that he is lost to you, my dear.' Lydia mellowed at her cousin's obvious distress and continued more kindly. 'Do you want to lose Allbright as well? Being courted and discarded by two beaux in one season would cause a great deal of speculation.'

Emma's head shot up, defiance shining in her eyes. 'But I never encouraged the lieutenant. I only followed your advice, for I could not bear the shame that I had been so cruelly treated and would be regarded with pity.'

'To lose one beau is regrettable. To lose two could tarnish your reputation irredeemably.'

Emma's blood ran cold. Her family was regarded in their village on the outskirts of Dorchester with pity, many believing that none of the Madison girls would marry. Emma had dreamed of marriage all her life; her sisters too often irritated her with their petty squabbling.

They had not left the house ten minutes when Mrs Durham, a middle-aged widow, and her older spinster sister accosted them. The sisters reminded Emma of two peas in a pod, both their short and very rounded bodies dressed in cloaks of Lincoln green. Both wore horn-rimmed spectacles and old-fashioned wigs contorted into childish ringlets. At any other time she might have found their figures amusing, but since both were quivering with the urge to impart new gossip, her heart seemed to stop and plummet to her pattens.

'Poor Miss Madison, you must be quite distraught. Indeed quite discomposed.' Mrs Durham rolled her fleshy eyes and her sister sighed dramatically. Mrs Durham hurried on, that myopic stare now fixed upon Emma's face, soaking up her every reaction. 'You poor dear woman. It is all the talk. Elizabeth Claythorpe is to marry your Captain Jevington, and they've known each other less than a month.'

The golden stonework of the elegant houses on each side of the street momentarily swirled crazily around Emma. Shock froze her features and mercifully her senses. The gushing commiserations faded to a far-off, incomprehensible twittering. The gossipmongers feasted like a succubus on their victim's emotions to enable them to lay them bare to the next passer-by hungry for diversion at another's expense. Dimly she was aware of her arm being bruisingly gripped as Lydia supported her body, which had lost the ability to function.

'He is hardly Miss Madison's Captain Jevington.' Lydia's voice was high and sharp, penetrating Emma's stupor. Her cousin could barely contain her venom. 'The man is a knave of the first order, Mrs Durham. I can assure you that my dear, sweet Emma believes herself well rid of him. Do you not, dear cousin?'

A painful pinch upon her upper arm jolted Emma enough to mumble words she could not later remember, wishing only that the ground would open up and swallow her.

'Of course, my dear,' Mrs Durham simpered. 'It is only dignified that you put on a brave face.'

The accompanying condescending smile, which Emma had witnessed so many times in her life, all but stripped her of her equilibrium. It took all her willpower not to turn and run home.

Lydia squeezed her forearm more gently and said breezily, 'My dear cousin has no need of a brave face. She deems she has had a lucky escape. A man who can change his affections so readily clearly has no sense of fidelity. It is Miss Claythorpe that I pity. She may find her future husband has a roving eye. And one has to question how important has been her fortune to the impoverished third son of a baronet? Good day, Mrs Durham.'

She propelled Emma forward at a brisk pace and swept her into a milliner's shop, which fortunately was devoid of customers. Their isolation allowed Emma to regain her composure.

The interior was lighter than many shops of its kind, the walls panelled with white-painted wood where hats of every colour and style were placed on stands of various heights. There was a lingering scent of roses, and a welcoming fire burned in a grate, with two comfortable armchairs placed nearby for the comfort of customers. From behind a curtain at the back of the establishment two low voices giggled. A sharp command stilled their chatter and the curtain was swung back. The scent of roses was more oppressive as the proprietress bore down upon them.

'Good morning, ladies. I am honoured that you grace

my humble emporium. How may I help you? There is not a finer milliner's in all Bath.'

Emma stood by the bow window, her face turned away from the effusive milliner, who gushed over Lydia as her cousin flitted from one straw creation to another. When the woman went to fetch a poke bonnet from the back of the shop, Emma whispered fiercely, 'I cannot bear this. I wish to return to Dorchester.'

'And let that knave and his milksop fiancée make a fool of you? Where is your spirit, Emma? I will not countenance you running back to your family in disgrace. Lieutenant Allbright is clearly enamoured of you to have called so often.'

She tugged at the ribbons on Emma's bonnet and lifted it from her head. Replacing it with a straw creation bedecked with silk daffodils and yellow ribbons, she stood back to admire her handiwork, her voice low and confidential. 'You must turn that to your advantage. No man can resist flattery. It is unlikely he will be recalled to duty for several months; many naval officers are without ships since the truce with France. This is the very time that a pretty woman who has caught his eye could win him as a husband.' She adjusted the bow tied at the side of Emma's head. 'That is perfect. Bright, cheerful and stylish. A bonnet for a woman without a care in the world. I will buy it for you.'

Emma frowned at her image in the looking glass. The bonnet did have an uplifting effect, and everything Lydia had said made sense. Until her heartbreak she had enjoyed all the entertainments that Bath could offer. She would be foolish to return to Dorchester, where she would endure more pitying glances. Life with her bickering sisters or the independence of marriage to a handsome officer was not a difficult choice. Had she not given her heart so easily to another, the charming manners and dashing looks of Lieutenant Allbright would have beguiled her. Surely love would come in time. She was determined to leave Bath triumphant.

Lydia was not giving her the chance to consider an alternative. She was fully determined to save Emma's reputation and find her a husband. Lieutenant Allbright had come to Bath at exactly the right moment. Emma should be grateful that another man had been so quick to pay court to her after her recent humiliation. Indeed, if the handsome officer had been a few years older, Lydia might have set her cap at him herself. She had been a widow too long, and after only a short time married to an army captain. He had served under Major Madison and been killed in a skirmish in India two years ago. She had always found it difficult to resist the lure of a man in uniform, although in the case of Lieutenant Allbright, she would have preferred he wore the more dashing scarlet of a soldier. But he was a gentleman, and that was what mattered. She had quite decided that he was perfect for Emma.

She chattered on brightly. 'We must count our blessings that Lieutenant Allbright is to call to take you for a carriage ride. I will naturally accompany you to observe the proprieties. You must do everything in your power to charm him.' She sighed, convinced her protégée could not fail, and continued to tweak at the bonnet, turning Emma's head from side to side as she inspected her in the mirror. Then she gave a conspiratorial wink. 'Now, my dear, what think you of this delightful piece? I always say a new bonnet raises the spirits, not to mention captivating a young man's heart.'

Chapter Thirteen

The afternoon was cloudy, with a swathe of blue sky over the hills to the west proclaiming that the weather was brightening. Richard had hired a curricle and driver and was to escort Mrs Kellerman and Miss Madison to an old school friend of Lydia's in the country, a half-hour's journey from Bath. A country lane led into a curving drive, taking them past a willow-lined stream to a square, three-storeyed porticoed manor house built in the local stone.

Mrs Cotterell airily apologised for the absence of her husband, who as a lawyer was attending upon a client on an urgent matter of business. She had three daughters all under the age of five, who, much to Richard's relief, were confined to the nursery. Mrs Cotterell obviously aspired to receiving large number of guests. The salon on the first floor was jammed with three sofas and a dozen armchairs, with every available space between filled with tables cluttered with porcelain figurines, vases of flowers and gewgaws of every conceivable nature. It was an oppressive room in spite of its attempt at magnificence. Every wall was crowded with paintings and portraits, with only a thin strip of the dark green wall covering visible between.

The greyhound-thin Mrs Cotterell was enthusiastic in her welcome and bubbling with gossip about her brother, who was to visit her next month. There was a desperation about her in her eagerness to please, and to Richard's surprise he detected a faint whiff of laudanum emanating from her person. From the constant restless fluttering of her hands he deduced she was of a nervous disposition, which was calmed by the opiate.

Richard was all too familiar with the smell. His own addiction to opiates had come from a wound sustained during a sea battle when a French cannon ball had crashed on to the quarterdeck, sending up a shower of wooden splinters, two of which had pierced his chest like arrows. Fortunately they had missed any vital organs, but his recovery had been slow and agonising. The only alleviation for all men similarly wounded was the indiscriminate use of opium by the ship's surgeon to silence their screams of agony. By the time his ship had returned to England, Richard had been in the power of its addiction. He had been finally able to overcome it only with the help of Senara, who had seen the horrors that withdrawal symptoms could induce and had been ruthless in ensuring he survived them. It had been a hellish few weeks and he had resented every moment of the pain, sweats and cramps he had endured. But eventually, when the craving had subsided and the strength had returned to his tortured and weakened body, he had realised that she had saved him from a wrecked naval career and certain early death.

Even so, that gratitude had turned to antagonism at the furious lecture he had received from Adam upon the rumours of his liaisons with the local women. For years he had idolised his stepbrother and had wanted to emulate his bold adventures at sea. Since taking on the responsibilities of the shipyard and parenthood, it seemed to Richard that Adam had forgotten the joys of a healthy young male's pursuits.

The carriage ride had not been the pleasurable interlude he had hoped for. Lydia had been too fulsome in praising Emma, and he was uncomfortable at realising that the foolish woman saw him as a match for her cousin. Now, within the house, the women's excited voices had risen to a high pitch, causing Richard to regret his decision to escort them on this drive. He had wanted some time alone with Emma to pursue his relationship with her. After half an hour he could not stifle a yawn of boredom as the formal, polite pleasantries became dominated by the reminiscences of the two school friends, and Lydia Kellerman's questions about the absent brother, Stephen Fanshawe. It was obvious that she had more than a passing interest in Mr Fanshawe and there seemed a conspiracy between the two older women to bring the couple together.

Halfway through their excited outburst, Mrs Cotterell put her hands to her cheeks. 'Your pardon, Lieutenant Allbright, it is unforgivable of us to exclude you from our conversation. Mrs Kellerman and I have much news to catch up on.' She looked anxiously at Emma. 'And my dear Miss Madison, our chatter must be tedious for you. It is such a fine afternoon; why do you two not stroll through the gardens? The daffodil walk down by the river is just coming into bloom.' She laughed nervously. 'One could say it is the perfect setting for your delightful bonnet. A gong will be rung in a half-hour or so to inform you we are about to take tea before your drive back to Bath. I promise that over our repast you will have our full attention.'

Richard rose and bowed to the two friends, then

offered Miss Madison his arm. 'A stroll will be most pleasant after our carriage drive.'

As the young couple left the room, Lydia anxiously chewed her lip. 'Should not a maid accompany them for the sake of proprieties?'

'Oh la, Lydie! You said in your letter that you wanted Emma betrothed before the end of the Season. Lieutenant Allbright is an officer and a gentleman – a perfectly personable young man. The grounds are in full view of the house. I thought he looked most smitten with your cousin. A quiet stroll where they can get to know each other better is just the opportunity he may need to declare himself.'

'I suppose if they are to stay in view of the house . . .' Lydia shrugged off her concern, and within moments was diverted by more information of Stephen Fanshawe and his need to find a mother for his children. A role she hoped to fill in the not too distant future.

As soon as they were out of the house, Emma apologised to Richard. 'I hope you have not found this afternoon too vexing, Lieutenant. Such gossip must have held little interest for you.'

Since learning of Jevington's forthcoming betrothal, Emma had masked her heartache behind a veil of pride. She had also endured long lectures from Lydia on the merits of Lieutenant Allbright's interest, wealth and position that would allow her to escape from the dreary existence in Dorchester. Although it was a large, thriving town, Aunt Myrtle, who lived a half-mile from their cottage, did not approve of her nieces attending social gatherings where young military officers might regard them as prey. Major Madison was too far away for his rank to hold any sway or influence over young bucks bent upon seduction. Any eligible gentleman introduced to Emma by her aunt was middle aged, stout and balding, and filled her with revulsion.

Lydia had finally convinced her that to regain her self-esteem she should encourage the lieutenant's attentions. In return he had been effusive in his compliments, and gradually his good looks and charm had channelled through her reservations and she found that she was enjoying his company. But since their arrival she had noticed the barely concealed boredom that had settled over his features.

'I would rather be out here in the company of a beautiful woman,' he enthused.

She was relieved that his mood had lightened considerably. The compliment lifted her own spirits and she cast a sideways glance at him. He was tall, slim and blond, with dark brows and lashes and a finely contoured face, and if she was honest she had to admit that he was far more handsome than the treacherous Theo. His wit was infectious, and as they walked through the daffodils she was surprised how easily she laughed at his humorous asides.

'Mrs Kellerman seems much enamoured of the estimable Mr Fanshawe,' he said drily. 'One would think that he was a hero the equal of Lord Nelson, or at the very least that his personage would outshine Beau Brummell himself.'

Emma laughed and at the same time felt a weight shift from her heart. It was the first time she had been happy since Theo had betrayed her. She brushed that thought aside. She did not want any reminder of that knave to spoil her happiness today. In defence of her cousin she was prompted to explain. 'They were childhood sweethearts, but Lydia had no dowry to speak of and Mr

Fanshawe's family home was in much need of an heiress to restore it. It is a tragedy when two lovers must be parted because of their lack of fortune, is it not?'

'Did Mrs Cotterell's brother marry his heiress?'

'Indeed, yes. A worthy woman who gave him six children.'

'Will she be accompanying him on his impending visit? Mrs Cotterell made no mention of her sister-in-law.' He frowned.

Emma gasped and blushed. 'Oh, you must think my cousin most forward the way she was discussing a married man. Mrs Fanshawe passed away last year.'

'Does Mrs Kellerman hope to renew her acquaintance with the recent widower? One assumes that his wife's death has made him financially independent.'

'My cousin is not interested in his wealth.' Emma defended Lydia's motives. 'Her own widowhood enables her to live comfortably.'

They had reached the daffodil walk and the sweet smell of the flowers scented the air around them as they crossed the grass towards the willow-lined stream.

'A man does a woman no service if he takes her to wife without the means of supporting her in the custom she deserves,' Lieutenant Allbright informed her with a note of hauteur.

'Yes, quite rightly so. But that leaves little room for romance in our world.'

'In matters of the heart a wise man or woman should be governed by the head. Or so my father once told me. But he died when I was young. Strangely those words are the only advice I remember him giving me. I cannot say that I agree with him.'

Emma realised he was teasing her. 'So you would allow your heart to rule in matters of a romantic nature.'

'Oh, the heart must always rule.' He grinned disarmingly. 'Although one can never abandon family duty.'

'Noble sentiments, Lieutenant. Is your family a naval one by tradition?'

'My stepbrother served for a time. His tales of the sea fired my imagination as a child and I resolved to follow in his footsteps. My father was a lawyer.'

'Where is your family home, Lieutenant?'

He frowned and did not answer immediately. In the silence a blackbird screeched a warning and flew up out of the daffodils, where it had been rooting for worms. 'My mother lives in Cornwall and is settled there. There is also property in London.'

'Cornwall is not so far away from Dorchester where I live.'

'It must be a day's journey,' he replied offhandedly.

'Then I shall see little of you after your sojourn in Bath is over.'

He heard the disappointment in her voice and inwardly grinned. She was not so averse to his company as she would have him believe. He cursed the obligations to his mother that could no longer be delayed, but there was a possibility that he could use them to his advantage.

'It saddens me that I must leave Bath shortly. My family is in mourning.'

'My sincere condolences, Lieutenant Allbright.' He did not miss the edge of alarm in her voice. 'When do you depart?'

They had reached the edge of the stream and turned to saunter along it. She was staring away from him into the clear running water. Until now Emma Madison had been an elusive conquest, which had heightened his interest. Too many women had fallen too easily to his persuasive charm. He had sampled three in his time in

Bath but none had held his interest once he had left their bed. He had heard the gossip surrounding Emma and Captain Jevington, and around the gaming tables there had been some speculation upon that liaison, for Jevington had a reputation that equalled Richard's own with the ladies. That Emma had not fallen immediately for his attentions made her a challenge to Richard's appetite.

'I leave in two days.'

Emma felt the first fluttering of panic. She feared that others would see his departure as another beau abandoning her. She glanced at him and her panic subsided. There was no mistaking the adoration in his gaze as it lingered upon her.

'Though I anticipate that it will be a visit of short duration to pay my respects. I find the attractions awaiting my return to Bath too irresistible to ignore.'

She glanced up at him, her heart seeming to leap to her throat in expectation of the meaning behind his words. Dare she hope that he referred to herself?

'Will you miss me?' He halted and took her arm to draw her round to look directly at him. 'Our acquaintanceship has been all too brief. I had hoped . . .' He paused and gave a regretful smile. 'Our family has suffered two recent bereavements, and those so close to the death of my stepbrother before Christmas. This is a difficult time for our family. Mama is deeply distressed and it is some time since my last leave. My duty is to offer her comfort at this time.'

'Then you are likely to be away from Bath for many weeks, are you not, Lieutenant?' Her gaze had lowered to fix upon the line of moisture that had soaked the hem of her dress from the wet grass. There was also a droop to her shoulders that he saw as a positive sign.

'Mama is surrounded by family. I should return to Bath in two or three weeks,' he said.

'Yet you could also be recalled to your ship at any time?' She still kept her gaze fixed upon the hem of her gown.

'Dare I hope that would trouble you, Miss Madison? I have yet to receive orders from the Admiralty as to whether I am given another ship or will remain ashore.' He still held her arm and she had made no attempt to pull it away.

'It would be a great sadness to me if you were recalled to duty too soon,' she said softly, looking up at him through her lashes. 'We have just begun to get to know each other.' She blushed, aware that she must have sounded forward.

His smile was captivating, his tone light and teasing. 'So you would miss me?'

His fingers caressed the skin of her wrist, causing a delicious shiver to speed through her body. 'Of course. I have few acquaintances in Bath. But your mama, she must also have need of you.'

'Fortunately I have a younger half-brother to divert her, and my stepbrother's widow and her three children also live with her,' he answered dismissively, unwilling to be drawn about his family. To deflect her questions he raised her hand and kissed her wrist, where he could feel the pulse racing. He could not delay returning to Cornwall but he was enjoying himself in Bath.

'I had began to wonder if my attentions displeased you in any way,' he continued, placing his hand dramatically over his heart. 'You seemed reluctant to receive me when I called.' He had guided Emma along the bank of the stream until they were no longer in line with the house and could not be spied upon.

'You must have thought me discourteous, Lieutenant Allbright. That was not my intention. I have been . . .' She faltered, her lips parted and trembling slightly in the most inviting manner. She still permitted him to hold her hand as she went on. 'It was not you.'

'You need not explain,' he said softly. The gossip about her and Jevington was all over Bath, as was the news of his recent betrothal. Clearly Emma was in need of consolation, needed to be shown that she was desirable.

'Please, Lieutenant Allbright, be assured that you were not at fault,' she reassured him.

His smile was tender and adoring. 'That makes me the happiest of men, dear lady.'

They paused by the outstretched branches of a cedar tree close to the stream. Two swans swam regally past. 'They say that swans mate for life,' Richard observed. 'One would not believe that a bird could form such strong attachments.'

'That is both beautiful and sad,' Emma sighed wistfully. 'If one dies, does the other spend its days in solitude?'

'One must assume so.' He had stepped closer and could smell the rosewater scent on her skin and hair. The rapid rise and fall of her breasts showed the heightened charge to her emotions. Seizing the moment, he leaned forward and kissed her. A gentle kiss, savouring the taste of her lips, which parted briefly in response. Then with a gasp she stepped back, her hand raised to lightly press against his chest.

'Lieutenant, I must protest, you are too bold.' Her voice was low and husky, carrying more enticement than conviction.

He placed his hand over his heart and bowed to her. 'A thousand pardons, dear lady. I am quite undone in your presence and beauty. I am your most obedient servant to command me as you will, a slave to your beauty and charm.'

She giggled. 'You have a silver tongue, Lieutenant Allbright.'

He sighed. 'I have never heard my name spoken from more perfect, kissable lips.'

'Again you are too forward, sir. Shame on you. A kiss should only be bestowed upon one's betrothed and then only on the most circumspect occasions. Would you ruin my reputation by the rashness of your speech?'

'I would worship the ground you walk upon if you would allow me to be your most ardent slave.'

Richard had spotted a boathouse built at the water's edge. It had no doors but protected the punt within from the worst of the weather. As they walked, he had deftly guided Emma towards it. Allowing her to digest his words, he stepped inside the shelter. It was surprisingly clean and tidy; only a few leaves had blown into the corners of the structure. The punt had been lifted out of the water and placed on the hard-packed earth, and there was a pole to propel it hanging across wooden pegs on the wall. The boat was long and sleek and could easily accommodate four people. It was clean inside and looked as though it had been revarnished in preparation for the spring.

Richard lifted the pole from its pegs and smiled at Emma. 'Would you care for a spell on the water, Miss Madison?'

Emma had cautiously followed him inside the boathouse and looked horrified at his suggestion. 'I have a fear of water. I fell in a pond as a child and almost drowned.'

'But there is nothing more pleasurable than a lazy day

on the river,' Richard declared. 'I would not have you miss such a delightful experience. Do you trust me enough to help you overcome your fear?'

'I could not. Oh, I mean, it is not that I do not trust you,' she blustered. 'I would be too afraid. How foolish you must think me, you being a naval officer.' Her eyes were wide with distress.

'I could never think you foolish, my dear.' He laughed. 'Then we shall sit in the punt in the boathouse and pretend we are on the water. It will help restore your confidence. That does not frighten you, does it?'

Still she hesitated, and he held out his hand to take hers, smiling enticingly. 'You cannot be that afraid. When you realise how safe the boat is, it will cure you of your fear.' He stepped into the punt, his voice low and coercing. 'Trust me, dear lady. We cannot sink upon dry land. Let this be the first step to overcoming your fear.'

'I think we should go back to the house, Lieutenant Allbright. The tea gong will sound soon.' She remained uncertain.

He stiffened with affront. 'You insult me. A few minutes and I could cure you of your fear.'

'I meant no insult,' she began. Lydia's instruction that she should encourage Lieutenant Allbright was uppermost in her mind. She had come so far in overcoming her heartbreak over Jevington, and that was all due to this charming man before her. When he had said he was shortly to leave Bath she had felt a stab of disappointment. Lydia might have advised her to captivate him so that she did not lose face as a woman abandoned by a suitor, but today she had been happier than she had been for some time. If the lieutenant also deserted her she was certain she would be condemned to spinsterhood. That was too mortifying to consider. She could not afford to risk losing this chance of making a match.

He gently drew her closer, his eyes gazing deep into her own. 'Join me. What is there to fear?'

A warning bell tinkled in Emma's mind. They were alone, and no chaperone was close by. Such impropriety could further damage her reputation. Or it could ensure she gained a husband. Richard certainly seemed enamoured, and was far more lavish in his compliments than ever Jevington had been. It gave her confidence. She stepped into the punt and he settled her in the stern. She had expected him to seat himself at the far end, but he placed himself beside her.

'I will hold your hand so that you will feel safer,' he said. 'There, that does not feel so bad, does it? And you can see the stream ahead so you can imagine that we are afloat.' He continued to talk soothingly until she relaxed. He smiled. 'To overcome a fear takes great bravery. I salute you, my dearest Emma.'

She knew she should upbraid him for breaking the proprieties and calling her by her first name, but when he raised her hand again to his lips, his free hand stroking the side of her cheek, her protest was swept aside at the devotion she encountered in his eyes.

'You are so brave and so beautiful, dearest Emma.'

He was staring at her lips as though mesmerised, and then he kissed her on the mouth with an expertise that sent her senses spiralling. Her lips parted in response and his tongue played along the seam of them, sending delicious waves of pleasure through her body. His arms slid around her, possessive and lightly caressing. Unaware that she was falling under the spell of an accomplished rake, she surrendered to the joy of the moment. So heady were the sensations created by his touch that her own passionate nature was fed by a craving for this moment never to end. His lips blazed a trail along her neck and a soft moan of pleasure escaped her. Her senses were bombarded with the unleashing of her sensuality. Then shock pulsed through her as she felt the heated touch of his hand exploring her inner thigh.

She jolted herself back from the maelstrom of sensations that had engulfed her body. 'No. We cannot. Please, you must stop.'

'You were made to be loved,' Richard breathed as his mouth travelled over a bare breast.

How had her clothing become so dishevelled? She was appalled that she had become so enslaved by her emotion that she had not realised the extent of the liberties she had permitted. Her cheeks flushed crimson with shame. In her embarrassment she tried to cover herself with one hand and push him away with the other. 'No. This cannot be.'

His face was inches from her own, and now the handsome features were suffused with anger. 'You little tease. There is nothing worse than a woman who leads a man on. Is that your game? You know I adore you.'

'I am not a tease. You tricked me.' Indignantly she pushed against him, but the body that lay half across her was heavy and unyielding.

'Oh, but I think you are the worst kind of tease,' he taunted. 'Is that why Jevington discarded you? I thought you the wronged party. So beautiful and so innocent. Was it but an act? No man likes to be made a fool of.'

Was that a threat behind his words? She had angered him. Was he also about to discard her? She had naively hoped that he had not learned how she had been humiliated by that knave's defection. It was too mortifying. How Jevington would laugh. How society would mock her. A spinsterhood trapped in Dorchester loomed before her. How could she bear it?

'But this is wrong!' she pleaded. 'If you cared for me you would have regard for my reputation.'

The hand that tried desperately to push him away was gripped and pulled over her head, her body crushed beneath his weight.

'Your honour is my most sacred regard. How can it be wrong when two people want it so much?' His voice was husky now, velvet with coercion. 'I adore you, sweet Emma.'

'Truly are your intentions honourable?' She ceased to struggle and held her breath, torn between the need for propriety and her wish to become his wife.

'You are an angel I cannot live without.' His kisses became more ardent and his hands again sought the intimate secrets of her flesh.

'But do you love me, Richard?' She managed to tear her mouth from his, tears flowing down her cheeks.

He kissed them away. 'As I have never loved another woman.' The onslaught of his persuasive kisses returned. She knew she should resist but she so desperately did not want to lose him.

Afterwards, as she sobbed against his shoulder, he was gentle and soothing, murmuring endearments until her mood brightened and she was reassured.

As she shook out the folds of her gown she was relieved it showed no telltale creases. Her cheeks flooded with crimson as she replaced the pins that had fallen from her hair. 'You did mean it, Richard? You do love me?'

The distant sound of the tea gong carried to them, and Richard planted a fervent kiss upon her lips. 'We must hurry or we will be late, and that will cause speculation.'

Stubbornly she held back. 'But I must know, Richard. You do intend that we shall wed?'

She looked about to burst into fresh tears and he was eager to avoid a scene. He stifled his irritation. 'How can you doubt, my love? But I have told you my family is in mourning and I must return to Cornwall. Our love must be our secret for now.'

'But you will speak with my cousin,' she insisted. 'I have risked my reputation for you. You said you loved me. We have to marry.'

The gong was being rung more forcefully. The conversation was getting out of hand. He had to silence her demands and keep her sweet. 'My beloved, I do not come into my inheritance for another three years. Unless my marriage is approved by my mother, how can I support a wife on a lieutenant's pay?'

'Then I am ruined!' Her voice rose in hysteria.

Richard panicked. The woman was infuriating in her persistence. His smile was fashioned from tense muscles. 'Surely you understand my situation. I am your devoted servant. Nothing can be said until I return to Bath.' He kissed away her tears and protests, murmuring against her ear, 'Be patient, my love.'

'But if you love me . . .' She continued to sob.

He gripped her shoulders and controlled the urge to shake some sense into her. From the house Mrs Kellerman was calling them.

'Trust me, my love. Let us for now enjoy a secret betrothal,' he coerced. 'Is that not romantic? When I return to Bath I will have my mother's blessing and an official announcement can be made. Now dry your eyes, or Mrs Kellerman will be suspicious.'

Her lips still trembled and she continued to regard him with uncertainty. He forced his most disarming smile. 'We have known each other such a short time. My family sets great store by loyalty and trust. You do trust me, do you not, sweet Emma?'

In the circumstances she had no choice but to agree.

The next day a curt note arrived from Richard saying that he had left for Cornwall. He did not mention the date of his return.

Chapter Fourteen

'How is your sister?' Amelia asked, putting aside her writing box. She had been composing a letter when Senara arrived at Reskelly Cottage.

'She is dealing with her grief by keeping busy. I called in at the parsonage on my way here. When I left, she was about to spend an hour reading to an elderly parishioner,' Senara replied. She kept to herself that she thought Bridie had become a spectre of her former self. The parsonage smelt strongly of lye soap and beeswax and every piece of furniture had a mirror shine from hours of vigorous polishing.

'Cecily says she sees little of her and Peter,' Amelia continued. 'And they leave for Launceston after Easter, do they not?'

'Work is a great healer, as is time,' Felicity said. Baby George had just woken up in his crib near the fire and was fretful from cutting his first tooth. Felicity picked up her son, which caused Thea to whine and clamour to sit on her mother's lap, jealous of the attention George was receiving. Felicity was a doting mother. She kissed Thea's head and insisted that the girl sit at her feet.

'Where are Rowena and Charlotte? I thought I heard Fraddon dropping them off in the coach from their lesson at Boscabel some time ago. They should be here, helping keep Thea from getting under our feet.' George began to cry, and with a sigh Felicity stood up and put him to her shoulder, pacing the parlour trying to pacify him.

'I saw them by the duck pond in the village with some other children of their age,' Senara answered and picked up a porcelain-faced doll to distract Thea, who ignored her and toddled after her mother.

Felicity rolled her eyes heavenwards. 'I told Rowena to come straight home. She is mixing too much with the village children and is a bad influence on Charlotte. I caught one of the older Wibbley boys hanging round here last week. They are not suitable company.'

'They are still young,' Senara stated. 'Adam and St John played with the children of Penruan village at their age. Mine mix with those on our estate.'

'I agree with Felicity. Rowena has a wayward streak.' Amelia looked disapproving. 'Although our circum-stances have changed, she must not forget that she is a Loveday. I would not have her gain a reputation as a hoyden. Too many people remember the waywardness of her mother.' She rang a bell, and when Edna Merrin bobbed an awkward curtsy instructed, 'Go down to the village and inform Rowena that she is expected here. And take Thea with you. A short walk may improve her disposition. Take care you wrap her up warmly.'

Felicity frowned as the maidservant took the girl to fetch their cloaks. George continued to cry, two coins of bright colour on his cheeks. 'I will take George to the nursery where his crying will not disturb you, Amelia.' The stiffness of her gait as she left the room showed the tension building between the two women.

Amelia sat with her fingers locked together, struggling to maintain her own composure.

'It cannot always be easy for you, with so many under one roof.' Senara voiced her compassion.

'It is little enough to suffer.' Amelia squared her shoulders. 'Felicity is finding it hard to cope with her husband's lies and deceit before his death, and St John left them so ill provided. Rowena grows more wilful by the day and is a disruptive influence upon Charlotte.'

'Would it help if Rowena came to Boscabel?' Senara suggested.

'Felicity will not hear of it. She takes her duties as stepmother seriously. Though it might help if Adam were to speak with his niece. She is very fond of her uncle.'

Senara nodded and Amelia noticeably relaxed, prompting the younger woman to offer, 'Adam would do more if you would let him. You have but to ask.'

'His father would have been proud of him. A pity he was not the heir to Trevowan.' She shrugged fatalistically. 'But I do not complain. I was born in a house much like this and I enjoy Felicity's company. You must miss your dear mother.'

'Yes, but it is harder for Bridie than myself. Leah was always protective of her, and she was used to her company at the parsonage.'

'I suppose you hear nothing of that brother of yours? It has been some years since he was in the neighbourhood.' Amelia regarded Senara steadily. 'Perhaps that is just as well, considering the trouble that was caused last time.'

The family never mentioned Caleph. None of them apart from Adam approved of Senara's gypsy blood. He accepted Caleph because of his wife's affection for her elder brother. Amelia's remark sent a cold shiver through Senara. She had awoken that morning having dreamed of Caleph. That his name had been so unexpectedly mentioned made her wonder if the dream had not been a premonition. She could not remember it clearly, except that Caleph had been ordering the tribe to break camp in the middle of the night. A common enough event when trouble was brewing for them in an area. But had the dream been a warning? The more she thought upon it, the more unsettled she became.

'Ma's last words were to give her love to Caleph. She never stopped worrying about him but accepted that he had his father's blood and would never give up his travelling. He stayed away to protect Bridie and myself from any criticism of our connection with the Romany way of life. And he was not responsible for the trouble that roused the villagers to attack his encampment. There had been thefts in the area but it was later proved that the gypsies did not commit them. Always prejudice points the finger at them, which is why he stays away from this part of Cornwall. I miss him and am not ashamed to call him brother. But I doubt I will see him again.'

To change the subject she asked, 'Have you heard further news from Richard about when he will come home? His last letter was written from Plymouth when he had just docked. Adam says that with the peace with France, many of the naval officers have been given leave to cool their heels on land.'

'He will be with us as soon as he can and will cancel his plans to accept an invitation to his friend Lieutenant Chandler's father's estate in Somerset.' There was a defensive light in Amelia's eyes as she hid her distress that her son had been so neglectful in calling upon her. 'Lieutenant Chandler has three younger sisters and a clutch of unmarried cousins.'

'You sound like Aunt Margaret, who could never resist matchmaking,' Senara said with a wry laugh. 'Richard is still young for marriage and I am sure in no hurry to lose his heart to a single woman.'

Amelia shot her a telling look. 'I would be happier if he was settled into a contented marriage; what mother would not be? During his last leave there was that regrettable incident with the governess who encouraged his attentions and had to be dismissed.'

Senara remembered that the governess was not the only female Richard had pursued. He had little care to the damage his interest brought to their reputation, and she suspected that he was something of a rake.

She stood up and shook out the skirt of her riding habit. It would take an exceptional woman to turn Lieutenant Richard Allbright's head towards matrimony, especially when so many flighty creatures were dazzled by a handsome face and uniform. She had no intention of pursuing this subject with Amelia. 'I also intended to visit Elspeth this morning. Adam refuses to step foot on Trevowan land since his cousin took possession.'

'At this time of the morning Elspeth will be at Tor Farm. She visits most days to watch the horses being put through their paces. Japhet has entered two of his two year olds at a race meeting, I forget where, and he will be away from home for another week.'

'Why do you not bind me in chains and lock me in the cellar?' Rowena's outraged tones preceded her presence flouncing into the parlour. Her blond hair was windswept and tumbled chaotically over the shoulders of her unfastened jacket, and there was an inch of mud on the hem of her fine woollen gown and tunic. A jagged tail of muddied lace from her torn petticoat trailed after her. 'Am I am prisoner here? Clearly I am allowed no friends.'

'You have friends. The Traherne girls,' Amelia snapped. 'And I will not tolerate your tone and manner. Go to your room. You will have no supper.' She then turned her attention to Felicity's daughter. 'And what have you to say of your conduct, Charlotte?'

The younger girl sidled into the parlour looking sheepish. 'I told Rowena we had to come straight home. We only stopped for a few minutes.'

'If you cannot be trusted to do as you are told, there will be an end to your lessons at Boscabel. I will instruct you myself here.'

'Uncle Adam will not allow my education to be jeopardised,' Rowena replied pertly.

'Your uncle will place more weight upon you keeping your good name and manners than upon lessons, young lady.' Senara added her censure.

'If Papa were alive—' Rowena began.

'He would be appalled at your conduct.' Amelia sniffed her disapproval. 'If you continue in this manner, your best interests may be served by packing you off to a ladies' academy. They will take no nonsense from you. In fact I think that would be the best solution. I will discuss this with your uncle when next I see him.'

Rowena stamped her foot, her pretty face reddening with fury. 'I will not go. I hate you. You just want an excuse to get rid of me.'

'Your attitude speaks for itself.' Amelia was equally incensed and stood up to bear down upon the young woman. 'This wilful disrespect will not be tolerated. Go to your room at once.'

Wild eyed, Rowena spun on her toes and before anyone could halt her ran outside.

'Come back this instant, young lady,' Amelia ordered.

Senara hurried after her niece. She was too slow. Rowena had snatched free the tether of Senara's mare and swung herself into the saddle. Her bare legs exposed, she kicked her heels to its sides and set off at a gallop away from the village.

Amelia joined Senara in the doorway as the mare disappeared over the crest of the hill in the direction of Trevowan Hard.

'The minx has gone to twist Adam around her finger,' Amelia groaned. 'She will not succeed. I'll get Merrin to hitch up the pony and trap and take you home, Senara. I cannot control her. She will have to go to an academy. Her wilful behaviour will not be tolerated there.'

'I fear you are right.' Senara was loath to agree. Rowena's world had been turned upside down by her father's death. She had adored St John and for too long had always managed to get her own way. She had the wildness of the Loveday blood and had inherited her hunger for worldly possessions from her mother. It was a dangerous combination for a woman. There was also a deep anger in her at having lost her home, her security and her father. In her pain she wanted to hit out at the world. Senara had felt the same when her own father had died, but she had known her place and the conduct expected of her. Such anger would have solved nothing and would only have brought further misery. Rowena was vulnerable and too wilful for her own good. Another girl might respond to love and understanding, but Rowena was cunning enough to use that against those who meant her well. Though it seemed harsh, some time away from the family within a strict disciplined regime could be the making of her.

'Adam is at the yard,' Senara added. 'I will ask Merrin to take me there. Rowena is more than capable of twisting the truth.'

'And I shall come with you to bring her home.'

★

They found Rowena in Adam's office at Trevowan Hard. They could hear her sobbing and pleading incoherently within. When Senara opened the door, she saw her husband in his shirtsleeves staring down in bewilderment at his distraught niece, who had thrown herself into his arms as she wept.

'Why do they hate me? I miss Papa so much. I am so unhappy.'

When she saw the two women, she became hysterical. 'Do not listen to them, Uncle Adam. Amelia hates me. She wants to get rid of me. Felicity has no time for me. She cares only for Charlotte, Thea and George. She would treat me like a servant, expecting me to be their nurserymaid. I want to live with you.'

'That is completely untrue,' Amelia declared, as evenly as her own anger allowed. Her flushed countenance showed the extent of her agitation.

Adam put his hands on his niece's shoulders and took a step back as he continued to look at her. 'Calm yourself, Rowena. No one hates you and you are certainly not regarded as a servant. Everyone has to adapt to the new circumstances since your father's death.'

'Not you. You still have your lovely house,' Rowena pouted mutinously.

'I still regard Trevowan as our family home. Its loss has been difficult to accept.' Adam checked his own anger. His grievances were focused upon Tristan, and clearly his niece needed comfort and understanding. He attempted to lighten the atmosphere and lifted a questioning brow towards his wife. 'I take it there is a reason for this theatrical drama.'

'Rowena is insufferably rude and out of control,' Amelia cut in. 'She is also wilful and too headstrong for her own good. She is a bad influence on Charlotte.'

'Stepmama has never liked me; neither does Grandmama. Let me stay with you, Uncle Adam. I will do everything you ask.' Rowena stared up at him with wide, pleading eyes.

'She has the manners of a hoyden,' Amelia added. 'Are her actions those of a rational child? Stealing Senara's mare and galloping here.'

'She has lost both her mother and father,' Adam reasoned, a frown lining his brow.

'I will be good, Uncle Adam. Please, I beg you, let me live with you. I am so unhappy.' Rowena flung herself back against her uncle's chest and wrapped her arms around him. 'I love you like a father. You have always been so dashing and brave. I adore you, Uncle Adam. I would be so happy to live with you.'

'I think you should heed Amelia, Adam,' Senara said quietly, annoyed at the deliberate way Rowena was seeking to win her uncle to her side.

'You gave Bryn a home.' Rowena squeezed out a fresh flood of tears. 'You cannot turn your back on me, Uncle Adam. Am I less than Bryn, who has no memory of his past or parents after his coach accident? I am your own blood.'

'Bryn faced being sent to a workhouse or orphanage had I not become his guardian. You are surrounded by family who have only your best interests at heart.'

'But they do not want me,' she sobbed. 'They want to stifle me and crush my Loveday spirit.'

For a moment Adam seemed on the point of wavering. 'Perhaps you could stay with us for a short time, but it would upset your stepmama and grandmother. You wrong them if you do not think they care for you.'

'I would do anything to live with you.' She became all smiles and sweet coercion. 'You are my dearest, closest relative. My father's twin. With respect, Stepmama and Grandmama do not understand me. They are not Lovedays. Not by blood. They bow to convention, and that is not always the Loveday way. They see my need to gallop across a moor with the wind in my hair as the act of a hoyden. It is because I want to feel alive and not smothered. You understand that, Uncle Adam. I am a true Loveday.'

His lips twitched with amusement. 'You are right to be proud of our independent spirit, but you are also a woman and fast becoming a beautiful one. The world is full of pitfalls for the naive and unwary. Before you can give in to the wild urges of your blood, you must learn how to control it. Today has shown you have no restraint. I would have you become a young lady your father would be proud of.' He stepped back from her entreating figure. 'This show of histrionics is unbecoming. None of us hates you. You are upset and grieving.' He glanced at Amelia. 'She needs time. This wildness will pass.'

His back was to his niece and a look of smug satisfaction replaced her wails. He turned quickly to catch her expression and his own darkened. 'I will not be lied to, niece, or taken for a fool. There is more to being a Loveday than the wildness you mistakenly see as strength. More importantly, there is honour, pride in our name and heritage, and family loyalty.'

'But I understand all those. I would never do anything to bring disgrace to our name.' Rowena's lips trembled and her eyes were wild with distress. 'Please, I entreat you, Uncle Adam. Do not let them send me away.'

Adam looked at Amelia. 'Is she capable of changing whilst remaining with us? How much has she learned from her lessons?'

'She pays no heed to anything Felicity or I say to curb

her wildness,' Amelia said with a sigh. 'She may have learned the rudiments from her lessons with her tutors, but she has the intelligence to be capable of so much more.'

'I do not intend to become a boring bluestocking or the wife of a parson, like Aunt Bridie,' Rowena retorted.

'A woman with a lively, intelligent mind can be an asset to her husband,' Amelia reminded her. 'You have also avoided your music lessons, and your painting and embroidery are a disgrace. A woman is expected to neatly sew her husband's cravats and linen shirts. They are accomplishments men prize in a wife.'

Rowena backed away, her eyes feral. 'I shall marry a man who will provide me with servants for all that. I've no intention of being a seamstress. Am I so plain that no man will look upon me with favour?'

'Beauty will attract a man, but it takes more than that to hold him,' Adam informed her.

Amelia inhaled sharply, clearly striving to keep her voice reasonable. 'If you are to marry well, you must excel in the refinements expected of a woman of respectable birth.'

Adam turned to his wife. 'Do you agree with Amelia?'

'I have said little, because Amelia has a better understanding of the upbringing of a gentlewoman, but I do agree with her.'

'That is unjust,' Rowena wailed. 'My father married my mother and she had no education. Neither did Senara, yet you married her, Uncle Adam.'

'Your father and uncle are exceptional men,' Amelia snapped. 'Senara learned quickly her role of gentlewoman and educated herself so that she brought no shame by her ignorance to our family. The same could not be said for your mother, Meriel. Do you want to end up like your mama, a whore who went from lover to lover in her need for riches and ended up abandoned by them all, diseased and a pauper?'

Senara gasped. 'That was cruel, Amelia.'

'But the truth.' The older woman remained unrepentant.

Rowena's expression became more mutinous with each word, and the flush staining her neck foretold of the tantrum about to erupt.

Adam cut her short. 'I am in agreement with Amelia. There will be no further discussion on this subject. A ladies' academy will teach you the correct decorum for a young lady. A suitable place will be found for you as soon as possible.'

Rowena's face screwed up and her hands clenched into fists; a wail rose from low in her stomach, building in resonance as it filled her body. As her mouth opened and her fury resounded in the office, Adam took his stepmother's arm, nodded to Senara to follow them, and guided Amelia outside. He turned the key in the lock.

'She can stay in there until she calms down. I will return her to Reskelly Cottage when she is in a more compliant frame of mind. Before we can even begin to turn her into a gentlewoman, she has to learn that histrionics of such magnitude will not be tolerated.'

Chapter Fifteen

Tristan was on the quarterdeck of his ship *Good Fortune*, returning from France, his body braced against the swell of the waves. Overhead the canvas creaked and flapped as the wind veered and the sails deflated. Captain Marlowe shouted orders to the helmsman to change direction and for the sailors in the rigging to haul in the topsails. The ship slowed its progress, the wind now taking it off course for Dartmouth, where the passengers had paid handsomely to disembark. The voyage could be delayed by anything from one day to a week if the wind did not change. From Dartmouth they would then sail to Plymouth, where Tristan had purchased a large warehouse to store his goods until they were catalogued and auctioned. He had employed an agent in France to purchase the gilded Louis XIV furniture from the desecrated chateaux ransacked in the revolution. A huge profit would be made when it was sold in England. The obvious place for storage would have been London, but it could take up to six weeks for a ship to be given a mooring and unloaded in the capital's overcrowded port.

Tristan squinted at the few clouds meandering across the sky. The sun was dipping lower on the horizon. He had taken a leaf out of Adam Loveday's book and intended to own a fleet of merchant ships trading throughout the world. It was a temporary setback that Adam had refused to build another vessel for him. That was his cousin's loss. There were other shipyards eager to take his money. For now he had purchased another smaller vessel, which had been used by smugglers and confiscated and sold by the revenue office. *Swallow* was not the fastest of brigantines, but she would serve him for shorter voyages to the Continent. When he had run away from Trevowan, he had lived in France for several years, working with a merchant who had contacts in many countries: wine merchants in Portugal and silk and spice merchants in Venice. Some of them had agreed to sell to him, and *Swallow* would return from this voyage laden with exotic goods.

The investment had taken the bulk of his fortune, which he accrued during his second marriage when he had lived in Boston. Many of the renovations and refurbishments he had planned for Trevowan had been put on hold. The main rooms of the house were already furnished in impressive style, and he had ordered the bailiff, Isaac Nance, to double the yearly harvest. If he succeeded, he could expect a rise in wages. If he failed, his job would be forfeit, as would that of his son as gamekeeper.

A movement on the lower deck drew Tristan's attention. The slim, upright figure of Lord Brienne had come on deck to take the air, along with his niece, the Lady Alys. His lordship was middle aged, with thick, greying blond hair swept back from a high brow. The woman was in her early twenties. Her velvet cloak hid the outline of her body, but the hood had blown back to reveal dark copper-tinted hair fashionably curled. Tristan's breath caught in his throat. She was stunningly beautiful: skin like porcelain; Cupid's bow lips; an angelic oval face.

He had made it his business to learn what he could about his lordship when he had booked his passage. The family were from Wiltshire. When they had dined earlier, Lord Brienne had been affable and charming, interested in Tristan's business ventures. Lady Alys had not joined them; she was suffering from a headache. Now, as the couple strolled around the deck, he noticed a protectiveness about Brienne's manner towards the woman, making Tristan wonder whether she was his mistress rather than his niece. He shrugged. Lucky devil if it was the case, but it was not his concern. He dismissed the matter as unimportant.

They were not the only passengers on board. *Good Fortune* had four passenger cabins, each accommodating a single person. Tristan occupied one and his lordship and companion two more. The fourth was taken by a stout fop in his late twenties, a Mr Walcott, who was over-dressed and overloud and full of his own self-importance. His single eyebrow crawled across his temple like a well-fed caterpillar. He had cut short his Grand Tour, saying he could not abide foreign food another day longer and that he had yet to visit any country whose culture was the equal of England. Since the peace with France, many young gentlemen who had delayed their Grand Tour because of the war had commenced the custom of spending a year or two travelling through Europe. Tristan had disliked the ignorant buffoon Walcott on sight.

He continued to scan the horizon as the light began to fade. The wind was still driving them off course and he hoped that they would be able to turn about without too much delay. He decided to go below decks and write some letters before they again dined at the captain's table. He bowed as he passed Lord Brienne, who remained on deck without his niece. He hoped she was not again indisposed. Any illness could turn even a short voyage into a tortuous ordeal.

As he descended the stairs to the passenger quarters he heard a muffled cry and the sound of a scuffle. No lights had been lit below deck and he could see little in the gloom. There continued the sound of movement from Lady Alys's cabin; nothing loud, but even so Tristan sensed that something was wrong. His childhood spent surviving the rigours of gang warfare in the poorest streets and witnessing sights of every degradation had alerted him to danger. The faintest groan followed by a thud made him dash forward. Without knocking, he flung open the Lady Alys's door. Across the narrow bed he saw the spread of white petticoats and the thrashing of a woman's legs that had nothing to do with passion and everything to do with desperation. She was fighting like a wildcat but had no chance against the superior weight of her assailant. One of the man's hands was over her mouth; the other was fumbling with his breeches.

Grabbing Walcott's shirt collar, Tristan hauled him up and smashed his fist into the blackguard's jaw. Then he followed through with another punch to his stomach, doubling him over. For good measure he slammed Walcott's head up against the wall. As he slumped unconscious, Tristan threw him bodily out of the cabin.

Lady Alys scrambled to pull down her skirts and rise shakily from the bed.

'That fiend burst in upon me!' she gasped. 'I cannot thank you enough. What makes a man act so like an animal?'

He held her tight. 'You are safe now. Did he harm you?'

She shook her head, but he could just make out a trickle of blood that ran from a cut lip where the knave must have struck her.

There was an outraged shout from Lord Brienne from the open door. 'What is this? Has this knave taken advantage of you?'

'Uncle, it is not what you think. Mr Loveday saved me. It was Walcott who attacked me.'

There was a groan from the corridor, and in the shadows Walcott levered himself to his knees. His lordship hauled him to his feet and pressed him up against the panelling. 'Mr Loveday, will you be my second? I will have honour satisfied. Though by rights the cur should be horsewhipped.'

'A ship is no place for a duel, my lord. But I will happily perform as your second once we land. Captain Marlowe may agree to act for Walcott.'

Brienne released the fop, who clutched his gut and whined, 'There has been a misunderstanding.'

Tristan lost his temper and lashed out twice more at the cringing passenger. 'Had I not chanced along, you would have raped the Lady Alys. Many would agree that you should be thrown overboard.'

'She led me on,' he blustered ungallantly.

'With respect, Mr Loveday, I will deal with this my way,' Brienne declared, taking hold of Walcott in a firm grip. 'If you would be so kind as to land in a deserted cove, honour will be served with pistols at dawn.'

Walcott cast around as though frantically searching for rescue. Lady Alys had retreated against the wall, as far away from him as possible. Her hands covered her face but she was remarkably composed. Tristan would have expected hysterics.

'That can be arranged, your lordship.' He eyed Walcott with disgust. 'Do you have the appropriate weapons?'

'I never travel without them,' Brienne tersely

informed them, before frogmarching Walcott into the fop's cabin and locking him inside.

In the circumstances Tristan admired his lordship's restraint. He would have given Walcott the thrashing he deserved before calling him out. His concern was now for his female passenger.

'Are you sure that the knave did not harm you, Lady Alys? Can I get you anything to overcome the shock?'

She shook her head. 'I will never forget my indebtedness to you, Mr Loveday,' she said shakily.

'I am ashamed that such an attack happened on my ship.'

'You are in no way to blame, Mr Loveday.' His lordship studied his niece with concern. 'I will not have the Lady Alys involved in a scandal.'

'That is understandable, my lord. You will have the complete discretion of Captain Marlowe and myself.'

Captain Marlowe was disturbed when the incident was explained to him. He had begun his life at sea as a cabin boy for the East India Company and for thirty years had worked his way through the ranks by his natural aptitude and initiative, taking his master's papers five years ago. He was a stout, bewhiskered, curmudgeonly old sea dog with a thin veneer of manners but a deep respect for authority. He also had an iron hook, which replaced the hand he had lost ten years ago when it had been blown off by a privateer's cannonball. He had bound the stump with a tourniquet and sunk the privateer before allowing the ship's surgeon to deal with the wound. Tristan had employed him by reputation and sealed the deal by doubling his normal salary.

'I don't hold with duelling myself,' Marlowe scowled. 'I'd give Walcott a taste of the cat-o'-nine-tails – a hundred lashes – or have him keel-hauled.'

'As I would expect if the man was one of your crew,' Tristan replied. 'However, since he is a passenger, such treatment would not serve the reputation of my shipping line. It is for his lordship to decide how he wishes the matter to proceed. I have the integrity of my business to consider. To attract valued customers, discretion must be part of our service.'

Captain Marlowe nodded, but Tristan knew that as captain he was the law upon the ship. The crew could be a motley assemblage, and any sign of weakness might lead them to take advantage of the rules in the future.

'I want us to put in to an isolated cove under cover of darkness,' Tristan informed him. 'One where his lordship and Walcott can be rowed ashore by ourselves round a headland and out of sight of the crew.'

'That be some order,' Marlowe frowned.

'That's what I pay you for.'

Marlowe shrugged. 'The wind is changing so it shouldn't be a problem. Though it will mean we won't make Dartmouth until tomorrow's evening tide.'

'I doubt his lordship will complain at that.'

At the sound of the anchor chain being run out, Tristan tapped on Brienne's door. It was opened by his lordship dressed in a dark jacket and breeches. He handed Tristan a box of duelling pistols to carry. Walcott was sweating and breathing heavily when Tristan unlocked his door.

'I unreservedly offer my abject apologies to your lordship,' the younger man whined. 'Having compromised her ladyship, I will save her reputation by marrying her. I believe a ship's captain can perform such a ceremony.'

'Do you think I would allow my niece to wed scum such as you?' Brienne gritted out. 'Or was that your ploy all along, to compromise her reputation and force my hand?'

'I do not know what came over me. I never meant—'

'Show some backbone, man,' Marlowe growled. 'This is a sorry enough affair without you being lily livered.'

A sound like a strangled whimper emanated from Walcott, but with a shake of his head he pulled himself upright, his lips clamped into a tight line to steady his nerves.

'The matter will be settled ashore,' Brienne declared, and strolled languidly in front as though he was out for an evening walk around his estate.

Walcott was flanked on either side by Marlowe and Tristan. On the captain's instructions the decks had been cleared of men, except for the bosun, who had received a gold sovereign from Tristan for his silence and loyalty. Tristan rewarded those who served him well, but amongst his men he had earned a reputation for dealing harshly with any who crossed him. The bosun had lowered the longboat, and the four men climbed down the rope ladder to settle inside. Tristan and Marlowe took up the oars. Dawn was lightening the sky to the east. Scanning the shore, he saw the white breakers washing over the beach and the outline of high cliffs. They were anchored in a horseshoe cove, the headland dipping down into the sea like a dragon taking a drink.

Accompanied by the splash of oars, they rowed in silence around the rocks to the next cove. Tristan reckoned they were somewhere east of the Lizard, on a stretch of uninhabited water. The cove was small, with a narrow, flat beach. The longboat scrunched over the seaweed that had come ashore in a recent storm.

Walcott stumbled as he stepped on to the sand, and Marlowe had to grab his arm to stop him from falling. Brienne had walked off to take his place by a boulder. Tristan laid the pistol box on the rock and took out the pistols, testing them both for balance before loading them.

The sky was brightening, casting long shadows over the cove from the cliffs above. It promised to be a cloudless day. He presented both pistols to Walcott to make his choice of weapon. The man's hand trembled slightly as it closed over the handle, then with Marlowe at his side he walked back along the beach.

Marlowe had paced out the sand and waited for the two opponents to join him. He stood with his legs planted apart, his arms crossed over his broad chest and his florid face showing as little emotion as a judge passing the death sentence on a prisoner. The two duellists stood back to back, the pistols cocked and pointed in the air.

'Gentlemen, you will take ten paces then turn and fire,' Tristan stated.

He held his breath as the two men stepped away from each other, his lordship's stride firm and determined and Walcott's nervous and stumbling. They turned together, and for a moment Walcott wavered. In that moment of hesitancy Brienne fired. The sound caused several dozen gulls to take flight from their roosts, screeching in protest. In slow motion Walcott swayed and staggered backwards. His knees buckled and he dropped his pistol, but he stayed upright, a dark stain spreading across his chest. Brienne walked back to the duelling case and replaced his weapon, at the same time tossing a leather pouch of coins to Tristan.

'Give that to the ship's surgeon to do what he can for the knave.'

Marlowe was assisting Walcott to walk to the longboat. The younger man's feet were dragging from loss of blood. He was unconscious by the time they reached *Good Fortune* and remained in the infirmary when they docked at Dartmouth.

Tristan was on the quarterdeck as the ship tied up. Lady Alys was the first of the passengers on deck, and she came to join him.

'I have much to thank you for, Mr Loveday.'

'It was an honour that I could be of service. The distressing incident is best forgotten.'

She blushed. 'I shall never forget what you did.' Her voice was low and tremulous.

Tristan saw the faint bruising along her jaw and the cut to her mouth where that brute had held her down, and was moved by her vulnerability. A tendril of hair blew across her cheek, and before he could stop himself he had brushed it aside with his thumb. Her eyes widened and he felt her hold her breath, not from fear, more from expectation.

A footfall behind him broke the spell that had been building and his hand fell to his side. Lady Alys lowered her eyes as Lord Brienne approached.

'Captain Marlowe informs me that Walcott is keeping to his cabin and will disembark at another port.' It had been agreed between his lordship and Tristan that nothing would be mentioned to Lady Alys of the outcome of the duel for fear of distressing her further.

'That is so. I trust you have a safe journey, my lord.'

Brienne smiled at his niece. 'Be so good as to await me at the gangplank, my dear. There is a matter I would discuss with Mr Loveday.'

Tristan watched the Lady Alys descend the steps to the lower deck, regretting that there had not been time to get to know her better.

'So, Loveday, Marlowe tells me Walcott survived the night.'

'He remains unconscious and the surgeon does not expect him to last until nightfall.'

'The authorities will be bound to ask awkward questions. Can't have my niece's reputation put in jeopardy, don't you know?' It was said in an offhand manner, but there was a fixedness to his lordship's stare.

Tristan knew exactly what needed doing. He weighed both the consequences to himself and the possible benefits.

'The Lady Alys's name must be protected. Walcott brought this business upon himself. Before dark we will dock in Plymouth. It is a rowdy port where many dangers lurk for the unwary amongst the quayside taverns. Fights and deaths are frequent in those dark alleys. A body could lie there all night and not be found by the watch until morning.'

Brienne nodded. 'Then I trust you will take great care, Mr Loveday. Your discretion over this matter will not be forgotten.'

Tristan bowed to his lordship as the man left him to escort his niece ashore. He had a feeling it would not be the last time he saw the couple. In fact he would make sure that they met again in more propitious circumstances. Brienne could be a useful contact in the future.

Good Fortune sailed out of Dartmouth on the afternoon tide. They made good time to Plymouth, and during the night a corpse was laid in the most notorious part of the dockside. When the constables found him in the morning it was declared that Walcott had been killed and robbed. From the information about his person, his family was notified of his tragic death.

Chapter Sixteen

Richard Allbright's arrival at Reskelly Cottage lightened the tension between the women. He had taken ship from Bristol to Falmouth and then paid a fisherman to bring him to Fowey, where he had hired a hack for the duration of his stay. He had presented an impressive figure as he greeted his family in his naval uniform, which he had worn as a forceful reminder that he was now a grown man who had risked his life in the service of his country. He still resented the lectures from his last leave by both his mother and Adam. Until then he had hero-worshipped his stepbrother.

He now considered that although he was Adam's junior by fourteen years, he had proved his manhood and would answer to his own conscience and not have his life dictated by another. Especially not by his mother. He also disliked the fact that she held the purse strings over his allowance for another three years. Even so he adored Amelia, and allowed her and Felicity to fuss over him for the first few days. He was shocked at how his mother had aged in the last two years. She had always found it difficult to overcome the shame when their family was hit by scandal. And there had been many scandals since her marriage to Edward Loveday, though this latest over the loss of Trevowan was one of the worst.

Felicity also seemed to be dragging the world around on her shoulders. Apart from her fair beauty, Richard had never seen what other attributes had attracted St John to her. Like his mother, she could be prim, and condemning of those who were not afraid to enjoy the varied pleasures life could offer. It was obvious that the two women were good friends, and bonded further by taking the moral high ground over anyone who fell short of their standards. To his surprise, that now included Aunt Elspeth.

His doughty aunt had called on his second day at the cottage, and although the two younger women were civil, the atmosphere became charged when Elspeth refused to answer any of their questions regarding Tristan and the changes he had made at Trevowan.

Richard had walked Elspeth to her horse when she left to visit Uncle Joshua before riding to Tor Farm. He stroked the mare's nose as Elspeth stood by the stone mounting block. 'Dear Aunt, pray do tell me of our new cousin. He cannot be all bad or you would not be living in the Dower House at Trevowan.'

Her pince-nez hung on a gold chain round her neck and she placed it on her long thin nose and regarded him over the top of the lens before replying. 'I have no cause to complain. He has treated me fairly.' Her mouth clamped shut.

Richard stared back at Reskelly Cottage, unimpressed with his new home. 'The cottage is not what Mama has been used to. Our London house is far grander and she would be surrounded by all her old friends, not to mention that the entertainment is finer.'

Elspeth viewed him disdainfully; he had not

considered the most important reason that his mother had stayed in Cornwall. 'Amelia would not part Rafe from his cousins. These are the people she cares for. Family is more important than the trappings of wealth.'

Richard shrugged, his tone deprecating. 'Apart from Tristan acquiring Trevowan, why do they hate him?'

Elspeth put her booted foot into the stirrup and swung into the saddle, hooking her leg over the pommel. From the advantage of her height she removed her pince-nez, tucking it inside her riding jacket, and regarded him sternly.

'I will not be drawn into family politics. You must ask Adam his opinion. Personally I believe Tristan is not as black as he is painted. That does not mean that I entirely trust him. I hope that by my presence at Trevowan I can prevent a major feud between Tristan and Adam.' She clicked her tongue and set her mare at a fast trot to her brother's rectory.

When Richard re-entered the cottage he could hear Felicity deriding Elspeth for her duplicity. In his opinion St John's wife was hypocritical to condemn Elspeth for choosing to remain in her childhood home when she herself was content to live on his mother's bounty. The pettiness of it all left him cold and he slunk back out again. There was a milkmaid he had met yesterday in the lane to a farm a mile away and he hoped to waylay her again. He had recognised the bold invitation in her smile and eyes.

Richard returned two hours later a satisfied man. When he led his horse into the stable, however, his sense of well-being dissipated as Rowena ambushed him. Her blond hair was loose and tumbling around her shoulders and her high-waisted muslin dress displayed her rounded curves in a way that would have aroused his desire had she not been his close relative. Instead her provocative giggle and slanted gaze made him uneasy. She resembled her mother not only in looks but also in her seductive wiles.

Her stare was bold and appraising. 'And where has our handsome officer been that he returns looking so pleased with himself? Have you found yourself a lover?'

'Less of your audacity, young madam. I've been riding.'

'Oh, I dare say you have.' Her laugh was low and throaty. 'What was her name?'

There was no sign of any servant, so he unsaddled his horse and picked up a currying brush to remove the mud from the gelding's coat. His tone was disparaging. 'You sound more like a sixpenny whore than a gentlewoman. Have you no shame?'

She leaned her back against the side of the stall and studied him through her lashes. 'Apparently not. I speak as I find and will not be hidebound by stupid convention.'

Such a statement coming from the lips of a common doxy would have tempted him to pursue the minx. But this was his cousin by marriage, and he was shocked at her words. Before he could reprimand her, she taunted him with brazen speculation.

'Well, my handsome officer, your mama has been asking after you whilst you dallied with your paramour. I hope she gave you pleasure. Your libertine ways will be cured if Amelia has her way. She'd have you wed before the year is out.' She giggled. 'That will not suit you at all, will it, my bold lecher?'

He dropped the brush and rounded on her. After all his mother's lectures, the insolent minx had pushed him too far. Grabbing her wrist, he pulled her over to a rainwater butt outside the stable. She giggled, no doubt thinking she had enticed him into a game.

'If you see fit to speak like a cheap whore, then expect to be treated like one.'

He gripped the back of her neck and before she could guess his intent had ducked her head under the water. He held her there for a few seconds. When he hauled her up, she was drenched, bedraggled and spluttering with fury.

'A pox on you!' she ranted, lashing out with her fists.

Another ducking silenced her.

'Never let me hear such filth from you again. I thought Mama was being too strict when she spoke of sending you away to a school for young ladies. Clearly she is not.'

'Adam will hear of this,' Rowena spat, her hair hanging in rat's tails around her skull. 'You'll pay for this.'

He laughed. 'Adam will be appalled at your conduct. If you wish to be treated as a gently bred woman, I suggest you start acting like one.'

He left her shivering, shocked and miserable, knowing she had lost her last ally. Her eyes blazed with impotent fury as he marched back into the stable. She had thought Richard would enjoy her teasing and had hoped to win him to her side to speak against Amelia's plans. Clearly she had misjudged him. She had heard him use similar language with the local girls when she had spied on him. She had thought that was what he wanted to hear. How wrong could she have been? Wrong, naive and less worldly than she had considered herself to be. It was mortifying. The village boys had found such comments amusing and she had provoked several of them to kiss her before she rejected them with a set-down. She had revelled in those moments of power. Now she felt ashamed and foolish. Had she sounded like a six-penny whore as Richard had accused? It was a sobering thought. She had heard the gossip about her mother and had no intention of following her path of greed and destruction. In her inexperience she had thought her boldness a sign of her independence and the adventurous spirit that refused to be crushed. That was one mistake she would not repeat.

She ran to her room, ignoring a call from Amelia, and locked the door to change her sopping gown and dry her hair. As she tore off the wet gown, her mouth set in an uncompromising line. Richard would not get away with what he had done. He might have taught her a valuable lesson in decorum, but he had also degraded and humiliated her. Her Loveday blood rebelled with outraged pride whilst her Sawle ancestry cried out for vengeance. Not for nothing was she the niece of the notorious and feared smuggler Harry Sawle. No one could treat her like that and not suffer the consequences. Richard Allbright would rue his actions this day.

Richard pursued the local wenches with enthusiasm. He had been at Reskelly a month when Amelia learned of his liaison with a milkmaid. He was astounded at the virulence of her condemnation. For three days he was subjected to her lectures on morality and the necessity for him to curb his lechery and take a bride. Felicity was constantly tearful. Mealtimes revolved around her woes, and the persistent cries from her two younger children stretched his patience beyond its limit. He resented that his mother had turned from a doting parent to a shrew. When he could no longer tolerate her sermons, he decided to leave Trewenna to pursue the peace and pleasures offered by the company of his friend Lieutenant Chandler.

As he stormed out of Reskelly Cottage, he noticed the gloating smirk on Rowena's face and guessed she had spied on him and reported his dalliance. That scheming minx had been all apologies for her behaviour and smiles to him since his punishment of her. She had pleaded with him not to mention her conduct to the family, as she regretted her actions and would never act so indecorously again. Like a fool he had believed her and had agreed to be silent. If he was not so furious with his mother – he knew he could not face her without more heated words – he would have retraced his steps and informed on Rowena.

He spent three weeks in Truro, but found it lacked the social amenities he had enjoyed in Bath. After two months away he returned to the spa. Lieutenant Chandler had left for his father's estate in Somerset, where Richard had earlier been invited to join him. He decided he would remain in Bath for a week before visiting his friend. If he gave any thought to Emma Madison, it was to hope that she had returned to her family in Dorchester.

He had enjoyed the freedom of the spa town for two days before he saw Emma and Mrs Kellerman in the Pump Room. Emma lifted her hand in a tentative wave across the crowded space. She looked pale and was not as pretty as he remembered. He had no intention of renewing that dalliance, so he affected not to see her and made a hasty retreat. For two more days he continued to avoid her.

But Bath was not so large that if you enjoyed the entertainments offered by polite society you could evade an encounter when another was determined to effect it. Richard remained wary as he promenaded through the elegant paved streets with their sandstone terraced houses favoured by the fashionable and wealthy. When he was invited to a musical soirée at the house of Mr and Mrs Hadford, cousins of his friend Chandler, he was put on his guard as soon as he arrived.

Mrs Hadford greeted him at the top of the stairs leading to the salon, where the guests were already gathered. 'There is one particular young lady who will be delighted that you have graced us with your presence.'

Richard parried his stab of unease by flirting with his hostess. 'How can we then escape the vigilance of your husband's attentions?' He bowed over her hand and raised it his lips.

'My dear Richard, if I were only ten years younger, I would be quite aflutter at your boldness.' She giggled. 'I mean of course Miss Madison. You were frequently in her company before you left for Cornwall. Have you been neglecting her since your return? That is too naughty of you.'

'I have not been the only caller upon Miss Madison this Season. I thought she had returned to the country.'

More guests arrived and Richard sidled into the salon, determined to delay any contact with Emma. When he saw her, he was appalled. Her face was without colour and her hair looked stringy and lacklustre. How had he ever found her attractive?

He circumnavigated the salon in the opposite direction to Miss Madison and joined a party of people he knew well. Throughout he watched her from the corner of his eye. When she manoeuvred her position to be closer to him, he moved around the room, making it difficult for her to approach him whilst appearing to be unaware of her presence. If he hoped that such tactics would discourage her usually timid nature, he was soon disabused of his belief.

'Lieutenant Allbright, how pleasant to see you again.' Her voice sent the hairs on the back of his neck rising. 'I trust your visit to Cornwall was pleasant.'

With half a dozen companions looking questioningly at him, Richard had no choice but to turn, smile and introduce Miss Madison before replying, 'It is always a joy to be reacquainted with my family.'

Mr Lane, who was a friend of Chandler's and something of a buffoon, chirped, 'Was the visit not a trial? I find the shorter time I spend with my family, the more pleasurable is the experience.'

'I was under the impression that Lieutenant Allbright was devoted to his family,' Emma said sweetly. 'They have recently suffered a bereavement. It must be a distressing time for them.'

There were murmured condolences. Then, to his further annoyance, Mrs Kellerman joined her niece, her voice high and carrying. 'What an elusive man you have become, Lieutenant. You promised to call upon us on your return. One does not expect a gentleman to be remiss upon his word.'

He veiled his displeasure at her accusation and bowed stiffly. 'I had many business matters to attend to.'

'Then I shall look forward to receiving you tomorrow.' She swept grandly away before he could reply.

'I would have thought that as your betrothed—' Emma began in an undertone.

'Let us talk elsewhere.' To stop her indiscreet chatter, he gripped her arm and propelled her towards an unoccupied corner, where they could not be overheard. 'Miss Madison, you are under some misapprehension,' he informed her coldly.

'How so?' Her lip trembled.

'Keep your voice down or I will leave,' he snapped.

'Why are you like this, Richard?' she gasped, her eyes brimming with tears. 'You declared your love and regard for me. You spoke of a secret betrothal.'

'And you seem determined to declare it to the world,' he responded, unable to conceal his contempt. 'I have taken great pains to be circumspect since my return to Bath.'

'What you may consider circumspect, I would consider neglect! People have remarked upon your absence in calling at our home.'

'It was to protect your reputation,' he hedged. 'Mama was too upset for me to mention our betrothal.'

To his astonishment, the light of battle glinted in her eyes. 'Then you must reconsider and inform her at once. For circumstances have changed. I am with child.'

A distant roaring like the gathering momentum of a tidal wave gushed through Richard's body. For a moment its force rocked him as it crashed through his emotions like a ship splintering on unseen rocks. He could not believe his ill fortune. He had taken the usual measures to ensure that she would not conceive. His eyes narrowed.

'Should I congratulate Jevington?'

Her cheeks flared with angry fire as bright as if he had slapped her. 'How dare you, sir? You know you are the father – the only man . . .' Her indignation was cut short by a sob, tears spilling on to her cheeks.

They left him unmoved. 'I know nothing of the kind. As I recall, you were easy with your favours. A woman who suspects that she is with child by one man has to act quickly if she seeks to dupe another.' He quelled his own panic.

Her face showed her horror at his words. 'Richard, why are you like this? You love me.'

As her voice began to rise, he hastily interceded. He

cast a covert glance over his shoulder and was relieved that no one was watching them. 'Your pardon. You must understand that this is something of a shock.'

'But we are betrothed, are we not?' Her eyes were dark and pleading. 'You must realise that we cannot now keep a secret our plans to marry.'

'They have to be secret until Mama will agree to them.' He was searching for excuses.

'You should have told her!' Emma twisted her hands in agitation.

'This is not the place to discuss such a matter.' He forced a note of reason into his voice. 'Naturally you are upset. The fact is that Mama will not hear of it.' The lie slipped easily off his tongue. 'If I marry without her permission before I am of age, I could lose my inheritance. How then could I support a wife and provide a suitable home?'

'In the circumstances she would not be so cruel.'

There was now a steeliness to her voice and a determined glint in her eye. Where was the sweet, compliant woman he had courted?

The unexpected change in her made him more defensive. 'In the circumstances, Miss Madison, she would regard you as rather too ready with your favours to be considered a worthy bride. Mama takes the highest moral ground of anyone I know.'

'But I shall be ruined.' Her face crumpled and he feared he could no longer forestall her tears and an unpleasant scene. Panic was gnawing his vitals and it increased his alarm that she was seeking to trap him and that he might not be the father of the child. 'We cannot discuss this now. I will call upon you tomorrow. It is but two months since our last meeting. Early days for you to be so certain as to your condition.'

'A midwife has confirmed it.'

His stock felt as if it was suddenly choking him, and he could feel the sweat running down his brow. When cornered, his instinct was to retaliate. He stood to attention, clicked his heels together and gave a mocking bow. 'I will not be tricked into a marriage and rear another man's child.'

He strode away, leaving Emma crushed and frightened.

He left Bath early the next morning and told no one of his destination.

Chapter Seventeen

May dusted the woods with bluebells and the air was filled with birdsong as they proclaimed their territory and reared their young. The changing season brought new beginnings for the family. Peter and Bridie said their emotional goodbyes and took up residence in their new parish in Launceston. A mutinous Rowena was sent away to her school, a reputable establishment in Exeter; Japhet's sister Hannah, who would be sending her eldest daughter Abigail there next year, had recommended it. After a short holiday, Adam's eldest son Nathan and his ward Bryn returned to their boarding school and were joined by Japhet's boy Japhet Edward, whilst the younger boys and girls continued with their studies at Boscabel under their tutor Mr Lancros, who rode to the house every weekday from Fowey.

For a time, life was more peaceful in Cornwall, although undercurrents of grief and anger still ran just below the surface.

Adam had immersed himself in work at the yard, where two keels had been laid down: one for a brigantine for a merchant in Falmouth and the other for the large merchantman that was Adam's latest design. The customer had been present at the launching of the vessel's sister ship *Good Fortune* last year and had been impressed by her size and performance. With the truce still holding with France, he had also been optimistic that England would again be a major importer and exporter of goods to all the continents. Another dozen shipwrights had been taken on, bringing an income to local villagers who housed them and their families as lodgers. A third merchantman had been commissioned for work to start next year. The yard had not been so busy for several years, and the only cloud over Adam's pleasure at his change in fortunes was that it was due to Tristan having commissioned *Good Fortune*, which had led to these orders. He resented any link with his cousin that made him beholden to him.

At least he was spared Tristan's presence. There had been no sign or word from him since his single visit to Trevowan upon taking possession. However, in the last month a flow of carts had arrived carrying expensive furniture and a score of workmen had been engaged to renovate the plasterwork in the main rooms. Adam had loved Trevowan for its simplicity and homeliness. Any changes were further proof that Tristan was a usurper and that the home Adam would have treasured meant little to his cousin.

Elspeth had become reclusive since the work began and close-lipped about the changes to the house. Most of the daylight hours found her visiting Tor Farm. Adam's last meeting with his aunt had been less than agreeable. There was a part of him that regarded her as consorting with the enemy.

Gwendolyn, who had suffered enough dissension within her own family over her marriage, was deter-mined to prevent any further rifts. Adam and Senara had been invited to dine at Tor Farm, along with Elspeth.

Throughout the meal Japhet had kept the mood jovial with his anecdotes and easy good humour. Adam had remained less communicative than usual. Finally Elspeth, never one to baulk at a fence, held him in a piercing glare over the top of her pince-nez.

'Since your family are in the best of health and the yard prospers, your lack of spirit at this table is clearly down to your disapproval of my actions.'

'You made your choice, Aunt.' His voice was clipped and his manner cool. 'What do you think of these changes he is making to the house?'

'He is master of Trevowan and has the money to renovate rooms in a way that your father could not afford.' She sucked in her cheeks. 'Your cousin has granted me permission to live where I was born. For that I am grateful. I will not spy on him.'

'Yet you have chosen to live in the Dower House rather than occupy your old rooms.' Adam remained unforgiving.

'It made more sense. It is too expensive to have the main house kept open solely for my convenience. The workmen are noisy. I prefer the quiet of the Dower House. Besides, I lived there before St John remarried,' she reminded him in equally terse tones.

At her own insistence Elspeth had moved into the Dower House with a single maid of all work to cater for her needs. She would not admit to Adam that she did not wish to witness the changes to the house – to her they would be a desecration. Every corner, every length of wainscoting and exposed roof beam, every cornice, door and window, damp patch and piece of scarred woodwork held memories of those she had loved and who were no more. Yet although the rooms at Trevowan were no longer the home she loved and cherished, the bricks and mortar were the same. Strangely, she did not blame Tristan for the changes to the house that had ripped out pieces of her heart. His own memories must hold more pain than pleasure.

Elspeth's great solace was her visits to Tor Farm. Several of the mares were carrying the foals sired by Emir Hassan, whose bloodlines went back to the Byerley Turk, one of the three stallions that had been imported from North Africa or the Middle East and from which all thoroughbreds in England had been bred. Japhet, despite his fall from grace and his transportation to lands across the sea for highway robbery, had returned a wealthy man with a hunger to succeed at his chosen dream of breeding racehorses.

Despite her show of unconcern at the censure many of the family had placed on her, Elspeth did regret the rift that was widening between Adam and herself. Both were too stubborn to seek a compromise upon what each regarded as a matter of principle. Tristan's manners might be newly acquired and his money undoubtedly nouveau riche, with all the ostentation of those wanting to stamp their mark upon society, but old Arthur, the first of the Loveday line to live at Trevowan, would have been proud of him. Perhaps Tristan was the fitting heir to the estate after all this time.

'Tristan is Arthur Loveday's great-grandson, as are you,' she reminded Adam now.

Adam snorted. 'You have to dig deep to draw from the taproot that links Tristan Loveday to this house. That root was transplanted generations ago by his grandfather and the seed has withered. A broken link has no strength in its chain. Tristan has the Loveday blood, but it has been blighted by bad breeding.'

'Good Lord!' Elspeth returned with an ironic twist to

her lips. 'How conveniently you forget how tainted that blood was in the beginning. Arthur St John Loveday was a rogue and adventurer of the first order. His wife, the genteel and wealthy Anne Penhaligan, was the heiress to Trevowan. Without her, my grandfather would never have been accepted amongst the gentry of Cornwall. I would say that Tristan is closer in nature and personality to old Arthur than any of my nephews.' She drew a ragged breath, and the stare she fixed on Adam was condemning. 'The past cannot be undone. You have to accept that Trevowan would have been lost to the family through St John's gambling.'

Adam pushed back his chair and stood up. 'Taking possession of Trevowan is but the start of Tristan's need to triumph over us. Nothing would please him more than to see us broken.'

Gwendolyn chewed her lower lip, anxious to restore peace. 'Adam, how can you say that, when in commissioning the *Good Fortune* he saved the shipyard when it was struggling because of the war?'

He bowed to his hostess and was at pains to batten down his anger. 'I would not expect someone of your sweet disposition to understand the skulduggery this man is capable of perpetrating. He has had many years to plan his retribution. He is wilier than a fox. To be accepted amongst society, he must show that he bears us no apparent ill will. He will work within the law, his actions insidious in their treachery, to trick us into a false security.'

Gwendolyn turned an imploring stare upon her husband. 'Do you think as Adam?'

Japhet spread his hands, the single gold signet ring he wore glinting in the late sunlight. 'None of us knows what Tristan is capable of. Neither do we know his true nature. He has little reason to love us and every reason to prove that he has been misjudged. He is a man coloured by his experiences, and those have been dark and mysterious. Adam is right not to trust him.'

'At least he has the decency to stay away until the scandal dies down,' Senara said to lighten the mood.

'I would rather my enemies were close at hand where I can be aware of their scheming.' Adam voiced his suspicions. 'This calm could be the eye of the storm.'

Elspeth sighed and rose stiffly to her feet. 'I have heard enough. I will take my leave. Why must you believe that he is hatching some conspiracy against you, Adam?'

'Because I know how I would act in Tristan's circumstances.'

Adam's words sent a shiver of unease through Senara. She hoped it was just grief for his twin that made him so unforgiving. He had always been a man who prized honour. Yet in the past he had shown how ruthlessly he could deal with those who set themselves against him. The years of conflict with the brutal smuggler Harry Sawle had shown Adam's refusal to allow any man to threaten his family. But Sawle had been an evil and corrupt smuggler, an unprincipled murderer who was hated and feared by the community yet who had always managed to escape justice. Adam had pitted his strength and wits against Sawle on many occasions and had finally emerged the victor, ensuring that the smuggler paid on the gallows for his crimes. Though always the Lovedays had kept within the law.

The change in her husband wounded Senara. His fierce sense of justice had always been something she respected. This was different. His anger fed the wildness in his blood. This time his enemy had struck far deeper than family pride and loyalty; he had struck at all Adam held sacrosanct.

Senara feared the consequences of a new rivalry with Tristan, and throughout the ride home she tried to reason with her husband.

'This anger against Tristan is so unlike you, Adam. He acted within the law. You must accept that St John lost Trevowan. Had he not taken his life, your anger would have been directed at him, not Tristan.'

'We lost Trevowan through trickery and deceit. How can I allow that to go unavenged?'

'Because Tristan did nothing unlawful.'

'It was a deliberate ploy to destroy us. Honour demands—'

'Men and their precious honour!' She lost her own temper. 'Why does it demand that you destroy all that is good and noble in yourself?'

They had reached the border of Boscabel land. 'I would not expect you to understand. Tristan may trick society into believing he is a gentleman, but he was born a guttersnipe, and his Loveday blood is tainted by that of miscreants and criminals.' He urged his gelding to a faster pace.

There was a coldness to Adam's tone Senara had never heard before. It shocked her and struck at her own pride. Her lowly birth made her too sensitive to a criticism that was not directed at herself. 'How would a common gypsy know anything of honour?' she flung back and veered her mare away to set off across the moor. Whether the wind had carried her reply away from Adam she did not know, but he did not come after her.

It was a small incident but it had sown the seed of misunderstanding. Senara had never been ashamed of her gypsy blood. Romany pride could be as fiery and as stubborn as any gentleman's. For the first time in their marriage a crack had appeared in the harmony and love they had shared. To begin with, it was so small it was hardly discernible, but as the days progressed Adam refused to listen to Senara's pleas for reason and spent longer hours at the yard. There he worked off a deepening anger fed by grief and by the guilt that he should have realised how St John's debts were escalating. He should have somehow stopped the obsessive gambling that had destroyed his twin. Any mention of either Tristan or St John sparked his temper, which was on a short fuse. To maintain peace within his home, he became withdrawn and no longer confided in his wife. Senara felt herself excluded, and the tension in their marriage widened the misunderstandings between the couple.

Senara was struggling with her own losses. She missed Bridie more than she had thought possible. All her sister's life Senara had been the one to watch over and protect her. She worried about Bridie doing too much to ingratiate herself with her new parishioners. The more she missed Bridie, the more her thoughts turned to her older brother Caleph, whom she had not heard from for some years. Caleph had remained true to his gypsy blood and led a nomadic life.

This evening she was quiet, the memories of the very different life she had led amongst the gypsies throughout her childhood constantly in her thoughts. It had been a hard life but she did not regret it. It had shaped her into the woman she had become today. The ties of blood were strong; she did not want to lose contact with Caleph, though she knew that he was uncomfortable sharing any part of her world. To visit him and take up even for a day that old life would also be a betrayal of her husband's faith in her.

When they retired for the night and she blew out the candle and stared up at the carved wooden top of their tester bed, those memories were still with her. Adam turned on his side and drew her into his arms.

'You have not been yourself this evening. I was wrong to take out my ill mood on you. You deserve it less than anyone.'

'I understand your anger and your pain. But I cannot forget my gypsy blood.'

'Is that what has upset you, my love? I should never have spoken such harsh words to you. Especially as I did not mean them.'

'But they were true in many ways. You mourn St John and your father. With Ma's death and Bridie moving away I have lost the threads that bound me to my childhood and my heritage. I worry about Caleph and the dangers he faces. Our race too often is accused of any villainy that has happened in a district and our men are arrested. Many have been hanged for crimes they did not commit.'

'If you need to find Caleph and assure yourself that he is alive and well, I will not stop you. But it will be dangerous, and so Eli Rudge will accompany you. Few men could match him in strength. He will protect you. But I would rather you did not go. Such a journey will only bring you pain.'

She wiped her hand across her eyes. 'I put that life behind me when we married. But your words mean a great deal. I was foolish to take offence when you were upset.'

He held her tight and kissed her with passion. 'Confound my hot blood and temper. You know I would never hurt you by word or deed. I love you, Senara. My life would have no meaning without you at my side. Am I forgiven?'

She ran her hand over his jaw, feeling the slight rough-ness of his night-time stubble. Her heart overflowed with love for this man who had faced censure to marry her and had given her a life she had never dreamed could be possible. She answered his passion with ardour, surrendering to his will and the all-consuming joy only he could give her. Replete and exhausted, she drifted into a dream-like euphoria in his arms.

Images swirled through her mind of the love and laughter that had filled their lives, deepening her sense of contentment. As sleep claimed her in its deeper embrace, the images changed. Her breathing became shallow and sweat broke out on her skin, followed by the sudden chill of gooseflesh raising the hair on her arms and the back of her neck. Terror rippled through her, her heart racing in panic, and she jolted awake, stifling a cry of alarm.

Beside her Adam stirred but did not wake. The dream continued to haunt her as she gazed fearfully at her husband's sleeping form. Soon destiny would separate them. The premonition was too strong to deny. And when it did, Adam would be drawn into the greatest danger he had ever faced.

Chapter Eighteen

Tristan had no reason to complain at how his life was progressing. He seemed to have acquired the Midas touch, and everything he involved himself in turned to gold, or at the very least to his advantage. The service he had performed for Lord Brienne had proved greatly to his own benefit. By covering up the death of Walcott and making it look like a robbery, he had earned the nobleman's gratitude and trust. Shrewdly, so as not to appear too eager, he had waited a month before taking up the baronet's invitation to visit his estate in Wiltshire. He had arrived during a week when his lordship was entertaining a houseful of guests.

Tristan had planned his entrance with style, driving his yellow phaeton. The house was not as grand as he had anticipated. It was a plain square three-storey construction in red brick with the date 1670 carved into masonry stone above a porticoed door. A dozen large casement windows faced the courtyard, reflecting the overcast sky. To one side of the house was a red-brick coach house and stables. The front two lawns were set out with the low box hedges of an old-fashioned knot garden.

A footman in worn red livery and a curled powdered

wig showed him into a small anteroom. There he was kept waiting half an hour before Brienne came to greet him. With a practised eye for pricing valuables, Tristan had plenty of time to examine the room, which smelt strongly of beeswax and the dried lavender and rose petals in a large Delft bowl on a table by the window. It could not completely disguise the aroma of damp, and his sharp eyes had detected a large mildewed area in the plasterwork not quite hidden by a window hanging. A tapestry of a hunting scene, the riders in long periwigs, covered one wall. The colours were faded with age and there were several holes scattered across it. A portrait of five family members in Tudor ruffs and padded breeches, and one of a dour aged man in a Puritan collar and high domed hat adorned another wall. The chairs were upholstered in red velvet, the seats and backs showing signs of considerable wear. A gilded and enamelled French clock on the marble fireplace ticked away the minutes.

'Your pardon for my tardiness,' Brienne said with a wary coolness. He was dressed in black satin breeches and a black and gold embroidered jacket that would not have been out of place at the King's court. 'This is an unexpected pleasure, Mr Loveday.'

'You said to call upon you if I was in the area.' Tristan smiled. 'But it appears I have arrived at an inopportune moment. You have guests. I did not mean to intrude. I have business in Salisbury and can return another time when it is convenient. I but wished to ascertain that Lady Alys had sustained no ill effects from her ordeal upon the *Good Fortune*.' He winced inwardly at the lack of subtlety to his reminder.

'Lady Alys is in good health.' Brienne remained stiff and on his guard.

Tristan bowed and kept his tone indifferent. 'Then no more need be said on the subject. Good day to you, Lord Brienne. I shall be on my way.'

'That would not be acceptable at all, Mr Loveday. This is but an informal house party for the week. I would be remiss in my duties as a host if you did not stay. It will be pleasant for Lady Alys to have company. My friends are somewhat old and staid in their ways. We dine in an hour. Time for you to freshen up and change. My niece has consented to play the pianoforte and sing for us this evening.'

'If you are certain I do not intrude.' Tristan kept his voice non-committal, unwilling to appear too eager to accept the invitation.

'Not at all, Mr Loveday. You are most welcome.'

Tristan sensed, however, that he was not as welcome as the courteous words intimated, and throughout the meal he set out to entertain the other guests. Most of them were middle-aged French émigrés and their wives, and at least one other English gentleman who was known for his support of the French Royalist cause. There was one younger nobleman, Viscount Atherton, who was in his twenties, seated next to Lady Alys, and the couple were locked in close conversation. The guests frequently lapsed into French, which fortunately Tristan had no trouble in following. In the same language he regaled the gathering with tales of his travels and dropped frequent references to his years living in France and to his French wife.

There were more men at the dining table than women, and unfortunately Lady Alys was seated some distance from himself. Several times he caught her gaze upon him, and she laughed at his anecdotes. Always a comment from Atherstone ensured that her attention was drawn back upon himself. The viscount had blond angelic looks and an engaging manner, and from his adoring puppy-dog expression was much enamoured of their hostess. Since their passage on his ship, Tristan had learned that Lady Alys was not as young as he had first surmised. Although her flawless complexion could easily pass for twenty, she was in fact approaching thirty. She was also a widow of three years. She had been married to Lord Brienne's nephew, who had been killed during street riots in Paris. Had he been fighting for the Royalist cause or supporting Napoleon? Nothing of any certainty had been revealed. But given Lord Brienne's political allegiance, his nephew was likely to have been involved in some Royalist plot.

After the ladies withdrew, the men enjoyed their port and Tristan found himself questioned by his companions about his politics and his opinion of the present regime in France.

'There is still much unrest,' he observed. 'I have visited Paris, Normandy, the Loire valley and Bordeaux in recent months. Trade is prospering during this period of peace, but the peasants are as impoverished and discontent as ever they were. Food remains scarce, for the land is poorly managed on many of the estates. The villages have a mournful air of neglect.'

'When the country is run by upstarts, what else can you expect?' scoffed a portly Frenchman by the name of Duval. He had the bulbous nose and broken thread veins across his cheeks of a heavy drinker. 'My country is in the hands of the *canaille*. It will be torn apart. Desecrated.'

'It is not the country it once was,' Tristan commiserated.

'Indeed it is not,' Duval retorted, and several other heads nodded agreement.

Earlier, before the company had gone in to dine,

Tristan was aware that conversations had stopped when he drew near, or became guarded if politics were under discussion. He suspected that many of the émigrés here were actively involved in plotting a Royalist revival in their homeland. That he found interesting.

The first strains from the pianoforte reminded them that the ladies were waiting for them to join them, and the men finished their port and sauntered to the music room. Lady Alys was an accomplished pianist. She was more beautiful than Tristan remembered, dressed in a high-waisted blue silk gown with diamonds sparkling at her neck and wrists. He quashed his irritation that an ageing beau, the Comte de Veronne, fawned over her; the lecher was almost drooling on the ivory keys as he turned the pages of her music. Viscount Atherstone was scowling, having been ousted from Lady Alys's side by Veronne.

When she finished playing, the applause was rapturous and admirers immediately surrounded her. Atherstone was predatory in his possessiveness of his former companion. Tristan stood back, content to observe the other guests. He had long ago concluded that to be noticed by a woman with many men clamouring for her attention, one never ran with the pack. When they all adjourned to the dining room, which was now laid out with a cold buffet, he again remained aloof. Entering last, he took a glass of wine from a footman and stood to one side to observe the gathering. Having charmed the guests as they dined, he deftly parried any questions that probed too deeply into his past. He had learned many years ago the art of evasion whilst maintaining an air of mystery. It was a habit he had developed to assess and learn about others when their minds were engaged elsewhere.

It was not long before Lady Alys, who was politely

circling the room as hostess, approached. He bowed and favoured her with his most disarming smile.

'Does our present company displease you, sir?'

'On the contrary, Lady Alys, there is nothing more boorish than a stranger foisting himself forward to claim all the attention. Many of your guests appear to be long-established friends.'

'They have many interests in common.'

'Mostly an interest in politics, if you had not noticed,' he said with deliberate casualness. 'It is rare a man does not share his opinion on the government of the day. These are times of much plotting and intrigue. King George's state of mind is a cause of concern to many. Though your uncle's friends seem to express more interest in what is happening in France.'

'There is always rumour and speculation. Are we not all concerned that war will again break out between France and England?' She smiled sweetly; her words were commonplace enough, or did they cleverly conceal her allegiance to her guardian and his interests.

Tristan studied her intently, and she held his appraising stare with equal candour. Her eyes were bright and intelligent. There was no quickening to her breathing. Clearly there was more to this woman than beauty and poise. She was a practised dissembler, her expression neither guarded nor showing any sign that she was either testing him or fobbing him off with platitudes.

'These are uncertain times,' he agreed.

'I hope you enjoy our stay with us, Mr Loveday.' She moved on to other guests, but as she continued to circle the room her gaze kept returning to him. It was not long before Atherstone had drawn her aside once more and they were laughing together in a corner.

When Tristan's host joined him, they were far enough

away from anyone so as not to be overheard. Brienne's manner was solemn as he said, 'I am greatly in your debt from our last meeting.'

Tristan looked surprised. 'The matter is forgotten. The reputation of my ship and myself depends upon it. I am your servant at all times, my lord. I believe we have many shared interests.'

The older man's eyes narrowed. 'How is that?'

'I have many connections in France. The tide of politics there is ever changing.'

'You are an importer of French furniture, are you not? Does it not trouble you that many of those pieces have been stolen from their original owners?'

'I have been charged to bring more than furniture back for past owners who still do not believe it is safe for them to return to their estates. They have been delighted with the funds that I have been able to return to them.'

He did not need to spell out that he had been entrusted with the details of where hastily buried valuables had been hidden. It had been a profitable enterprise both from the commission percentage he had charged and in some cases from the valuables he had kept back for himself.

'I had heard your name mentioned in this connection amongst my associates.' Brienne's stare hardened. 'Although not everyone had all their heirlooms returned.'

'Sometimes the cache had already been looted. Or lost if the chateau was destroyed by fire. Only once did I return completely empty handed. But that is the cost of rebellion. Many priceless possessions are lost. It always saddens me when I fail. Many of the émigrés have lost loved ones during the Terror and had their wealth stripped from them. It is unjust.'

'Yet it has become profitable for you. And it is not without its dangers.'

It was a loaded question, almost as though Brienne was testing him. 'Many who know our family would say that the buccaneering spirit is in our blood.' He parried the questions with an ironic laugh.

His lordship's expression remained serious. 'As you may have noticed, some of my guests fled France with only what they could carry.'

'If any require my services, I would be happy to oblige.'

Across the room he saw Atherstone and Veronne competing for Lady Alys's attention. Tristan bowed to Brienne and decided to retire.

As he walked silently through the corridors with their closed doors, he was drawn to try their handles. Most of them were locked, unless they were a chamber in use by a guest. He noted that apart from the main reception rooms, only about half the house appeared to be in use, and that the money was not available for urgent repairs.

The next morning he arose early and was one of the first to break his fast. In the harsher light of day, his practised eyes noted many scuffs and chips to the wooden furniture and cracks as wide as a man's index finger appearing along several of the walls and cornices. Patches of plasterwork had fallen off walls and others showed the staining of damp, and no amount of fresh or dried flowers could disguise its musty smell.

It was too fine a day to be cooped up indoors, and he went for a stroll around the grounds. Away from the immediate vicinity of the house, less care had been taken in the maintenance of the lawns, and many were over-grown. He was also surprised to see few servants or labourers working on the estate. Fences were broken in many places and the ditches clogged with rushes provided poor drainage for the land.

He walked the grounds for another hour reviewing all that he knew and had learned about Brienne. Some of it did not make sense. There were too many Frenchmen here talking in veiled terms, which again made him suspect that they were Royalist sympathisers. As to his lordship, he showed a face of wealth and position to the world, but there was also the obvious neglect to the house and grounds. Apart from a small beef herd, Tristan had seen no fields of livestock or crops growing. There was no visible means of income generated by the estate. He had met many villains in all walks of life, from the lowest footpad to wealthy businessmen and noblemen little better than shysters in their double-dealing and treachery. Brienne was not who he gave the impression to be. Tristan would keep a close eye on him and his companions during his stay here. He could learn much that was to his advantage.

Chapter Nineteen

Japhet Loveday was battling with an inner demon that threatened all he held dear. He had awoken before dawn from a recurring nightmare that had haunted him in recent weeks. He was bathed in a cold sweat and his pulse was racing. The acrid taste of fear filled his mouth. Fear born of the memory the dream evoked.

He wiped a callused palm over his face and swung his feet to the floor of the bedchamber, moving stealthily and in silence so as to not awaken his wife. He wrapped a velvet dressing robe around his naked figure and strode through the house, avoiding any creaking floorboards that would alert his family or servants. He needed to be alone, to escape from the confines of enclosed spaces and breathe deeply of clean fresh air.

The fear was irrational. The vivid images of the dream were long in the past and unable to harm him. Images he had turned from defeat into victory and that he had thought long ago buried and forgotten. Images of the only time in his past that had ever seeped through his fearless and confident nature. Yet the dream clung more tenaciously than leeches. His heart continued to pound in a frantic rhythm, his mind cloyed with the heaviness of oppression. His dream had relived his days on the transport ship to Sydney Cove. The taint of despair and terror clung to him, his nostrils scenting the rank odours of sweat, defecation, death and decay. He heard voices shrill with threats, screams of torture and beatings, cries of hunger, pitiful weeping from men whose spirit had already broken. The stench was as vivid now as it had been all those years ago: fever, blood, vomit, fear and despair.

There was suppressed violence in his movements as he swung open the door and stepped outside. He ignored the dew-soaked earth beneath his bare feet and marched to the railing of the nearest paddock. The field was empty, the horses shut in their stables. A knee-high mist rose from the grass, and on the far side several red deer does and their young grazed. The females lifted their heads to sniff the air, but Japhet was downwind from them. He remained still, watching them, and they sensed no danger. The breeze carried only a trace of the sea from the coast five miles away. It rustled through new leaves on the trees like a soft whisper, instead of the heavy slap of canvas and the creak of rigging that echoed in his mind. He breathed deeply of the scent of damp earth and dew on meadow grass, the tension gradually relaxing through his figure.

The crown of the sun peeking over the horizon revealed the undulating hills behind the stud farm, and the limewashed walls of the double row of a dozen stables were tinged with an ochre glow. The beauty that was Cornwall could not be more different from the bleak, fetid hold of the transport ship in his dream. A blackbird was already trilling in the hedgerow, and high on a tree branch a robin added his song. Japhet willed the familiar sights and sounds to calm his emotions.

The fear within the dream was irrational. He had not felt such terror at any time during his transportation.

Mostly he had felt anger at the careless lack of judgement that had led up to his arrest and trial for highway robbery. He had been innocent of the crime for which he had been convicted, but it had been an ironic judgement, for some months earlier, when in a pit of desperation to pay his gambling debts, he had robbed another coach. Justice would not be mocked. The man he had held up, Sir Pettigrew Osgood, had become his enemy – not because of a robbery, but over a mistress they had shared. The actress Celestine Yorke had spurned Osgood and fallen in love with Japhet. Celestine had also been in Osgood's coach when he had robbed it. He had thought the mask over his lower face and his disguised voice would hide his identity. Believing that he had lost Gwen, Japhet's reckless nature had sought danger to smother his pain. Celestine was as beautiful as she was promiscuous, and she never took a lover unless they paid highly for her favours with expensive jewels. He wanted to win her but his pride demanded that it would be without pandering to her greed. And he had succeeded. But did they not say that pride came before a fall? Or was it fate that would not be mocked?

Japhet shook his head to clear the firmament of those memories. Pride had been his downfall. His affections were elsewhere. He loved Gwendolyn but believed at the time that her family would never allow her to marry a notorious rake who made his money by selling horses and gambling. He had reckoned without Gwendolyn's determination to marry for love or not at all. And for that he would be eternally grateful and would devote his life to ensuring her happiness. Or so he had believed.

But old habits were not so easily vanquished. Throughout his two score years he had lived by his wits and by a code of honour ruled by pistols or the sword.

When nine years ago Gwendolyn had followed him to London and he had realised the truth of his love for her, he had ended his relationship with the actress. That was when Celestine had declared that she recognised him as the highwayman who had robbed Osgood's coach and for a time, to ensure her power over him, had attempted blackmail. Japhet had charmed her into acquiescence, laughing aside her threats to denounce him by denying that he was a highwayman. When finally he ended their relationship, her vanity could not abide the rejection of her love. She had returned to Osgood and denounced Japhet to her lover. Osgood did not care if her statement was true or false; it was a weapon to use against his enemy. When Lord Sefton's coach was robbed, he convinced the peer that Japhet was the thief and also made charges against him. Japhet was arrested within hours of marrying Gwendolyn and taken to Newgate.

With two peers giving evidence against him, Japhet was found guilty and condemned to transportation for a period of fourteen years. His wife had remained loyal to him and throughout the year of his incarceration following his trial had worked to obtain a pardon from the King. Their son Japhet Edward had been born during his imprisonment. On the night before the royal pardon had been granted, Japhet had been drugged inside Newgate and taken unconscious aboard a transport ship. It had sailed before the pardon could secure his release. Reviled by her family for not abandoning a man who had brought dishonour to their name, Gwendolyn had within a couple of months sailed on another ship bound for the new penal colony in Australia, determined that Japhet would not suffer the rigours of convict life. The voyage took nine months.

There was only one man who had hated him enough

to bribe the guards to drug and abduct him – Sir Pettigrew Osgood. Because of the cowardly knave, Japhet had spent nearly two years in hell in Newgate, the prison ship and those first months in New South Wales. Against the odds he had survived and triumphed over every adversity, his wits gaining him privileges during the voyage and his courage earning the respect of hardened criminals. Prison and deprivation could not break his spirit, and when Gwen arrived in Parramatta with his pardon, he had seen the opportunities in the new land for a free man to make his fortune. But always buried deep within him was a resolve to bring Osgood to account for his treachery.

On their return to England, Gwendolyn had begged him not to seek out Osgood. By his survival and by returning a wealthy man in his own right, he had proved he was a better man than ever Osgood could hope to be. He had a dream to build one of the finest stud farms in England. Every accolade Japhet received for his prize-winning horses would be a further snub to Osgood, proving to his adversary how pathetic had been his attempt to destroy him.

But the dream, and the memories and anger it evoked, had shown Japhet that he could never find peace whilst his enemy escaped justice. He did not want to break his word to Gwendolyn, but he knew that one day it would be inevitable.

He cursed the restlessness that had begun to plague him since his return to his homeland. A craving for new experiences and adventure had always driven him. Despite the hardships of the last six years, no two weeks had been the same, except for the return voyage from Sydney Cove. Even the nine-month voyage to the penal colony had been a time when survival was dependent on keeping one's wits one step ahead of those of his gaolers and hardened criminals. In his early twenties Japhet had lived on the edge of the criminal fraternity in London, and the information he had gained from his time in Newgate had given him a high standing amongst the criminals; his prowess at street fighting had also earned their respect. He had managed to win a greater freedom on board ship because of his skills with livestock, especially the horses that had sickened. Husbandry knowledge had served him well on his arrival, and he had won the trust of the new governor of the settlement.

Once his pardon arrived, they were not the only skills that had stood him in good stead. There was also the carpentry he had learned as a youth in the Loveday shipyard, and the farming expertise by helping on his sister's farm with both crops and animals. All these had enabled him to succeed as a farmer where other settlers failed. They had also enabled him to run a sawmill supplying wood for buildings for the expanding colony, and later to invest in the building of shops in the developing settlements away from the main port. When Adam and a group of investors had sent ships filled with provisions to the colony, Japhet had been appointed their agent to avoid the investors being cheated of their profits, and he had built a store to house the goods. His success had earned him enemies amongst the officers who had run a monopoly on all goods arriving in the port, whilst his ability with sword, pistol, rifle or knife had made the military wary of picking fights with him.

The challenges he had faced had been diverse and had often tested the limits of his endurance, but he had enjoyed every moment of it. Since his return, life had fallen into a pattern. The stud farm was slowly building a reputation, helped by the foals that had been born from the first mares he had selected before his arrest. He had earned a fortune from his enterprises abroad and could afford any luxury he and his family desired. The purchase of the Arab stallion Emir Hassan had assured the future of the stud, and within a few months the first of the foals he had sired would be born. There was still the matter of overcoming some of the prejudices of old neighbours who had not approved of his lifestyle before his marriage and still regarded him as little better than a criminal despite his pardon. But they presented no threat to his security or safety, and therein lay the source of his restlessness.

He had always thrived on adventure and overcoming challenges and adversity. It was why he had lived by gambling for so many years. But gaming was not the answer. He needed to find a new challenge, for despite the devotion he had for his wife and family, and his desire to breed the best racehorses, it was not enough to replace the intoxicating excitement of danger and adventure.

He tightened his jaw and drew a harsh breath. The dream that had disturbed his sleep continued to darken his resolve. He wanted to keep his vow to Gwen not to pursue Osgood unless the baronet crossed his path. But his blood demanded action. There must be some way he could channel his energy and interest, some new challenge to uplift him that would divert his thoughts more fully from Osgood.

Japhet was not the only Loveday who felt constrained by responsibilities and the need to curb a desire to bring an enemy to justice. Adam's anger towards Tristan ran just below the surface and would rise up in an unguarded moment when his mind was not engaged in estate or yard activities. It added to an underlying frustration that had been growing in the months since his twin's death. He had spent many hours in Japhet's company enjoying his descriptions of his travels and adventures. It made him realise that it had been some years since he himself had travelled or captained his own ship on a long voyage. Like Japhet he loved his family and wife and was proud of all he had achieved by expanding the shipyard and designing new ships. He too had thrived on the love of adventure and the thrill of overcoming danger. Apart from his years in the navy, he had commanded his brigantine *Pegasus* and rescued French émigrés during the height of the Terror in their country. At that time he had also worked as an English agent in France and rescued another of his kind who had been taken prisoner, Sir Gregory Kilmarthen, who was known to his friends as Long Tom. They had been exciting days, and there were times when Adam's adventuring spirit missed the danger and thrill of action overcoming difficult odds. His friend had been much on his mind of late, as it had been a great many months since he had heard from Long Tom.

Something was going on at Brienne's home that the guests wanted Tristan excluded from. This was the second time he had suddenly found that the other men were nowhere to be seen. Tristan had been reading the *Gentleman's Magazine* in the main salon after breakfast with three other companions when one by one they drifted away. He had thought nothing of it at the time and continued reading. Gradually the house had fallen quiet apart from the chatter of female voices in the next room. Snatches of their conversation on children and fashions drifted to him. Unused to spending time inactive, Tristan rose to seek out companions for more stimulating conversation than was offered by the women.

He strode out to the terrace to survey the gardens, but found them deserted of male guests. A leisurely stroll through the billiard and smoking rooms met with an equal lack of success.

His suspicions were aroused that the men, who had openly expressed their Royalist sympathies regarding France, might have agreed to meet for the purpose of conspiring to aid the Royalist cause. His arrival must have caused them some alarm and they had had to resort to subterfuge. He would give much to have overheard their plans. He wandered apparently aimlessly through the deserted rooms for several minutes before he heard his name called by Lady Alys. As he emerged from an anteroom, she was hurrying down the passageway. Her relief at discovering him was obvious.

'Mr Loveday, I have woefully neglected you during your stay. Would you care to see my aviary? I have a great fondness for songbirds.'

'That would be an honour, Lady Alys. Are the other men there with your uncle?' He threw out the question wondering how she would answer.

'Oh, I should not think so,' she said with apparent surprise. 'I believe two have taken the carriage into town with their wives. Some have possibly gone to the wine cellars; I heard my uncle discussing some vintage wine earlier. Would you prefer to join them instead?'

She was either an accomplished actress or a consummate liar, so confidently had she made the excuses. Tristan had enough secrets in his past and business dealings he would not want discovered to see this as no failing. In fact it made him admire her more. 'I can think of nothing more pleasurable than to accompany you, dear lady.'

She blushed. Throughout his visit she had played the perfect hostess and was always attentive to the needs of her uncle's guests. She was the youngest woman present by several years, yet she mixed easily with the other women. The only person she showed any coolness towards was Veronne. Tristan did not blame her for that, for he did not trust him. There was something sly about his manner.

'You have not ignored me, Lady Alys, you have been busy with your guests,' he said gallantly. 'Viscount Atherstone occupies a great deal of your time.'

'He is a valued friend. I have known him since childhood.'

'I would say he would prefer to be much more than a friend, Lady Alys.'

She laughed. 'What gave you that impression?'

'The way he looks at you with such adoration.'

'You are mistaken, Mr Loveday. Julian Atherstone is just a friend.' She giggled. 'Can you imagine how dreadful it would be for me to be Lady Alys Atherstone? It is such a tongue-twister.' Her expression sobered. 'I am delighted you have called upon us. But I have not forgotten how much I owe you for your kindness and bravery on board ship.' Her blush deepened.

'Any gentleman would have done as much.'

'You are too modest, sir.' She glanced sideways up at him as they walked to the aviary. There was no mistaking the admiration in her eyes. Tristan was flattered and he felt his heartbeat quicken. Lady Alys was beautiful, vivacious and loyal, from an old and revered family – in fact all that he wanted in a wife. But would he ever be able to break through the class barrier and win not only her heart but also her hand? That could be a problem. From the dilapidation and neglect of the property and grounds, it was likely Brienne would insist on a suitor for his ward of immense wealth as well as position. Tristan had the wealth, but by many of Brienne's station he would be regarded as a parvenu – an upstart. The mystery surrounding his early life might appeal to the romantically inclined, but to the marriage market it made his background doubly suspicious.

The aviary had been built on to what once had been the falconry mews. A male servant in his twenties was sweeping the floor with a besom. He shuffled awkwardly at the appearance of his mistress. The inane grin on his pumpkin-round face was as witless as that of the village idiot. His hair was thick, long and matted, his shirt sleeves frayed and patched, but the cotton had been recently pressed. Someone clearly looked after him.

'Good morning, Brody. How are the birds today?' Lady Alys enquired.

'They be well, your ladyship.' His voice whistled through several missing teeth. 'Two more have laid eggs. Old Sergeant here,' he indicated the blue and yellow macaw, 'he's been fighting again with Harlequin.'

Lady Alys went over to a red parrot and held up her arm for him to fly to her. A couple of long feathers were missing from his wings, and when he landed and Lady Alys scratched his head, there was a raw bald patch on the back of his neck.

'You have cleaned the wound well, Brody.' Lady Alys smiled at the keeper, who continued to grin widely. Her attention again given to the bird, she crooned softly, 'You have been in the wars, old boy. Put Sergeant's chain back on, Brody. He's too bad tempered lately to fly loose.'

She took the bird back to its perch and gave it a grape she took from a velvet reticule she was carrying. She gave another to each of the four other parrots, and when Sergeant made a stab at her finger, she waved it admonishingly at him. 'You are a grouchy old man, Sergeant. Shame on you.'

The bird ran along its perch swaying its head from side to side and squawking, 'Shame on you. Give us a kiss. Kiss. Kiss.'

She blew one to him and laughed.

Tristan admired her naturalness with the birds. He looked around the old barn. Brody continued with his sweeping in slow, rhythmic movements. The building had a high-beamed roof, and extra windows had been added. Along one wall was a collection of large, exotic birdcages made of thin slivers of cane. Four perches were placed along another wall, each holding a brightly coloured macaw. One cage housed the smaller English songbirds: robins, linnets, nightingales and goldfinches. Another held more exotic birds – bright yellow canaries and some species he did not recognise. Many of them had bred and raised young, and there must have been more than a hundred birds flying round the cages and singing.

'You have an impressive collection, Lady Alys. It must be quite unusual, is it not? I have seen single birds in cages and the occasional popinjay as pets, but never so many all together.'

'They fascinate me. Some are quite tame and will come upon your hand. The birds and my two horses are my oldest friends. I spent many years alone here with just a governess for company when Papa was at court. Mama died when I was four.'

'This is your family home, not your husband's?' He had not expected that.

'Family millstone more like.' She shrugged. 'My father and grandfather served at court for little reward. The land brings in income enough but the house has suffered a century of neglect.'

'How long has Brienne been your guardian? I thought you had married his nephew.'

'I did, and Brienne is not my guardian. Marcus and I married when we were sixteen. My father was dying and he wanted to see me settled. Brienne was Marcus's guardian and all the family we had after Papa died.'

'You seem devoted to him.'

Her attention was on the birds flying in their cages, and it was some moments before she asked, 'What of your parents, Mr Loveday? You have an estate in Cornwall?'

'My parents died when I was a child. And Trevowan has been the home of the Loveday family for five generations.' He skirted over the truth whilst not exactly telling a lie.

'And are you, like me, without other kin?'

He gave an ironic laugh. 'I have many cousins, though I do not see that as a blessing. They are an unruly and quarrelsome brood. But an elderly aunt lives at Trevowan. She never married and lives for her horses. She can be quite a martinet at times.'

'Your family sound formidable.' She gave a mock shiver.

'Many see us as unconventional. One is a parson, another a horse-breeder, one a shipbuilder. He built *Good Fortune*. Another is a playwright who once owned one of London's most prestigious banks and is now building his own theatre. Another is married to the guardian of the young Lord Eastley.'

'They sound fascinating.' Her eyes widened with interest. 'Your family reunions must be filled with tales of adventure.'

'Our family reunions are very different from most.' His sarcasm was covered by a disarming smile.

Lady Alys moved to another of the cages and opened

a small door. She held her hand inside and immediately it was covered with half a dozen brightly coloured finches.

'They are very tame,' Tristan observed.

'Some days I spend hours in here.' She walked towards the door. 'They are nervous of strangers. I do not usually bring guests to visit them.'

Tristan put his hand over his heart and bowed to her in acknowledgement. 'I am deeply honoured, Lady Alys. I have never seen the like of this. Thank you for sharing something so special with me.'

She dipped her head and her cheeks again were a becoming shade of pink. Tristan opened the aviary door, and as she passed through he reached for her hand and laughingly pulled her round to face him. A hasty survey of their surroundings showed that they were unobserved. He raised her hand to his lips, feeling the pulse quickening beneath his fingers. He breathed softly against her warm flesh. 'You are the most captivating of women. If I were a dozen years younger . . .' He let the promise hang in the air between them.

'What has age to do with anything, Mr Loveday?' Her answer was low and breathless. 'You place too much importance on it, sir. I have no interest in bragging young bucks with no thought but the next conquest or caper. Maturity and experience count for much more. A woman wants a man who can protect her and be solicitous of her every comfort. A man she can respect and trust.'

'And love?' he prompted.

'Most assuredly love.'

He drew her closer, drinking in the perfume of her hair and skin. Their lips were a finger's breadth apart, hers parting in anticipation as she waited for his kiss.

The moment was shattered by Veronne's voice closing in on them. The words were indistinct but Tristan detected menace in the demanding tone. Brienne answered him, but again the words were inaudible.

Lady Alys gasped and the colour drained from her face. 'You must take me away from here or I am lost.' She wrenched her hand from his and fled round the corner of the barn, away from the direction from which Brienne and Veronne were approaching.

As the two men came into sight, Veronne did not trouble to hide his displeasure at encountering Tristan. 'What the devil are you doing here, Loveday?'

'I was taking a stroll around these magnificent grounds. You have not got contraband hidden in these old buildings?' he laughed. 'Rather too common an occurrence in my county. The smugglers do not even trouble to ask for permission.' He raised a questioning brow at Brienne, who looked equally disgruntled but with an effort regained his composure and his manners.

'They do say Cornwall is a wild place not fit for decent folk,' Veronne sneered.

Brienne cleared his throat. 'The best walks are on the far side of the house. There is not much here of interest. Just a few barns.'

'They are what fascinate me.' Tristan played for time to ensure Lady Alys had every chance to make good her escape. 'Take this one, for instance.' He nodded to the building behind him. 'It is possibly three or four centuries old. It tells much more about the origins of the estate than the main house, which has often been rebuilt. I would say this was from the late fourteen hundreds. Is that right, your lordship?'

'Quite possibly.' Brienne remained ill at ease.

'Are old buildings of interest to you, Comte?' Tristan

turned his attention upon the older Frenchman.

Veronne spluttered. 'Indeed not. Brienne and I were discussing business. We walked this way to avoid being interrupted by other guests.'

Tristan bowed, hiding his anger at Veronne's rudeness. 'I will not intrude further upon you. Your servant, my lords.'

As he strolled away, he whistled jauntily but his thoughts were far from pleasant. Lady Alys had bolted like a frightened doe. What had she feared? Was that why she had played the coquette and flattered him, to escape from her circumstances here? Was it Brienne she feared, although she had shown no previous signs of distress in his company? Or was it something or someone else? Tristan did not flatter himself that she was truly interested in a man so much older than her. Nevertheless he was intrigued. He did not like mysteries.

Chapter Twenty

Adam was in the timber yard of Trevowan Hard, selecting tree trunks to have their bark removed and be shaped into supporting pillars between decks. The scrape and rasp of the four men working in the two sawpits drowned out the noise of a horse approaching.

'Avast, me hearties,' boomed a voice.

Adam whirled round. A grey gelding pawed the ground as it came to a halt. The sun was in his eyes, shadowing the rider's form. But there was no mistaking the short, stocky rider, who would come no higher than Adam's chest when he dismounted.

'Long Tom, where the devil did you spring from? I was thinking about you just the other day.' In his surprise, Adam reverted to the name Sir Gregory Kilmarthen had used when they had first met. The name only his closest friends could presume to address him by.

'Gawd love us, but I be glad to hear you've not forgotten yer old comrade in arms, Cap'n Loveday.' The baronet continued to play a role as he leapt to the ground with the agility that always amazed Adam for one so short and thickset. One of Long Tom's disguises when he had worked as a British spy had been as a street entertainer, and he was an accomplished acrobat. Not that you would mistake him for anyone so humble now. Sir Gregory Kilmarthen was dressed in the height of fashion. His cinnamon hair, although now woven with grey, had receded to the crown of his head, his broad face was speckled with light freckles and his lips turned up at the corners as though waiting to break into a wide smile. A monocle was released from one crinkled eye and he guffawed, the rough accent replaced by a voice that rang with the authority of a long line of knights whose family had served several dynasties of royalty.

'I am not one to let the grass grow under my feet,' he announced with the swirl of a hand and an elaborate bow. 'I am just back from France.'

'Duty or pleasure?' Adam raised a dark brow, leaving much unsaid. He suspected that his friend had been on government business.

'Both. Paris is at its gayest for many years. One would hardly know there had been a revolution only a decade ago.'

Adam signalled to a passing apprentice to take Kilmarthen's mount to the yard's stables and walked with his friend towards his office, saying, 'It is good that those terrible days of suffering are behind the people. No one seemed to be safe from Madame Guillotine. Yet if one can believe the news-sheets, the French have replaced a monarch with a man who would rule all Europe. How many thousands of its citizens who demanded liberty and equality have been slaughtered in the war machine created by Bonaparte?'

'I did observe that there is more frenzy to their gaiety, which covers a smouldering discontent,' said Sir Gregory as they entered the single-storey cottage that served as an office.

'I doubt the Royalist faction are content; they still

regard Bonaparte as an upstart and a usurper.'

'As ever, *mon capitaine*, you have a keen wit to discern current politics.' Long Tom gave a mock salute. 'Indeed, they continue to plot behind closed doors, and many are active in England.'

Adam crossed the room and opened a wall cupboard to take out a brandy decanter and two glasses. As he did so, Long Tom wandered around the room inspecting the paintings on the walls of the most recent ships that had been built in the yard. They were used as a showpiece for any prospective visiting customer.

'This place has certainly changed from the early days when I first knew you. Then the ships built here were much smaller.'

'We have been fortunate.'

'Because of your skill as a shipbuilder and most of all as a designer. The yard looks busier than I remember,' Long Tom praised.

'I was lucky that my father had faith in my endeavours. He took a risk building *Pegasus*, my first brigantine.'

'Do you miss captaining her, my friend?'

'There is much to occupy me on land, but the sea is in my blood. Yes, there are times when the lure—' He stopped abruptly and shrugged. 'But the shipyard has brought many rewards. I have been fortunate.'

'Not to mention having a lovely wife and four children. Though as a confirmed bachelor I have yet to discover the merits of such an existence. And my family have never been close. I never wanted the responsibilities of an estate and am content to allow my cousin to supervise it. It will be his one day.'

Long Tom supped his brandy and changed the subject. 'This is good. Must be French and no doubt contraband. Surely you miss the excitement of the old days?'

'Sometimes,' Adam conceded with a roguish smile. 'They were certainly never boring.'

Long Tom raised his glass. 'To old adventures.'

Relaxing in the company of his friend, Adam found that the years rolled back. Sir Gregory had been a British spy working in France when they had first met. It was shortly after Adam had been cashiered from the navy and Squire Penwithick, who worked for the First Lord of the Treasury, Pitt the Younger, had sent him on a mission to rescue the captured agent known as Long Tom. The older man's dwarfish height had enabled him to take on countless disguises, the enemy never suspecting that such a diminutive figure could pose any threat. How wrong they had been. Sir Gregory had a sharpness of mind that could outwit Machiavelli himself. After his rescue the two men had become close friends. It was Sir Gregory who had found the evidence to prove St John's innocence when he had been on trial for murder. Later, when Japhet had been found guilty by false evidence laid against him for highway robbery, Kilmarthen's investigations had again proved his innocence. Sir Gregory might have retired from government work, but he had not lost his craving for adventure. The family had been indebted to him when he had escorted Gwendolyn as they conveyed Japhet's pardon halfway around the world.

Momentarily, the baronet's expression sobered as he turned from examining the pictures. 'I heard when I docked in Falmouth that St John was dead. My sincere condolences.'

'Thank you, my friend.' Adam rose above the wave of sadness that assailed him and forced a cheerful reply. 'We have other news for you to rejoice in. Japhet is home. He returned to England last year and is living at Tor Farm.'

'So I had heard. Rumour is that he is a wealthy man,

and there is much speculation as to how a freed convict made such a fortune. The new colony in the southern hemisphere is a place ripe for opportunity. It is a land that suited your cousin's talents. I did wonder whether he would find the country irresistible and might not grace these shores again.'

'Having made his fortune he considered that after all Gwen had sacrificed for him, she deserved a life of greater ease than Australia could provide. He also had unfinished business here.'

'Is he still bent upon calling to account the man who betrayed him?' Long Tom shook his head with misgivings.

'Honour demands it. Although the last we heard, Sir Pettigrew Osgood was no longer in England.'

'I had learned the same.'

Adam sat forward on his seat. 'Do you know where the blackguard has gone to ground?'

'My information is some months old; it will need verification,' Long Tom evaded. 'Is this course wise? Japhet suffered a heavy price for Osgood's treachery, but he turned it to his favour.'

'Osgood destroyed Japhet's reputation. No amount of money can redeem that. Would you allow such a point of honour to go unavenged?' Adam replied.

Long Tom shook his head. 'I shall find out what I can and inform you.'

Adam's blood quickened and he felt his body flush first with heat, then with cold. Japhet would relish the information. Finally the whereabouts of the man who had laid false evidence against him would be discovered. It was the news Adam both exulted in and dreaded. Japhet wanted revenge against his adversary and Adam would not let his cousin pursue him alone. But it was an action that whether he succeeded or failed could destroy all Japhet had worked towards and his dreams for the future.

After her strange outburst Lady Alys seemed to be avoiding Tristan. When he sought her company amongst others she became flustered, and her gaze when it settled upon him was beseeching, as though begging him to forget the incident. It served to intrigue Tristan further, though he was not about to confront her when others could overhear.

He spent the afternoon in the company of several of the Frenchmen who had been absent during the morning, dropping hints into his conversation of his empathy with the troubles that had followed the fall of the *ancien régime* in France. He also dropped reminders of his time in France and his French wife and her family. Gradually their wariness of him lessened as he convinced them of his Royalist sympathies.

When they became more interested in such events, he intimated that his ship, his resources and his income had all been pledged in the past to the Royalist cause, though he frequently worked in disguise and covered his trail so that his true identity was seldom known to his associates. The opportunities here to fill his coffers were too good for him to trouble his conscience at his duplicity.

However, he did not pursue this line of information too deeply, wishing only to sow the seeds of interest and ability. Politics was a dangerous game where lives and fortunes could be destroyed overnight. Having laid the groundwork, it was now up to them to approach him. It never did to appear too eager. He kept the dialogue light and interspersed it with amusing anecdotes. Then, when he sensed that their interest had been heightened, he casually excused himself and joined another group in the billiard room. For the rest of the afternoon he worked the groups of men, always at his most charming and entertaining. He had set his bait and soon the snare would be sprung.

His interest now returned to the Lady Alys. Throughout the day she had been less in Atherstone's company. Once he had seen them arguing and Atherstone had stormed away. Lady Alys had stared after him sadly. The more Tristan observed her, the more he came to the conclusion that the woman was clearly a consummate actress. She was calm and poised in her role of hostess, and nothing in her demeanour showed the distress he had witnessed outside the aviary. She was solicitous of all the needs of her guests, fussing over the women by plumping up cushions behind them or fetching footstools for their greater comfort. She also summoned the servants to bring shawls and cordials to ensure the guests were warm and refreshed. When an al fresco picnic was abandoned in the grounds, the women adjourned to the grand salon, where Lady Alys's showmanship came to the fore as she introduced a game of charades for their amusement. All were lavish in their praise and compliments, the women as avid as the men to seek her company. Tristan contented himself with studying this vivacious woman from a distance. Was he the only one to see the sadness and insecurity behind her ready smile and good humour?

Everyone retired to their rooms to change before they dined; the ladies also to rest for an hour before the entertainment for the evening. Tristan was the first guest down and filled his time exploring the house. He had hoped Lady Alys would be present but was disappointed. His assessing gaze noted that much of the silverware on display was plated; the paintings were by no known masters and of an inferior quality; and the crystal chandeliers were missing many of their droplets or were otherwise damaged. It reinforced his opinion that Brienne was not the man of means he wanted people to believe.

Hearing the voices of guests gathering in the salon, he joined them but again had no chance to talk his hostess alone as she moved from one group to another. When they went in to dine she was at the far end of the table from him, so any conversation with her was impossible. Afterwards the card tables were set up for an evening of faro. The wagers became intense, with Brienne increasing the stakes with every game and often losing. Lady Alys laid modest wagers, winning most hands. Tristan would have found it easy to fleece every guest of their fortune, having watched card sharps throughout his travels and learned their tricks and sleights of hand. That was not his purpose on this occasion, however. He chose to allow others to win and waved aside his losses with aplomb. By the end of the session Brienne had lost heavily, mostly to Veronne, to whom he had written several promissory notes. As the game progressed, it was obvious that several of the other male guests had little liking for Veronne. He would pick on any man's failings or weaknesses and humiliate them with his derision. Yet no one retaliated. It made Tristan wonder whether Veronne had some hold over them.

Tristan continued to watch the Comte, certain that he was cheating. If he was, it was in an accomplished manner that would equal Tristan's own skill. Veronne had all the vices Tristan despised. He was arrogant, ungracious, a bore and a bully. The Frenchman would bear careful surveillance. Neither did Tristan like the way Veronne followed Lady Alys with his lecherous gaze.

When the card game broke up, Tristan wandered outside to smoke a cheroot. The more time he spent in the Comte de Veronne's company, the harder it became for him to control his need to bring the Frenchman down a peg. He strolled across the stone terrace and down a dozen steps into the gardens and along the side of the house. The windows were open, as the evening remained mild. There were no clouds and enough moonlight to light his way. His cheroot finished, he was about to return indoors when he heard Veronne talking in one of the anterooms. What alerted him was the Frenchman's tone. Tristan moved closer to the window to investigate. A single candle burned within the room, throwing the tall shadows of two men high up on the walls.

'I shall be leaving before noon tomorrow,' Veronne tersely informed his companion. 'I expect full payment of your debt before I leave.'

'I do not keep that amount of money in the house.' It was Brienne who replied, and there was an uneasy note to his lordship's voice.

'Then I shall take a promissory note drawn on your bank.' The command was rapped out with intended threat.

There was a long silence before Brienne answered. 'I would appreciate you giving me more time to settle the debt.'

'I am not a moneylender.' Veronne barked out his disdain. 'A gentleman settles his gaming obligations without delay.'

'I need more time. A week or two at the most.' Brienne did not plead, and it was a reasonable enough request.

Again there was a weighty silence. Then Veronne scoffed, 'I will give you another chance. Double or nothing on the turn of a card.'

'That is a fool's game,' Brienne announced coolly, all politeness stripped from his tone.

'Then there must be another way to settle a debt of honour. The Lady Alys is a tempting prize.'

The menace evident between his host and Veronne disturbed Tristan. Something sinister was building here.

'I will accept her hand in marriage as payment of the debt,' Veronne announced on a note of triumph.

Brienne did not immediately answer. His lordship was no doubt fighting to control his anger. 'My niece will not agree to such a match.'

'It is for you to persuade her that it is in her best interests and also your own.' The threat now smacked of blackmail.

Brienne had shown by killing Walcott that he could be ruthless. However, Veronne's next words stunned Tristan.

'Do you wish me to inform your new friends and your sweet niece of the truth about her husband's death?'

There was a creak as the door to the room opened and Lady Alys was silhouetted in the doorway. 'Your pardon, I did not realise you were with the Comte, my lord. It is Lady Myrtle. She tripped on the stair and has hurt her ankle. It is very swollen. It looks like a sprain but I think Dr Williams should be summoned to ensure it is not broken.'

'I shall come at once.' Brienne was eager to attend to this new emergency. As he marched out of the room, following his niece, he announced sharply to the Frenchman, 'We will discuss this later.'

Tristan felt his blood boil at the thought of Veronne

possessing the beautiful Alys. The arrogance of his threat roused a need in him to protect her. Not only that, but he would gain great satisfaction from bringing the Frenchman to heel.

He made his way back to the faro tables and chatted amiably to his companions as they waited for other players to return. There remained an empty seat at his table. As yet Veronne had not returned to the gambling. Atherstone was also absent, no doubt hanging around the anterooms waiting for Lady Alys to reappear. The young nobleman was slim, with a self-conscious awkwardness to his stance. Tristan doubted he was proficient with a sword, or strong enough to beat a man in unarmed combat. He would be no match for the wily Veronne in protecting Lady Alys. Briefly Tristan wondered why Brienne had not shown the ruthlessness he had witnessed in his treatment of Walcott on board ship. Veronne must have condemning information about him.

The Comte paused in the doorway of the card room, his manner disdainful as he surveyed the gathering. Before the cards were dealt, Tristan threw out his challenge. 'My lord, you won a great deal of money from our friends here earlier. Will you not join us so that they can recoup their losses?'

'Another time.' The Comte was looking round, clearly searching for someone. Tristan had no intention of allowing him to seek out Lady Alys.

'In England it is considered fair play to give your opponents the chance to win back their losses. Do the French prefer to hoard their winnings like misers?'

'Sir, you insult my countrymen,' sneered the Comte.

'I am offering you the chance to uphold the reputation of fair play honoured by gentlemen.'

Veronne flipped open a gold snuffbox. He sprinkled

some snuff on the back of his hand and sniffed it before answering. 'A Frenchman has more honour than an Englishman any day. But can an Englishman lose with good grace? That is also a matter of honour.'

'Please join us so that we prove that the honour of both our countries is not in jeopardy,' Tristan taunted.

The Frenchman's nostrils flared as he regarded Tristan with unconcealed hatred. 'Very well. I hope you are prepared to lose, Englishman.'

'When the honour of my country is at stake, I never lose.' The challenge sparked between them, and as Veronne sat down, several other men were drawn to stand around their table and watch.

'The Comte rarely loses,' another Frenchman announced, but there was no admiration in his tone.

Tristan studied every movement of Veronne's hands. It was when he was dealing that he scooped the largest winnings. After they had been playing for an hour, he was dealing again. The pile of coins in front of Tristan had tripled and the same could be said for Veronne. The other gamblers had lost most of the money on the table in front of them, particularly another Frenchman, Lapoitiere. He had come to the table with the highest stake, and only a few coins remained. Three times he had lost a pot to Veronne when only the two of them remained in play. Tristan threw in his hand, leaving the two old adversaries to play out the final round.

The sleight of hand was fast. Everyone was watching Lapoitiere and had not noticed.

Lapoitiere spread his cards on the table. 'At last I win.'

As he made to draw the money towards him, Veronne scoffed, '*Mon ami*, yet again you lose.' He laid down each of his cards with a smirk.

Lapoitiere leapt to his feet. 'You have the devil on your side tonight.'

'You are a poor loser.' Veronne reached forward to take his winnings.

Faster than a striking viper, Tristan snatched at the older man's wrist, flicked back his lace cuff and withdrew three low-scoring cards from inside.

'I think Lapoitiere is the winner.'

All the men at the table rose to their feet. 'You cheat! How many of us have you fleeced of our money in this manner?'

'There has been a mistake,' blustered Veronne, backing away from his outraged companions.

'Those cards upon your person do not lie. You will answer to us. Take him outside, gentlemen,' Lapoitiere demanded. 'He is not fit to be in our company.'

'I do not know how those cards got there.' Veronne was sweating profusely. 'I swear . . .'

'Do not add to your dishonour by lying. You were caught. You will be banished from our society and this infamy will be broadcast amongst all our country-men. No man of honour will receive you. Return all the money you have cheated from us, then get out of our sight, and if you have any sense, out of the country.'

'I have been insulted. I demand that honour be satisfied. My seconds will attend upon my accusers.' Veronne glared at the men who were closing in on him.

'I would not sully my sword with a blackguard's blood,' Lapoitiere retorted. 'Your guilt is clear. Your name will be spat upon. You shame all Frenchmen.'

Veronne was roughly escorted out of the room by two of the men. In the hallway they met Brienne. 'What is happening?'

'Mr Loveday exposed this scoundrel for a cheat and a

liar. He will return the money you lost to him and we intend to escort him from the house. He is no longer one of us.'

Brienne was frowning as he entered the gaming room and bowed to Tristan. 'I have much to thank you for, sir. I am ashamed that such a man preyed upon my friendship and that of my acquaintances. Again I am indebted to you.'

'Think nothing of it.' Tristan waved aside his gratitude. 'No one will tolerate a card sharp. I was happy to be of service in the circumstances.'

To his surprise, Tristan received a round of applause from the others present, one saying, 'I would never have suspected him for a scoundrel. We are all indebted to you, Mr Loveday.'

Tristan inclined his head in acknowledgement. As he walked from the room, he put his hand into his pocket, where he had secreted the cards he had planted upon Veronne.

Chapter Twenty-one

Adam, Japhet, Joshua and Long Tom were sitting at the dining table at Boscabel with their port after the women had retired to the saloon. With the absence of the fairer sex the conversation had turned to politics. Sir Gregory expanded on what they knew of the European situation, particularly regarding France and its warrior First Consul.

'This so-called peace treaty is farcical,' he declared as he poured himself another glass of port and passed the decanter to Japhet. 'The Corsican is amassing ships in all the major French ports. It is clear as day that he is planning an invasion. And our government does nothing.'

'Surely they are aware of the danger.' Joshua puffed on his clay pipe. Through the veil of blue smoke he was frowning.

'So far our navy has kept the Little Corporal at bay.' Adam used the derisory title for the man who saw himself as the leader of the French. 'Only an all-out trouncing will finally deter him.'

'There is unrest throughout Europe,' Long Tom went on. 'It is not only our country Bonaparte would invade.'

'Is not our navy the finest? The French fleet was no

match for us at the Battle of the Nile.' Japhet leaned forward, his elbows resting on the table.

'We cannot afford to sit on our laurels. Bonaparte should never be underestimated.' Long Tom subjected the cousins to a warning glare. 'One battle, no matter how glorious, does not necessarily win a war. Bonaparte is an injured tiger licking his wounds. That makes him unpredictable and dangerous.'

'So in your opinion this peace will not last,' Joshua said heavily.

Sir Gregory shook his head. 'He has his sights on building an empire. Only death will stop him. But for now he gathers his strength behind the pretence of this treaty. When he is ready, we will again hear his roar.'

He looked pointedly at Adam and changed the subject. 'Has the peace been beneficial to the shipyard?'

'I've orders to keep the men in work for the next two years. But if as you predict war will again break out, it will inevitably affect further orders. Merchant ships are too much at risk from foreign privateers attacking them.'

'You survived through the recent troubles,' Sir Gregory stated. 'Surely you will again?'

'The revenue office have placed no further orders for the cutter I designed, and though the ships are popular with the free-traders, war makes such commerce difficult, with the Channel full of patrol vessels. The yard nearly faced ruin and was only saved by the order for the merchant ship *Good Fortune*, but that brought unhappy consequences from its anonymous client.'

Adam's expression darkened. He had refrained from speaking of St John's death, unwilling to cast a shadow over the reunion with his friend. 'It sticks in my gullet that I now owe the continued existence of the shipyard to a man who brought such misery to our family.'

'How is that?' Long Tom was genuinely concerned.

Seeing the pain etched upon his nephew's features, Joshua briefly explained Tristan's involvement, St John's death and the loss of Trevowan.

Long Tom shook his head sorrowfully. 'I had heard only of St John's death and had discounted the gossip that he had brought ruin to his family. There had always been idle talk about his gambling. My deepest condolences.' He stared from Japhet to Adam. 'A long-lost cousin appears from nowhere and manages to dispossess St John of his home. And you have allowed this?'

'He has the law on his side,' Adam fumed. 'Nothing he did was illegal. It was underhand and the action of a treacherous dog – but it was not illegal.'

'Have you not contested the manner in which he plotted St John's ruin?' Recovering from his shock, Sir Gregory was flushed with outrage.

'Cousin Thomas in London consulted one of the country's best lawyers. There is no case. St John was too deeply in debt. He had gambled his inheritance away.' Japhet clenched a fist and banged it down on to the table, making the crystal glasses judder. 'Tristan Loveday bought up St John's debts and loans. When he called them in and St John could not pay, he was entitled to recoup his money by demanding the estate as payment.'

'Did he bear a grudge against your whole family, or against St John in particular?' Long Tom asked astutely. He was too experienced in judging men and the demons that drove them not to guess at some hidden agenda behind these actions.

'He had no reason to have affection for us,' Adam admitted. 'His branch of the family had been disowned by my great-grandfather. Apparently his mother lived in extreme poverty and drank herself to death. A belated spate of conscience prompted my grandfather to offer Tristan a home when St John and I were young. He lived at Trevowan for a few years before he was condemned by St John for a crime my grandfather could never forgive. Tristan ran away. We only discovered after St John's death that Tristan had forced him to write a confession admitting that he had lied. My brother was the guilty party.'

'That must have been painful for you to learn,' Long Tom commiserated. 'St John was involved in some underhand schemes in the past, with his smuggling and that episode in Virginia when he became engaged to that wealthy heiress whilst his wife in England still lived.' In his secretive work for the British government Kilmarthen had learned how to assess the character of an individual. He could not have survived so long as a spy had he not. His first impressions of Adam when the younger man had rescued him from a French prison had been that he was brave and enjoyed the excitement danger could bring, but also had high principles, steadfastness and loyalty. A man he could trust implicitly. His impression of Adam's twin had been the opposite. The Lovedays were a complex and diverse family, and although Japhet had been a rakehell and adventurer before his marriage, he too was a man to count on in a fight, and would never betray his family or a friend even if his life depended upon it.

Sir Gregory drew on his knowledge of the law. 'A civil case could be brought against your cousin if he deliberately planned St John's downfall. It would bring to light any underhand dealings.'

'Unfortunately it would bring as much harm to our reputation as Tristan's,' Adam groaned. 'St John could not control his gambling. He frequently lost vast fortunes at the tables.'

'Was this to Tristan?' Long Tom asked.

'Only at the end did he play against Tristan,' Adam replied. 'Before that he refused to have anything to do with him.'

'Could it be that Tristan engaged card sharps when your brother lost so heavily?' Long Tom persisted. 'Were there witnesses who would testify that he was urged to give IOUs when he was in his cups and his judgement impaired?'

Adam dragged his fingers through his hair, trying to calm his anger as he recalled his twin's compulsion to gamble. 'Half the young bucks at the gaming halls St John frequented were in their cups. His friends knew it was impossible to reason with my brother when his blood was fevered by the run of the cards or dice.' He sighed. 'I suspect he lost heavily to the knave's agents, but that could be difficult to prove. I made enquiries, and none of the gentlemen present suspected foul play. St John was drunk and was drawn in deeper than he could repay. There were dozens of IOUs in Tristan's possession.'

'At least you did not allow your hot blood to call this knave to account.' Long Tom eyed Adam warily. 'That would only have fuelled the gossip about your brother's state of mind and his death.'

'I was tempted,' Adam admitted.

'And wisely saw reason,' Joshua cut in. 'How would a duel have solved anything? If Tristan had been killed, Adam would have been implicated in his murder.'

Long Tom regarded the three men. The atmosphere in the dining room was simmering with tension. 'Given the circumstances, your restraint is admirable.'

'Do not imagine that this state of affairs is other than temporary. The knave will not get away with his treachery,' Adam informed him.

Japhet voiced his own feelings. 'For months after my return I was prepared to give Tristan the benefit of the doubt when he seemed intent on establishing a link with our family. I liked him when he first came to Trevowan. Beneath his bluster and boasting he was desperate to fit in and be accepted. The confession he forced St John to write showed us all a side of St John we had refused to acknowledge – the lies and deceit he was capable of to save his own hide at the expense of another were unacceptable. Yet in his retaliation against St John, Tristan overstepped the line. He cannot be allowed to get away with his treachery.'

'And what will you do about it?' Long Tom demanded.

Japhet's eyes narrowed. 'Somehow he must be discredited. Honour demands he be brought to justice for his treachery against our family. It was not only St John who suffered.' He grew more incensed with every word, his eyes blazing with affront and condemnation. 'The repercussions of Tristan's vengeance have affected our womenfolk, leaving them in much straitened circumstances. That is intolerable.'

Long Tom saw the Loveday men exchange heated glances. No doubt it had been a topic much discussed without conclusion. Their anger was contained on too short a fuse and at any moment the powder keg could explode. He knew Japhet and Adam were fearless and driven by the need for justice. He was surprised that they had restrained themselves so far from some rash action that would be as disastrous for them as for their opponent. Joshua clearly had had his work cut out making these fiery men restrain their emotions.

Joshua spoke forcefully. 'It must be done legally, or Japhet and Adam could lose their own property and liberty. That would achieve nothing.'

'Rightly so,' Long Tom agreed.

'Then your visit is most opportune.' Joshua smiled at the baronet. 'Keeping these two from bringing Tristan to account has taken all my reasoning powers. What would you suggest?'

Kilmarthen frowned and considered the matter.

Ever impatient, Japhet confessed, 'We've racked our brains for months to devise a plan. All could destroy our family's reputation. That must be avoided.'

'I am glad you see the sense of that,' Joshua said, not unkindly.

Adam sprang to his feet and paced round the table. 'If it was just my reputation at stake, I'd run him through tomorrow without a qualm. But I don't want my sons to carry that stigma through life. And Tristan is too shrewd a businessman not to have made a will leaving Trevowan to some unknown heir. It is reclaiming our family home and estate for the rightful incumbent, St John's son, that is the question of honour here.'

'Japhet is right,' Long Tom announced. 'Tristan Loveday must be publicly discredited and in a way that does not rebound upon your own reputations.' He spread his hands and a calculating light shone in his eyes. 'What Tristan did in the years after he left Trevowan must be discovered. How did he make his money? He clearly has no little fortune at his command. I doubt he came by it entirely honestly.'

'Yet does not any discredit brought against him also reflect upon us as his kin?' Joshua counselled.

'I doubt it. Anyone of consequence in this county knows that you have had nothing to do with him since his childhood,' Long Tom advised. 'What do you know of those years?'

'Only what he told my half-sister Tamasine,' Adam

said, his anger again breaking through. 'After her marriage he inveigled his way into her company, no doubt lured by her husband's wealth and position. Tamasine had some misguided idea of reuniting us. Her illegitimacy had excluded her from our family throughout her childhood and she empathised with Tristan over his own childhood exiled from our family. He told her he had married a Frenchwoman and lived in Marseilles for some years. His wife died during the Terror. He spent some time in the Channel Islands and then travelled extensively through Europe and settled in Boston, where he married a second time before his wife and son died in a boating accident.'

'You say he married a Frenchwoman. What if he still has connections there?' Long Tom suggested. 'They could be construed as treasonable. Emotions run high and many of the French émigrés are viewed with suspicion that they could be Bonaparte's spies. The other side of the coin is that Bonaparte fears a Royalist plot to restore the French monarchy. There is doubt cast upon any who lived through the Terror in France, where treachery became the rule of the day in order to survive. I have contacts who can make enquiries if you wish.'

It was agreed, and Adam said, 'From his guttersnipe beginnings our ne'er-do-well cousin has led an eventful life.'

Japhet rocked his chair back on to its rear legs, his long lashes shielding his eyes as he twisted an oval emerald ring on his little finger. He was uncomfortable at condoning a conspiracy that investigated how their cousin had acquired his fortune. Not all his own enterprises in Sydney would be viewed by polite society as gentlemanly or even honest pursuits. When he had seen an opportunity to make money he had seized it. Apart from the emporium he had built to sell the goods Adam and his investors exported to the colony, and the houses he constructed in the expanding townships of Sydney and Parramatta, there were also the dozen inns he had owned, with their drink, gaming and women. These had been popular with the increasing number of ticket-of-leave men who had served their time and had yet to find the money to pay for their passage home.

Sir Gregory studied the older cousin closely. Japhet was the wild card. He doubted his years in the penal colony had tamed him. Japhet became more impassioned as he vented his anger upon teaching Tristan the error of thinking he could cross the Lovedays and not face the consequences. As the conversation around the table grew more heated, Sir Gregory decided that he had been right not to reveal the whereabouts of Japhet's sworn enemy, Sir Pettigrew Osgood. He did not want to be the instrument of his downfall.

He sat back in his chair. The cousins should be using this time of peace to safeguard their investments for the future. But he sensed a restlessness within them. Especially Adam. His twin's death had affected him deeply. There were times when Sir Gregory had glimpsed a faraway look in his expressive eyes – a yearning for fresh adventure. The responsibilities of the shipyard weighted his broad shoulders. It had been several years since Adam had captained his own ship, *Pegasus*, rescuing émigrés from the Terror in France. Those days had brought out his buccaneering spirit, and he had never hesitated to take on a French corsair in battle. Sir Gregory was again working for the British government, and he needed men like Adam whom he could trust. Adam had given up that life when he took over the running of the shipyard, but if Long Tom could discover the means to discredit their cousin, Adam would be beholden to him in the future. The Lovedays had endured a turbulent year. He would be travelling on tomorrow. Let them have a few more months of peace before he revealed Osgood's where-abouts and any information he could discover about their faithless cousin.

'For now, your cousin seems to have right on his side,' Long Tom said with heavy emphasis. 'And to dishonour him, or any adversary,' he glanced at Japhet with equal warning, 'you must ensure that your own honour remains unquestioned.'

Chapter Twenty-two

Tristan was doing what he did best, and he could not remember the last time he had felt this thrill of excitement and frisson of danger that made him feel so alive. Whilst Veronne was being made to pay back all his winnings and Lapoitiere and the other Frenchmen prepared to escort him from the premises, Tristan had sped upstairs, collected a leather saddlebag and escaped from the house unobserved. He still had unfinished business with Veronne.

He sneaked into the tack room and carried away a bridle and saddle. With so many guests, the stalls in the stables were full and several horses had been put into a paddock. It was not a good night for travelling. There was only a thin sliver of the crescent moon visible, and clouds obscured most of the stars. In places the night was so black it was like looking into a barrel of pitch. Once his eyes became accustomed to the darkness, he was able to make out silhouettes against the lighter colour of the grass. He singled out a bay mare with no white markings to ride and hid in the trees by the entrance to the estate. Veronne's coach approached, two lanterns burning on each side of the vehicle. They gave little illumination on to the road and the horses proceeded at a slow pace.

Tristan hoped the Comte did not plan to travel far before he decided to stop for the night.

The carriage bumped along the highway, the coachman unable to avoid all the ruts. They had only travelled a few miles through country lanes when they entered a sprawling village with several shops and three taverns, one of which, the Plough, was a coaching inn. The vehicle turned under the archway leading to the stable yard.

Tristan watched from the shadows. The Frenchman hobbled into the inn, his body sore from the battering of his ride. His surly voice demanded a bottle of brandy and a room for the night. Tristan kept the inn under surveillance whilst allowing his mount to drink at the village trough opposite. He could be in for a long night if Veronne remained in the taproom for hours.

A candle flickered as it was carried past the window by the stairs and another was lit in a front bedroom. Briefly Tristan saw Veronne outlined within before the shutters were closed, the light showing through a broken slat.

Satisfied that his quarry intended to retire for the night, Tristan rode to the edge of the village. He tethered the mare in a coppice near the road, where there was plenty of grass for her to eat. Then he walked back to the inn and peered into the dimly lit taproom. The coachman was stretched out on a settle, his greatcoat serving as a blanket. The only other customers were three men in rough work clothes quaffing from quart tankards and singing a nonsensical folk song.

Tristan sat outside on the ground under the shade of a twisted oak tree and waited for the inn to grow quiet. The light in Veronne's window was doused but it was some time before the three labourers staggered outside, one singing tunelessly as they wove their way on a precarious route to their cottages. From inside the inn came the sound of a wooden bar being lowered into place to secure the door, and it was not long before the candles were extinguished and the place became quiet.

There was just enough moonlight for Tristan to have surveyed the outside of the establishment. The branches of the oak tree stretched across the front of the building. Tristan climbed into the foliage and edged along the branch that was nearest to Veronne's window. Fortunately the sill was wide enough to take his body as he listened at the shutter. The sound of snoring came from within. Tristan flicked the long black cloak he was wearing over his shoulders. Before leaving Brienne's house he had exchanged his finery for dark, serviceable clothing, donned a padded waistcoat to change the appearance of his build, and taken a theatrical long wig and beard from his saddlebag to complete the disguise. In recent years he had become a master of deception, learning all the tricks he had needed to transform his identity. Even St John had not recognised him when he had adopted a foreign accent during one of the attacks upon his cousin. Forced to make his preparations in the darkness, he knew the disguise would not have looked natural in daylight. On a night like this, however, it was good enough to conceal his identity.

Drawing his dagger, Tristan slipped it between the two shutters and manoeuvred the inner latch open. It clunked as it fell aside and he paused frozen on the sill to ensure that the snoring continued. There were a couple of loud snorts from the chamber's occupant before the snoring again built to a steady rhythm. He pushed open the shutters and silently lowered himself into the room, crouching low so that he was not outlined against the window. Veronne continued to sound like a boar snuffling for truffles, his body turned away from him on the bed.

'Call out and 'ee be a dead man.' Tristan pitched his voice higher than normal and adopted a thick, guttural accent.

At the pressure of the knife against his throat, Veronne's eyes shot open, rounded with terror.

'Don't 'ee make a move,' Tristan warned, playing out his role. 'I'd plans fer tonight and 'ee ruined 'em. All set I were to rob them guests at the manor afore 'ee cheated them. Lost me chance of a fortune. 'Ee owe me. 'Ee owe me good.'

'Take what money I have,' Veronne whined. 'Take it all.'

'Happen I will, but it be small fry against the pickings I were after, until 'ee spoilt me chances.' The blade slithered across his victim's throat, drawing a thin line of blood that trickled down the Frenchman's neck. 'I reckon 'ee got information worth a guinea or two. I be hidden in that room when 'ee were threatening your host. Nothing like blackmail to earn a pretty turn of a coin.'

'I do not know what you are talking about,' Veronne blustered. 'Here, take my purse.' He fumbled under his pillow, but Tristan grabbed his wrist and pinioned it to the bed.

'Try a move like that again and 'ee be dead.' He shoved his victim on to the floor and knelt on his back as his free hand searched under the pillow and found not only a leather purse but a knife.

'Thought 'ee'd prick me with this, did 'ee?' Tristan sneered, his knee digging deeply into his victim's spine. He jerked Veronne's head back so that his neck was fully exposed, and the point of the dagger sank deeper.

'I'll tell you. Don't kill me.'

Some minutes later Veronne was bound and gagged on

the floor and Tristan left as silently as he had arrived. He was richer by some two hundred guineas, having taken the Comte's money. He had also learned some interesting information about Brienne's activities that could be used to his advantage. He had been certain that Veronne had not recognised him and that he would not report back to Brienne or his associates of this robbery. No one who had been party to his treachery this evening would take the word of a man who had acted with such dishonour.

With Rowena away at school, the atmosphere at Reskelly Cottage became more agreeable. Felicity was content to allow Amelia to take charge, and without her stepsister's disruptive influence Charlotte was happy to entertain her half-sister in the nursery. Since both women were happy to live quietly, their time passed pleasantly with visits to Boscabel, Tor Farm, Trewenna Rectory and a fortnightly visit to Traherne Hall. The only cloud in Amelia's life was the continued absence of Richard. Since he had returned to Bath there had been only one letter, saying he would be spending the next weeks of his leave with friends on their estate but giving no addresses. There was something almost secretive in his evasion. The close ties Amelia had once shared with her son had altered since his adolescence, and she suspected that he was avoiding her to escape her censure. His father had been a libertine and had caused her much unhappiness in her marriage. At least his affairs had been discreet. She could not say the same for her son. After his last leave there were rumours that a dairymaid who had often been seen in his company had been hurriedly married to an ageing widower when Richard had been called to sea. Six months after the wedding she had been delivered of a daughter. It was a rumour Amelia chose to ignore. There was always speculation and gossip where a six-month baby was concerned. But she could not rest easy until Richard was married with his own family. Was that not every mother's dream?

Fears if allowed to fester too often became manifest. A week of sunshine in May changed abruptly to a deluge, which did not ease for three days. Amelia had been anxiously watching the swelling stream at the end of the garden, which had flowed over its banks and was advancing towards the cottage. Fortunately the rise of the garden to the building and the sloping away of the ground on the far side of the river meant that although the lower meadows were flooded, she doubted the cottage would be in danger. At the front of the residence the track widened to the unpaved main street of Trewenna. The downpour had churned it into a quagmire and the villagers who ventured forth were ankle deep in mud. As she passed the front parlour window she was surprised to see two well-dressed women clinging together, their fashionable clothes and bonnets sodden, as they climbed the incline to the cottage.

Amelia frowned. What gentlewomen travelled in such ungodly weather and on foot? It was not unheard of for friends of the family or acquaintances to pay an unsolicited call, though usually they would send a servant first to present their cards. She certainly did not recognise them, but there was no mistaking that they were heading for the cottage, as the village was now behind them and it was three miles to the next farm.

As she watched, they paused and looked up at the cottage, their faces hidden by the deep brims of their bonnets. They were wet and bedraggled, their skirts lifted above their ankles to protect them from the mud. Their wooden pattens had done little to protect their shoes and ankles from the deluge. Even so, the younger of the two seemed reluctant to approach, and her companion wrenched her arm and was clearly angered by her hesitancy.

Amelia's natural hospitality was roused by their obvious plight. It would be unthinkable to turn away a gentlewoman who was in dire need. Perhaps their carriage had broken its axle. Their first place of refuge would have been the rectory, though she would not have expected Joshua and Cecily to be away from home in such weather. There was no suitable inn in the village for them to take their rest, so perhaps they had been guided by a villager to approach Amelia for shelter.

She smoothed the folds of her black silk gown and called up the stairs to where Felicity was feeding George in her bedchamber. 'It appears we have visitors, my dear.'

She went into the parlour and waited for Jenna or Mo to announce them. To distract herself from an unaccountable feeling of unease, she rearranged a vase of bluebells that were beginning to wilt.

'Mrs Kellerman and Miss Madison, ma'am.' Jenna Biddick held two sodden cloaks over her arm; they dripped on the polished floorboards.

'You had better spread those before the kitchen fire to dry,' Amelia instructed.

Her gaze took in the women's bare feet, from which they had removed their muddied shoes and pattens on entering the cottage. Their gowns were damp where the rain had soaked through their cloaks and the hems were mired despite their efforts to keep them away from the ground. They were as bedraggled as half-drowned cats, and the younger one looked exhausted and ready to burst into tears at any moment. Their distress roused Amelia's compassion, although she remained suspicious of their unexpected visit. The older woman was assessing the room and looked far from approving or appreciative at being received in her home.

'I do not believe we have met,' Amelia said with cool politeness. 'What brings you to Reskelly Cottage? Or has your coach suffered some mishap on your journey?'

'Our business is with Lieutenant Allbright,' the older of the two replied tartly. 'This is his home, is it not?'

Her tone and manner put Amelia further on her guard. 'Then I fear you have had a wasted journey. My son has not been here for some weeks.'

'Have you an address where we can find him?'

Amelia stiffened. The older woman was barely civil and her companion became more agitated by the moment. Her fingers were gripped together, her knuckles white with tension, her stare fixed upon a knot of wood in the polished floorboards.

'Lydia, he is not here. We must leave,' the younger woman urged.

'Not until we learn his whereabouts—' Mrs Kellerman's grim-faced retort ended with a gasp as her companion suddenly crumpled and fell in a faint to the floor.

Felicity, who had just walked into the room, screamed and then belatedly recovered her wits. 'Is the woman ill?'

Mrs Kellerman crouched beside her companion and lifted her hand to gently chafe her wrist, her manner now distraught. 'Emma. Emma. Can you hear me?'

Amelia glared at Felicity, who was frozen to the spot. 'Fetch your smelling salts. She has swooned, most likely from exhaustion.'

As Felicity hurried to comply, the only sounds were the rustle of her black taffeta and the deeper tick of the grandfather clock in the corner of the room. The rain had finally stopped beating against the windows. Amelia hooked her arms under the legs of the woman on the floor and addressed Mrs Kellerman. 'We should lift her on to the chair closest to the fire. You are both wet and cold. This is hardly the weather for a social call.'

'Our visit is not social.' Mrs Kellerman remained antagonistic as they settled Miss Madison into the chair. Felicity reappeared and Amelia took the smelling salts from her and waved them under the unconscious woman's nostrils. It was several moments before she wrinkled her nose and stirred, pushing the bottle aside, her eyes watering from the pungency of the smell. Her face was ghostly and her wits were slow to return. Whilst Amelia pushed her head down between her knees, Felicity went to the door and ordered tea for their guests.

'Your pardon,' Miss Madison groaned as she regained her senses. 'I do not know what came over me.'

Her voice was soft and cultured and she glanced anxiously at Mrs Kellerman.

'If this is not a social call, what is your business with my son?' Amelia demanded, fixing her stare upon Mrs Kellerman. 'Few people know our address, as we have but recently moved here.'

'We were directed first to the big house at Trevowan.' Mrs Kellerman continued to rub her companion's hands and Miss Madison's colour was gradually returning. 'A servant informed us that you no longer resided there and that if Lieutenant Allbright was in the area he would be here.'

'Unfortunately, he is not. He is spending his leave with friends. I fear you have had a wasted journey. I have no idea when to expect him.' Amelia remained wary, but the wretched state of the two women, who were obviously of good birth, did concern her and reminded her of the fact that hospitality extended even to strangers. 'Ah, here is the tea. It will bring some warmth to you and restore you both.' She indicated for Mrs Kellerman to sit on the chair opposite her, close to the fire. Felicity sat on the padded settle where Edna had placed the silver teapot and tray, together with a plate of sliced fruit cake baked that morning.

Amelia joined her daughter-in-law, an uneasy silence stretching between the women as she poured the tea and passed the cups to the visitors. Her gaze sharpened upon the younger woman as she handed her the crockery. Miss Madison's nervousness increased under Amelia's scrutiny. The cup rattled in its saucer and the teaspoon clattered to the floor.

'Your pardon.' She blushed and retrieved her spoon. 'You must find this all very singular.'

'How do you know my son?' Amelia dismissed any further prevarication. She had a feeling she was not going to like what she was about to hear, and wanted it over with. Better still, she preferred to put these women in their place and send them on their way.

Miss Madison, who had been sipping her tea, spilled some into her lap as her hands continued to shake.

'Lieutenant Allbright has not mentioned his acquaintanceship with Miss Madison, I presume,' Mrs Kellerman declared in icy tones. 'Did he not visit here recently?'

'We had the pleasure of his company for a few weeks, but he has many friends and commitments. No mention was made of Miss Madison, or any woman who was not of our family.' Amelia fixed the older guest with a piercing stare. From the corner of her eye she saw the younger woman shrink into herself, her stare again fastened upon the floor.

Internal alarm bells were ringing for Amelia. The extraordinariness of this meeting carried an ominous portent. She stamped down her fears, her voice harshening. 'And what exactly, may I ask, is the nature of this acquaintanceship?'

'Miss Madison is my niece. Mr Allbright and Miss Madison are betrothed.'

Amelia placed her cup firmly on the table, needing a few moments to overcome her shock. She drew a calming breath, linked her fingers in her lap and fixed both women with a cool stare. 'That is not possible. My son does not come into his majority until he is twenty-five. During his visit he certainly mentioned no betrothal, or asked my permission as to any future intention. Indeed he seemed quite set against any mention of marriage.'

'He said you would object.' Miss Madison spoke softly, her voice tremulous and hesitant. She did not lift her gaze from the floor. 'It was to be a secret.'

'A clandestine subterfuge! My son would never so deceive me,' Amelia protested.

Abruptly Emma Madison stood up, the fine porcelain of the cup and saucer wobbling precariously in her hands. 'Lydia, we have imposed upon Mrs Loveday's kindness for too long. I knew no good would come of this. It is Richard I must speak with.' Her demeanour was one of total wretchedness.

'Sit down, Miss Madison,' Amelia announced. Without the shadows of exhaustion tightening her face and her hair unbecomingly flattened by the rain, this nervous young woman would be pretty enough to catch any man's eye. There was also a certain vulnerability and innocence about her, overlaid with an air of misery and hopelessness. 'Since you have seen fit to call uninvited with some preposterous tale of a secret betrothal to my son, I would have the whole story from you.'

'We met in Bath . . .' Miss Madison sank back on to the chair, unable to hold Amelia's stare. She shook her head, clearly too overcome to speak, and her gaze was beseeching as it lighted upon her companion.

Mrs Kellerman tutted. 'I will speak for Emma. Lieutenant Allbright pursued my niece with great persistence and passion. Before he returned to Cornwall he declared his love and devotion and asked for her hand in marriage. When she accepted, for reasons of his own he insisted that the betrothal remain secret. He explained that your family was in mourning and left Bath to visit you. When he returned, his manner was different and he denied their betrothal.'

'My stepson died recently.' Amelia nodded to Felicity. 'This is his widow. Your visit is an intrusion upon our mourning. We are not receiving visitors.' She reminded them curtly of conventional etiquette, though her emotions were still reeling from shock. There must be some mistake. Richard would never treat a woman so falsely, would never betray her in this base manner. Despite her faith, however, a nagging at the back of her mind made her choose a wary path when she continued. 'Even the most suitable engagement would be a breach of our sensibilities at this time.'

'That does not change Lieutenant Allbright's responsibility to honour his word,' Mrs Kellerman declared with a haughty sniff. 'You have our sincere condolences at your grief. Under normal circumstances we would not intrude upon your mourning. Understandably my niece is distraught at this breach of contract. A jilted fiancée faces ridicule and loss of reputation. Miss Madison comes from a good family, gently reared and well educated.

Unfortunately her father, Major Madison, is serving with his regiment in India at the present time, or he would be calling Lieutenant Allbright to account for his conduct.'

Amelia stood up, her expression stony and her body rigid with affront. 'My son is not here to answer your accusations. Neither will I tolerate his name being blackened in this manner. I must ask you both to leave.'

Mrs Kellerman rose also, equally stiff with anger and outrage. 'My niece was seduced by your son and is now carrying his child. A child he refuses to acknowledge. She is eighteen years old. Young and innocent. He took that innocence and has ruined her reputation and her life. Do you intend for him to do the honourable thing and stand by her?'

Amelia gripped her hands together. Her heart was pounding frantically. Felicity was staring with open-mouthed shock at their guests, and Amelia shot her a warning glare to remain silent. She did not want her blurting out some comment that would prejudice Richard.

'If my son has wronged Miss Madison, and your accusations are correct and her innocence is beyond doubt, then he is duty bound to wed her. However, I have yet to hear his side of the story. He is a man of no little fortune and has risked his life for his country. Such a dashing figure will turn many a foolish maid's head, or attract a scheming fortune-huntress to snare him into marriage. I do not know your niece well enough to pass judgement upon her character, but I know my son.'

Unfortunately Amelia knew Richard's failings only too well, and she was devastated by this news. She suspected that the accusations were true, but loyalty made her steadfast. She had survived too many scandals to be intimidated by some scheming Jezebel, and there was a coldness and calculation about Mrs Kellerman that she distrusted.

'When do you anticipate being in contact with Lieutenant Allbright?' Mrs Kellerman demanded.

Amelia ignored the question, her attention focused upon Miss Madison. Her gown although travel stained was of fine wool and in the latest mode. She wore discreet gold eardrops and a gold and amethyst pendant. Amelia looked pointedly at the third finger on her left hand. It was devoid of a betrothal ring.

'Miss Madison, did my son propose marriage and formally ask your guardian for permission to offer for your hand? Or did he merely declare his affection, as many men do if they believe it will sway a woman to grant them her favours?'

'I believed his word as a gentleman. He said he loved me and asked me to marry him, and I accepted.' She still did not hold Amelia's stare, either from embarrassment or because she was evading the truth, but rushed on, her cheeks staining crimson. 'He said there could be no announcement until he had spoken to you, as is only right. He said that a secret engagement until he returned to Bath would be romantic. Naturally, I then expected him to write to my father and at the very least inform Mrs Kellerman of his intentions. I have no other male relatives.'

'Did he make this declaration before or after you had given him your favours?' Amelia asked coldly.

'I would not have . . .' Miss Madison stumbled in her distress. 'It would not have been right, but is not a betrothal as binding as a marriage?'

'You are naive indeed if you were seduced so easily,' Amelia informed her. 'But matters cannot remain as they are. Leave an address where you can be contacted.'

She rang a bell, and when Edna appeared too quickly not to have been eavesdropping, Amelia announced, 'Mrs Kellerman and Miss Madison are leaving.'

'This matter must be settled.' Lydia Kellerman faced her boldly.

'Until I have spoken with my son, nothing can be decided,' Amelia informed them curtly. 'Miss Madison has been extremely foolish, and clearly she was not adequately chaperoned. You have neglected your duties. I would leave now, Mrs Kellerman, before you say something that may make me regret being so generous in listening to your tale. The good name of my son – a war hero – has been put to question, and I do not take kindly to that.'

Emma Madison bobbed a curtsy. 'I am sorry; this must be a shock to you, Mrs Loveday. I do love Richard and I know he loves me. I'm so frightened. Papa will disown me.'

'You should have considered that before you acted in so wayward a manner.'

Despite the cruelty of her words, Amelia understood the young woman's plight, and that moment of honesty convinced her that Richard would have been more than capable of charming and seducing so innocent a maid.

Chapter Twenty-three

'Where were you last night?' Lady Alys challenged Tristan the next morning. She had found him after breakfast in the billiard room, where he was waiting for Lapoitiere to join him for an arranged game. 'After you denounced the Comte de Veronne, you disappeared.'

He delivered his practice shot and straightened, holding the cue like a spear at his side. 'Had I known you were eager for my company, I would have made myself available. It was an honour I had not expected. Did Atherstone not dance attendance upon you as usual? Is one ardent admirer not sufficient?' He could not resist teasing her, and was rewarded by her cheeks becoming pink.

'Will you stop insisting that Julian is anything but a friend? And it was not for myself that I asked.' She fidgeted with the fan hanging from a chain on her wrist, clearly flustered by his insinuation.

'Then I am quite undone. I had dared to hope for a more favourable consideration from you.' He moved closer, lowering his voice to a husky whisper. 'We shared so much yesterday in the aviary, and then you avoided me. I thought I had displeased you in some manner. I was distraught.'

She glanced at him through her lashes. 'You did not

displease me. I have other guests. My uncle is very strict that I show none of them undue favours.'

'He is a wise man. How can I now be of service to you?' He saw that he had discountenanced her by his swift change of subject, and was sure that he had not imagined the flash of disappointment in her lovely eyes.

Her chin came up, her composure recovered, though there remained an intriguing brightness in her eyes as she held his regard. She cleared her throat and ran her tongue across her lower lip. How sweet would those lips taste if he kissed them? They had come so close yesterday, and from the shallowness of her breathing she was also remembering that moment.

As he closed the gap between them, her lashes shielded her eyes. 'Many of our guests wished to thank you for exposing a man who had cheated them. It called into question more serious dealings that Veronne had been undertaking.'

She was cool and composed, the perfect hostess. How well she guarded her emotions. Beyond the open door, the sound of voices drifted to them. Lady Alys was discreet, the secret smile now playing across her lips, an invitation of pleasures to come. Tristan felt his blood quicken. She never failed to stimulate him, her beauty holding him enthralled.

Aware that anyone could come upon them, he took his cue from her. 'I did not expect gratitude. A man who cheats on his friends has no place in polite society. I went for a long walk through the grounds and then retired early. I had planned to depart this morning and have some distance to travel. I have intruded enough upon your uncle and his friends.'

'You cannot leave.' This time she did not hide her distress. 'Not after you saved my uncle from dishonour.

He would be distraught that he could not extend the hospitality you deserve. Veronne won more than my uncle could afford to pay at this time. That knave would have declared that he had reneged on a debt and we would have been shunned. I cannot believe the audacity of the man.'

'I was delighted to be of service in exposing a fraudster, but I do have an appointment elsewhere.' His tone expressed his regret. He did not wish to appear too eager to extend his visit.

'Can you not delay it for another day? Yet again our family is much beholden to you. You must allow us to show our gratitude.'

'I am rewarded enough if I have unwittingly been of service to you.'

Brienne strode into the room, breaking the intimacy that was again building between them. Tristan concealed his annoyance.

'There you are, Loveday. What an elusive man you can be. My friends and myself have much to thank you for.'

Tristan waved his lordship's words aside. 'I did little enough when you have extended to me such hospitality and I had encroached upon your house party.'

'Nonsense, my dear fellow. Indeed, it is most fortuitous that you are here. In these troubled times I place great stock by men with impeccable honour. This is the second time you have prevented dishonour tainting my name.'

'Mr Loveday is talking of leaving today, my lord. You must persuade him to stay,' Lady Alys insisted.

'I will not hear of your leaving.' His lordship shed his aloofness and became more affable. 'Fate has brought you to us at this time and there is much I would discuss with you. The gentlemen are assembled in the library. You have shown loyalty not only to us but upon matters of greater importance and have impressed us. You are the very man we need for our enterprise, and you will find it greatly to your advantage. Will you join us, Mr Loveday?'

This was the invitation Tristan had been working towards. 'It will be my pleasure, my lord.'

As they walked to the library, Viscount Atherstone passed them. Shooting Tristan a sullen glower, he addressed Brienne. 'Have you seen Lady Alys? We were to ride this morning.'

'Lady Alys was on her way to the green room, but she was not dressed for riding,' his lordship informed him, and the young nobleman quickened his pace.

Brienne sighed. 'If my niece had an ounce of sense she would wed the lovestruck fool. Pity is, she regards him as a brother. She holds you in high esteem because you saved her reputation. She will listen to you. If you can convince her to marry Atherstone, I would be greatly beholden to you.'

'My lord, you overestimate my influence upon Lady Alys.' Tristan did not relish the role of matchmaker. This was something he had not expected. 'I believe Lady Alys knows her own mind upon affairs of the heart.'

'She could do far worse than Atherstone. It is time she remembered her duty. In my day we married for advantage, not where our hearts led us.'

When they entered the library, the guests who had previously regarded Tristan with suspicion as an interloper now openly welcomed him. The room had the musty smell that came with old books. The walls were lined with shelves of gilt-tooled leather volumes that had probably been bought by the yard a half-century ago and never been opened.

Monsieur Lapoitiere smiled ingratiatingly. 'Mr Loveday, you have proved yourself a man of keen observation and a superb judge of character, with the courage to act upon your convictions.'

'Well done, sir.' Monsieur Gautier added his praise.

'Any one of you would have done the same had you noticed his sleight of hand,' Tristan responded.

Brienne handed around a box of Havana cigars and there was a pause in the conversation as the men snipped off the ends and lit them from a taper that was passed around. Wisps of blue smoke swirled around their heads as they drew on the cigars to ensure that they were fully alight. The men then sat back in their chairs, relaxed and at ease.

'We understand that you are a man of many business interests, Mr Loveday, which includes being of service to many of our exiled countrymen,' Lapoitiere declared. 'Do you frequently travel to France upon your ship *Good Fortune*?'

'As often as is required. As I said before, my first wife was French. I lived in your country for several years and have many contacts there.'

'And this present government – do you approve of them?' Lapoitiere continued his inquisition.

'Bonaparte is the enemy of the British people.'

There was a heavy silence as the men puffed on their cigars. The atmosphere became tense. They were waiting for Tristan to be more explicit. If these men were loyal to Napoleon, they would be in France, not living in exile.

'Bonaparte will only achieve greatness by war,' he informed them. 'France needs a time of peace and prosperity to restock its coffers and enjoy rich harvests. In 1649 Britain shook off its monarchy for a short period and it was riven by dissent. The Restoration returned this country to its present greatness.'

There was a nodding of heads. 'Replacing governments is ever a time of danger for the conspirators,' the lantern-jawed Monsieur Gautier observed.

'Should not a man be prepared to make the ultimate sacrifice for what he believes is right?' Tristan threw back at them.

'When you next sail to France, would you be prepared to act as our agent in political affairs, Mr Loveday?' Brienne cut straight to the point of the meeting. 'We have influential friends who would pay very generously for the services of a man like yourself.'

Tristan controlled the glow of satisfaction at the ease of his success in achieving their trust and confidence. 'I am sure it will be a mutually beneficial arrangement.'

'So when did you plan to tell me that you were engaged to be married?' Amelia demanded of her son. He had arrived the previous evening, talking animatedly throughout the meal of the friends he had stayed with during the last two months. He had dismissed any questions she had raised about his time in Bath and changed the subject. After breakfast this morning he had announced that he would ride to Tor Farm on the horse he had hired from the inn in Fowey.

'Since the peace with France, most of our officers have spent months on land, and I have received no word from the Admiralty that I am to be recalled to duty in the near future. I thought I would get Japhet's advice on a decent mare to keep here for my use.'

Amelia had cut short his words with her deadly shot across his bows. She had told Felicity to keep the children out of the way whilst she confronted him. Richard had his back to her and was staring out of the parlour window to the stream. His hands were clasped behind his back, but the set of his shoulders had tensed, his jaw lifting to a stubborn angle, although he chose to ignore her words. Or more likely he was searching for a plausible excuse.

'I am waiting for your answer, Richard.'

'Sorry, Mama, I was miles away. What did you say?' He turned slowly to face her, but the bright June sunlight shining directly into the room made it impossible for her to see his expression. A beam of light speckled with dust motes haloed his golden hair like a saint or an angel in a biblical painting. The image had never been more false. She knew he was being deliberately evasive.

'You heard exactly what I said. Are you not secretly betrothed?'

He spread his hands in mock astonishment. 'Mama, where do you come by these absurd notions? Or is this a trick at matchmaking?' He moved away from the window, an amused smile set rigidly in place.

'Do not look at me as though my wits have gone begging.' Her stare was coldly appraising. The haughty guardedness in his eyes was a painful reminder of her first husband. 'You look just like your father when he was caught keeping yet another mistress. I will not tolerate lies and deceit. You are betrothed, are you not? A secret engagement! How clandestine and sordid was your scheme to seduce an innocent woman barely out of the schoolroom?'

'Dearest Mama, have I not made myself plain that I have no intention of marrying for some years?' His voice was velvet with coercion, his look one of hurt pride.

'Do not think to bamboozle me with your slick words. Or lie.' She stood up abruptly, her hands gripped tightly together as she controlled the rage sweeping through her. 'If you had no intention of marrying, why seduce a young woman who clearly believes you are to wed?'

'This conversation is absurd, Mama. I will not listen to more of such talk.' He swaggered to the door.

Her hand shot out to grip his arm. 'You will sit down and tell me the truth. Miss Emma Madison. Is that not the name of the young lady you asked to marry whilst you were in Bath?'

'Miss who? I have spent no more than three weeks in Bath since I returned to England. Where did you hear such ridiculous gossip? Who is spreading such lies?' Although he blustered in hearty denial, his colour had drained away.

'I have met Miss Madison.' Amelia flayed him with her fury. 'She was very explicit about the nature of your relationship and your insistence upon a secret betrothal.'

'Then the woman is under a delusion.' He paced the room with measured strides.

'Yet you are acquainted with her?'

'I was introduced to Miss Madison in Bath,' he finally admitted. 'I danced with her a few times. I even escorted her and a companion when they wished to visit a friend out of town. Nothing untoward occurred. Mrs Kellerman was her chaperone.'

'You would be more than capable of eluding a chaperone.' Her anger lashed him. 'Have you no remorse that you have destroyed a young woman's reputation without thought of the consequences? Did you think you could act in so dastardly a fashion and not be found out? I am talking about a gentlewoman from a good family, not some trollop you have picked up from the streets. I am appalled at your conduct. Quite appalled!'

'And so am I, Mama.' He assumed an air of indignant outrage. 'That you have listened to some scurrilous gossip. When I met Miss Madison, her beau had recently jilted her. The woman was quite deranged and indecorous in her conduct.'

Amelia did not believe him and her body burned with shame. 'Do not add to your lechery by blackening a gentlewoman's name.'

'She was little better than a whore!'

Amelia lost control and slapped his face. 'I have met Miss Madison. Do not lie to me.'

He blanched at her information but his discomposure was short-lived. 'Do you want me to marry a whore who gives herself so freely? I would not so besmirch our name.'

'Miss Madison is carrying your child.'

'It could be anyone's.'

Her disgust was chiselled into the deepening lines about her eyes and mouth. 'I brought you up to have more respect for women, especially those of our own class.'

'I will listen to this no further. I am not marrying this creature, and that is an end to it.' He strode towards the door.

'Your father was a lecher of the worst order, but even he did not abandon his own child to face the ridicule of bastardy.'

'And what child would that be?' he jeered.

She continued to glare at him and his mouth gaped in astonishment. Then he gave a snort of derision. 'You mean you and Papa had to get married. You are a fine one to take the high ground.'

'Despite your actions I can at least keep my head high, knowing you are no son of mine. I did my best by you, Richard Allbright, but bad blood will always out in the end.'

His ridicule turned to shock. 'You are not my mother? Then who is?'

'A servant. And if you have one shred of decency and honour left you will marry Miss Madison, or I will ensure that hers is not the only reputation that is destroyed.'

'You are not my mama,' he said dazedly, pain etching his features. Then he wheeled about and marched out, slamming the door behind him.

Amelia was haunted by the shock and misery her disclosure had aroused. She bit her lip, wishing she could retract her words. If she had not been so angry at his cavalier manner, she would never had told him. For she did love Richard like a son.

Her distress intensified when he did not return to the cottage that night. Was it because he was upset, or because he had again run away from his responsibilities? Amelia found it impossible to sleep, and the next morning she drove the pony trap to Boscabel before Adam left for the shipyard.

Jasper Fraddon appeared at the sound of her arrival.

'Captain Loveday and Mrs Loveday be in the stable. Mrs Loveday be tending a plough horse who be lame.'

'I will not take them from their work. I will go to the stable. There is no need to announce me, Fraddon.'

When she called out to the couple, they both showed their surprise at the earliness of her call.

'There is a matter of some urgency. A word in private, if you have the time. I will not keep you long from your work.' She cast a nervous glance at young Will Brown, the son of Adam's servants, who was mucking out another stall.

'Leave that until later, Will,' Adam ordered. 'Or shall we go into the house?'

'This will only take a few minutes.' Amelia quickly informed them of the visit she had had from Miss Madison and Mrs Kellerman, and her quarrel with Richard.

'If the woman is with child, then he has no choice but to wed her,' Adam said sternly.

'But he rode off in a temper. And . . .' Amelia paused to regain her composure, which kept threatening to desert her. 'I said something I should not have. I told him he was not my son. He was upset. What reason has he now to return to the cottage?'

Senara finished wrapping a poultice around the plough horse's hoof and patted his neck, her expression saddened by the news.

'His deep regard for you,' Adam reassured her. 'He has had time to calm down. He probably spent the night at a tavern.'

'You did not see the way he looked at me.' Amelia's voice caught on a sob. 'It was as though I had betrayed him.'

Senara wiped her hands on her apron and put her arm around the older woman. 'That does not excuse his conduct.'

'But what if he ignores his obligations?' Amelia gasped. 'He could ask for a transfer to the first naval ship to leave our shores.'

'You may be worrying unnecessarily,' Adam said. 'I will go to some of the haunts he has frequented in the past. I will also check that he has not taken a ship from Fowey. I shall find him, Amelia.'

'I hope you are right, Adam,' she said heavily. 'It has grieved me to tell you the whole sordid story. I have never been more bitterly ashamed.'

'Richard must marry the girl.' Adam was emphatic.

In that moment he looked and sounded so like his father, Edward, that Amelia found the emotion too much to bear. 'I failed him. I thought I had taught him to be decent and upright.'

'You cannot always curb a man's nature. You taught him to be a gentleman. He will do what is right,' Adam assured her.

Senara remarked, gently, 'Though it is the most extraordinary story, the way those women sought you out.'

'What choice did they have?' Amelia shrugged. 'Mistress Kellerman is not the type of woman I would have chosen for a chaperone – there is a flightiness about her – but Miss Madison is young, and despite her conduct she has an innocence about her.'

'Not so innocent it would appear,' Adam declared.

'Regrettably not!' Amelia's lips thinned with disapproval. 'But her father is a major. She is of a good family. She swore that Richard protested his love and devotion and that they were secretly betrothed.'

'Which Richard denied.' Adam regarded Amelia sternly. In the past his stepmother had been condemning of his own marriage. She had a strong puritanical streak where morals were concerned, and he was surprised that she had taken such a fervent stance against her son and not condemned Miss Madison.

Amelia regarded him with a determined tilt to her chin. 'Do not for a moment think I approve of what has happened. The girl is young and foolish. But Richard has acted disgracefully. That my son has shown himself to be a seducer and lecher disgusts me. His disappearance but proves his guilt. I will not have him be the ruin of this woman.'

'You are right, of course.' Adam crushed his anger that Richard had brought this fresh scandal upon the family. But the greater disgrace would be to let him escape his duty. 'I shall search for him. I doubt he has gone too far. He has been ashore for two months and could be recalled by the navy at any time. He will face disciplinary action if he is not here to answer their summons.'

Chapter Twenty-four

It was not difficult for Adam to track Richard down. His stepbrother was angry, feeling trapped and hurting at Amelia's revelations. He was probably running scared from the situation he had landed himself in by getting a woman of gentle birth with child, but he would soon realise that there would be nowhere for him to run. Eventually he would be called to service in the navy. If he did not return to duty he would be condemned as a deserter and would be hunted down and shot. He would not risk his life or career. He was a creature of habit and not a man of great imagination. Any flight to join his friends would be an obvious direction for the family to look. With nowhere to safely run, he would seek oblivion for a time from his troubles.

Adam set out for Fowey, the nearest busy seaport. He arrived as the tide made it possible for three ships to dock from their overnight moorings in mid-channel. The quayside was packed with horses and carts waiting to be loaded, the noise of the gulls drowned out by the shouted commands from sailors and dock workers. Normally Adam would have stopped to enjoy the sights of a prosperous port at work. Men ran up gangplanks pushing in front of them barrels of provisions to be stored in the hold for the next voyage, and carts jostled for space near the docks, laden with tin from the local mines to be unloaded on to a vessel. Another ship was disgorging its cargo of heavy wooden crates, which were hoisted ashore by a pulley. The fishing fleet was setting out to sea, whilst a ferryman rowed through the melee taking villagers across the estuary to Polruan on the far shore. Adam's experienced eye scanned the slope of the Polruan shipyard. A lugger and a ketch were under construction, smaller vessels than those now built at Trevowan Hard.

He started his search at the more respectable bawdy houses and taverns. His patience shortened as the establishments became seedier and he still had not discovered anyone who had seen Richard. It was the fifth den of ill repute where he finally achieved success. A woman whose voluptuous figure was tightly corseted and swathed in a gown of scarlet and gold lace ambled towards him. Her auburn wig was adorned with three curling white ostrich plumes, her white-powdered face splattered with black silk patches to hide the blemishes of a skin raddled by a score of years pandering to the demands and pleasure of men. Rouge the colour of a high fever painted her flaccid cheeks and a few stumps of yellowing teeth flashed in a vulpine smile through carmined lips.

'Cap'n Loveday, 'ow 'onoured we be to be graced by your company. Your brother be a regular caller, not so yourself. That we must remedy.'

He bowed to Madame Rosa. 'I am not here for my pleasure but to seek my stepbrother, Mr Allbright.'

'My girls will be disappointed.' She fluttered her lashes and waved her hand towards the row of women in various stages of undress reclining on day beds or lounging against the wall. Although it was little past noon, the bawdy house was filled with sailors. The air was thick with tobacco smoke and the smell of stale ale.

He pressed a gold coin into Madame Rosa's hand, the fleshy fingers of which were indented with semi-precious gems set in tight gold bands. 'Is Mr Allbright here?'

The coin disappeared down the front of her deep cleavage. 'End room at the back upstairs. But are you sure we canna interest you in—'

Ignoring her invitation, Adam pushed past some women seated on the stairs, which creaked at every tread. Their hands roamed across his thighs and groin as they promised an hour of whatever pleasure he desired. The cheap smell of their perfume held no allure, and he wondered at Richard's taste in choosing so lowly a dive.

The corridor was poorly lit with guttering candles, their wax dripping like icicles over the sconces and down the walls to be squashed underfoot on the bare boards. The fetid stench of unwashed bodies and the pervading smell of sex had permeated into the flaking plasterwork of the walls.

The end door was almost in total darkness. Adam flung it open shouting Richard's name. The single candle by the crumpled bed showed the naked figure of a woman snoring drunkenly. Draped across her was Richard's equally comatose figure wearing his shirt but not his breeches. Adam slapped his bare rump.

'Get up! We are going home.'

The whore opened bleary eyes. 'What the . . . I don't do two at once and he's paid for the day.'

'Get out!' Adam ordered her, and picking up a cracked ewer of water by the washing bowl, he threw the contents over Richard.

The woman got equally drenched and reared up, snatching the sheet around her. 'Bastard, what you do that fer?' There were several yellowing bruises along her arms and legs from the fights that frequently broke out between the girls and amongst the customers.

Adam glared at her. 'Leave us. This is my brother.' He flipped a silver coin in her direction, which she caught in mid-air before scrambling from the bed.

Richard was holding his head and groaning. 'Leave me alone, Adam. I'm not going back to the cottage. And I'm not getting married, if that is why you're here.'

'Don't make me drag you from the bed,' Adam warned. He watched in disgust as a cockroach scurried across the wainscot and disappeared under a broken floorboard. There were red marks on Richard's shoulders and legs, testifying to the fleas and bugs inhabiting the bed. 'And you are going to face the music.'

He snatched up the younger man's breeches from the floor and flung them at him. 'I'm ashamed at your conduct, and if I have to give you a thrashing or worse, then I shall be happy to oblige. Good Lord, how could you choose such a squalid establishment? At least at Mrs Merryweather's you know the girls are free of disease. Have you no pride?'

Richard sat up and scowled. 'It's a fitting place for a bastard, wouldn't you say?'

Adam heard the pain in his voice and his anger mounted. 'Wallowing in self-pity solves nothing. You have hardly had a disadvantaged life. No one would question your birth. And it is all more reason for you to stand by your duty to Miss Madison.'

'I'm not a child any more. You can't rule my life.' He squinted against the pain of a hangover pounding through his head.

'In the absence of a father, I am head of the family,' Adam shouted. 'You are a disgrace. You have shamed your name and your honour as an officer and a gentleman. Amelia is distraught.'

Richard held his head to protect it from the buffeting of the harsh words and became truculent. 'She is not even my mother.'

'She is more of a mother to you than I ever knew. She reared you as her own, and if you were not so pig-headed, you would acknowledge that she loves you. Do you intend to shame her, and not only your name but ours?'

Richard rose unsteadily, refusing to look at his stepbrother as he pulled on his breeches and tucked his shirt into the waistband. The linen was stained with sweat and spilled drink.

'You stink like a midden,' Adam snapped. 'You'll come back to Boscabel and get cleaned up before you present yourself to the women.'

'I'll see you all in hell first. I am not going to ruin my life by marrying a stupid whore – a common fortune-huntress out for my riches.' He was petulant and sullen.

'Is that your opinion of your real mother – a whore after your father's money? According to Amelia, Mr Allbright's reputation left much to be desired.' Unable to tolerate Richard's sneering self-pity, Adam's knuckles cracked as they slammed into the younger man's jaw, knocking his stepbrother back on to the bed. Still burning with rage, he grabbed the young officer's shirt and hauled him back on to his feet. 'The eighteen-year-old daughter of a major is an innocent girl and no whore, though you treated her as one.'

'You can't make me marry her.'

'Can I not?' Adam's voice was low and dangerous. 'Would you rather I informed the Admiralty of your true birth? Bastards do not become officers. You would be thrown out of the service and ridiculed by your peers.

Bastards also do not inherit their father's fortunes.'

Richard swung at Adam, but missed and fell back on to the bed. He glared in defiance. 'You would not ruin me. It would kill Amelia if the truth were known. Neither will it do the reputation of your family any good by association. There's enough scandal and speculation over Tristan Loveday and the way St John died.'

'I do not make idle threats,' Adam warned, making another grab at the supine figure. Richard rolled away and stood up on the far side of the bed. Adam flung out an accusing finger. 'Our family will be seen as the benefactors of a child who threw all we had done for him back in our faces. You will face poverty and disgrace. Amelia swallowed her pride to bring you up as her own. Would you repay her by treachery and dishonour? You still have a brilliant career and future ahead of you. Marrying the daughter of a major is a good match. Act with honour and no one will know of your birth. The family is behind me in this.'

Richard dragged a shaking hand through his dishevelled hair. 'So you would all conspire against me?'

'For the good of all, Richard,' Adam snapped.

His bloodshot eyes lost their defiance. With his hair tousled and flopping over his brow, he looked very young and frightened, but Adam had no pity for him. 'Get dressed and deal with this with dignity.'

Richard raised his hands in resignation, although his voice remained sullen. 'Then I had better prepare for my nuptials. I dare say Amelia will take pleasure in making the arrangements for a hasty wedding.'

'It will be done with honour and pride.' Adam flung Richard's jacket at him. 'Do not give me the excuse I would relish to hand you the thrashing you deserve.'

*

To deflect speculation and gossip away from a hasty marriage and the arrival of a baby six months later, a quiet wedding was arranged. The ceremony was to be a discreet service performed by Peter in Launceston. The date and time were conveyed to Miss Madison and Mrs Kellerman, who were advised to be the only two members of their family present. They were to lodge at an inn in the town, and after the service the couple were to leave on honeymoon for a few days in Plymouth. When Richard had returned to Reskelly Cottage, a letter from the Admiralty had been awaiting him, summoning him to report to duty next week.

Adam attended his stepbrother as groomsman, and Senara insisted upon accompanying them, eager to visit her sister and see Bridie's new home. Relations between Richard and Amelia had remained chilly, for Richard still resented being forced into this marriage. In consequence Amelia stayed at home looking after Sara, Adam's younger daughter.

The wedding was arranged for eleven in the forenoon so that the couple could leave for Plymouth the next morning. The Lovedays had arrived in Launceston drenched from travelling through a storm, and the rain continued throughout the afternoon. Launceston was dominated by its ruined castle, the ancient keep and ramparts squatting atop the crest of the steep hill from which all roads wove down to the plain below. The vicarage was opposite the church on the slope of a hill on the outskirts of the town. It was a plain three-storey grey-stone building that was no older than half a century; the previous vicarage had burnt down. The windows and rooms were larger than the parsonage at Polruggan, and were far less gloomy. The house had been well kept and showed no signs of damp or decay, and although it was sparsely furnished, Bridie had ensured that it had a homely atmosphere. However, the district it was situated in had deteriorated in the last century and was now one of the poorer quarters, housing the families of miners, who had a long trek every day to work in the local mines.

Senara felt the fragility of her sister's body as they embraced on meeting. Her black mourning gown accentuated her thinness and pallor. Peter looked equally gaunt. There was a harsher set to his lips and his eyes remained shadowed in his grief for his son. She was relieved that when the couple caught each other's stare, the tenderness remained between them. Adversity had strengthened their bonds, and Bridie was stoical in her acceptance of her loss.

'How do you like your new parish?' Senara asked as Bridie showed her around the vicarage.

'We are still viewed with suspicion as incomers, though some of the women recognised me from market days, when I came here to sell the lace made by the women local to Polruggan.'

'Will you start up the same venture here?'

'I suggested it but met with little response. There is more employment within the town for the women. I take the Bible classes and have helped some with their reading. I thought to work with adults who are illiterate, as there is a school in the town for the children, but I have only two who occasionally attend. These things take trust and time.'

'And how does Peter view his congregation?'

'They are sadly much given to spending most of their wages on drinking. He has delivered some fiery sermons and has mounted a crusade to reclaim lost sinners to the fold.'

'That sounds more like the Peter of old. Has he regained his zeal along with his faith?'

Bridie shrugged. 'His faith remains tested, but he would improve the lot of the poor and educate them with his sermons to spend more of their income on food rather than cheap ale and gin. It has not made him popular.'

'I expect not. The poor drink to escape the misery of their poverty and long hours of labour.'

Seeing Senara's frown, Bridie smiled. 'Do not worry about us. There is much that can be done for the parish when they learn to trust us. Now you must tell me all about this young lady that Richard is to marry. Adam's letter delivered by Billy Brown on market day was a surprise.'

'I am sure you must have guessed the reason for the haste. Miss Madison is with child and Richard has been reluctant to stand by her, though she is young and innocent and from a good family. Let us pray that they will find happiness together. I have not met Miss Madison, but Amelia said she seems amiable and obviously has spirit to have sought out her seducer rather than face her shame alone.'

'Will she live at Reskelly Cottage whilst Richard is at sea?'

'That is yet to be decided. She has sisters in Dorchester. Richard may set her up in a cottage and have one of them live with them. It can be a lonely life as a naval wife.'

Richard had spent his last evening of freedom getting gloriously drunk and Adam had carried him unconscious to his bed. Now, as they waited at the church, the groom was deathly pale and sat in the front pew with his head in his hands, his eyes closed against the pounding pain of his hangover.

Adam took out his hunter and glanced back over the pews to where his wife and her sister hovered anxiously by the door. Senara caught his stare and shook her head.

'What time is it?' Richard groaned.

'It wants five minutes to noon.' Adam replied.

Richard stood up. 'I've been jilted. They are not coming.'

'Give it five more minutes. Perhaps they have mistaken the time of the service.'

Richard glared at his stepbrother. 'The damned woman has made a fool of us.'

'Why should she do that? Something must have happened.' Adam guessed that Richard was looking for an excuse to abandon the wedding.

'She could have lost the child and decided to keep her shame secret.' Richard's tone was brighter than it had been for some days.

'That does not excuse that you dishonoured her.' The shackles Adam had put on his temper were rapidly sliding loose.

'I have a ship waiting for me at Plymouth. This nonsense has gone on long enough.' Richard marched towards the exit, and Adam stormed after him, grabbing his arm and spinning him round.

'You are not running away, Richard.'

'Running away from what? A scheming minx who has played me for a fool!' He shrugged off the bruising hold and straightened his jacket.

'We will wait until quarter after the hour,' Adam reasoned. 'Then we have stood by our side of the bargain.'

He did not mention that when last night he had visited the inn where he had booked a room for the two women to ensure that they had arrived safely, they were not there.

Chapter Twenty-five

Emma Madison was locked in a blind panic. Waves of nausea had been assaulting her ever since they boarded the coach engaged by Adam Loveday to convey them to Launceston. She had spent a miserable few weeks living with Lydia in Bodmin. Despite the lowering presence of the prison, which dominated one end of the town, she found the people friendly when she ventured into the streets. But for the most part they lived in seclusion, so that no difficult questions could be asked of her status and family. Every day she was on edge, waiting to receive the summons. She was terrified that Richard would not marry her. Her faith in him had been destroyed by his cruel words in Bath. What would happen to her if he abandoned her? She could never return to Dorchester. Any chance of her sisters finding husbands would be blighted by the shame she had brought upon her name. And if her father learned of her disgrace, he would disown her.

Just the thought of the alternatives that awaited her in the future filled her with terror. She would not be able to hide her pregnancy much longer. With no one to support her, the horrors of the workhouse loomed closer. Or she could live in secret and when the baby arrived leave it on the steps of an orphanage. But she knew she could not condemn her own flesh and blood to a life of uncertainty and probably abject poverty. Lydia had spoken of places in the country where a wetnurse would raise the child, providing she received a regular payment. Again such a route seemed heartless and callous. She had felt the baby move within her, a life blossoming and dependent on her, trusting her to safeguard its future and provide the best she could for its life. Could she live with the guilty secret of deserting her child? Would not such a sin cast her into everlasting hell? How could she have been so stupid as to believe Richard's lies? How many other innocent women had ruined their lives by placing their trust in a lecher bent only upon his own gratification? Those images and fears invaded her sleep and together with the pregnancy had drained her of energy. Even the sickness would not go away, adding to her misery.

Then the summons had come and hope had flared that all would be well. Yet fate continued to punish her. Her sickness had made travelling a nightmare and they had been forced to stop every few miles for her to alight and vomit into a ditch. The constant rain had added to her wretchedness as the road churned into a quagmire and the coach lurched violently in deep ruts hidden by flooding.

Her stomach and throat were raw from heaving, and by late yesterday she had been too weak to travel further. They had stopped at an inn some miles from Launceston. Her intention had been to rise early and continue her journey in the morning so that they would arrive at their destination in plenty of time for the wedding. But the torrential rain had continued through the night, and although the morning had dawned with a clear, bright sky, in many places where streams crossed the road, the way had remained flooded and their passage had been slow. Then, two miles from Launceston, disaster had struck. The driver was easing the horses slowly through a ford that had swollen to a dangerously high level across the road. Halfway across, the coach had lurched to one side and there was an ominous splitting of wood.

The women were thrown forward and struggled to regain their seating, which was difficult due to the acute angle of the floor. Lydia held on to the door and managed to help Emma on to the seat.

'Are you unharmed, my dear?'

Emma nodded. 'I am just shaken.'

'That fool of a coachman could have lost you the baby,' Lydia groaned as she peered out of the window.

The driver was standing in the middle of the highway calming the horses, which were prancing nervously.

'You could have killed us!' Lydia shouted in her fury. 'How long before we can continue? We were due in Launceston last night. It is urgent we are delayed no longer.'

The man continued to calm the horses for some moments before walking back to the coach, which listed at an angle. 'We won't be going anywhere this morning. Wheel's broke. Nearest wheelwright be Launceston.'

'But the wedding,' Emma gasped. 'I am to be married in an hour.'

He shrugged. 'Nothing I can do. It be a fair way to walk and the road be all washed out. Best you wait in the coach. Happen someone will come along soon and get you to town.'

Emma burst into tears. 'We will never make the church on time.'

'It is not much further.' Lydia tried to calm her cousin, who could not control her hysteria. 'A cart will come along and give us a ride. This is the main road to Launceston. You must calm yourself, my dear, or you will harm yourself and the child.'

'If we are late, Richard will think I have jilted him and all will be lost,' Emma sobbed. 'He will leave town and I shall be abandoned.'

'He will do no such thing. The family will hear that the roads are flooded and guess we have had trouble on our journey,' Lydia consoled, although her own face was drawn and anxious. 'Of course the Lovedays will wait for your arrival. In your condition they know you would not miss the wedding.'

Her words caused Emma to cry harder. 'But what if Richard does not love me? He did not want this marriage. All is lost, I know it. How could fate be so cruel?' She was close to swooning.

'Take deep breaths, my dear,' Lydia ordered.

'I have to marry him.' Emma was trembling in her panic. 'I have to. Papa will kill me if he learns of my disgrace. His regiment will not stay in India for ever.'

Lydia wiped her cousin's eyes. 'Do you want to ruin your looks? You are worrying needlessly. A cart will come along soon. Parson Loveday is to perform the service. Richard has a special licence. You can marry tomorrow. Richard will not abandon you. Dry your tears. You do not want to arrive with your eyes red and your face swollen.'

Emma groaned and put her hand to her mouth. She just managed to get her head outside the window before she was sick again.

'Take heart, my dear.' Lydia patted her hand and waved her smelling salts under the younger woman's nose. 'I can see a farmer coming in his cart. It looks to be empty. We will pay him to take us to town if he is not going that way. He will take pity on a bride, I am sure.'

Emma allowed herself hope as the cheerful farmer helped them on to the cart. 'You on your way to be wed? Looks like the weather is gonna be fine for the rest of the day. Don't you worry none. I'll get you there, you see if I don't.'

He flicked the reins, and after negotiating the ford they set off at a pace that threatened to jolt every bone in the women's bodies.

'Not so fast, sir.' Lydia clung to the side. 'I am in a delicate condition. Please, sir. A little slower if you will.' After having gone to such lengths the last weeks to avoid any gossip about Emma's condition, she did not want the farmer either refusing them aid by judging Emma a fallen woman, or tittle-tattling to his family that the bride was in the family way. Better if he thought it was herself.

'The bride do look a bit peaky,' the farmer snorted.

'And why should she not? She is all overset with nerves that she will be late,' Lydia reprimanded fiercely.

Emma closed her eyes as they rattled along and prayed that there would be no more delays. As they climbed the slope into town, the road became more crowded, and when they entered the main street, a herd of cattle was blocking the road.

'We will walk from here,' Emma announced. Her heart was pounding in her chest and she was struggling to keep her nausea under control. They had to push their way through the solid mass of cattle, their bodies jostled and bruised. The pedestrians crowding the busy town were little better, and once Emma was almost knocked to the ground. It took them another twenty minutes to find the church, and as they entered, Emma was holding her side, which had knotted into a stitch.

The chill interior of the church was deserted. Emma

let out a long wail and sank to the cold flagstones, inconsolable in her tears.

'I am undone. Richard never intended to wed me.'

'They will be at the vicarage,' Lydia declared stoutly.

'I cannot go on. I feel so ill.' Emma clutched her side, too weak and exhausted to rise.

'Then rest in a pew,' Lydia encouraged. 'I will go to the vicarage. Do not despair. All will be well. You will be married today.'

Lydia Kellerman hurried next door to the vicarage and rapped loudly on the knocker. Expecting a servant to answer, she was taken aback when a tall, handsome, elegantly dressed man opened the door.

'Parson Loveday?' she queried.

'Captain Loveday at your service.' His sharp eyes studied her agitated state, adding, 'Miss Madison?'

Lydia bobbed a curtsy and explained breathlessly, 'I am Mrs Kellerman. Miss Madison is in the church. She is quite overcome. The weather delayed us, and this morning the coach broke a wheel. Where is Mr Allbright?'

Adam digested this news with dismay. 'We had better fetch Miss Madison,' he said softly. 'Has she been taken ill? Does she need a physician?'

'There has been delay enough,' the woman answered with a challenging glare. 'She needs a husband, not a physician. Please inform Mr Allbright that we are here. I take it that Parson Loveday can still perform the service and has not been called away?'

Adam hesitated. 'The wedding was to take place two hours ago. Mr Allbright was greatly distressed that Miss Madison left him standing at the altar.'

'But it could not be helped.' Lydia now fought to keep her own panic from her voice.

'There is no easy way to say this.' Captain Loveday

cleared his throat in embarrassment. 'Mr Allbright has left town for Plymouth, where he has been ordered by the Admiralty to report for duty.'

'But surely there was to be a honeymoon and he would report for duty next week,' Lydia protested. 'He must have known that Miss Madison would not have forsaken him.' Her face mirrored her horror. 'When did he leave? He could not have gone far. He must be brought back.'

Hearing the raised voices, Bridie had come to the door to investigate. Adam briefly explained what had happened.

'Take Mrs Kellerman into the parlour.' Bridie took charge. 'I will bring Miss Madison from the church. She will need a moment or so to compose herself. Then over tea we will discuss what must be done.'

It was half an hour before Bridie appeared with Miss Madison. Adam was relieved to see that the woman was composed, although she remained very pale. She looked very young, with a frail beauty and vulnerability. Nothing suggested the calculating wiles Richard would have had them believe.

'My dear, all has been arranged,' Mrs Kellerman quickly asserted. 'There is nothing for you to distress yourself further over.' She then introduced the Loveday family to Emma before informing her, 'Captain and Mr Loveday will accompany us in their coach to Plymouth. They still have the special licence, and Mr Loveday will marry you and Richard before he reports for duty. All will be well.'

Emma sank gratefully on to a sofa. 'It is all my fault. I was so ill yesterday we could not complete our journey. Richard must be angry with me.'

'He will understand,' Adam consoled. He did not

elaborate that Richard had been in a towering fury when his bride had left him at the altar and stormed out of Launceston, refusing to listen to reason that he should postpone his departure for another day so that they could ascertain if she had been unavoidably delayed.

'The woman has made a laughing stock of us.' Richard had turned his anger on Adam. 'I would not marry her now for all the money in the King's treasury.'

Miss Madison was visibly struggling to retain her composure. 'I am ready to leave as soon as you are, Captain Loveday. Though I do not believe my betrothed will be pleased that we pursue him. If he had loved me, he would have stayed to ensure that no harm had come upon me.'

'Love grows in time,' Senara observed. 'None of this is your fault, Miss Madison.'

'Yet fate conspires against us.'

'And God is on the side of the righteous, Miss Madison,' Peter declared.

Although Miss Madison had appeared tearful on their first meeting, Adam was relieved that as soon as she entered the coach and they began their journey to Plymouth she was much restored in spirit. She did however remain quiet and subdued, although Mrs Kellerman's constant chatter was so relentless she never paused for breath to give another the chance to speak.

'Captain Loveday, you have been most understanding throughout this whole unsavoury affair.' She kept repeating the same praise. 'Although one must say that we have been vastly disappointed in the failure of Mr Allbright to honour his obligations. This last unseemly flight from Launceston shows a distressing reluctance to do the honourable thing by my cousin.'

'He was at the church at the agreed time,' Adam pointedly reminded her. 'A young man's pride is quick to wound in matters of the heart. He felt humiliated in front of his family.'

'He left in undue haste,' Mrs Kellerman pursued.

'Please, Lydia. Mr Allbright was justified in believing I had forsaken him.' Emma Madison defended her lover, though her eyes were shadowed as she fought against her own fears. 'There have been misunderstandings enough without further recriminations.'

'You are too loyal to your sweetheart, Emma. But that is no failing.'

'Indeed not, Mrs Kellerman.' Adam smiled at the younger woman, who was putting on such a brave and uncomplaining face. His admiration for her grew. There was an innocence and trust about her nature that she would certainly need in dealing with Richard in the future. He was disheartened at how shamelessly his stepbrother had used those qualities to seduce her.

The navy could be the making or the breaking of a man and the officers were no exception. Richard had changed greatly from the idealistic youth who had joined as a midshipman. There was no disputing his courage, for eighteen months ago he had been grievously wounded in serving his country. That the incident had resulted in his addiction to morphine showed a weaker side to his character. Also with maturity he had become more arrogant; the power wielded by officers over the common seamen often corrupted men who believed themselves invincible in their control of others.

Adam acknowledged that Mrs Kellerman was right in her opinion that Richard had fled his responsibilities in Launceston too quickly. His flight had the urgency of desperation to escape the consequences of his actions. Yet

Miss Madison was attractive and had so far in her manner shown a sweetness of nature. He had every reason to suspect that she would make Richard a good wife. Whether Richard would return the same courtesy towards her was another matter.

There was also the matter of finding Richard in the sprawling, busy port. All the precautions the family had taken to avoid gossip concerning the speed of the marriage would come to naught if Richard were found carousing with friends. Adam suspected that the young officer would not continue to Plymouth today. He was festering with resentment; he was more likely to get drunk at a nearby inn. There was a slim chance that if this was the case, they would discover him on the road and their task could still be accomplished without too much delay.

Adam had ordered Jasper Fraddon to stop at every wayside inn so that he could go inside to search for Richard. The eighth inn they passed, in a hamlet of nine cottages and a small church, yielded success. They were over halfway to Plymouth and within an hour it would be dark. The inn looked respectable and would prove suitable enough for the ladies to take a room for the night. Adam had entered first and discovered his stepbrother in his cups sitting in a darkened corner with a barmaid on his lap. Richard scowled as Adam approached the table.

'Get rid of the woman,' Adam ordered. 'I have not come alone.'

Richard pushed the barmaid away from him. 'Bring my brother a quart of your best ale.' He stared belligerently across the table. 'We've said all there is to be said. Why the devil have you followed me?'

'Can you not guess? Miss Madison and Mrs Kellerman

are in the coach, and also Peter. There is a church over the road. If it is open, you can say your vows.'

'I played my part. I will not be made a fool of by that hussy,' Richard slurred.

Adam grabbed him by his necktie and hauled him up out of the seat. 'You'll marry the woman. I meant what I said about informing the Admiralty of your perfidy if you refuse. You will not be received by decent society and the scandal will follow you through life.'

'But I was left standing at the church.'

'Your fiancée had been taken ill the day before the wedding and this morning their coach broke its axel, delaying them further. There will be no more prevarication.'

Their gazes locked in silent combat. Richard was weaving unsteadily on his feet. 'Was ever a man more beset with ill fortune?'

'It is Miss Madison who had the misfortune to meet you,' Adam accused. 'At least have the grace to conduct yourself with dignity.

Richard stood to attention and saluted, his voice slurred. 'Aye, aye, Captain. Lead me to the slaughter.'

Adam marched him outside to where Miss Madison and Mrs Kellerman had remained in the coach. Richard opened the door of the vehicle and bent in an elaborate bow. He held out his hand to the younger woman, who was staring at him with apprehension. 'Miss Madison, it appears my resilient brother has at his means the facilities for us to be wed after all. I trust you have recovered from your indisposition.' The words were cuttingly polite and without warmth.

Emma Madison flinched and nodded. Adam could feel her tension.

Mrs Kellerman stepped down into the inn yard. 'Let us

delay no longer. Mr Loveday is waiting in the church.'

It was like no wedding Adam had ever attended. Peter had secured permission from the church's minister to perform the marriage. Richard remained rebellious and sullenly mumbled his vows. Miss Madison whispered them so quietly Peter had twice to ask her to repeat them.

When the ceremony was over, the party walked back to the inn in silence. Fortunately the establishment had a parlour where they could take their meal in private. The conversation remained stilted throughout, with Richard continuing to drink heavily.

'Where will you provide a house for your wife, Lieutenant Allbright?' Mrs Kellerman broke through the strained silence.

Emma hung her head. Ignored by Richard, she had picked at her food and was again looking as though she would burst into tears. Under cover of the table Adam kicked the groom and shot him a warning glare to be more sociable.

'I assumed that Emma would reside at Reskelly Cottage,' he replied. 'It will enable Mama to become acquainted with my wife.'

'That is one option.' Adam struggled to keep his anger from his voice. 'But the cottage is rather overcrowded as it is. An establishment of your own would be more fitting.'

'Emma is always welcome to stay with me. Or I could visit when Lieutenant Allbright is away at sea. The life of a naval officer's wife can be lonely,' offered Mrs Kellerman with a satisfied air.

Richard gave a derisory laugh. 'You have proved how inadequately you protect a woman's reputation. I would not have the honour of my wife's name called into question by further association with yourself, Mrs Kellerman.'

'That is unfair.' Emma found her voice to defend her cousin. 'Lydia is my friend.'

'An unworthy one in my opinion,' Richard returned. 'Mama will help you look for a suitable home for us if I am given a ship. What did you think of Bodmin?'

'I liked it well enough,' Emma replied dutifully.

Richard nodded, apparently satisfied. He rose and held out his hand towards his wife. 'We will retire now, Mrs Allbright.'

Emma took her husband's hand dutifully and allowed him to lead her to their chamber.

Adam raised his glass in a belated toast. 'To the happiness of the couple.'

'Amen,' said Peter.

Adam turned his attention upon Mrs Kellerman, who now appeared ill at ease in their company. He bowed to her. 'I suggest you also retire to your room. The inn can become rowdy of an evening. Tomorrow we will return to Launceston, where I will procure a hired coach to return you to Bath.'

Peter glanced wearily at the staircase where the couple had disappeared. 'Not an auspicious start to a marriage.'

'If Richard has any sense he will make the best of it,' Adam snapped. 'Emma seems a better match than he deserves and is still half in love with him despite my brother's surliness. Time apart will give him a chance to come to terms with his marriage.'

Chapter Twenty-six

Tristan walked slowly around the warehouse filled with the French furniture he had imported from *Good Fortune's* recent voyage. He had bought land between Fowey and the Loveday shipyard, where the river was still deep enough to navigate, and had built a jetty and warehouse. He also employed a chief clerk to run the office and a carter to deliver the goods. His clerk had already prepared an inventory and catalogue to be sent to customers likely to be interested in his wares. That last voyage had shown him a great many possibilities for his future. The forged papers and money he had deposited in a reputable bank would ensure his entrée to the circles he needed in the future. His French was flawless from his years living in France when he had fled England after St John's lies had destroyed his chances of being accepted by the Loveday family.

His eyes narrowed at the memories of those first years in France. Living in St Malo, he had taken a French wife, and he could now pass as easily as a peasant or a nobleman when the need arose. That wife was long gone, dying on board ship after they had fled France at the height of the troubles. The marriage had given him his first fortune, for she had been the only child of his employer, a merchant, and his years with the company had taught him all there was to know about trading. But that money had dissipated in the years he had spent travelling through Europe and succumbing to the decadence and debauchery of Venice. Facing bankruptcy, he had fled Europe and after travelling through the Caribbean had finally ended up in Boston, where he had met his second wife, another heiress. But he had never forgotten his roots in England and planned always to return and prove to the Lovedays his innocence and St John's treachery. With the war with France continuing, his wife had been reluctant to undertake so dangerous a voyage. Living a life of wealth and ease in Boston, Tristan had been content in those years to enjoy the privileges of the New World. But when his second wife and son had drowned in a yachting accident during a sudden squall, he had been driven to return to England and prove to the Lovedays that he was not only their equal but also their superior. With an English estate he wanted a wife and heir – and not just any wife. It must be a woman with wealth and position. And in these times, a man of ruthless ambition and courage could carve his own destiny if he was not afraid of the consequences. Boldness had served him well in recent years. It would not fail him now.

His friendship with the French aristocrats during their stay in England led to many salon doors opening to him. The exiled noblemen plotted for a return of the monarchy, which would ensure the reinstatement of their estates and position. But with Napoleon's star in the ascendancy, Tristan did not believe that the time was right for a counter-revolution. Other Frenchmen in exile were of the same opinion. They were concerned that the valuables they had hastily hidden before their flight abroad would be discovered and forever lost to them.

Many of those men had commissioned Tristan to make investigations as to the condition of their estates; some had trusted him enough to confide the whereabouts of those valuables and paid him well for returning the treasure to them. It was a profitable enterprise and he charged a high fee for the work undertaken, which was not without its dangers.

In later years he had travelled to Paris and formed links with the supporters of the Directory. Napoleon's star was brighter than ever. During his last visit to Paris, Tristan had overheard Lord Whitworth, the British ambassador, intimating that the First Consul was set upon establishing himself as emperor. The mood in the capital was one of enforced gaiety, but underlying it was a sense of deep-rooted suspicion. Furtive glances were cast over shoulders and caution was taken in expressing allegiance, for no one could be certain they were not being spied upon. Bonaparte had elevated his family, but they were unpopular, with their ostentatious show of riches and haughty demands for precedence. Behind the scenes the Royalists continued to plot.

Tristan admired Napoleon's ambition and expertise, which had enabled him to rise from an impoverished corporal to First Consul. That First Consul would now be ruler of his country. His ability to command and organise was undisputed, but he was not popular with the people. Too many heavy taxes had been imposed and a ruthless will to conscript into his formidable army made many regard him as a tyrant. The new regime was built on the shaky foundations of the revolution and all the terrors that had been sketchily papered over. It was not enough for Napoleon that France could rise from the ashes of its past; it must also conquer and subjugate Europe. When he rode through the streets in a military parade there were few cheers. Too many of the populace had lost their brothers and sons in his merciless war machine, in which lives were sacrificed as cannon fodder.

Tristan had taken a calculated gamble in giving his support to the French Royalist cause. It held the highest risk and the chance of the greatest rewards. Once *Good Fortune* was reprovisioned, he would return to France with Brienne on a secret mission.

'Be sure that you treat your new wife with respect and tenderness.' Adam took Richard aside as the couple prepared to leave for their honeymoon. 'This marriage may have started inauspiciously, but it is within your power to make it a success or a living hell.'

Emma was saying her farewells to Lydia and looked far from happy.

Richard snorted with derision. 'That is easy for you to say. You married the woman you loved.'

'Stop resenting the mess you have made of your life and do not blame your bride,' Adam retaliated, barely resisting the urge to shake some sense into his stepbrother. 'Look at Emma and count your blessings. She is beautiful, accomplished, sweet natured and for her sins is clearly still smitten with the boorish oaf she married. Win over that sweet nature, Richard. A happy and compliant wife will make your home a haven. If you continue in the navy, much of your time will be spent at sea. Provide your wife with a home to be proud of, a dress allowance that befits her station, children to occupy her time and upon whom she can lavish her affection, and you will reap the rewards of your consideration. Is that too much to ask?'

'You sound like Pious Peter,' Richard said cuttingly. He bowed with equal sarcasm. 'I would stay for more of your sermon but I have to report for duty. Mrs Allbright can return to Trewenna with you.'

'She is now your responsibility. You are on honeymoon. Even if you are to join a ship, it will be some time before it is provisioned and ready to sail. I advise you to use that time wisely and leave your wife on loving terms. If you then wish her to live at Boscabel or Reskelly Cottage, we will all make her welcome.'

For the first hour of the journey the couple sat in an uncomfortable silence, and although Emma's head was turned away from him, Richard was aware of the occasional sob that shook her figure. Adam's words burned through his brain. He might have derided his stepbrother's advice but he could not deny that his words made sense. Since he was now saddled with an unwanted wife, it would be wise to make the best of the circumstances. Last night Emma had at least proved her eagerness to please him and be a dutiful and biddable wife.

They were the only passengers beside an elderly gentleman who had fallen asleep within minutes of the post-chaise leaving and was snoring loudly. Richard took Emma's hand and gently squeezed it.

'A thousand pardons, my love. I have acted like a boorish clod. I never could abide being told I was in the wrong.'

It was a poor apology, but Emma seized upon it. 'You do not hate me?'

'How could I hate a woman of such beauty? You know I was lost the first time I saw you.' The lies tripped easily off his tongue. He kissed her gloved hand. 'Let us put the past weeks behind us and start anew.'

Her smile had been so easily won, he wondered if he had not wedded a simpleton. The pleading in her eyes was pathetically eager. Richard had always favoured the chase rather than the winning. Even so, he put his misgivings behind him. A fawning wife was a biddable wife in his opinion. If she was so eager to accept his lies as truth, his marriage might not contain the shackles he feared. He would be magnanimous and keep her sweet with the words she wanted to hear. In a few weeks he would again be at sea and every port would provide him with a new conquest.

Unfortunately, when they arrived in Plymouth the Admiralty had other ideas. Instead of a ship, he had been given indefinite shore leave. It meant he could no longer defer making permanent arrangements for his wife. He was still angry with his mother for her interference. Although it would have been an easy option for Emma to live with Amelia at Reskelly Cottage, the accommodation there would be cramped with so many women. Also he would be constantly under his mother's scrutiny. Upon his marriage he had come into his inheritance and could now afford to live wherever he chose. He would have preferred to take a house in Plymouth or Falmouth, but realised that whilst he continued his naval career he would be spending many months away from Emma at sea.

He finally settled upon a house in Bodmin where the family could visit Emma. As they waited for the lawyer to sign the final papers, Emma became agitated.

'Is this house really what you want?' she burst out in a rush, her eyes flashing with a defiance she had not shown since her marriage.

'Do you not like it?'

'The house is lovely but it is so far from anyone I know. Could we not live closer to your family? Your mama was very kind to me.'

'Mama can visit when I am away. She will wish to be involved with her grandchild.' He brushed aside her request. 'You will have three servants who will look after your every need. And much to occupy you. More furniture is needed for our house and new hangings to be selected and made.'

'But what of when you rejoin your ship? You could be away for months or even years. Would you then allow me to have Lydia to stay? You do not approve much of her.'

Richard frowned. 'She was a bad influence on you.'

'But I do not know anyone in Bodmin.' Emma tried to be brave but was daunted by the thought of living in a strange town without people she knew around her. Although Richard's family had been welcoming and she had particularly liked Bridie and Senara, they did not live close enough to visit often. She was also in awe of Amelia and had sensed the older woman's disapproval of her condition, although she had insisted on the marriage. If Amelia were to visit Bodmin she would expect to stay for some days, and that prospect filled Emma with trepidation. 'If you do not approve of Lydia, could not my younger sister Meredith stay with me when you are away? You have yet to meet my sisters. They do not know that we have married. It would be a wonderful surprise if we could visit them.'

'It is not convenient to travel to Dorchester.' Richard certainly did not want another gaggle of women gossiping about the wedding and the baby.

'A visit would take only two or three days, if you did not wish to stay. Meredith could return with us.'

Richard was about to protest when he considered that having Emma occupied with a sister would stop her prying too closely into his own activities in the town.

'Very well, it is only right I should meet your family.

And Meredith must be prepared to return with us. We will have a seamstress call today. You may choose all you need for a trousseau and some new gowns.'

She flung her arms around his neck and kissed him. 'I love you, Richard. You are so kind and generous.'

If that were all it took to keep his wife happy, then mayhap marriage would not be as onerous as he had feared.

Chapter Twenty-seven

It was a day's carriage ride to Dorchester, and as they would not arrive until the light was fading, Richard took rooms at the King's Arms. On arrival Emma had written to her sisters to tell them of her marriage and to prepare them for their visit in the morning. Her home was on the outskirts of the town. She wanted to give them time to prepare the house so that it looked its best for Richard. She was nervous that he would find it lacking the comforts and luxury he was used to. On her original visit to Amelia she had first gone to Trevowan and had been surprised at the vastness of the estate and the splendour of the house. It had been a shock to discover that the home had recently been lost to the family and that Richard and his mother now resided at Reskelly Cottage. Yet although the size of that residence was similar to her own home, the quality of the furniture and furnishings had been far superior. Although her husband had not discussed his finances with her, she had heard that he owned several properties in expensive districts of London. Would he despise her more lowly childhood home? Her father's rank of major made him more than her husband's equal, for Richard's father had been a lawyer.

She tried to brush her anxiety aside but it continued to nag at her. Her relationship with Richard this last week had been like the first days of his courtship. She was proud of her handsome naval lieutenant, and when he was in a good mood his charm and wit were infectious. She was also relieved that nothing of her pregnancy showed. Her elder sisters would be scathing in their condemnation and would be quick to write to their father with their criticism. At least with the major in India she would be spared the violence of his fury. To calm her thudding heart she smoothed the front of her burgundy velvet pelisse, which matched her military-style hat. Her gown was pale green silk, its hem and neck embroidered with burgundy leaves. The gold and garnet necklace, earrings and bracelet, sent to her as a wedding gift from Amelia, complemented her attire.

The carriage drew up outside the limestone house set back from the main road into Dorchester. They were a half-mile from the town's limits and a dozen pretty cottages with well-tended gardens lined the highway. The small parish church could easily hold the community of fifty souls who also attended from the surrounding farms.

As Richard alighted to hand Emma down from the carriage, there was a squeal of delight and a fair-haired young woman ran out of the house to embrace his wife. Her russet gown was high-necked and shapeless and a cream shawl was draped over the short sleeves.

'How wonderful to see you, Emma,' the young woman squealed. 'Though I am heartbroken you did not invite us to your wedding. It was too cruel to make us miss such a grand occasion.' Her enthusiasm and vivaciousness bubbled over as she hugged her elder sister.

'It all happened so quickly, Meredith,' Emma laughed. 'Was it love at first sight and Lieutenant Allbright swept you off your feet?' Meredith giggled infectiously and Richard found himself smiling.

'Something like that,' he teased. The young woman could not be more than a year older than Rowena and was already a beauty, but whereas Rowena displayed a knowingness of the power her looks could hold over men, Meredith was delightfully fresh and innocent.

They were interrupted by a sterner voice. 'Bring yourselves inside. I would not have us as a spectacle for the whole of the village.' In the doorway stood a prim woman some years older than Emma, with her dun-coloured hair pulled back in a tight chignon. There was no welcome in her eyes, only disapproval. 'Meredith, you are making an exhibition of yourself.'

Richard glanced at his wife and saw her pale. She had told him little of her family, except that they were strict Wesleyan. The grim-faced woman in her unflattering brown gown with no adornment looked puritanical. Richard was not about to tolerate any criticism when he had already faced so much from his own family. Pride made him sweep off his hat and bow to the two women, affecting his most charming smile.

'Cupid's arrow flew straight to my heart as soon as I met Emma.' He took his wife's arm in the manner of the most doting of husbands. 'Fearing I would soon be recalled to my ship, I could not bear to leave England without making her my wife. It was a whirl-wind romance. May I present myself to you? Lieutenant Richard Allbright of His Majesty's Navy at your service.'

'Better late than never, I suppose,' snapped the older woman, glaring at Emma as she stood back for the couple to enter the dwelling. 'We heard of this wild escapade from Cousin Lydia. There is only one reason why a couple marry in such haste. Have you brought disgrace to us, Emma?'

They had entered a dark and gloomy hallway, which was chilly and uninviting. Richard felt his wife trembling and countered protectively, 'With respect, Miss Madison, you insult both my wife and myself by your accusation.'

'Temperance, can you not be more welcoming?' Emma begged. 'We are all family.'

'And who are these two delightful creatures?' Richard ignored Temperance Madison, who could not have been more inaccurately named, and turned his smile upon the two younger women.

'This is Meredith, who was so enthusiastic in her welcome.' Emma laughed. 'And this is my sister Clemency.'

A darker-haired version of Emma curtsied to Richard. He knew she was only three years older than Emma, but there was already a matronly air about her manner. 'Cousin Lydia said that Lieutenant Allbright was handsome and charming. She was not mistaken. Welcome to our home, Lieutenant.' Although the words were genial, there was a brittleness to her tone, which had an unpleasant ring. 'You have come at an opportune time. Though you will find us not quite as you expect us.'

Unaccountably, Richard felt a stab of unease. There were undercurrents of tension and something malicious surrounding their arrival. He had not expected them to fall on him with affection, but he had thought they would be excited for Emma. Even Meredith had now grown silent and subdued and was tugging at the shawl around her upper arms. He squared his shoulders, continuing to feel the hostility emanating from the two older women as they walked into the sunny morning room. He had a brief impression of a sparsely furnished parlour devoid of the usual female adornments of flowers and ornaments. A colossus of a man stood in front of the unlit hearth, legs planted firmly apart and bull neck thrust aggressively forward. His broad face with its flamboyant white moustache and side-whiskers was red with anger. His bulbous eyes narrowed and were as condemning as any assize judge pronouncing the death sentence.

Richard felt his smile freeze on his lips and a rush of icy dread pervaded his body. Emma gasped with alarm.

'Papa!'

'So this is the knave who seduced my daughter with a false promise of marriage and then sought to jilt her,' Major Madison barked.

'Papa, you insult Richard. We are married,' protested Emma, her expression tight with fear.

'Not without extreme coercion from his family, so it would appear,' the officer returned. 'I had not expected to learn on my return to England that one of my daughters had become a whore.'

'Papa, what lies have you heard?' Emma drew closer to Richard.

'Silence. Your shame goes before you.' Major Madison scowled, his colour heightening. 'As for this knave—'

'Papa, there has been a misunderstanding,' Emma protested.

The major snorted in disbelief, his glare bayoneting Richard. 'Do you let your wife speak for you? What manner of churl are you, sir? What have you to say for yourself? Speak up.' With the force of a bully he rapped out belligerently, drowning Richard's answer, 'Did you think to seduce her and discard the foolish girl, believing she had no male to protect her whilst I served abroad?'

'You could not be more wrong, Major Madison,'

Richard forced out from a mouth leached of all moisture. 'During our courtship I was recalled by the Admiralty. I had no choice but to obey. And there had also been two tragic deaths in my family. The plans for the wedding were delayed.'

A movement behind them revealed a pale spectre edging into the room. Lydia Kellerman had a black eye and a swollen and cut lip. Her arm was also in a sling.

'I am sorry, Emma,' she said in a quavering voice.

Richard summed up the woman. She had clearly been beaten. His anger erupted towards the bully who had used brutality to vent his own fury. He could feel the malevolence of the family closing in upon them. Clemency was now openly smirking. She had Emma's beauty but none of her sweet nature. Temperance was sucking in her prim lips, relishing the prospect of Emma receiving the same treatment from their father for her wanton behaviour. Meredith was sobbing and obviously terrified. Only Emma did not cower. She was trembling, but from indignation not fear. Such courage raised her in Richard's estimation.

He moved to stand protectively in front of his wife, eyeing Major Madison with all the arrogance of a naval officer who regarded the undisciplined troops of the army as little more than scum. The navy had brought glory and greatness to England. They were the senior service. It was the navy who had brought the upstart Napoleon to heel at the Battle of the Nile. It was the navy who defended the nation's shores from invasion. This man might be his superior in rank, but in Richard's opinion he did not match him in status.

He puffed out his chest and clicked the heels of his top boots together as he stood to attention. 'I am not one of your subordinates, Major Madison. And take care how you address my wife. I would have no slur cast upon her name. What manner of knave beats a woman to gain information? Mrs Kellerman was not aware of many of the facts surrounding my courtship of your daughter.'

'She knew enough to learn that she was pregnant when you deserted her.' Madison lashed him with his disgust. 'I did not raise her to become a whore. She is no daughter of mine.'

'Papa!' A wail of distress was torn from Emma.

'Take the strumpet out of my sight. I never want to see her again,' her father raged.

'Papa, please,' Emma begged. 'Richard is a man of honour from a good family.'

'Do not beg, Emma,' Richard said. 'He is unworthy of your loyalty.' He put his arm around her, feeling her shoulders shaking beneath his hand. 'Come, my dear. The arms of my family are wide as well as wise. They know your true worth.' He guided her out of the room, pausing before Lydia, who hung her head.

'Can we convey you to your home in Bath, Mrs Kellerman? It will be more congenial than here.'

'I did not know he had returned,' she whispered. 'He is my only male kin. How can I disobey him?' She pulled away and ran upstairs, and there was the sound of a door slamming.

Richard led the now sobbing Emma out of the house, fighting to control his anger at the scene he had encountered. Meredith ran after them and threw her arms around her sister.

'Emma, you cannot go like this. I hate him. No one could stop what he did to Lydia. And Temperance made it worse, spouting her own lies. I hate her. I hate Papa. Take me with you.'

'Papa would not allow it.' Emma folded her sister in her

arms. 'He would send the authorities after us. He could even send them after me and try and have my marriage annulled, as I am under age and he has given no permission. I am lucky he chose to disown me.'

'You were the only one who stood up to him,' Meredith sobbed. 'Even Clemency has become mean and nasty. She has been worse since he returned last week. She is jealous that you have wed before her and have a good life with more freedom ahead of you. They will never let me marry. I will remain a prisoner here. It was dreadful how Papa punished Lydia. If anything his rages are worse than ever.'

Emma pressed a small purse holding five pounds into her sister's hands. 'Hide this. If things get too bad, I have a house now in Bodmin. Keep the money safe and it will pay for your fare.'

'Meredith, get back in here this instant, or you will be locked in your room,' Major Madison bellowed.

The young woman continued to cling to her sister as though she was a life raft. Gently Richard disengaged her hands and whispered, 'I can do nothing without your father's permission. But as Emma says, there will always be a sanctuary for you at Bodmin.'

The officer continued to shout. 'Get back here, girl. I will not have this disregard of my orders. I've had men whipped for less insolence.' He stamped out of the house and made a grab for the young woman. Instinctively Richard stepped in front of Meredith. 'You will not harm her.'

'I will do exactly as I please to a wilful daughter. Get to your room, girl. I will deal with you later.'

Meredith trembled but continued to stand her ground. When her father raised his fist, she held her hands to her head to protect her face.

'Get to your room at once,' Major Madison snarled and planted a bruising grip upon her shoulder.

The shawl slipped, showing livid bruises across her arms from a recent beating.

'Still you defy me,' the officer raged.

Richard grabbed the mammoth hand and in one lithe movement shoved it aside and put Meredith behind him. Despite the soldier being several stones heavier than himself, he pushed him back against the wall of the house. 'Your bullying tactics do not scare me. I will not allow you to abuse the girl.'

'Get to your room, Meredith,' her father repeated, taking a lumbering swing at his adversary.

Richard ducked but was loath to strike his wife's father, even though the bully deserved a thorough thrashing. When a blow landed on his jaw, however, snapping back his head, he had no choice but to attack, landing a punch in the older man's stomach that doubled him over.

'I cannot stay here,' Meredith beseeched. 'Emma, you must take me with you. He'll beat me to within an inch of my life after this.'

'Get into the coach, Meredith,' Emma urged.

Richard stood over his opponent, his fists clenched, ready to strike again. From the corner of his eye he saw his wife and her sister climbing into the coach.

'Get back here, girl,' the major raged, 'or you are no longer my daughter.' He took another swing at Richard, who nimbly sidestepped and slammed his hand into a fleshy eye. He had never witnessed such appalling behaviour from a gentleman, and it made him fiercely protective of the two women. With a guttural snarl the major lurched forward, his arms outspread to clamp him in a bear hug and crush his ribs. Richard leapt aside, seeing his death written in the hatred sparking from the officer's eyes. If he were caught in that lethal hold, he would stand no chance of overcoming the larger man. With only one choice left to him, he locked his hands together and with all his strength brought them down on the back of that bull neck, feeling the bones in his fingers crack from the force of the blow. The soldier dropped down on one knee, shaking his head to clear his wits.

'If beating your daughters into submission is how you see yourself as their protector, then you are a sorry excuse for a father and they are well rid of you.' He turned on his heel and jumped into the coach, shouting to the driver to whip up the horses as he slammed the carriage door behind him.

'Richard, that was so brave of you. No one stands up to Papa.' Emma stared at him with admiration. Both women were white as parchment and still clung to each other in their terror.

'It seems you both had the courage to stand up to him. It is a privilege to defend such valiant women. Yet it was not how I planned to make my acquaintance with your family.' He tried to lighten the mood.

'How could he treat us like that?' Emma wept as she covered her face.

'He cannot bully or hurt you again. Either of you,' Richard reassured them. 'May Temperance and Clemency have joy of him. Though I have to say, I thought Mrs Kellerman had more fight in her.'

'A woman cannot fight the weight of a man's fist. You were so brave, my love, to stand up to him.'

'Men like that should be horsewhipped.' He could understand now Emma's eagerness to be married and escape the misery of her home life. He felt a stab of conscience that he had used her vulnerability to seduce her. No wonder she had been such easy prey; she was desperate for some form of affection. Some of his resentment towards her mellowed.

Meredith was also staring at him with hero worship in her eyes. 'Can I really live with Emma?'

'It looks as though we have burned our boats.' Richard basked in the adoration of the two women. He had always been in the shadow of Adam's bravery, and his pride swelled that he had been able to save two beautiful damsels in distress.

Chapter Twenty-eight

A period of calm settled over the family during the summer and autumn, but as the festive season neared, Elspeth found her loyalty severely tested. Carts of French furniture had arrived at Trevowan with instructions as to the rooms they were to be placed in. There were ornate gilded and canopied beds for every bedroom, a table with twenty matching chairs and two sideboards for the dining room, padded couches and armchairs for the morning room, salon, winter parlour and orangery, together with carved Venetian mirrors and exquisite crystal chandeliers for the main rooms, a pianoforte and harp for the music room, crates of Sèvres crockery, elaborate dining silverware, paintings by Canaletto, Gainsborough, Rubens and Caravaggio, to name but a few of the renowned artists. Silk hangings for the beds and windows were accompanied by the arrival of four seamstresses to fit and make them. Even three life-size marble goddesses had been placed in a newly landscaped part of the garden.

Trevowan had been transformed into a grand country house but it was no longer the home Elspeth had cherished. She was content in the Dower House with her old familiar furniture and furnishings. She had seen Tristan twice, each time only for a short overnight visit.

When she had questioned him as to why he had not taken up residence, he had given a sardonic laugh.

'I would first banish all the ghosts of my connection with Trevowan's past,' he had replied.

'You cannot suppress such forceful personalities by new paintwork and hangings. The spirits of your ancestors are in every brick, floorboard and blade of grass,' she had thrown back at him. 'And what of me? Am I not the living reminder of those who came before me?'

'You are my nemesis, Aunt Elspeth. A role you enjoy. I can disguise my roots but I can never run away from them. Once Trevowan has my mark firmly stamped upon it, then I will live here.'

Tristan had been mistaken. Elspeth had walked through the rooms and corridors with their changed appearance, but in her mind she could hear the gruff laughter of her grandfather, Arthur, and her father, George, mocking the pretensions of the young outcast.

'Mock him if you will, Arthur,' she had challenged the voices. 'You were the most ruthless and cold-blooded of us all. Your blood runs thickest in Tristan's veins. There was honour and loyalty during my brother Edward's time as master here. Only Adam would have preserved that, but would Trevowan have survived under his honourable charge? The very mortar of Trevowan is steeped in a ruthlessness I have only witnessed in the new master. Tristan is Trevowan's destiny. For good or bad.'

She gave a dry laugh that she was talking to the house as though it was a person. ' 'Tis a sign of madness, old girl, talking to yourself. Yet I never feel alone walking through these rooms. They are peopled by memories.' To her, the ghosts of the past still lived and breathed, her recollections undiminished.

She wandered outside to inspect the stables. No new

head groom had been appointed to replace Jasper Fraddon. Isaac Nance's grandson Jeb was diligent enough as a stable lad, but like all youths he shirked some of his duties if a watchful eye was not kept upon him. She found him mucking out a stall, using a pitchfork to transfer the soiled straw into a hand barrow. It was the stables that upset Elspeth the most. Once every stall would have been filled with the family's hunters, carriage and work horses. Now there were only two plough horses, at the moment clearing trees that had blown down in last month's storms from the four-acre wood. They would later be cut and stored as logs for the fires.

A whinny greeted her entrance to the stables and her two bay mares, Bella and Kara, hung their heads over the gate of the stalls. She gave them both an apple and stroked their muzzles. The mares were five and seven years old, with valiant hearts that had served her well in the hunting field. They were the last of a long line of mares she had enjoyed and loved over six decades. Once she had owned five mares, but age and ill fortune had thinned their number down in recent years. She still rode every day, despite the increasing pain in her hip from a hunting accident over twenty years ago.

She breathed in the scents of fresh straw, oats, horses and the leather of their gleaming halters. This was where she had always found peace and happiness. She ordered Jeb to saddle Kara. A hard ride would dispel the disquiet caused by the letter she had received from Tristan that morning. He would take up residence in a fortnight. The beds were to be made ready for thirty guests, who would be staying for three weeks. A cook, housekeeper and major-domo would arrive tomorrow, together with six servants to perform the duties of maids – upstairs, downstairs and kitchen – and footmen. The wives of the estate workers were expected to prepare the servants' quarters. He also instructed Elspeth to ensure that rooms were made ready over the stables for the new head groom. It seemed he wanted no one working in the house who had previously served the family and might gossip with guests. The housekeeper and major-domo would arrive with full instructions for the entertainments planned, the first of which would be two days of shooting for the gentlemen, to supply game for the later part of the feasting. Tristan had requested that Elspeth act as his hostess.

This was where her loyalty would be tested. She was beholden to Tristan for allowing her to remain in her home and providing the upkeep for her horses, but the family would frown upon such lavish entertainment at Trevowan close to the date of St John's death.

A memorial service at Penruan church had been arranged for the anniversary of St John's passing. The Loveday family were interred within a vault in the village church. Afterwards Adam had planned restrained entertainments over the festive season at Boscabel. A group of rowdy strangers descending upon Penruan church for the Yuletide services would be singularly inappropriate and would cause further friction between the two branches of the family. Also Adam had invited Elspeth and the women from Reskelly Cottage to Boscabel for Christmas.

Elspeth's role of peacemaker was clearly to be a thorny one. With Kara saddled, she set off for a confrontation at Boscabel before Adam left for the shipyard.

She found him still breaking his fast with Senara. The older children did not return from their boarding schools until next week and the young ones were noisily playing tag through the upper rooms of the Tudor house.

Adam threw down his napkin and stood up as Elspeth was announced. 'Aunt Elspeth, you are abroad early this morning. What problem has curtailed your morning ride? Something serious? You look as though you have the weight of the world on your shoulders.'

'The good name and reputation of our family could be called into question. I ask for tolerance and forbearance on your part.' She fired her opening salvo and did not take the seat her nephew had offered to her.

'Is Tristan involved in some further treachery?' Adam's eyes narrowed and his manner chilled several degrees.

'Treachery is too strong a word, but there has been lack of consideration. Unfortunately, I have no knowledge of his present whereabouts to address it with him before events will be put in hand.'

'Do sit down, Aunt.' Adam impatiently held a chair out for her. 'Can I offer you refreshment before we do battle? I have a feeling I am not going to like what you have to impart.'

'Tea will suffice. I have already eaten.'

Jenna Biddick was hovering by the sideboard laid with devilled kidneys, kedgeree and gammon. Adam signalled for her to bring his aunt a cup, and as Senara poured her drink he dismissed the maid.

Without preamble Elspeth announced, 'Your cousin has invited a houseful of guests for Yuletide.'

'When do they arrive?' A muscle twitched along Adam's jaw.

'In two weeks.'

'Damn his eyes!' Adam flushed with mounting fury. 'It is an insult to St John's memory. A deliberate slur upon the memorial service.'

'He has no knowledge of the service,' Elspeth hotly defended. 'It is no doubt his wish to celebrate the completion of the refurbishing of Trevowan and a year of him being its master. He has not lived there during that time.'

'I trust you intend to boycott this debacle?' Adam glared at his aunt.

'Your cousin wishes me to be his hostess.'

'Thereby proclaiming to society that he has our family's approval of his treachery.'

Elspeth sighed. 'Does it not also show our neighbours that our family remains united? That there was no scandal attached to St John's death? Your brother signed documents declaring that he forfeited Trevowan to repay his gambling debts. That saves his reputation. There has been no word from your cousin to dispute this.'

'Because it puts him in a favourable light. The saviour of our family home,' Adam raged. He sprang out of the chair to pace the dining room, pointing an accusing finger at his aunt, ignoring the fact that she had gone deathly pale. 'You have accepted our invitation to spend Christmas here with Amelia and Felicity. Do you abandon those plans to bask in the glory of being hostess at Trevowan?'

'Adam, that is unfair!' Senara protested. 'Elspeth is in a difficult position. Trevowan is still her home.'

Elspeth rose wearily to her feet, but her voice was no less blistering in its scorn. 'I came here out of the respect and esteem in which I hold you to inform you of your cousin's plans. And you should hang your head in shame if you think my family loyalty is divided. We are one family with a common ancestry. This is what you have chosen to forget. If we discredit Tristan by our censure, then how long will it be before the truth behind St John's disgrace and death is public knowledge?'

She straightened her slender frame and there was such

fire in her eyes that her face was transformed, her features bearing an unmistakable likeness to Adam's late father Edward.

'Whatever our pain or internal rivalry, the Lovedays show a united front to the world. That is our way. In case it has escaped your notice, Tristan has stayed away this past year to allow tempers to cool. I do not expect you to embrace him in friendship. Polite civility is all that is needed.'

She turned and limped from the room. Senara shot a pleading look at her husband and saw the brief battle of pride against duty.

'Your pardon, Aunt Elspeth.' His tone still carried the threads of his anger, but it was now without its heat. 'You are right. At least in public there should appear to be a truce.'

'Finally some of your father's wisdom has rubbed off on you.' She regarded him with a nod of satisfaction. 'As an act of his contrition I will expect your cousin to attend the service at Penruan church. There is no other need than an exchange of civilities between you.'

'You drive a hard bargain, Aunt.'

She regarded him over the top of her pince-nez, the glint of battle in her eyes. 'I have yet to convince your cousin of the merits of this public truce.'

When Tristan arrived at Trevowan two days before his guests were due, it was more difficult for Elspeth to persuade him to attend the memorial service. And who could blame him for his reluctance when those who believed him the villain of the family would outnumber him?

'You will escort me to my nephew's service, and I will give thanks that Trevowan still has a Loveday as its master.'

'So I must face a lynching mob to prove my worth!' Tristan's black humour did not amuse her.

'Triumphing over your cousins by winning Trevowan is one thing. Gaining the respect of our neighbours is another. Had you planned to live as a hermit or outcast in your new home?'

'I have been an outcast most of my life,' he reminded her. 'There will always be acquaintances eager to enjoy the entertainments Trevowan will provide.'

'Would they be true friends whom you can rely upon in time of need, or sycophants ready to bleed you dry and spit you out in a time of crisis?'

He laughed bitterly. 'Your tongue is more vicious than a scorpion's sting, old woman.'

'I never flinch from the truth,' she parried. 'And I always have the best interests of my family at heart. The service is a private affair for members of the family. You are not only master of Trevowan but landlord of half of the cottages in Penruan. They may pay lip service to their landlord, but in the past they were loyal to Edward. Do not forget that St John married one of their own. You may find yourself the loser if they are forced to take sides between you and Adam.'

They rode together to the church and left their horses stabled at the Dolphin Inn. Japhet had arrived by coach with his family and parents. Amelia, Felicity, Rowena and Charlotte had squeezed into the pony trap and Adam and his brood had journeyed by coach from Boscabel.

The family had expected the service to be a private affair, but to their surprise, most of the villagers were present. Clem Sawle, who now owned the Dolphin, was in the first pew with his wife Keziah, mother Sal and son Zach. St John had been married to Clem's sister Meriel, and when Rowena saw her young cousin after so many months away at the ladies' academy, despite her new-found sophistication and elegance she ran to the pew and hugged him.

'You've grown so much, Zach.'

'The same can be said of you.' Sal beamed toothlessly at her granddaughter. 'You be a fine beauty.'

Sir Henry and Lady Traherne were also present, together with Squire Penwithick and Dr and Mrs Chegwidden and their daughter.

Leaving Zach, Rowena dipped a curtsy at the altar, where the Reverend Mr Snell stood in his vestments, a bible clutched close to his chest. She took her place in the Loveday pew by the altar until Adam took her arm and guided her to the front row of seats across from the Sawles. Three rows of Lovedays filed into the pews behind them.

The old family pew had been their place of worship until recent years, when they had visited Trewenna church every Sunday to enjoy Joshua's sermons. It was now very different from how they remembered it at St John's funeral; the last time they had seen it. Then the upholstery had been worn and faded, the carving scuffed down to the bare wood. Now it gleamed from a renovation, the wood highly polished and the seats covered in gold brocade.

'Why have we been relegated here?' Rowena seethed in a husky whisper.

'The family pew is no longer our place,' Adam curtly reminded her.

There was a rumble of conversation from the congregation as they became impatient for the service to commence. Then, like a sabre slicing through silk, all talk stopped. A firm tread and a more hesitant one resounded on the flagstones. Adam prodded Rowena in the ribs to stop her from glancing round. His own face was set in rigid lines.

Tristan and Aunt Elspeth took their place in the family pew and Adam bowed curtly to his aunt, his expression rigid with tension as his gaze flickered over his cousin. Tristan bowed, and with only the barest inclination of his head Adam returned the greeting.

Beside him Rowena gasped, her voice ominously loud in the continued silence. 'What is that blackguard doing here?'

'Showing respect for your father,' Adam ground back in a harsh whisper. 'You will be civil, young lady. The Lovedays always show a united front.'

'Even to traitors?' Rowena hissed glaring at her uncle.

'It is as much to safeguard your father's reputation as his,' Adam warned, gripping her arm to add weight to his words. Rowena turned her shoulder so that her back was presented to Tristan.

Felicity stood next to Adam, dabbing at her eyes with a lace-edged handkerchief. Amelia was on the far side of her, steadfastly ignoring Tristan and Elspeth. Her relationship with her sister-in-law had been strained all year.

Joshua read from the Bible and Snell gave a short sermon before Sir Henry Traherne delivered the eulogy exemplifying St John's life. Adam and Squire Penwithick also spoke before the final hymn was sung.

His flesh stinging with antagonism at the nearness of Tristan, Adam marched out of the church in Snell's wake. He could feel the eyes of the villagers burning into him as they waited for a confrontation between him and the new master of Trevowan.

Adam spoke briefly to Snell and stood aside for the rest of his family to join him. Amelia had linked her arm through Rowena's and together with Felicity they moved towards the family vault to place a wreath by the tomb. Rowena was arguing with Amelia, and as soon as she had laid her tribute she ran back to stand with the Sawle family, with a defiant show of a different kind of solidarity towards her own kin. Adam, who was having difficulty restraining his own anger, hoped that she would not make a scene.

Japhet sauntered to his side, his expression strained. After the solemnity of the service, Adam's and Japhet's sons had run off across the village square and along the harbour arm to where some local lads were fishing for crabs.

'That went relatively well, though I doubt it fooled anyone,' Japhet observed.

Elspeth and Tristan were emerging from the church, the villagers pushing behind them to make sure they did not miss any of the expected conflict. Elspeth was leaning heavily on her cane, supported by Tristan's arm. She paused as she drew level with Adam and Japhet. Both men bowed to her and she extended her hand for them to kiss. As they straightened, they silently inclined their heads to Tristan.

'May the blessings of the season be upon you, cousins.' Tristan greeted them stiffly.

Adam could not stop his hand clenching into a fist but managed to grate out a civil 'And to you, cousin.'

Tristan laughed, adding quietly, 'But you would rather see me roasting like a chestnut on hot coals.'

'It is a pleasure I look forward to,' Adam returned.

Elspeth limped away, relieved that in the circumstances, the show of reconciliation had gone better than she had expected.

Chapter Twenty-nine

There was one boy amongst the Loveday family who felt
the tension and rift between the older cousins more
acutely than the others. Although at twelve Bryn was the
eldest by at least a year, he did not join in the other
boys' exuberance. As the coach took the inland track to
skirt around the Trevowan estate, a volley of gunfire was
heard and the distant clamour of beaters rattling sticks on
metal and wooden surfaces to put the pheasants to flight
echoed through the surrounding hills. Several more
volleys followed their passage. The number of guns
fired heralded to the neighbours how popular Tristan was
amongst his acquaintances. It did not improve Adam's
mood, and when they arrived at Boscabel he changed
his fashionable clothes to start work on a dilapidated
outbuilding that needed its roof repaired. The old shingles
had been stripped off and stored in a barn and any rotten
timbers cut away. The new rafters forming the A frame
were already in position, and over half the crossbeams. He
wanted the building completed before the worst of the
winter storms.

Bryn followed him outside. The liver and white
spaniel Scamp was at his master's heels, carrying a bone
he had scavenged from the kitchen.

'Captain Loveday, the situation today could not have been easy for you,' Bryn said hesitantly.

Adam picked up a saw. Holding familiar tools in his hand always had a calming effect on his mind, and a few hours' work cutting the crossbeams to size would chase away the demons that lay perilously close to the surface of his anger. He regarded his ward with a frown. 'Not easy, Bryn. But necessary.'

When Bryn did not pursue the conversation and stood scuffing his boots in a gesture of unease, Adam said more gently, 'Did it bring to mind any memory from your past?'

The youth shook his blond hair, which fell to his shoulders, his eyes fixed on the ground in front of him. 'I think that there were many heated arguments in my family and much unhappiness because of them. It is an increasing feeling. I do not forget that if your brother had not chanced upon our wrecked carriage I would not have survived that night. I owe him so much and regret that I will never be able to repay him.'

'St John did what any man would have done. The tragedy was that he was too late to save the woman who travelled with you. Do you still remember nothing of your family or past?'

Bryn shook his head. 'I heard some of the villagers call your cousin who now lives at Trevowan an interloper – a cuckoo in the nest who destroyed your brother.'

Adam frowned. 'Is that how you think the villagers view you – as an interloper? It is not the case with us, Bryn. I am proud to be your guardian until your memory returns. You were undoubtedly born a gentleman. One day I hope you will remember your heritage. It could make a great deal of difference to your future.'

Bryn continued to kick at pebbles on the ground and

Adam sensed the lad was not being entirely truthful. In the last four months he had grown a great deal and looked much older than Adam had first assumed. That could explain the boy's high level of education. He put his hand on the youth's shoulder. 'You are not the same as Tristan. There was much he resented about his early life. His grandfather was the black sheep of the family and he turned his back on all that was decent and right. Tristan was brought up in poverty and he hated us because our childhood had been so privileged. As youths, the rivalry between us was intense, and it got out of hand between him and St John. When our grandfather took St John's side against Tristan, he ran away.'

When Bryn remained silent, Adam asked, 'Do you have problems like that with Nathan or Joel?'

'No, indeed not. We get on well – especially if we let Joel win.' He grinned, for Joel's temper and competitive spirit became fiercer with each year, and Adam was more than aware of his younger son's failings.

As if on cue, Joel's voice piped through an open window, 'I won. I won.'

'Only because you moved the markers on the board,' Nathan shouted back.

'I did not.'

'Cheats never prosper, Joel,' Nathan responded, and there was the sound of scuffling as the two boys rolled across the floor in a fight.

Adam sighed but did not attempt to stop the tussle. He believed his children should work out their own problems. He and St John had fought regularly through their childhood. He was more concerned about Bryn. He selected a piece of wood and marked it up to be cut to size. 'If there is anything you want to discuss with me, any feelings or ideas you have about your past – even if they are frightening – I am always here for you and on your side.'

'But what if I am not the gentleman's son you believe me to be?' There was a new note of uncertainty in Bryn's voice. 'Or there is some taint upon my background? I would bring shame to you.'

'There is nothing in your character or behaviour that would make me believe that was possible,' Adam again reassured him. 'Do you think that could be the case?'

When Bryn would not raise his eyes, he added, 'All families have skeletons they would prefer not to be discovered. But from what I know of you, I do not believe you are capable of doing anything to destroy my faith in you.'

'Is it true you asked your friend Sir Gregory Kilmarthen to trace my family?'

'Sir Gregory has many friends who can discover these things.'

Bryn hugged his arms about his chest, and as he lifted his gaze to hold Adam's there was stark terror in their depths. 'What if they were bad people? Would you make me return to them?'

'Is that what you fear, Bryn? Are you sure you have not remembered something? I would never place you in danger.'

'I have violent dreams, Captain Loveday.'

'Mayhap they are just nightmares, Bryn.' Adam wanted to reassure the lad – Senara had often heard him crying out in the night and gone to his room to find him shaking with fear – but he also felt the need to be honest with him. 'You had a very bad concussion. It is likely from the speed the coach was travelling that the woman who accompanied you was fleeing someone.'

'I think we were fleeing for our lives,' the boy confessed. 'I should have told you before but I was too scared.

That time you took Nathan and myself to Falmouth, I saw someone on the docks. A foreign gentleman. Just his voice terrified me. I ran and hid.'

'As any youth would have done in the circumstances.' Adam reined in his disquiet that this had been a lost opportunity to learn Bryn's identity.

'You are not angry with me, Captain Loveday? I have worried about it ever since. You have given me a home and I was too scared to let you know that this man was familiar to me.'

'You said he was foreign. Did you recognise his accent?'

Bryn chewed his lip, still unhappy at making a disclosure.

'Do you think it was the man who used to beat you?' Adam persisted. 'You had many old injuries when we found you that had nothing to do with the coach accident.'

Bryn nodded. 'He sounded Spanish. How would I know it was that language if the man was a stranger?'

'The woman travelling with you was of a darker complexion than yourself. She could have been Spanish or come from the Mediterranean.'

Josephina. The name sprang to his mind. Bryn pressed his fingers to his temples as his whole body began to shake. 'She was my friend. No, sister. No, my stepsister, I think. Josephina, that was her name.' Images spun through his mind, distorted by a mist. 'She was like a mother to me.' Pain tore through him and he felt that his heart had been torn asunder. 'My mama is dead. I saw her lying at the foot of the stairs and that monster was standing over her.'

'What was Josephina's full name? Can you remember?'

Echoes ricocheted through his memory. Overriding all of them was terror. A violent trembling seized his body. The name had begun to haunt his dreams. Yet even with all of Captain Loveday's assurances, he was terrified that if he spoke it aloud and investigations were made, his guardian would be in mortal danger. And not only him, but this family who had shown Bryn nothing but kindness.

Bryn gripped his head in his hands and fell to his knees. 'It has gone. I cannot recall the name. Just Josephina. I'm sorry, Captain Loveday.' He hated the lies. But to save himself and the family he had come to love, he had no choice. His body shook with uncontrollable sobs.

Adam put both his hands on the boy's shoulders, his voice gentle. 'Do not upset yourself, Bryn. You are safe here. If there is danger lying ahead for you, you will not have to face it alone. So far no one has come forward who is searching for a lost ward or youth. That in itself is suspicious. Nothing has changed, Bryn. You will stay here and continue your education. Time enough to find out about your past when you have put childhood behind you and are a man.'

Two days after the memorial service, Jasper Fraddon drove Amelia to Bodmin in the Loveday coach. It was close to the time of Emma's delivery, and without a mother to support her, Amelia had insisted that she would stay until after the birth.

It was a gruelling journey across the moor, where the landmarks were obscured by mist. At this time of year, with so much rain, the roads were often deeply rutted or partially flooded. Amelia was aching in every bone when she arrived at the Allbright house. Fraddon was to stay the night at an inn and travel back to Boscabel in the morning.

What she found awaiting her shocked her to the core. Emma had been in labour for two days. Meredith was hysterical with fear and the midwife was drunk. Of

Richard there was no sign. Amelia's arrival was greeted by the sound of Emma's screams, which were hoarse from the hours of her travail. Throwing off her cloak and gloves, she ordered Fraddon to fetch Dr Knightley, who had the best reputation in Bodmin, and pay him whatever it took to get him to the house without delay. She then ordered Meredith to strip off the soiled sheets and instructed the maid to boil more water.

'There bain't nothing to fetch Doctor for. You be wasting your money,' sniffed Mrs Riddley, the midwife, sour ale fumes heavy on her breath. She flopped down on the end of the bed and wiped her sweating face with her sleeve. Her skirt was hitched to her knees and several holes were on view in her thick woollen hose. 'First one always takes its time.'

Emma bared her teeth, her face contorting with the violence of another pain, her hair plastered wetly to her skull.

'Where is Richard?' Amelia angrily demanded.

'He was called away three days ago.' Meredith hovered by the door, reluctant to enter and witness her sister's ordeal.

Emma said, 'The baby was not due for another two weeks. Some lout pushed into me on the street. Knocked me down and stole my purse.' Another spasm contorted her body and she screamed.

Amelia had never felt so helpless. She wished that she had brought Senara with her. 'There must be something you can do?' she said, shoving Mrs Riddley off the end of the bed.

'She be doing fine,' the midwife grunted. 'Some makes more fuss than others. Bain't used to pain, that be all.'

Amelia rounded on the woman. 'If the child is not delivered in the next few hours, mother and baby safe and well, you will not receive a penny of your fee and I shall have you whipped through the town as a fraud.'

She had not attended another woman's confinement, and Emma's suffering seemed far worse than she herself had endured during the births of her three children. She wrung her hands. It must be nearly an hour since Fraddon had gone for help. Where was he?

Mrs Riddley swayed to her feet and belched. 'I bain't no fraud. Best midwife in Bodmin, I be.'

'Then prove it!' Amelia demanded.

There was a loud banging on the door and Fraddon pounded up the stairs. Amelia sighed with relief that the doctor had arrived. Her hopes were rapidly dashed.

'Knightley's bedridden with gout and won't come out,' Fraddon informed her from the landing.

Her heart raced with growing panic and she forced herself to take several calming breaths.

'Then try another doctor,' she snapped in exasperation. 'Didn't he give you a name?'

'Ay, man by the name of Priest. He were out of town for the day. Bain't no one else.' He stamped back down the stairs.

Emma screamed again and the midwife elbowed Amelia out of the way, lifting the sheet to examine her patient.

'Emma is not going to die, is she?' Meredith wailed. She had opened the door but was still too terrified to enter the room.

'Out of my way, all of you.' The midwife rounded on Amelia. 'I've delivered more babies than most folk have had hot dinners. Lost no more than half a dozen of them and the same with the mothers.'

Far from reassured, Amelia refused to leave. 'Get downstairs, Meredith. This is no place for an unwed maiden.'

'I can't leave Emma. What will we do if she dies?'

There was another piercing scream from the bed and the midwife's bulk obscured what she was up to under the sheets. Then suddenly Emma's scream was cut off and she fell back unconscious.

Amelia's hand flew to her mouth and she muttered a hasty prayer, fearing the worst. A sharp slap was followed by a soft mewing sound, and then the baby gave full voice to its indignation at being so rudely presented to the world. The midwife cut and tied the cord and wrapped the baby in a piece of sheeting, then thrust it at Amelia. 'Hold on to the babby. I've still got the mother to tend.'

Tears misted Amelia's eyes as she stared into the wrinkled face of her granddaughter and gently wrapped the sheet around her tiny body. The midwife continued to work in sullen silence, kneading Emma's stomach. 'Got to make sure all the afterbirth is out, or she'll be a goner.'

Finally there was an exhausted groan from Emma. The midwife straightened, took the baby from Amelia and laid it on the mother's chest. Then she sniffed and cuffed the sweat from her upper lip. 'Mother and babby be just fine. Let her rest and give her some beef broth to strengthen her. I said no doctor be needed. Not when Ma Riddley tends a birth.'

'Thank you, Mrs Riddley. It was a shock arriving as we did and finding my daughter-in-law in such a weak state.'

'Some women just don't take well to having babies. It will be easier for her next time.'

Amelia and Meredith sat each side of the new mother as she dozed peacefully. 'We will need to engage a nursemaid in the morning, and a wetnurse.'

'I believe Emma wishes to feed Jane herself,' Meredith answered softly. She was still nervous in Amelia's company, as the older woman had such outspoken views. However, she was grateful to Amelia for insisting upon the marriage; many mothers would have refused to acknowledge a woman carrying an illegitimate child.

'Jane? Is that to be her name?' Amelia sounded disappointed.

Meredith blushed and twisted a handkerchief between her fingers, hesitating to explain.

'Jane is a good, wise name without affectation. Jane Allbright sounds very well indeed.' Amelia did not want to be seen to criticise.

The younger woman smiled and relaxed. 'Mr Allbright said if it was a girl Emma could choose her name. Jane is for our mother. If it had been a boy it was to be called after Richard's father.'

Amelia bowed her head to hide a jolt of pain. Was that a deliberate slight to herself? Richard's way of getting back at her for allowing him to believe that she was his mother? She drew a steadying breath, refusing to be upset. Jane was a good name. It was only right that Emma would wish to name her daughter after her late mother.

She frowned, all the worry and drama of her arrival finally giving way to the anger that had been gnawing within her. 'I shall have a great deal to say to my son when he returns. How could he have deserted his wife at such a time?'

'It was not his fault, Mrs Loveday.' Emma roused herself to defend her husband. Amelia thought the young woman would have been furious at her husband's neglect; instead she was smiling proudly. 'Richard had no choice. He was summoned by the Admiralty to Plymouth. They have made him a commander and he has been given his own ship.'

Chapter Thirty

Pasting on a cheerful smile and playing the dutiful wife of a vicar tested all Bridie's skill in not allowing her pain to ruin the festive season. She had already endured the misery of Michael's birthday, with all the memories of happier years and the reminder of what had been forever denied her in the future. Christmas with its nativity celebrations bludgeoned her grief even harder. She tried to throw herself into the care of the parish poor but her heart was never in it. It was also her first Christmas without the love and guidance of her mother and sister.

Oppressive as bruises, dark clouds loomed over the rooftops of Launceston, rain and wind battering the shuttered windows and adding to the gloom that pervaded every room of the vicarage.

Bridie had never liked towns, her limp too often a source of derision. The parishioners were wary of the new vicar and his wife, and Bridie found them too quick to judge her crippled leg to mean that she could not perform her duties. She worked hard to show them that they were wrong, but feeling tired and unappreciated, she missed her old home. Most of all she missed teaching at Trevowan Hard. She worried about her less able pupils, who had needed extra encouragement to learn their numbers and letters. Did the new teacher understand their needs? Many of the pupils from nearby villages came from troubled families, having to deal with their parents' drunkenness or severe illnesses. If they missed too much time at school she would check on them and take provisions or any remedy needed from Senara.

'They are no longer my responsibility,' she chided herself. 'Have I not similar duties here?' Yet it was not the same. Here she was again viewed with suspicion for being a stranger. At Trevowan Hard and Polruggan she had fought hard for years to be accepted. She could do so again but her heart was not in it, especially when Peter also had not settled into their new parish.

'Pull yourself together, Bridie. That's what Ma would say, and she was right. Your duty is to your husband. You will overcome this.' The words echoed hollowly around the empty vicarage. Peter had left the house early that morning with no word of where he was going and had not returned.

A sigh was dragged from her. 'My love, why will you not talk to me of your problems? I know you find this as difficult as I do.' She feared that despite loving her husband with all her heart, following the death of their child they were growing further apart.

She shook her shoulders to dispel her despondency. The poverty and prejudice she had faced throughout her childhood had given her the resilience to accept the hardship and deprivations of life. She had witnessed the ravages of cholera and typhoid on a community, known too many women who did not survive childbirth and children who did not live past their first year. She could accept Michael's death, but coming to terms with the void that his loss had brought to her life was a constant challenge. She did not blame God, for death struck the rich as well as the poor and it frequently took the good as well as the bad. Michael had been one of life's angels and she could understand why God wanted him at his side. She wished, though, that they could have been granted longer to enjoy the blessings of his life.

She was worried about her husband. Peter ate little and slept less. He spent long hours praying in church and each week his sermons became more fervent, lecturing on the evils of drink, fornication, gambling and blasphemy. His words condemned the temptation presented by the devil, but his voice had lost its strident ring of conviction. The light of religious ardour no longer brightened his eyes or pulsated through his sermons. The longer he spent at prayer, the more reluctant he became to discuss the problems that faced them. Bridie's own prayers were that he would regain peace from his faith.

Throughout the Christmas services his sermons became shorter and he cut down on the number of hymns. He spent less time visiting the sick and debating points of theology with the church elders.

Bridie watched him from her place in the front pew and saw the vibrancy and passion seeping from him. The day after Christmas he disappeared and did not return until nightfall; he would not speak of where he had been. In the following weeks his absences became more frequent, and one Sunday morning he failed to take the service and left it to his curate. When he did not show for evensong, Bridie feared some harm had come to him. She was haunted by the fear that he had been attacked, as he had when the smugglers had abducted him for preaching against their practices.

The days were lengthening as the sun rose higher in the sky. Yet the rebirth of spring with its burst of new life and beginnings still seemed far away.

★

It was a time of adjustment for all the Lovedays. The once close-knit family of Cornish cousins, who had lived within half a dozen miles of each other, were now spread over distances that involved several hours' travel, and two resided in different counties. A prolonged wet spell in February kept the family in their own homes.

Where once Trevowan had been the monthly meeting place to dine and catch up on news, the gatherings were now fragmented. Cecily was often short of breath and found it difficult to travel, so Japhet and Gwendolyn dined at the rectory after the Sunday service at Trewenna. Felicity was often exhausted with two young children to cope with and rarely mixed with her neighbours, preferring her own company and the avoidance of gossip that was still rife concerning her husband. To everyone's surprise, Elspeth visited Reskelly Cottage daily, dividing her time between Felicity and calling upon Joshua and Cecily.

With the men so occupied, Senara visited Trevowan Hard every morning to tend any of the local villagers who needed her remedies, and twice a week Gwendolyn and Senara called upon each other. They had become close friends. Senara missed the companionship of her sister, whom she had seen only once since Richard and Emma's wedding.

Outwardly life settled down to quiet country normality. Adam spent long hours at the shipyard, the wet winter having caused delays in the schedules for the shipbuilding. At Boscabel two extra fields were put to the plough to increase the crop yield, whilst at Tor Farm Japhet eagerly awaited the birth of the first foals sired by his prize stallion Emir Khan. By mutual consensus Trevowan and Tristan were never mentioned. That did not mean that old scores were forgotten.

Early-morning sword practice remained a twice-weekly occurrence for Japhet and Adam, and as the weeks passed a growing restlessness consumed the cousins. Their hot blood demanded retribution, their patience stifled by the need for justice. Their wives sensed it but held back their protest. They had seen the darkness of revenge festering behind their husbands' eyes and chiselling into their hearts. Honour demanded that they defeat their enemies before they themselves were defeated.

Another unexpected visit from Sir Gregory Kilmarthen sent the thrill of anticipation through the men's veins, and fear for their loved ones jeopardised the happiness of the women.

Tristan was never the happiest of sailors, and as *Good Fortune* was tossed and buffeted by rough seas he cursed his lack of sea legs. He would have thought that coming from a seafaring family, and after all the voyages he had undertaken, he would no longer be beset with *mal de mer*. It was madness to take to sea in the middle of winter, and this was the second voyage he had undertaken on Lord Brienne's behalf. The earlier one had been extremely profitable, and this time he could not in honour refuse his lordship's request to escort his niece to Paris. Brienne had been taken ill with a sudden ague and had been unable to accompany Lady Alys. The beautiful young woman had been adamant that she did not intend to cancel her plans to visit friends.

The French capital had shaken off the shackles of revolution. Napoleon had taken up residence in the palace of St Cloud and spent millions of livres on its redecoration and refurbishment. To further enhance his status, Josephine, with her ancient lineage, was given a prominent role, taking her place next to him at daily receptions and audiences. The First Consul was setting up a glittering court and protocol as he strode purposefully towards declaring himself the new monarch. In the past, Royalist plots to assassinate him had failed, and many believed him invincible. He had declared an amnesty to French exiles where previously they would have been condemned to death. He was seeking the acceptance of the Royalist supporters by further dividing the monarchist parties. The Pretender, Louis XVIII, remained in exile in Poland.

As the peace with France continued, English nobles and gentry joined the throng of returning exiles. Where once terror had hung like storm clouds over Paris, now gaiety was the order. The restaurants and parks were filled with people parading in the latest fashions, seeking to fill their days with entertainments. Crowds were drawn to watch the military parades. Grand balls filled the streets with carriages by night as well as day, and the theatres flourished.

The poverty following the revolution was replaced by displays of extravagance. Jewellers, goldsmiths, even carriage-makers worked night and day to supply the increasing demands of the populace.

As escort to Lady Alys, Tristan was drawn into this sparkling chameleon world. A world of undercurrents and desperate gaiety; old values resurrected together with an almost frantic need for stability and normalcy. Yet he was not fooled by outward appearances. Intrigue throbbed just under the surface. Resentments and suspicion smouldered.

He had expected to feel ill at ease in the company of so many of the *ancien régime*, with their impeccable bloodlines. Although he had prospered in his years in

France, it had been amongst the bourgeoisie, the wealthier merchants. His life in America, where he had married a socialite and lived amongst the elite, had given him a veneer of polished manners and taught him how to be accepted in the higher echelons of society. Yet rooted within him were the old insecurities of his impoverished childhood. However much he wore his confidence like a protective cloak of sable, he could still awake sweating at night with dreams of being exposed and persecuted as an outcast.

Neither did Tristan trust his new acquaintances. Too many conversations halted or abruptly changed course when newcomers approached. Behind the smiles and compliments, eyes were carefully masked of emotion. The hairs at the back of his neck constantly prickled, a warning that he was being observed; that he was being assessed as to how he could be of advantage to another. Words professing friendship held a hollow ring. Tristan could not believe that the nobility, who had lost kin and property during the revolution and who now pandered to the new regime, did not smoulder with hatred and the quest for revenge. And France was also the sworn enemy of the British, for all they had welcomed them during this period of peace. Tristan trusted no one. He even had his suspicions about Lady Alys.

They were staying with Louis Lapoitiere and his wife Marie-Ann. The Frenchman had introduced Tristan to a number of noblemen in his circle, many of whom pandered to the new court at St Cloud. There were so many rumours about the scandalous past and lovers of the First Consul's wife that Tristan had been intrigued to meet her. He had only seen her from a distance and was surprised that she was not the great beauty he had expected, but she did have a certain presence and was witty and vivacious when surrounded by admirers. Yet there was talk that Napoleon was no longer the devoted husband he had been at the outset of their marriage. Even from a distance Tristan could sense a tension within Josephine. She was no longer young and it was rumoured that she would never bear Napoleon an heir. Many suspected that her days were numbered. A man with ambitions to be king would surely require a dynasty to follow in his greatness.

Although in the first days of their visit Lady Alys was much in demand, she frequently sought Tristan's company. Then there were unexplained absences, which became more frequent as their visit progressed. When questioned, she was elusive.

Tonight they were alone in the Lapoitieres' salon, their hosts attending the theatre. Alys had earlier cried off with a headache and insisted that Tristan accompany them. He had gone instead to a gaming house but found that he was in no mood to gamble. Lady Alys was like no woman he had ever met. It infuriated him that she was so independent. That her emotions towards him could blow hot and cold. Her eyes would offer the boldest of invitations, yet if he tried to get closer to her, she would evade his advances.

'Are you jealous, my friend?' she would tease. 'There is no need.'

'Jealousy has nothing to do with it,' Tristan countered. 'Lord Brienne has charged me to be your escort and protector.'

'And you are. But sometimes I need freedom to be myself.'

It was an outrageous statement and one he never thought to hear from a woman. Yet it echoed his own inner struggle. There were times when he had painted such a realistic picture of himself as the perfect gentleman that he had obliterated a fundamental part of his soul: the wild side of his nature, which cared not a whit what anyone thought and would have thumbed its nose at the devil.

'Paris is a dangerous city,' he reminded Lady Alys.

She laughed. 'I am always with friends. But not friends like you and me.' She moved closer so that the scent of her skin and her perfume swirled around his senses. Her hand rested delicately over his heart. 'We understand each other, do we not?' Her voice was low and husky with promise, her lips parted invitingly.

'I know you not at all, Lady Alys,' he replied coolly. This was not a woman he could use as he had others in his past. Even his wives had not captured his heart. They had been a means to advancement, to the acceptance he had needed at the time. None had broken through the armour that had for so long protected his emotions. He pulled her to him, his lips claiming hers, needing to subjugate and dominate. He felt their heat and fullness quiver and respond all too briefly, and then she wrenched herself out of his arms. But he was faster and caught her hands, drawing her back to him.

'This cannot be!' Her words contradicted the desire in her eyes.

'Why do you lie to yourself?' His lips again captured her mouth. He felt the pounding of her heart against his chest, and her body soften and quiver.

Then her hands were again firm against his torso. 'It is not possible.'

'Because of my birth?' he forced out as he continued to hold her.

She did not struggle. 'Because of mine.'

He released her as though her skin had branded him and stepped back.

'Then you would do well not to play with fire, Lady Alys.' He marched from the room, cursing his need and his pain at her rejection.

'You do not understand.' Her voice was a harsh whisper.

Unfortunately he thought he understood all too well.

Chapter Thirty-one

Adam, Japhet and Long Tom were frequently closeted together during Sir Gregory's visit. It had been reported that Osgood had been seen for a time at the court of the exiled Louis XVIII, though the hopes of the French Royalists had been thwarted when Louis relinquished his fight for the throne after Napoleon had made peace with England.

Long Tom explained, 'Our agents in France believed that Napoleon would prefer to offer favourable terms to Louis if he renounced his claim to the throne. That has caused the Royalists to redouble their efforts with plots to depose Napoleon. Furthermore, Osgood was seen in Paris last week.'

'So Osgood is working for those who would restore Louis to the throne, which would be to England's advantage.' Japhet cracked his knuckles, a muscle pumping along his jaw. 'How does that serve us bringing about his disgrace?'

'You know him better than I.' Long Tom regarded him with speculative amusement.

Japhet held the older man's stare, his voice gruff as he answered. 'Osgood seeks to feather his own nest rather than place himself in danger by supporting a lost cause.'

'Precisely.' Long Tom smiled.

The tension left Japhet's body and he sat forward, eyes bright with anticipation. 'He is more likely to use what information he gains for his own ends.'

'That is what concerns some of my friends,' Long Tom said. 'Are you interested in discovering if he has remained loyal and that our allies are not in danger?'

'I would deem it a privilege.' Japhet grinned broadly.

'And I shall accompany you,' offered Adam. 'Your French is not as good as mine, and since you would be recognised by Osgood, I may be able to get closer to his associates.'

'I would welcome your company, cousin.' Japhet raised his glass in salute. 'A traitor will be brought to justice.'

Long Tom hesitated before drinking the toast. 'As a British agent I cannot countenance you killing Osgood in a duel, Japhet.'

'After all the humiliation and degradation I faced because of his spite, death would be too easy for that cur. The shame of being brought to trial as a traitor will terrify his craven soul.'

'If you are to act for our government, I will need you to take an oath of allegiance to our king and country. Adam took it many years ago when he rescued me from a French prison.'

'I would willingly serve my country to bring any traitor to justice,' Japhet vowed. 'Such a duty will be all the sweeter when it is Osgood.'

'As British agents we will all be shot if our mission is discovered by the French,' Long Tom soberly reminded the cousins. As the men downed their brandy, all thoughts were already on the dangers ahead and what fate held in store for each of them in France.

★

Sitting alone by the parlour fire in the vicarage at Launceston, Bridie stared into the flames. It was at times like these that she wished she had her sister's sight for knowing when ill had befallen someone or danger loomed. Her husband had again been absent for many hours without telling her where he was going. She knew he was not drinking because he never returned with the smell of it on his breath. The town watchman was calling the hour of ten in the evening when he at last returned.

She bit back her concern, determined not to scold him for his thoughtlessness at how much she had been worrying about his safety. 'Husband, come sit by the fire. You must be frozen. The rain has drenched your cloak and jacket. I will fetch you hot food.'

'I cannot go on like this,' Peter abruptly declared. The light from the fire showed the gaunt hollows of his cheeks and eyes and the droop of his once proud shoulders.

'There is nothing we cannot get through together.' Fear set her heart racing.

'I have lost my faith.' The confession was delivered in a tortured voice. 'You deserve better than the life I have given you.' He dropped his head into his hands.

She knelt at his side and reached out to clasp his fingers. 'You have given me a wonderful life.'

'I have failed you.' The words were dragged out painfully and slowly. 'I failed Michael. I failed my family. I gave my life to God but he has turned his face from me.'

'My love, you have failed no one.'

'You deserve more. We live little better than paupers on my stipend. What have I achieved? Nothing compared to my family. Japhet turned his life and fate around and achieved wealth through his misfortune. Hannah lost the man she adored and met another who has showered her with riches.'

'I have no need for riches,' Bridie began, but he cut her short by placing a finger against her lips.

'All my life I have fought my demons and temptations for the greater glory of God. How have I been repaid – by him taking the life of my son?'

'That is your grief talking.' She slid her arms around him but his body was stiff and unyielding in her embrace.

He turned away to stare into the fire, his voice harsh with accusation. 'It is my conscience that mocks my failure. I thought that to serve God brought its own rewards, but God helps those who help themselves. I praised him and sat back waiting for him to provide.'

'You were his most conscientious servant.' Tears rolled down Bridie's cheeks to witness his torment.

'I betrayed my family. How my ancestors must ridicule me. We fight for what is ours. We carve our own destiny.'

'Your father is content as a village parson.' Her heart was aching at witnessing his despondency.

'But he had lived a fulfilling life before he turned to the Church. There is so much I regret. Not marrying you, I hasten to assure you.' He looked at her then, the tenderness in his eyes overcast by pain. 'I love you. But the wildness of my blood calls to me to make something more of my life. As did Adam and Japhet. Even Tristan has returned and shown the world the success he has achieved. I need to do this for myself. For us.'

'Then that is how it must be,' she said without hesitation.

He stood and drew her up against him, and kissed her with a passion he had not shown her in months. 'Thank you for understanding. I love you, Bridie. Never doubt that.'

Tristan regretted his decision to travel to France. He was angry at the way Lady Alys had rejected him. He had visited a gaming house, but found that even after winning several hands his mood remained weighted and restless. The laughter and music sounded too loud and discordant. The excited babble of French voices rang falsely in his ears. The glittering chandeliers were too bright and the darkened recesses too gloomy. The wine was tainted with the sourness of discontent and the food was sickly, over-spiced with the taste of conspiracy.

Frigid smiles never reached shadowed eyes. Few people held his stare, casting nervous glances at companions as though suspecting treachery to be unleashed. The air was fetid with a restless desperation.

Tristan left the gaming rooms before midnight. The success of his business deals no longer exhilarated him. What was he doing embroiling himself in this lair of intrigue and underlying treachery? He had proved he could triumph over his adversaries. He was master of the estate in England he had long coveted. Why was he pandering to the French when he could be at his ease in Cornwall? He was not a pawn to be picked up and discarded when the mood claimed Lady Alys. Tomorrow he would return to England. If she insisted on remaining, Lapoitiere would be as good an escort as any.

When he entered the Lapoitieres' house, few candles were lit, as his host and his wife had not returned. He waved aside the servant who appeared to take his greatcoat and hat and offer him refreshments, and took the stairs two at a time to his room. To his surprise the door was ajar and a single candle burned on the table beside the bed. He drew the dagger that he carried inside his top boot and with it held before him scanned the room. No one lurked in any of the corners. Silently he advanced towards the bed. Lady Alys was asleep on top of the covers, her closed lids still reddened from crying. He laid the dagger aside and sat on the edge of the mattress, softly calling her name.

Her eyes flew open and she gasped. 'Oh, I must have fallen asleep. I wanted to apologise to you.'

'You could have done that in the morning.' He remained wary of her motives.

'It would not have been the same.' She pushed herself up on to her elbow. Although she still wore the gown he had seen her in earlier, her hair had been loosed from its pins and draped in soft curls to her waist.

He brushed his hand across her cheek and could feel the dampness of tears upon her lashes. 'You have been crying.'

'You are mistaken. My eyes are sore from the smoke of the candle.'

His gaze hovered briefly upon her lips. She was beautiful and so desirable. With a soft groan he crushed her to him, his kisses travelling along her neck to the rise of her breasts. Her fingers twined through his hair as her body arched against him. It sent his blood pulsing to a white heat as he reverently peeled the gown from her shoulders, kissing every inch of exposed flesh. Then her own hands became impatient, pushing his jacket from his arms, their bodies heated with molten fire as their clothes were tossed to the floor and the room echoed to their soft sighs.

Later, they fell asleep entwined in each other's arms, but when Tristan awoke in the middle of the night he found himself once more alone in his bed. It seemed emptier than it had ever done before, but he understood that Alys would wish to preserve her reputation and not want a maid finding her bed unoccupied in the morning.

He rose early and was disappointed when Alys was not there to take her breakfast with him. His host was the first to appear, with a list of acquaintances he had seen at the theatre who were eager to meet the Englishman. Tristan made vague excuses that he had several appointments that day. An hour later, when Alys had not still not emerged from her bedchamber, he left the house before Lapoitiere could pester him to accompany him on his visits. He did not go far. There was a coffee house on the corner where he could keep watch. When he saw Lapoitiere leave, he returned to the house expecting Alys soon to join him. Another hour had passed when Madam Lapoitiere came into the salon talking to her maid about the shops they must visit.

She smiled at Tristan. 'Monsieur Loveday, you are all by yourself. Did my husband not have appointments for you together?'

'I have previous engagements. And I also wondered if Lady Alys would be requiring me to escort her this morning.'

The woman's smile faltered and she coughed in embarrassment. 'Oh dear, this is most unfortunate, Monsieur Loveday. Lady Alys has already left. At some ungodly hour this morning according to her maid. I do hope that you have not been inconvenienced, monsieur.'

'I must have been mistaken.' He managed to stretch a smile across his lips though inside he was blazing with fury. 'Do you happen to know where she went?'

'That she did not say.' Madame Lapoitiere pulled on her gloves and adjusted the braid of the reticule hanging from her wrist. 'I will not delay you, Monsieur Loveday. Can I ask my coachman to take you anywhere?'

He shook his head. He needed to walk and gather his

emotions. Again Lady Alys had led him a merry dance. He was now convinced that she was hiding something from him and that last night had been nothing more than a ruse to gain his trust. She had underestimated him and would regret using her wiles to make a fool of him. Clearly this bold, independent woman was far different from the vulnerable female she had shown when they first met. Then she had played the damsel in distress. Who was the real Lady Alys?

Tristan excused himself from dining with his hosts and Lady Alys that evening. He took up a position in a darkened corner of the street and was prepared to wait there all night if it meant he could discover where Lady Alys kept disappearing to and the company she preferred to his own.

There was the bite of frost in the air. The moon was three quarters full in a cloudless sky and was bright enough to throw the centre of the street into light. Fortunately the tall buildings gave protection from the wind. Not that the cold troubled Tristan. As a pickpocket in his childhood he had spent many nights lying in wait for a victim. He secreted himself from the patrolling watchmen, and not long afterwards a cloaked figure emerged from a side door of the Lapoitieres' house. The hood was pulled down low over the features but the figure was unmistakably that of a woman. Her grace and bearing was not that of a servant. It must be Lady Alys. The figure kept to the shadows and Tristan's step was silent as he followed his prey.

The journey was short and they turned right at the first crossroads. Four houses from there he heard a rap on a door and sprang deeper into the shadows. The portal swung open and the woman disappeared within. It was not a residence Tristan was familiar with, but he would make it his business to find out who lived there and the nature of any visitors. No lights were visible behind the shuttered windows, adding to the clandestine atmosphere of the visit. He did not have to wait long before the door opened again and the figure of a young man in a greatcoat emerged, a low-crowned broad-brimmed hat concealing his features.

Tristan dismissed him as unimportant. He could not be who the Lady Alys was meeting as she had not re-emerged. He frowned when the figure returned within the hour and after a knock on the door slid silently back into the building. Had he been remiss not to follow him and discover the man's identity? Too late now. He must learn more of the house and its inhabitants.

As he mulled these events over, his stare was fixed on the dwelling. There was the slightest stirring in the air around him. Tristan reacted instinctively, his hand snaking out and clamping around a bony wrist about to dip into his pocket. He spun round and twisted his assailant's arm high behind the man's back, with his free hand pulling a dagger from his top boot. There was the stench of rotting teeth on a harshly expelled breath as he slammed the figure up against the wall of a house. He pressed his dagger against a bewhiskered throat.

'Make a sound to call your gang and I'll slit your gullet,' Tristan whispered against the unwashed ear, the rancid smell of the lank hair sour in his nostrils. 'Thought to lighten me of my purse, did you?' He spoke rapidly in French. 'It will be a long day in hell before you get the better of me.'

'This is our patch,' the man snarled. 'Snatcher don't take kindly to others poaching our game. It will be you who is dead.'

As the thief attempted to wriggle free, Tristan jerked the limb higher and the man groaned in agony.

'Try that again and I'll break your arm. I am not working your patch.' Menace dripped from every word. 'And if I did, I would not be caught, nor would I be at the call of some chancer who thinks he can lord it over me. Understand? I've more important work.'

Another twist on the wrist and the thief sagged against the wall. Tristan tersely informed him, 'Now, I can break your arm, or you could make yourself useful to me, seeing as how you are familiar with these parts.'

'The devil take you! Snatcher will cut out your liver for this.' The thief hawked and spat at Tristan's feet.

'All I want is information.'

'What's it worth?'

'Your life. Though that strikes me as worthless enough.'

'I ain't welching on Snatcher. He'd kill me for sure.'

'I've no interest in Snatcher,' Tristan returned. 'Who lives in that house over there?'

The man in his clutches stopped wriggling. 'You another damned aristo?'

'I'm the man losing patience with some lowlife who tried to rob me.' The tip of his dagger pierced the grime-encrusted skin, and the iron smell of blood mixed with the stench of the robber's stale sweat. 'Not only will the information save your life, but I may make it worth your while.'

Tristan had often used his knowledge of the underworld to gain the trust of men who could slip unnoticed through crowds. They could discover facts that others preferred kept secret.

'I'm no aristo,' he added. 'I grew up on the streets of St Malo.' He did not want the man to suspect that he was

English. 'You should heed that I've worked for the most unprincipled rogues you could imagine. How else would I have known you were about to steal my purse before you even got close to my pocket? Or were you just careless in your old age? I doubt Snatcher will want anyone working for him who is likely to be caught by the law. Many a thief has snitched on his friends rather than face Madame Guillotine.'

The moon had moved over the rooftops, and in its light Tristan could clearly see the thief's pockmarked face. He shoved him back into the shadows. 'Who lives in the house?'

The man again attempted to wrench himself free. The blade slipped deeper into flesh. As his captive turned his head aside, Tristan saw that one ear had been sliced off, either as punishment for a crime or in a knife fight.

'Do you really want to die tonight?' he threatened.

The robber went limp. 'Some foreigner's been living there for months.'

'His name?'

'I don't know his name.'

'Nationality?'

'They ain't French. That's all I know.'

'You're a poor excuse for a thief if you don't know who lives on your own patch.' Tristan considered whether to run the knave through. Yet there was still a chance he could be useful to him. He eased the dagger away from the man's throat.

'Don't kill me,' the thief pleaded. 'I got a wife. Seven kids. I could find out for you. Just don't kill me.'

'What's your name?' Tristan did not believe his tale of a family. It was too common an excuse for mercy.

The man hesitated. Tristan changed tactics. With such distinctive features the thief would be easy to track down.

The people he mixed with would sell their own souls for a price.

'Get the information for me and I'll pay you well,' he offered. 'I'll be on the steps of Notre-Dame tomorrow morning. If you think to feed me a lie or set your gang of robbers upon me, then you won't live through the day. I don't work alone and I know your face.'

He gave the man a shove and released him. As he heard him scampering away, he hoped the robber's greed would bring him to the ancient church tomorrow.

Tristan adjusted the cape of his greatcoat and leaned back against the wall, expecting another long wait. In that he was proved wrong. Within minutes the door opposite opened and Lady Alys stepped into the street, hurrying back to Lapoitiere's house. His own encounter with the thief had shown him how unsafe the streets were. What meeting was so important that she would risk her life? And if she had met a lover, what knave would allow a woman to walk the streets alone of a night?

Chapter Thirty-two

'Did Adam tell you the real reason he and Japhet have sailed to France with Long Tom?' A worried Gwendolyn had ridden to Boscabel the day after the men had left. It had been dawn when Japhet and Adam had bidden goodbye to their wives with promises that they would be safely home soon. The dark shadows under Gwen's eyes showed Senara that she had slept little.

Senara sensed that Adam and Japhet were upon business other than that they had stated. Since St John's death she had been aware of the restlessness within her husband. The need for adventure was as much a part of him as was his love for his family. Even though she feared that he would again be placing himself in danger, she would never curb the wildness in his blood.

'Long Tom asked for their help to bring a traitor to justice. It was a request our husbands were unlikely to refuse.'

'You know that they meet most weeks to practise their swordplay?' Gwen pressed a hand to her temple. 'We both know what is behind that. Their need for vengeance. I had hoped Japhet would have put that behind him after all these years.'

'It is not the Loveday way.' Senara shrugged. 'We love

them for their courage and daring, and no matter how much they love us, we could never change their sense of honour. Nor would it be right.'

'But I hate the secrecy and deception of the last weeks. I know we have much to thank Long Tom for, but I wish he had not involved them.'

'Japhet and Adam owe Long Tom a great deal. They would want to repay him. And if they sought to deceive us, it was to spare us the worry of knowing the danger they would face.'

Gwendolyn sighed and raised her eyes to the wintry sky. She forced a brighter note into her voice. 'At least they have each other. One Loveday is a force to be reckoned with. Two fighting for the same cause are invincible, are they not?'

'We have to believe that. Nothing could have stopped them pursuing this line of duty. It would only have made it harder for them if we had caused a fuss.'

'Do you think Osgood is somehow involved?' Gwendolyn's eyes were dark with fear.

'It is likely. But Japhet is not facing his enemy alone. And if Osgood is a traitor, he deserves to be brought to justice. Perhaps then Japhet will find peace and put his wild ways behind him.'

'And what of Adam and Tristan?' Gwendolyn persisted. 'There is no sign of that rivalry abating.'

'It must take its course. I trust Japhet to be the reasoning force in that vendetta as Adam will be between your husband and Osgood. Let us hope that they will be home soon, safe and unharmed.' To change the subject, Senara said, 'There are no problems at the stud, are there?'

Gwendolyn shook her head. 'Joshua has promised to call by when he can, and so has Sir Henry.'

'Your brother-in-law is a good man. He promised as

much to Adam. But we both have servants to protect us. Not that I am expecting any trouble. Besides, as Loveday women, are we not formidable ourselves?' she jested to cheer Gwendolyn.

'Indefatigable.' Gwen laughed. 'Anything you need, do not hesitate to ask.'

'And you.'

They made their farewells, but after Gwendolyn left Senara remained unsettled. She could not forget an earlier premonition that Adam would face the greatest danger of his life. Her thoughts also dwelt upon other members of her family. It was some weeks since she had seen Bridie, and she often wondered how she had adapted to life in a bustling town. She did not doubt that soon her sister would win the hearts of the people in her husband's parish as she had done at Polruggan. She did miss her company, though, as she missed all her family, not least the most elusive member. She had not seen or heard of her brother Caleph for several years. His gypsy tribe no longer came so far west, even though Adam had given them permission to camp on his land. She knew Caleph kept his distance to protect her from malicious gossip. Yet he was often in her thoughts. Life was hard on the road, and during a freezing winter his family could be facing starvation.

It also troubled her that Caleph might not know of Leah's death. Her instinct was to search for him, but with Adam away she was reluctant to leave Sara and Rhianne at Boscabel with their tutor and servants. Amelia was in Bodmin and Felicity had enough to cope within without adding to her burdens. Even so, she could not shake thoughts of Caleph from haunting her days. Every instinct told her that her brother was in trouble.

★

The sun was low in the sky, and when Tristan passed into the long shadow cast by Notre-Dame, the temperature dropped several degrees. As an atheist, he had no feelings of awe or splendour at this ancient edifice.

For his meeting with the thief, Tristan had donned a shabby greatcoat with a torn cape and a sleeve ripped out. He was unshaven and wore a woollen cap pulled low on his brow under a battered tricorne hat. He mingled inconspicuously with the beggars demanding alms and shambled up the church steps to flop down behind the man who had tried to rob him. He had learned earlier he was known as Gargoyle. He was certainly ugly enough.

'*Bonsoir*, Gargoyle. You are not much valued by your associates. A couple of sous bought me your name and where I could find you if you were not here. Do not turn round. I prefer us not to be seen talking together. What did you find out for me?'

Gargoyle scratched his neck, a bloodied bandaged hand extended towards a merchant's wife as he whined, 'Alms for an old soldier. For my sick wife and seven children.'

She took one look at him, shuddered and rapidly crossed herself, dropping a single sou at his feet as she hurried in to mass. Gargoyle spat on the ground as her skirts swept past him. 'Rot in hell, pinchpenny.' He kept his hand extended whilst his head was averted from Tristan. 'The house belongs to the Comte de Duchon. But he is reported to live quietly at his chateau in Bordeaux. Or what is left of it,' Gargoyle sniggered derisively. 'An English aristo has rented the house for the winter. He is rarely seen there, although some fancy trollop is a regular visitor.'

Tristan swallowed against a rise of bitter bile. 'If you are lying, your throat will be slit before nightfall.' He tossed down several livres and disappeared into the crowd before Gargoyle had a chance to see his face. He ducked through the press of Parisians, fury burning his gut. For the Lady Alys to spend so long in that house could only mean that she was no different from any whore intent upon her own pleasure. She was visiting her lover. How wrong he had been about her. Like a lovelorn fool he had been taken in by her false air of innocence.

He spent an hour prowling the streets before his temper had cooled enough for him to return to Lapoitiere's house. He'd be damned if he'd be at the beck and call of some harlot. He did not need Brienne's patronage any more. He had made enough contacts for his business to prosper. Even so, he was furious at how easily he had been taken in by Brienne's play-acting. His mood turned his thoughts savage.

He was not pleased to encounter Lady Alys when he returned to Lapoitiere's residence. As they were alone, she ran to him and threw her arms around his waist.

'There you are, my love. Where have you been? I have missed you so much. The Lapoitieres are visiting friends. We have at least an hour before they return. A whole hour for me to tell you how much I adore you.'

Tristan stood unyielding as marble. He turned his head away from her kisses, his arms loose at his sides.

'My love, what is amiss?' Her stare was anxious upon his face. The steel she saw in his eyes made her step back.

'What manner of whore are you?' he clipped out, his lip curled with contempt.

Her hands went limp at her sides and her face drained of colour. 'Is that what you think of me? It is not my custom to offer myself to a man. I was mistaken in you.'

The anger was burning too strongly for him to consider his words. He wanted to hurt her for betraying

351

his trust. 'My mother was a whore. Yet at least she sold her body so that we could eat. And she was frequently beaten by the men who used her. What is your excuse? Hardly poverty.' His scorn lashed her.

His cheek stung with fire before he had even realised that she had raised her hand. He was shocked as much by the speed of her reaction as he was that his reflexes had not been fast enough to counter the blow.

'Get out of this house,' she raged. 'If that is what you believe, I never want to see you again.'

He stormed away, packed his bag and marched down the staircase. He ignored her when she appeared in the hall, her voice low and beseeching.

'Tristan. Let us not part this way. I do not know what lies you have heard. Tell me so that I can put your mind at rest.'

He was too angry to reply. What was the point of listening to more of her falsehoods?

He did not trust her or Brienne. He was expecting a final delivery of goods to his warehouse in two days. He had already engaged three carters who would load up the furniture and valuables and transport them to Calais. He had decided to travel with them to ensure the more fragile porcelain and china he had acquired did not meet with an accident. He had also employed two men as armed guards. Some of the furnishings and ornaments were for his own use at Trevowan. The rest would go to his warehouse, where they would be catalogued and brochures printed for his growing number of clients.

By the end of the week he would be leaving France and the intrigue that he had almost been embroiled in.

Adam and Japhet were beginning to wonder if they were on a wild goose chase. They had visited all the main places of entertainment and there had been so sign of the hedonistic Osgood. Discreet enquiries had also yielded nothing about the whereabouts of a man with a scarred cheek. After a week Japhet had met an old acquaintance from his gambling days who had recognised Osgood at the theatre two nights ago.

'Finally he is within my grasp,' Japhet announced to Adam as they returned to their rooms in an inn close to the Tuileries palace.

'And how do you plan to bring him to account?' Adam responded. 'I thought you wanted his disgrace to be known in England. If he is siding with the Royalists and is not a supporter of Bonaparte, our government will not regard him as a traitor. Many will view him as a hero, for if the king is restored with British support, France will be our ally.'

'Osgood must be the means of his own downfall.' Japhet flopped down on his bed and, stretching out his long legs, put his hands behind his head and frowned. 'I have no plan as yet. It depends on what we learn about that treacherous dog. But I have a feeling that our first confrontation will provide the source of his undoing.'

'If Long Tom were here, he would know the best course to take,' Adam remarked.

'He has his own investigations to make. We do not need him.'

'I am not so sure he does not need us.' Adam paced thoughtfully. 'He should have joined us in Paris by now. He could have been arrested. The mood of the people is changing. Our ambassador is warning the English to leave. He might suspect that war will soon break out.'

Elspeth had assumed that Tristan would be settling at Trevowan now that the furniture was in place and the renovations completed. Yet he and his guests had left after two weeks. The windows were again shuttered and dust sheets made ghostly shapes of the furniture. Stubbornness had driven her through cold and isolated weeks. Although the family had welcomed her whenever she visited them, she was not so thick skinned that she could not sense their disapproval. They believed that she had taken sides with Tristan by supporting him over the festive season.

Adam and Japhet had since gone on their travels, ostensibly to drum up more business for the shipyard – though Elspeth did not believe a word of it. The family had been reticent in explaining the nature of their business and to her it smacked of secrecy. Knowing her nephews, there was also bound to be danger. The strained faces and sombre moods of Senara and Gwendolyn confirmed this.

In Japhet's absence she had more of an excuse to visit the stud, though she was careful of giving any advice to their new trainer, who was far too ready to take offence and clearly had not learned his place when addressing his betters.

The weather had turned colder and a permanent mist added to the chill in the air. Today Elspeth had ridden across the moor to dispel the restlessness that consumed her. Her pride would never allow her to admit that often of late she had been lonely. Trevowan had become more of a mausoleum than a home. Tristan had brought in more servants and labourers. All had been given detailed instructions of the work they were to carry out on the home farm, grounds and house. Although Elspeth kept a watchful eye on them, they were diligent in their labours, obviously intent upon proving their capabilities to their new master.

By the late afternoon her entire body ached after the

exertions of her ride. Her injured hip stabbed deep inside the joint with every stride of her mare. She was used to such pain and gritted her teeth, refusing to allow it to spoil the pleasure of her ride. The mist was thickening and she was eager for the warmth of her hearth to ease the discomfort in her bones.

In the distance the sound of baying hounds was eerie in the mist. There was nothing she enjoyed more than the thrill of the hunt, but the dogs sounded different and as far as she knew Lord Fetherington's pack were not hunting today or she would have been invited to join them. Two shots echoed sinisterly from a wood and a pheasant flapped noisily out of the undergrowth across the field. It was hardly the weather for a pheasant shoot. It was more likely that a hungry farmer was after rabbits. There was no more gunfire and she forgot the incident, cutting across a field and giving Kara her head as they jumped a low hedge into a narrow lane with overhanging branches. The light was fading and she urged her mount to a faster pace.

Suddenly ahead of her a dark shape darted across the road and seemed to fall into a ditch. Suspecting that it was a deer, she expected to hear it breaking through the dead bracken on the other side. Instead there was silence. As she neared the place where it had crossed, Kara began to prance nervously, the side saddle jarring Elspeth's inflamed hip until she gasped for breath. She reined Kara in and took several deep breaths to combat the pain. It was then that she heard the agonised groan and a bearded, unkempt figure, his shirt covered with blood, threw himself at Kara's bridle.

'Give me your horse,' the man threatened.

Elspeth raised her whip and brought it down on the brigand's wrist. 'Unhand my mare. I'll have you flogged and imprisoned for this outrage.' Her heart beat rapidly. This was the first time she had ever been accosted during a ride, but she was not frightened, she was angry.

The man's wild eyes regarded her, his voice hoarse. 'Miss Loveday. Help me.'

'Who the devil are you? And get away from my horse if you value your freedom.' She struck him again, this time across the shoulders, incensed that he intended to steal Kara.

'It is my life I fear for, Miss Elspeth. Help me.'

'You'll hang as a horse thief all right,' she raged.

'Do you not recognise me? I'm Caleph. Senara's . . .' His body swayed against the neck of the mare.

'Get away.' Elspeth was about to strike him again when her hand froze. The man was ragged, grime encrusted, no better than a beggar. Thickly lashed green eyes stared up at her. A beggar or a gypsy . . . Her brain slowly focused. She did not recognise him apart from the eyes. They were the same colour as those of Adam's wife. And was not Caleph the name of Senara's brother? A shudder passed through her at hearing the sound of baying hounds much closer.

'They're after me. Help me. Take me to Senara.' He leaned heavily against Kara's neck and seemed close to collapse.

'What crime have you committed? That they would set the dogs on you?'

'Nothing bad. I was in the wrong place at the wrong time.' He released the bridle and staggered backwards. Blood was now running down his arm.

'Have you been shot?'

The dogs were breaking through the hedgerow on the far side of the next field. They would be upon them in moments.

'I should not have asked. Too dangerous,' he muttered and turned away, reeling from loss of blood.

Elspeth urged Kara closer and reached out her hand. 'Be quick. Get up behind me. And hang on tight.'

He clasped her fingers and used his failing strength to vault on to the mare behind her. The trees, sky and ground began to spin crazily around him. Caleph had ridden bareback since a child, and as he hovered on the edge of consciousness he had wits left enough to fold his arms around Elspeth's waist.

She kicked her mount to a gallop, leaving the track to weave through a wood before splashing along a stream and doubling back towards Boscabel.

Chapter Thirty-three

The baying of the dogs had changed, signalling that they had lost Caleph's trail. Elspeth could feel the man losing his hold around her body and gripped his arm with one hand. It had also started to rain, which would further aid their flight and prevent the hounds from again picking up their scent.

'Stay awake, man,' she ordered fiercely. 'If you fall off I will never get you back on the horse. The dogs could pick up your scent at any moment. It is not far to Boscabel.'

There was a slight tightening of his hold but she feared that loss of blood would cause him to tumble to the ground. She would not be able to dismount even to drag him to cover while she rode for help. Her hip no longer allowed her to remount without the use of a block or a groom cupping his hands to assist her into the saddle. If Caleph fell to the ground he would have to stay where he lay until Billy Brown brought a cart from Boscabel. But in that time he could be captured. And if his identity were known, it would rebound upon Senara and Adam.

Fortunately Elspeth was a skilled horsewoman, and even though Kara was spirited, the mare was obedient to all commands. They were close enough to Boscabel for

Elspeth to ease their pace and keep a firm hand upon Caleph, who was leaning against her back.

The sound of the dogs searching for their scent was far behind them. Laughter rumbled in Elspeth's throat and her blood was racing through her body. It was years since she had felt this buzz of excitement. It made her feel young again, and carefree. Even the seriousness of Caleph's plight and the consequences it could bring down upon her family did not lessen her euphoria.

She knew that the Brown family and Eli Rudge, the bailiff, were loyal to Adam and would never betray Senara's brother to the authorities. She was not so sure about some of the other servants, although many of their families were beholden to Senara for tending them during illness.

It was dusk when Elspeth clattered through the arched entrance to Boscabel. Billy Brown came out of an outbuilding in the stable yard at the sound of her horse's arrival. He was clearly shocked to see the ragged figure of a man clinging to the staid elderly woman.

Elspeth rode straight past him into one of the empty stalls.

'Lay him down on the straw over there,' she ordered as he followed her. 'Then fetch your mistress. It is her brother, but tell no one else for now. I trust your mistress is at home, or she may return to find a corpse in his place.'

Brown had lost a hand in the navy, where he had once served with Adam. He used his stump to support Caleph as he laid him down on the straw. 'Mrs Loveday has just come in from tending her herb garden.' He hurried out as Elspeth dismounted and loosened Kara's girth.

Senara was breathless as she ran into the stable. Elspeth had placed a horse blanket over the gypsy and brought two lighted lanterns from the tack room, where Brown had been cleaning the harnesses of the work horses. She hung one lantern on the nail for the horse's fodder net and held the other over the prone patient. Beneath his tattered jacket, blood had seeped across the red flannel of his shirt. It also dripped from one hand and was beginning to soak through the horse blanket. His breathing was so shallow, Elspeth was no longer sure whether he still lived.

'He's been shot. Quite bad from what I can tell,' she informed Senara.

Adam's wife put her basket of remedies on the straw and knelt beside her brother. She lifted the blanket and peeled away his jacket. Her hands shook as she tore open his shirt and saw the blackened holes of two bullet wounds. One of them had ploughed through the top of his shoulder, just missing the bone, and this was bleeding profusely. The other had passed through the fleshy part of his torso just below his ribcage. From the size of the holes he had been shot in the back. Exit wounds were always larger than where the bullets had entered the body. Even so, Caleph had been lucky. A fingernail's length difference to either of them could have resulted in a fatality. No major organ had been penetrated.

Elijah Rudge, their bailiff, also came into the stable just as Senara had taken a handful of old sheets that had been ripped into bandages and pressed them against the wounds to stop the bleeding.

'I cannot treat him here.' She glanced up at the tall, stocky man. 'Take the tack room door off its hinges and carry him up the back stairs to the blue guest room. Elspeth, can you keep some pressure on these bandages while I fetch what else I need from the herb room.'

Her aunt obeyed without comment, and as they made

their slow passage to the house, Senara ran into the kitchen shouting for water to be boiled and also collected some prepared herbs and steel instruments. She entered the bedroom as Brown and Rudge slid Caleph on to the bed. The room was in darkness as the last of the daylight faded. Elspeth lit a taper from the lantern she was carrying and touched it first to the kindling and logs in the hearth and then to the candle at the side of the bed. Then she drew back to the fire, her wet riding habit clinging to her shoulders and back.

Senara closed the shutters. Not that anyone could see into the room from outside, but she was always extra cautious where Caleph was involved. The bullet wounds were a warning that her brother was in danger, and not only from the shots themselves.

'I shall leave you to tend to him,' Elspeth said, limping to the door. 'I have to tell you that someone was hunting him with dogs when they shot him. If he has broken the law . . .' She broke off, her stare grim with warning. 'Well, you know the consequences.'

'Thank you for bringing him here, Elspeth. Especially in such circumstances.' Senara had eased off her brother's jacket and was removing his bloodstained shirt.

'It is what Adam would expect,' Elspeth replied. 'I may not approve of the manner of his living, but he is your brother.'

'And that makes this deed even more special.' Senara paused in her work and smiled at the older woman. 'I shall never forget it. I doubt from these wounds that Caleph could have made it here alone. Even if he had escaped capture, he could have died from a night in the open.'

Elspeth waved her hand dismissively, and as the light from the lantern moved across the floorboards, Senara noticed the damp trail left by her riding skirt. The heat of the fire caused a faint vapour to rise from her garments.

'Aunt Elspeth, you must be soaked. Gilly will bring you a change of clothes and she will heat you water for a bath, if you so wish.'

Elspeth was about to refuse both offers when her aching hip almost gave way and she grabbed hold of a chair back for support. 'A change of clothes will be welcome and a hot toddy of brandy will chase the cold from my bones. A servant should ride to Trevowan to inform them that I am here. Otherwise they will be sending out a search party suspecting I have fallen from my horse. Tristan has threatened the jobs of the Nance family should they fail in their duty to me.'

Gilly Brown had followed Senara to the bedchamber. Senara had now removed the bloodied bandages from Caleph's body. She did not look up from cleaning the wounds as she instructed the servant, 'See to Miss Loveday's needs, and Trevowan must also be informed.'

Elspeth left with the maid and could be heard giving her own instructions. 'Get that man of yours to rub down and stable my mare. She's been ridden hard and needs extra food.'

Alone with Caleph, Senara studied him more closely as she cleansed the bloodied flesh. She was shocked at how thin he had become. His family must have endured a hard winter and those hardships of near starvation she knew so well. Her heart went out to him. Now that he had come to her she hoped that he would allow her to help his family. It troubled her that he was still unconscious, but that enabled her to probe more deeply as she inspected the wounds. The shots might have passed cleanly through him, but if fibres from his shirt remained in the wound, they would fester and could kill him from blood poisoning. He groaned as she worked over him, and as she was lifting a thread of coarse cotton from the gore, his eyes flickered open. They widened in alarm and, disorientated as to his surroundings, his hand went to her throat as he fought to free himself from the clutches of an assailant.

'Caleph, it is me, Senara. Be still. You are safe at Boscabel.'

Her words penetrated his fear and the wildness left his eyes. Slowly the light of recognition dawned and his fingers loosened from her neck. 'Is it really you?'

'Yes.' She swallowed against a lump of emotion in her throat. 'Are your family close by? Can I send word to them? They can camp in the wood. Rudge will take them all the food they need.'

He screwed shut his eyes and his face twisted in a spasm of pain. 'They've gone. All gone. My fault.'

He struggled to sit up.

Senara eased him gently back on to the mattress, worried that he would start his wounds bleeding. He had already lost so much blood and was very weak. She struggled to regain her own composure, needing to be calm and clear headed to attend him. 'We will not talk of it now. You must rest and regain your strength.'

He pushed against her restraining hand. 'I cannot stay here. It is too dangerous for you.'

'You cannot go anywhere until you are stronger,' she said firmly. 'You need rest and food.'

'Then warn Adam to be vigilant.' His voice became fainter with every word and his eyes closed.

She felt his pulse and was relieved that it was stronger. From the even rhythm of his breath she was certain that he had fallen asleep and was not unconscious. Sleep was what he needed most. It was the best healing.

Tears welled into her eyes as she held his hand and stared down at him. What had he meant about his family being gone? And why did he blame himself?

Senara left Gilly Brown watching over Caleph, with instructions for the servant to summon her if he awoke. She then sought out Elspeth, who was in the winter parlour. The walls were covered with tapestries depicting hunting scenes. Her aunt was seated by the fire and put aside the book she was reading.

'How is the patient?' she asked.

'He is sleeping. You saved his life, Elspeth.'

'How came he to be shot?' She sniffed her disapproval, which Senara guessed was for her brother and the crime he might have committed.

Senara sighed. 'He did not say. His wounds are recent.'

'They do not set the dogs after a man for no reason. Could he have escaped the prison?'

'It is possible,' Senara had to admit.

'And if the authorities visit here, will you hand him over?' Elspeth's manner remained stiff and accusing.

'Would you have given Adam, St John or Japhet over to the authorities when they transgressed? Especially if it was likely they would hang.'

Elspeth studied Senara over the top of her pince-nez. 'I suppose that would depend on the severity of the crime. If they were guilty of a heinous murder – then it would not be so easy to ignore the law.'

'And if they had killed in self-defence, what then?'

'My nephews have dealt with many unsavoury characters. If the murder was not premeditated, then I would do all I could to help them escape arrest.'

Senara folded her arms across her chest. 'A man can also be hanged for stealing a horse or a rabbit from the land of the gentry; even a starving child has been so condemned for stealing a loaf of bread.'

'I am no judiciary, but such a punishment does seem harsh for those crimes.' Elspeth pinned her with a forthright stare. 'But without the power of the law, we fall into anarchy.'

A loud knocking on the outer door startled both women. A maid screamed and there was the clump of heavy boots in the hall.

'Where's your master?' demanded a gruff voice.

When Senara stood up, Elspeth said quickly, 'Sit down and look as though you have not a care in the world. We are two women enjoying a pleasant evening of conversation.'

The door banged open and a surly militia sergeant and three men thrust themselves into the room. Their scarlet uniforms were splattered with mud, and rain dripped from the peaks of their bicornes and their sodden horsehair wigs. Behind them Gilly was pale and shaken.

'I'm sorry, Mrs Loveday. They forced themselves in.' The servant wrung her hands.

Senara smiled at her. 'It is not your fault, Gilly. No one expects to have their home so rudely invaded.'

Elspeth had risen to her feet and brandished her cane in accusation at the soldiers. 'What do you mean by such unseemly conduct? Good Lord, man, you've tramped mud all over this Persian carpet with your filthy boots, and your men are dripping water on the polished floorboards.' She advanced on them, striking at their ankles with her stick. 'Get back into the porch. The floor and carpet will be ruined. This is a gentleman's residence, not some wayside kiddley.'

The soldiers stepped back, taken by surprise by the old woman's attack. The sergeant stayed where he was and raised his rifle. 'I am here on official business. A convict has escaped. He was seen heading in this direction.'

'I can assure you that no convict has entered this house,' Elspeth thundered. 'Though you may search the outbuildings if you insist. It is possible that he could have taken shelter there from the rain, but I doubt it. It would be foolhardy, would it not, to risk discovery by our servants when there are barns on the outskirts of the estate?' She continued to hold her cane in a menacing manner. 'Your name, Sergeant? And take that weapon away from my face, sir.'

The rifle was lowered and the sergeant's face darkened with anger. He was a head shorter than either of the women, with several days' beard stubble on his jutting jaw.

'Sergeant Harris,' he announced belligerently.

'Then, Sergeant Harris, I suggest you learn to mend your manners.' Elspeth stood her ground, imperious in her outrage. 'Your commanding officer will learn that you have forced your way into the house of an old and revered family and threatened their women at gunpoint.'

'The prisoner were a gypsy.' The sergeant scowled at Senara. 'It be said the master here let them use his land – and he's been known to show them favour in the past.'

'My husband is away on business, Sergeant,' Senara informed him coldly. She breathed deeply to combat her rising fear that at any moment they would search the house and find Caleph upstairs. The soldiers resurrected her deepest dread. During the years she had lived with the gypsies, she had seen her kind arrested on any suspicion or misdeed. Many of them were never heard of again. In those days she had faced many prejudices. The poor had no rights against the authorities. But she was no longer that ragged, helpless gypsy girl. She was the wife of Adam Loveday, the respected owner of a shipyard. She squared her shoulders, taking her cue from Elspeth's fury upon this invasion of her home. Her cultured voice rang with the hauteur of a woman who expects obedience to her commands. 'There have been no gypsies on our land for some years, or in the area as far as I am aware.'

'You won't object to us searching the house then, will you?' Harris sneered. 'Heard tell you were no better than a gypsy wench yourself.'

'Take care, Sergeant Harris, how you address the wife of a respected gentleman.' Elspeth banged her cane on the floorboards.

Harris scowled and murmured an apology.

Senara knew the folly of antagonising the man. It would only make him more vigilant in his search. 'My duties as mistress of this estate would allow nothing to jeopardise my husband's reputation. Apart from my aunt, there have been no visitors to Boscabel this day.'

The sergeant's eyes narrowed. 'Then why would you not wish us to search the place?'

'I can think of a hundred good reasons why I object to loutish soldiers stamping through my nephew's home.' Elspeth prodded him in the stomach with her walking cane.' Not least that you have already ruined this fine carpet. The house is full of valuables. No thieving gypsy would be welcome inside. 'She jabbed him again, her voice thick with disdain. 'Besides, we are about to retire to our beds, and I will not have you tramping mud and water all through the house at this ungodly hour. Our good neighbour, friend and justice, Sir Henry Traherne, will hear of this outrage. As will Lord Fetherington. Mr Adam Loveday is godfather to his lordship's youngest daughter.'

'The convict is dangerous. For your own safety the

house should be searched,' the sergeant blustered.

'We have four male servants living adjacent to the house,' Elspeth continued to bear down on him, and though the sergeant took two paces back, his rifle remained raised across his chest. 'If the alarm bell is rung, another half-dozen tenants will run to our aid. No gypsy, however dangerous, is a match for them. Your commanding officer will be furious that you have wasted time here. If this prisoner is so dangerous, you should be searching for him in some derelict barn, old mine workings or disused shepherd's or charcoal burner's hut.'

The accompanying soldiers looked uneasy at Elspeth's challenge and glanced nervously at the sergeant. Senara almost felt sorry for them, Elspeth in full rage made many of the family quake in their shoes, including the men.

The oldest of the soldiers grunted to his superior, 'It bain't likely he be here, Sarge.'

Harris glared at the two women, clearly resentful that his authority had been questioned.

Senara stepped forward, tactfully extending her hand and lowering Elspeth's cane to the floor. 'Sergeant Harris, as two women alone, we are grateful for your warning that a prisoner is on the loose. You may be assured that the doors and windows will be tightly barred and our servants vigilant in searching the outbuildings at first light. If the prisoner should be found, he will be locked in the woodshed and your commander will be informed.'

Harris hesitated as he considered her words. 'Very well, Mrs Loveday. I hope you will not live to regret your decision and find yourselves and your children murdered in your beds.'

'Forewarned is forearmed, Sergeant. My bailiff is diligent in training our male servants to protect us from thieves and even poachers,' she conceded.

'Outside, men. There's a prisoner to be found,' Harris bellowed.

'You may wish to search down by the river. There is a rowboat kept there. He could have stolen that and gone upriver,' Senara suggested as the soldiers tramped out of the house.

She shut the door behind them and leaned back against the frame. 'Thank you again for your support, Elspeth. I am not sure I could have dealt with them alone.'

Despite her earlier scepticism, the older woman's face was etched with lines of worry. 'It may only be a short reprieve. They could be back. It is not safe to keep your brother here.'

Senara nodded. 'Not where he can be easily found, that is now obvious. Let us hope that in the morning he is stronger. Last year when Adam had some of the floors repaired in the old wing, he found a priest's hole. That is why I put Caleph in the blue guestroom. The original owners of the house must have been Catholics. A watch will be kept on the entrance to the estate, and if the soldiers return, Caleph must hide in the priest's hole. He will be cramped but at least he will be safe.'

Overcome with gratitude and emotion, Senara gave way to the impulse to embrace the formidable woman. She felt Elspeth stiffen with surprise and kissed her cheek before drawing back. 'Adam was wrong to judge you so harshly, Aunt.'

Elspeth cleared her throat. 'Really, my dear, such emotion is scarcely warranted.'

Senara grinned. There was a softened light in the older woman's eyes. 'Dear Aunt Elspeth, I suspect you are not so crusty in your own feelings as you would have us believe.'

'I must be getting mellow in my old age,' Elspeth responded, and then her voice again became sombre. 'You realise that it is not safe for your brother to remain here for long. They will keep watch on the estate.'

When Senara returned to Caleph, he was of the same mind.

'You cannot leave until you are well enough to travel. How far do you think you will get in your condition?'

She persuaded him to stay for the night. But when she retired to bed, Senara could not help but fear the dangers her brother's return might have unleashed.

Chapter Thirty-four

Japhet was hunched in a darkened corner of a tavern, his cloak wrapped around him and a slouch hat pulled low over his brow. His clothes were dark and nondescript, blending in with the homespun of many of the customers, and his boots were worn and scuffed. A quart of ale was in a pottery tankard on the table before him and he puffed on the short stem of a clay pipe. The air was thick with tobacco smoke and weighted with the shrill voices of whores and gamblers. The tavern was on the border of a dilapidated area of the city near the River Seine. It had been a favoured haunt of revolutionists in the days of the Terror. Earlier Japhet had had his first sight of Sir Pettigrew Osgood when he and Adam had seen him in a market square talking to a pedlar with a tray of brass buckles and cheap trinkets suspended from his neck.

Although he had been told that Osgood frequented that district, the cousins had been prowling the area for two days before they had seen their prey. Japhet would not have recognised him if it had not been for the scar on his cheek. Osgood's long face was thin to the point of gauntness, with deep lines carved around his mouth and across his broad brow. A plain woollen cloak hid the baronet's fine clothes and a muffler concealed his lower face. It could not completely hide the telltale scar that puckered his cheek. Although he had tried to disguise his mode of dress, his boots were too polished for any ordinary citizen. To any casual observer, it looked as though Osgood was purchasing a trinket for his mistress, but Japhet had seen the scrap of paper that had changed hands together with payment for the gewgaw. The pedlar was clearly a messenger whom Osgood used to pass on information.

Since Osgood would recognise Japhet, Adam had been the one to follow him, hoping to discover his lodgings. Japhet had stayed observing the trinket seller, following him as he ambled through the streets and finally entered this tavern. A few customers had nodded a greeting to the man, who had taken a paste brooch from his tray and waved it as a lure for one of the whores. The woman sauntered across to him and he pulled her down on to his lap.

Japhet suppressed a sigh. This could be a long vigil. He was hoping the pedlar would meet an accomplice and pass on the paper given to him by Osgood. He was drinking the last swallow of ale from his tankard when a thickset, straggly-haired man with cheeks oozing pus-headed sores squeezed on to the bench opposite the pedlar.

'Get rid of her,' Japhet heard him growl. His bare fist resting on the table was misshapen and scored with the scars of a lifetime of brawling.

The whore opened her mouth to give him a stream of abuse, and then closed it with a scowl. She stood up and sullenly shook down her skirts.

'I'll see you later, *mon chéri*,' she said, sidling away from the table.

There was a deft movement from the pedlar's fingers, but not so fast that Japhet did not see the flash of the paper passing hands.

'That all you got for me?' His companion did not sound pleased, his voice hissing through the gaps of missing teeth.

'It will more than satisfy your master.'

The folded paper disappeared into the newcomer's pocket and he rose from his seat. Japhet waited until he had opened the door of the tavern before he followed him.

To bring Sir Pettigrew Osgood to the justice he deserved, Japhet needed proof of his latest treachery. It had so far been no easy matter. Osgood was no longer so rash and impetuous, driven by his greed or injured pride.

In the days when they had both been rivals for the favours of Celestine Yorke, Japhet had been equally ruthless and headstrong. Believing that Gwen's family would never accept him as her husband, there had followed months when the wildness of his blood had driven him to find escape from his heartache in the mindless pursuit of pleasure. That had led to gambling debts, and it was in his desperation to settle them that he had turned to a single act of highway robbery.

Even before he had reached twenty, Japhet had walked a narrow line teetering on the wrong side of the law. Always his quick wits and charm had saved him from discovery. It had given him an insight into the ways of the criminal underworld and a sharpened instinct of how to survive and judge the worth and reliability of his fellow man. Those strengths had worked in his favour during his transportation and early days in Australia before his pardon had arrived. They continued to give him an edge over adversaries to this day.

Yet he did not underestimate Osgood. It had been seven years since his rivalry with the arrogant baronet. Japhet knew that in the intervening years his own experiences had shaped him and changed him in many ways. Osgood could also have altered. Long Tom had said that he had until the last year shied away from mixing with society, which had shown its disgust at the dishonour of his actions at the time of Japhet's arrest and trial.

Osgood had always been vengeful and malicious and Japhet doubted that he had mellowed in the intervening years. Adversity would have hardened and embittered such a man, and that would make him even more dangerous.

Long Tom had informed them that Osgood was involved with French Royalist sympathisers, and that was in the interests of the British government, but he suspected that the baronet was also in the pay of Napoleon's Minister of Police, Joseph Fouché. That could place many British spies at risk of discovery. If Osgood had any hint of the true reason Japhet and Adam were after him, he would not hesitate to have Fouché's men arrest them. The formidable prison of the Bastille might have been torn down stone by stone since the start of the revolution, but the Temple, which had housed the aristocrats and later those who were considered traitors to the new regime as they awaited their journey to the guillotine, was equally feared. Even now it was a place where incarceration too frequently led to death and prisoners had disappeared without trace.

Japhet was expert at trailing a man without him being aware that he was followed. The man who had left the tavern was more cautious than most. He paused to look into a shop window and use the reflection to see if he was being observed. He also stopped to scrape dirt from the sole of his shoe, whilst glancing over his shoulder. He swerved and doubled back on himself, his gaze searching the pedestrians who had been behind him. Each time he performed such an action, Japhet either stopped to help a pretty woman cross the road or ducked into a door or alleyway.

When he recognised the street where Long Tom had informed him that Fouché lived, he knew he had to recover the paper if he was to have any information with which to condemn Osgood. Japhet moved swiftly. The press of people was beginning to thin as the daylight faded. He wove in and out of the hurrying citizens, and as he cut behind the man from the tavern, his fingers dipped into his pocket. For a moment his heartbeat increased. It had been years since he had used the skill he had acquired as a pickpocket. Was he still able to perform the task without being detected? It was over in a split second and the paper was palmed into Japhet's sleeve. He immediately turned away, losing himself amongst the crowd.

To his relief there was no shout of anger or sound of pursuit. He did not stop to read the paper until he reached his lodgings. His cousin was in the taproom of the inn, his expression dark and brooding.

'I lost Osgood in the crowd,' he groaned. 'There was a street fight and I could not get through. We still do not know where he lodges.'

'That may not be so important for the moment.' Japhet sat opposite Adam at the table and ordered a bottle of brandy. With a grin he produced the paper and unfolded it in the light of the smoking candle. Three words were scrawled on it.

Wednesday. Noon. St Cloud.

'That could mean anything.' Adam remained pessimistic.

'But it is something to go on,' Japhet countered. 'It is more than we had before. And it is not for another four days. Time enough to get more information.'

'St Cloud must be a connection with Bonaparte.' Adam was frowning. 'It is his residence.'

'And who stands in the way of a Royalist revival?'

'Our beloved First Consul. But he is too well protected at St Cloud,' Adam stated, dropping his voice to a whisper. 'Could it mean an ambush on the road?'

'That is one possibility.'

Adam leaned forward, his eyes narrowed with puzzlement. 'But why would Osgood send a written message? It would be safer to pass it on by word of mouth.'

'I wondered about that.' Japhet rubbed his jaw. 'He must be covering his back if he is working for both the French and the English. He might have thought it was some insurance against the French arresting him as a spy.'

'That could be, but it is a foolish move.' Adam was not entirely convinced.

'Osgood is sly and greedy, but not necessarily that clever.' Japhet tried to make sense of the action.

Adam pinched the top of his nose as he analysed what he knew of the man and what was required to stay safe when spying for the enemy. Such an act was a huge risk, unless . . . 'What if he suspects someone is on to him and this information is false, to throw them off the scent?'

Japhet shrugged. 'Then whilst we act on this we do not stop our investigations. We will step up our hunt to discover Osgood's lodgings and keep a twenty-four-hour watch on him.'

It was late in the evening when Lady Alys halted in the shadows of the street, away from the main thoroughfares. Her heart was thumping unnaturally fast and the hairs at the back of her neck prickled. There were few people to observe her passage, but that brought with it its own dangers. The area was known for its footpads and cutpurses. A chill of fear coated her brow. Was that a soft footfall she had heard? Was she being followed? She had taken care to cover her tracks, but the moon was brighter tonight and there were fewer clouds to obscure it. She forced herself to breathe slowly and silently. Her knuckles tightened over the dagger that she carried for protection, her eyes straining to discern a human form in the darkness. All was still. All was quiet. Then she froze at hearing a faint rustling. Two rats were foraging in the debris of the gutter. She relaxed and drew a steadying breath. It was not like her to jump at ghosts, but she could not quash the feeling that within the shelter of the overhanging houses someone was waiting and watching. A black silk vizard covered half her face and her long black cloak should have concealed her from spying eyes in the darkness.

More rodents joined the scavenging rats. Surely they would be alerted if anyone else were close by? She was already late for her meeting. It had been difficult enough to prove to her co-conspirators that she was capable of overcoming danger and evading capture by the authorities. She did not allow herself to consider what would happen to her if she were caught. Death was certain, but it would not be without first being subjected to torture to reveal the names of her associates. She had a high threshold for bearing pain but she knew she would not be able to withstand the horrific hot irons invading her flesh or the gouging and mutilation men could devise for a woman suspected of treachery. To evade that nightmare she carried a vial of hemlock and prayed that she was given the time to drink it before they dragged her away in chains.

She shook her head to stop the images robbing her of courage. She had been aware of the risks from the outset and was prepared to pay the price.

There was no movement or sound from the street, and when she turned a corner she pressed herself close to the wall of a house. Another hundred yards and she would be safe. The short distance was covered without incident. She tapped on the side door and was admitted into the deserted servants' quarters and led up narrow stairs to a shuttered room lit by a single candle.

Four masked figures sat at a table. She knew them only by the names they had chosen for this subterfuge. Bleu. Blanc. Vert. Noir. She was Rouge.

'Gentlemen.' She inclined her head in the briefest of bows. 'Your pardon for my tardiness. I had to ascertain that I was not being followed.'

'I also thought I was being observed earlier,' Blanc informed her. 'We must strike before our cover is blown.'

Noir, who had assumed the role of leader, was curt. The man was arrogant to the point of rudeness. 'We strike on Wednesday. You each know your positions. There must be no errors.'

'We have our instructions.' Alys stared at Noir. 'What is your role? You have not made that clear.' She had an uncomfortable feeling about their leader and did not entirely trust him. They were the ones taking the greater risk.

Noir banged his fist on the table, his eyes glinting savagely in the candlelight. 'I will be where I am needed most. Someone must be on hand to cover your backs if anything goes wrong.'

'You will be safely out of the way,' Vert sneered. 'While we could face the bayonets of the soldiers.'

Chapter Thirty-five

The ballroom was so crowded that the dancers rubbed shoulders as they moved through the intricate steps, and the strains of the sweating musicians were muted by the drone of voices from the guests huddled around the walls.

One man stood alone, away from the lights of the glittering chandeliers, his hooded eyes searching the press of figures. Anonymity suited him. There was no chance of advancement for him in England, whilst the intrigue and politics underpinning the new regime in France had offered him the opportunity to seek his redemption.

Sir Pettigrew Osgood had spent lavishly to win the trust of the conspirators. The meetings he had attended with those who plotted in secret boded well for the success of a double conspiracy. The danger to him was minimal.

'There's Loveday. I must introduce you to him,' a man declared loudly as he pushed past him with a companion.

He froze at hearing that name, then moved slowly and cautiously through the gathering. His quarry would be easy to pick out, for he was tall, his dark features handsome and menacing as a satyr.

'There you are, Loveday!' The older of the two men he

had been following spoke as he approached a dark-haired man with his back to them.

The announcement spun the newcomer round. What the observer would not have given to have a dagger in his hand to plunge into that broad back and pierce his enemy's heart. When Loveday turned to greet those who had hailed him, Osgood lifted a hand to shield his face. Tension tightened the puckered scar on his cheek.

Unmistakably this was a Loveday before him. Through narrowed eyes he noted the difference in features from his old adversary. Bringing any Loveday down would prove extremely satisfactory.

Loveday bowed to the man who had greeted him, though Osgood detected wariness in his voice. 'Lord Brienne, you have made a speedy recovery. I had not expected you would join us in Paris at this time.' He certainly did not sound pleased at the arrival of his acquaintance. He bowed to the younger man. 'Atherstone, what brings you to Paris?'

'Business and pleasure. We were concerned when we called at Lapoitiere's that the Lady Alys was not in residence and that you had taken rooms elsewhere.'

'I have not had contact with the Lady Alys for some days,' Loveday answered stiffly.

'Were you not her escort whilst she was here?' Atherstone challenged.

'Lady Alys had many friends she wished to visit. I have been engaged in business.'

'I say, old chap, it was a poor show for you to abandon her,' Atherstone blustered.

There was an animated exchange between the men at the same time as laughter rang out behind Osgood. He was annoyed he could not hear what was said. Then

Loveday strode away, the tense set of his shoulders betraying his anger. The older of the two men put a restraining hand upon his companion's arm and Osgood leaned forward to eavesdrop.

'Let it go, Atherstone. You could create more harm than good.'

'How do we know he will not betray our cause?'

Again laughter from the group behind Osgood prevented him hearing the reply. Intrigued as to the nature of the cause they had mentioned, he watched as Atherstone parted company from his friend. They were English. Would they be of use to him? For an instant Osgood caught Lord Brienne's gaze. Its cold, merciless depths sent a quiver of unease through him. This was not a man he would want as an enemy. But it could be a man who would be of interest to his other master. That was the purpose of playing the English off against the French, and the French off against the English. Whoever won, he could not lose.

The scar on Osgood's cheek throbbed painfully. That was the legacy from another Loveday meeting, when he had lost a duel with Japhet's cousin Thomas, who had sought revenge for Japhet's transportation. Osgood's fury towards the family continued to fester. No other adversaries had outwitted him in the past. For that reason alone he would continue the mission that had brought him to Paris.

Even so, the incident had unsettled him and he remained uneasy as he spoke to the man he had come here tonight to meet. Shortly afterwards he left the ball to return to his lodgings. His mind was on the plans he had so carefully laid, and he did not notice the young woman who ducked behind a marble pillar to avoid being seen.

★

Lady Alys's eyes narrowed as she observed Osgood and the man with whom he had been conversing. It set her skin prickling with alarm. Why was Noir talking to a man she suspected was an agent of Fouché?

If that encounter were not disturbing enough, moments later Viscount Atherstone waved to her and hurried over.

'What are you dong in Paris, my lord?' Her voice lifted at her shock.

'Like many of our countrymen, I thought to take the opportunity of the truce to visit the treasures of the Louvre and see how the city has changed.' His gaze flickered over her with a superiority she found distasteful. 'It would appear we have arrived in time to save your reputation. I've just learned that that rogue Loveday has deserted you.'

'Mr Loveday did not abandon me,' she tartly informed him. Atherstone's high-handed manner annoyed her and she resented his interference in her affairs. 'He had business to attend upon and I was perfectly safe visiting my friends.'

'Who would they be? You must introduce me.' His manner continued to be condescending as he surveyed the guests. 'Are they here tonight?'

'With respect, my lord, I am not accustomed to being interrogated about my companions.' Her chin tilted at a stubborn angle. 'And I object to your tone. You are not my kin, or my guardian. You presume too much upon our acquaintance.'

'Because we have been worried,' protested Atherstone, his face flushing now in his eagerness to please her. 'And I thought we had an understanding. Brienne would be delighted at a match between us.'

'I have no intention of tying myself to a man who would dictate to me as though I was a child. And with respect, my lord, I have never given you any encouragement to be other than a friend.'

His cheeks darkened to crimson. 'My pardon, dear lady, that I had dared to presume there was more to our friendship. Naturally Lord Brienne and myself were concerned to discover that Loveday had left Lapoitiere's house. We feared something dreadful might have happened to you.'

'I did not think that Lord Brienne would miss this opportunity to visit Paris,' she replied sweetly.

'It seems we have arrived not a day too soon. We know little of this Loveday fellow and it appears we were wrong to place our trust in him.'

It was then that she saw Brienne, and also Tristan, who was some distance from him on the opposite side of the room. Thankfully his lordship had his back to the younger man. All her plans could be ruined if Atherstone caused trouble tonight. Her instinct was to get Tristan to leave.

'There is Brienne,' Atherstone pompously declared. He grabbed her wrist and pulled her forward. 'We will see what he has to say about your recent antics.'

She jerked back from his hold, her eyes bright with anger. 'How dare you lay a hand upon me. Release me.'

In her desperation to escape, she kicked him on the shin and ground her heel down on to his instep. At his grunt of pain his hold loosened and she spun away and dashed through the crowd. She skirted the dancers to seek out Tristan and tapped him on the arm with her fan.

'Sir, it is most imperative that you come with me at once.' She headed out of the ballroom before he could protest, and heard his companions laugh.

'Better go after her, Loveday. You'll not get a better invitation than that tonight.'

Before she was halfway to the door her elbow was taken in a firm grip and he snarled, 'What are you up to now?'

'My uncle and Atherstone are here. They cannot learn where I have been.' Her gaze scoured the room to ensure that they had not been noticed. 'Please, I would not have my uncle discover my plans at this time. And Atherstone is a fool. He could ruin everything.'

'And why should I trust you?' His dark eyes glittered menacingly.

'Because if you do not, all our lives could be in danger. This is not the place to discuss it. Will you help me?'

Wondering if he was the biggest dupe alive, Tristan nodded tersely. 'But I want the truth, and no more lies.'

Adam and Japhet stepped down from a carriage just as a man and a woman hurried out of the townhouse where the ball was being held.

'Good Lord! That looked like Tristan.' Adam voiced his astonishment. 'What the devil is he doing in Paris?'

Japhet followed his gaze. 'You must have been mistaken.'

'Do you think I would not recognise him? I've a mind to follow him.'

'He is not the reason we are here,' Japhet tersely reminded him. 'We know that Tristan will eventually go back home. For now we have more important quarry.'

Adam reluctantly dragged his gaze away. Japhet was right.

Long Tom had given them the information they needed to bring Osgood to account. They had so far uncovered no further details about the events in the note.

The crush of people inside the ballroom assaulted Japhet's senses. The chandeliers were dazzling after the darkness of the evening. The smell of perfume and cologne barely masked the scent of stale sweat from the feverish dancers. The atmosphere was frenzied, the gaiety appearing false and founded on desperation for normalcy. After the wide-open spaces of Australia and Cornwall, it made him uneasy. The air itself pulsated with an underlying hysteria. He found the French too excitable and his natural caution made him distrust them.

Their enquiries had led them to believe that Osgood would attend the ball tonight. Japhet was hopeful. He no longer sought a duel with his enemy. The contest would be unequal and death was too easy a sentence. Honour would only be satisfied if Osgood suffered the same humiliation and disgrace that the knave's lies had heaped upon Japhet. Despite Long Tom's information, they had yet to discover the proof that would destroy his enemy's reputation.

The cousins circled the gathering and after half an hour were convinced that Osgood was not in attendance.

'Dammit, Loveday, you will answer for your foul knavery.' The angry outburst swung both cousins round to regard a red-faced young man.

The stranger's eyes rounded in alarm. 'My pardon, sir. I thought you were someone else. From behind, the likeness was astonishing.'

'And who may you be?' Japhet challenged, his husky voice dangerous with outrage.

'Lord Atherstone. It was an honest mistake.'

'You make a serious accusation.'

An older companion whose countenance was haughty and antagonistic joined his lordship. There was a tension in his stance that Japhet recognised as that of a man who would challenge you to a duel rather than ask you to account for an action.

'The likeness is too close for you not to be related. Are you a Loveday?' the senior of the two Englishmen demanded.

'We both are,' Adam informed him, for the moment willing to appease the men and prevent a scene. Clearly they had mistaken one of them for Tristan. And he had no intention of becoming embroiled in any of his cousin's trickery.

'And are you related to a Mr Tristan Loveday?' the older man persisted.

'Loveday is not an uncommon name in Cornwall,' Adam returned.

'Is it not a strange coincidence that you are in Paris at the same time as your namesake?' The older man eyed him haughtily, mistrustful of his evasion.

'I doubt we shall have the pleasure of his company,' Adam said and walked away fuming. Tristan could ruin their mission if he was stirring up trouble. When he was alone with Japhet he ground out, 'We should have followed Tristan when we had the chance. He's up to his old tricks. I'll not have him dishonour our name.'

'Tristan is not the reason we are here. It is unlikely that our paths will cross.'

'They had better not. This time he will be answerable to me.'

Chapter Thirty-six

Once they were in the street, Lady Alys hurried along the row of waiting carriages where many of the drivers were dozing over the reins. She opened the door to hers and stepped inside. When Tristan hesitated to follow, she addressed him sharply. 'Get in. There is no time to lose or we will be discovered.' His body was rigid with disapproval as he seated himself opposite her. 'What address shall I give to the driver where we can take you?'

'You can drop me around the corner and I can walk.'

'How serious were you about helping our cause? Or was it just a ruse to win the trust of important business associates?'

'Is that what you think of me?'

She could not see his expression in the dark interior of the carriage, but his voice was cold and condemning.

'You judged me quickly enough without troubling to hear an explanation.' Her own pain broke through.

'I know what I saw,' he accused. 'I followed you to your lover's tryst.'

Her fists clenched at his stubbornness and she struggled to check her own rising temper. 'You saw what you were expecting to perceive, which was but part of what happened.'

'How glibly you would turn the truth to a lie, my lady.'

'How little you know me, sir.' She banged on the roof of the carriage for the driver to stop. 'You may alight now if you wish.'

As soon as he had leapt to the ground and the carriage began to pull away he regretted his action. Why did Lady Alys make him act so irrationally? Even at this late hour the streets were busy as people returned from the theatres for the evening. He kept the carriage in sight as he walked and was not surprised when it stopped outside the house he had seen Lady Alys enter the other evening. The windows were shuttered and only one of them showed a thin sliver of light. A few minutes after Lady Alys had entered, a chink of light appeared through a crack in a shutter on the first floor.

He continued his watch for a few minutes, but his own uncertain temper was creating images of Lady Alys and a lover he would rather not bring to mind. Convinced that he had been right about her all along, his mood was bleak as he decided to walk back to his lodgings. He had covered only a few yards when he detected a faint noise behind him. Remembering the attack on him by Gargoyle, he stepped into the cover of a doorway. The slight figure of a man hurried past his hiding place. From the brief glimpse of moonlight on his face, Tristan recognised him as the one who had left the house that Alys had entered on the previous occasion he had spied on her.

The furtiveness of his manner kindled Tristan's sense of danger, not to himself but to Lady Alys. Was Brienne using her as an emissary between Royalist groups? The idea increased his anger. Did her guardian not realise the danger to her? And what of this man? He had left the rendezvous shortly after Lady Alys arrived; was he intent on betraying her accomplices? Tristan did not like unsolved riddles. There was only one way he would find the answer.

He silently followed the young man, who kept to the shadows. When his quarry approached an alleyway, Tristan sprang forward, grabbed his arm and pushed him up against the wall. The unexpected prick of a dagger point pressed into his neck froze his movements. No light penetrated the alley and neither could see the other's face.

'One move and you are dead,' a low voice murmured. 'You seem too well dressed to be a thief. Why were you following me?'

Tristan brought up his elbow to jab it into his attacker's ribs but was kicked on the knee before his blow met his mark. Instinctively his fingers snapped on to his opponent's arm and he twisted it up behind his back, wrenching it until the blade clattered to the ground.

'Stop struggling or I'll break your wrist!' he ordered.

'Tristan! Is that you?'

Although the voice was husky with pain, he was shocked at its familiar tone.

'Good Lord, Lady Alys. What the devil is this about?'

'It is none of your affair. Let me go, I am late for a meeting.' She struck his chest with her free hand.

'You fight almost as well as a man. And why the disguise?'

'Let me go!' She continued to struggle, each movement sending spirals of pain through her hand and arm. 'Oaf! I think you've broken my wrist.'

'You are lucky I did not kill you.'

'Huh! I was the one with the knife at your throat.' Her scorn lashed him.

He was confused about her actions. Why was she

sneaking about the city dressed as a man? He was also furious with her, not only for the danger she had placed herself in, but also for getting the upper hand so quickly in a knife fight. A life of ease must be dulling his reactions. Few men had ever bested him.

He released her arm and she cradled it with her other hand.

'You cannot go anywhere until that is tended. And you have some explaining to do, my lady.'

'I do not need to explain myself to you.' Her voice, although low, dripped with hauteur.

'Pig-headed wench,' he growled. 'Tell me why I should not hand you over to Lord Brienne for your own safety?'

She was braced ready to dart past him. 'No doubt you are well meaning, but I do not need you or any man to protect me. Now kindly step aside. I have matters to attend.'

He gripped her shoulders and shook her. 'Not until you tell me the truth. You did not come to Paris to visit friends, did you? When I visited your home it was a hotbed of intrigue. Are you a French spy? I could forgive you much, but not that.'

'What a vivid imagination you have, Mr Loveday.'

Her flippancy goaded him further. 'I may have been mistaken in some things about you, but do not take me for a fool. How can I help you, or trust you, if you do not confide in me?'

'There are some things better left unsaid.' She held his stare.

'And what if I could not forgive myself if any harm came to you and I could have prevented it?' His voice cracked in his exasperation.

A sigh sent a tremor through her body, her voice

barely audible. 'If only it were that simple. Just let me go and—'

Tristan tensed and put a hand over her mouth to still her words. He had sensed rather than heard movement closing in upon them. Lady Alys also stood rigid. Clearly she was no novice at subterfuge. The alley smelt like any other: stale urine, rotting garbage, the odour of rats, but tracing through this was the whiff of unwashed bodies and musty clothes.

An instinct that danger lurked in the darkness raised the hairs on the back of Tristan's neck. He retrieved the dagger that had fallen from Alys's hand and returned it to her before drawing his own knife from his top boot. Straightening, he placed himself between his companion and the direction of the smell of humans. For an instant the stench of the detritus of mankind assaulted them; the next moment four figures loomed around them.

Tristan kicked out and caught one of the attackers in the groin, and as he crumpled to the ground, he plunged his dagger into the arm of another. Even in the thick of the fighting he was astonished to note that Lady Alys was putting up an equal struggle. There was a grunt of pain and an attacker staggered back clutching his gut, and from the corner of his eye he saw her slash her blade across the face of another, who toppled to the ground, blood pouring from his nose and cheek.

Three more figures appeared, and when Tristan saw her swing round to confront them, he ordered, 'Make a run for it. I'll defend your back.'

He cursed when she continued to fight, but at least she seemed to be holding her own. He took on two men with raised cudgels, his dagger parrying a blow before he ducked and managed to swing a punch and heard the bone of a nose crunch under the impact. A follow-through jab at his jaw felled his assailant. He could not avoid the second cudgel, which struck his shoulder, and pain flared through his body, momentarily robbing his arm of its use. He kicked the man's knees from under him and a slash from the dagger again skewered flesh. Rolling away from him, the attacker staggered into the shadows, where he could be heard running away.

At a cry of pain from Lady Alys, Tristan spun round to protect her. She had been pushed against the wall and a large-set man was viciously punching her. Tristan hauled him away, delivered a jab to his gut that doubled him over and then kicked him on the buttocks to send him sprawling into the gutter. Other dark shapes were stirring on the ground but the way ahead of them looked clear.

He grabbed Lady Alys around the waist to give her swaying body extra support and together they ran across the main street and back to the house where Alys had first emerged. There was no sound of pursuit, but even so they did not slow their pace.

Gasping for breath, they sank against the door. Alys gave two slow knocks followed by another two rapid ones. As the door started to open, they staggered inside, and in the light of a single candle Tristan glimpsed the terrified face of a maid. He recovered his wits enough to push the heavy door shut.

'Your mistress has been hurt,' he said in French. 'Which is her room?' He lifted Alys into his arms, clamping tight his jaw at the pain throbbing through his injured shoulder.

'Put me down, Tristan,' Lady Alys commanded. 'I am not that badly hurt.'

He kept her arms around her and she sighed. 'Marie, show Mr Loveday to the downstairs salon and then bring us a flagon of wine and some hot water to bathe our cuts.'

Tristan followed the maid, who fussed ahead of them, lighting more candles in the salon and dragging dust sheets from some of the furniture. He laid Alys on a chaise longue, and as the full light of the candles fell upon their faces, the maid gave a cry of dismay.

'My lady, who has done this to you? I knew it was madness to risk your life in this manner.'

'Marie, the wine and water. Hurry.' Alys halted the woman's chatter. When the maid had left them, she swung her legs round to place them on the floor and could not stop a grimace of pain.

'If you had not followed me this would never have happened.' She lashed him with her scorn. 'You have done untold damage to important matters.'

'Those thieves would have attacked you. They strike at any likely victim. Now will you kindly tell me what the devil you are playing at?'

'It is not your concern.'

'Tonight made it my concern.'

They glared at each other, the tension crackling in the room between them. She had lost her hat in the fight, and many of the pins had fallen from the sleek coil on top of her head, allowing curling tresses to drape around her neck. The light from the flickering candles showed a darkening bruise on her cheek and a cut to her chin. From the slight hunch to her shoulders he guessed her body had taken a harsh beating. The maid returned and set down a tray with a bowl of water, some cloths and a decanter and glasses.

'Leave us, Marie,' Alys instructed. She poured two large drinks and drank hers quickly, then closed her eyes as the alcohol seeped through her exhausted and aching body.

'I am sworn to secrecy,' she finally informed him. 'I

393

trust you enough to tell you that, but no more. You would not expect me to break that vow.'

She was being maddeningly evasive. But he would not give up. 'Is Lord Brienne involved in this?'

'No.

'Atherstone?'

'That fool,' she scoffed. 'Certainly not.'

'Then who?'

She put a hand to her temple. 'My head aches. I ache all over.'

'You were lucky you were not killed.'

'The only danger I was in tonight was from your crack-brained attack.' She pointedly rubbed her sore wrist.

Contrite at the damage he had inflicted, he was momentarily diverted. 'Does it pain you? I could so easily have broken it. But then that may keep you out of further trouble.'

She yawned. 'The wrist will be well enough come morning.'

Her stoicism played havoc with his emotions; he both wanted to shake some sense into her and at the same time protect her from whatever madness she was involved in. His curiosity got the better of his anger. 'How came you to fight like that?'

'Ah, that would tell you too much.' She laid her head on the pillow and closed her eyes.

He knelt and shook her shoulders. 'Oh no, you'll not escape telling me the truth that way.'

'In the morning. I must regain my strength.' Her breathing deepened. 'After having to fight for my life, and all that brandy, I am exhausted. Let me sleep. We will talk in the morning.'

'Alys. My lady.' He shook her again.

'Stay here if you do not trust me,' she murmured.

Tristan sank his head in his hands. He admired her bravery and at the same time cursed her stubbornness. Yet surely if she was in any immediate danger from whatever plot she was involved in, she would not be able to sleep.

He lay down on the floor by the chaise longue. She could not escape the room without stepping over him. For the moment he had to be content with that. He stared at the dust sheets still covering the furniture. They would only be used if the house was shut up and the owners away. Perhaps she had not met a lover here as he had first concluded. When they had first entered, the house had smelled musty, a sign that it was not in general use. Had he misjudged the Lady Alys? It was possible, and until he heard her story in the morning he was prepared to give her the benefit of the doubt.

At the same time as Tristan and Lady Alys were fighting for their lives, Osgood was pacing his rooms. He touched the scar on his cheek, which prickled from the tense line of his jaw. The Loveday family had much to answer for.

His reflections turned sour as the memories of his vendetta against Japhet filled his mind. After Japhet Loveday had received the King's pardon and the charges against him for highway robbery had been declared false, Osgood had been ostracised by society. In return he had taken his anger and frustration out on those who had no power to retaliate: his servants and estate workers. Any man who did not kowtow to his punishing demands and long hours of work was turned from his home, his family made homeless. No young woman of even moderate looks escaped his lechery. For years he had been governed by terrifying rages fed by his bitterness and isolation. He had no love for his fellow Englishman. He wanted revenge for the ills that had beset him. Here in France, intrigue was as virulent as dysentery. For a man without scruples, information could be bought or obtained by force. In this circle Osgood had found his niche, treachery as natural to him as breathing. There was nothing he enjoyed more than playing one faction off against another whilst making sure that he was the victor claiming the spoils.

Chapter Thirty-seven

Two days after the soldier's visit when Senara entered the blue guestroom, she found Caleph sitting on the edge of the bed wearing an old robe of Adam's. His expression was antagonistic.

'What have you done with my clothes?'

'I had to cut your jacket and shirt to tend your wound. Adam's clothes will fit you. Your breeches have been washed and are drying in the kitchen.' She put down the tray of broth she was carrying on the bedside table. 'You should be resting.'

He rubbed his hand across his jaw, his usual swarthy complexion grey with tiredness and loss of blood. 'It is not that I do not appreciate your help, but you must bring me what I need. I cannot stay here, it is too dangerous for you.'

'You will stay until you are strong enough to travel.'

'Then I should be at Ma's old cottage. I went there but it was deserted. Where's Ma living now?' A flash of disapproval glinted in his eyes. 'Clearly she is not in your grand house, or she would have come to see me.'

Senara suppressed her irritation at his accusation. He had always felt that Leah had betrayed their father by leaving their tribe. Her voice lowered with compassion.

'Ma is dead, Caleph. She died at the end of last winter from a seizure. I sent word by other travellers, but they could not have met up with you.'

He hung his head and exhaled sharply. 'I was never much of a son to her. Yet I suppose you and Bridie made sure she wanted for nothing.'

'She was happy at the parsonage with Bridie and Peter and looked after their son Michael. Michael died the same day as Ma, from croup. He was Bridie's only child.'

'So your children are the only ones who continue our blood.' His sarcasm was bitter. 'I doubt your husband is proud of that. Where's Ma buried?'

'At Polruggan cemetery. She was laid to rest with Michael.'

'I should have done more for her.' He rested his head in his hands, which were callused, from his years of hard toil. 'I should have done more for my own family.' He raised red-rimmed eyes. 'They're all dead. Maddie and the children.'

The shock of his news sent waves of pain through her chest and for a moment she thought she was going to swoon. As a child Maddie had been her best friend, and Caleph's children had been cheeky imps with a spirit for mischief. She had adored them. 'I am so sorry, Caleph. I was proud of my nieces and nephews. How did it happen?'

He stared into the embers of the fire, his voice hollow. 'We were on our way to celebrate the winter solstice at Avebury and were about a dozen miles from our destination when a wheel on my wagon broke. The others of our band carried on while I went to the nearest village to find a wheelwright. Maddie and the children tried to sell some heather. The villagers took against us. The children managed to run away, but Maddie was arrested and dragged to the stocks. I fought to free her but was beaten and thrown in the lockup. The villagers set fire to the wagon. When they released Maddie, she and the children spent the next week living in a shallow cave. It snowed heavily. The ground was frozen. When they let me out of the lockup, I found them huddled together, the cave dripping with icicles. They were all dead, covered with a coating of frost.'

Senara reeled from the shock. 'Caleph, I am so dreadfully sorry. Your lovely children and wife.' Tears spilled from her eyes. There were no words that could give him comfort after such a tragedy.

'I tried to drown my grief in drink. I was always in fights and stabbed a man. He lived but they arrested me. I escaped when a village blacksmith tried to put the shackles on me. I've been on the run for days. Thought I'd lost them. They put a price on my head. I shouldn't have come here, but I wanted to see you and Ma, and I suppose I hoped Adam would be able to help me get away. Then the dogs picked up my scent.'

He pushed himself up from the bed. 'I've got to leave here. I'll bring trouble to you. I'll stay at Ma's cottage.'

'That is one of the first places they will look if they know your identity. Adam is not here, but you are not going anywhere,' she insisted.

'I will not put you in danger.' He snatched up a shirt and breeches. 'If you want to help, give me a horse. I shall leave as soon as I am dressed.'

'You are still weak,' she reasoned. Her panic rose that if he left Boscabel now she would never see him again. 'And why should the soldiers return? Elspeth convinced them that we would not harbour a felon.'

'They will not give up their search until I am found. Senara, you know what they can be like. Do you think that they would spare you if I was found here? They would arrest you as an accomplice.'

She was about to protest when a violent knocking on the front door of the house made her gasp. Caleph whitened.

Downstairs Gilly Brown had raised her voice in protest. 'It bain't done for you to barge in unannounced. Mistress will see you in the drawing room. Wait in there.'

'Out of my way, woman,' a man shouted, sending Senara's heart scudding with alarm. 'A violent attacker is on the loose and was last seen heading in this direction. I'll throw the damned lot of you into prison for obstructing the course of justice.'

'Quickly, over here, Caleph,' Senara ordered. 'There's a priest's hole. You can hide there.' She ran ahead of him and pressed one of the carved wooden Tudor roses on the panelling by the chimney breast. A small section of woodwork a foot from the floor slid open. It was just wide enough for him to crawl into and dropped down four feet. 'They will never find you here. I'll fetch you when it is safe.'

He disappeared from sight and she could hear Billy Brown's voice added to that of his wife as he tried to keep the soldiers from searching the house. Her hands shook with mounting terror as she scooped the bloodied sheets off the bed and thrust them down after her brother.

Caleph gripped the sides of the panelling, about to haul himself back into the room. 'You have not even got Miss Loveday here to help you. She returned to Trevowan yesterday. I must give myself up. I cannot put you in danger.'

'It is too late for that. Stay where you are. They cannot harm me if you are not found.' To her relief he did not

400

protest. She scanned the room to check that there were no other signs that it had been occupied before closing the panel. Quickly she straightened the counterpane on the bed. She could do nothing about the fire burning in the grate, so threw on another log. If the soldiers searched here, she hoped to bluff her way through an explanation.

'What is all this commotion?' she demanded as she descended the stairs. Two soldiers carrying muskets with bayonets attached were about to charge towards the staircase. Her presence brought them to a halt. Their captain appeared at the foot of the stairs. He was barely in his twenties and must have recently purchased his commission, yet there was no softness of youth in his features. He was below medium height, his fair hair curled to disguise the patches of pink scalp already evident, and his broad side-whiskers showed him to be something of a dandy. His brow was heavy and his eyes revealed more arrogance than intelligence. She summed him up as a short man, too full of his own self-importance. A dangerous combination in a man of little experience and too much authority.

She could hear other men searching through the lower rooms. 'Gentlemen, can I be of assistance to you?' Senara was relieved her voice sounded composed. 'I trust there is a reason for this intrusion into my home.'

The officer glowered and Billy Brown positioned himself at the foot of the stairs. 'Captain Durrant insists on searching the house for a hidden fugitive, Mrs Loveday. I told him Sergeant Harris found no one and there has certainly been no sign of an escaped prisoner anywhere on the estate.'

'Sergeant Harris informed us that he was prevented from searching the house.' The officer rested one hand on his hip and the other on his sword belt, his gaze sweeping over Senara with an insolence she found offensive.

'He was no respecter of property,' Senara said cuttingly as she descended, at the same time willing her shaking legs not to collapse under her. She paused by the two soldiers blocking her passage. Clearly their intent was to intimidate her. Their lack of respect triggered her pride and aided the recovery of her composure. She looked over their heads at the officer. 'It was an ungodly late hour and we were about to retire, without the benefit of the protection of the master of the house. Their boots were thick with mud. But that was two days ago. Is this felon still at large? With so much time passed, he could have taken a ship to the Continent by now.'

'Not if he is being protected by those who think themselves above the law.' Durrant remained repugnantly officious.

Senara held his stare. 'I can assure you, Captain Durrant, that no escaped prisoner is being harboured here.'

'Where is Captain Loveday now?' Captain Durrant remained hostile.

'Away on business for another day or so,' Senara informed him coldly.

'Then stand aside and allow my men to search, madam.'

His rudeness strengthened her resolve and she answered with haughty disdain. 'Since you doubt our word, Captain Durrant, and your men are presentable enough today not to despoil our floors, then please search as you will. Though I insist you accompany them into every room to ensure that no damage is done to our possessions.'

'You will accompany us also, Mrs Loveday,' the officer demanded.

'As you wish, Captain. Shall we start with this staircase?' She retraced her steps and stood back against the wall of the landing for the soldiers to pass. Apart from her fears for Caleph, she was concerned that her daughters would be frightened by the ruthlessness of this invasion.

The first two bedrooms were empty and dust sheets were draped over the furnishings. Captain Durrant proceeded to the blue room, where his eyes narrowed with suspicion. 'Why is there a fire here? Who occupies this room?'

'At the moment no one,' Senara improvised. 'We are expecting guests. The room is being aired. It is uncommonly damp.'

'Yet there are no fires in the other rooms.' His stare remained condemning.

She held his glare, unflinching. 'Why would there be when only the one room will be occupied?'

'Who are the visitors and when do they arrive?'

'Family members who are expected sometime this week.' Senara was equally cool in her manner, reminding this man that she was his equal.

His lips curled into a sneer. 'When was the last time you saw your brother, Mrs Loveday?'

She felt her heart plummet to the soles of her shoes before she steadied her voice enough to answer. She took courage in the knowledge that they had not discovered Caleph's hiding place. 'That is difficult to say. Several years. There had been some local robberies and my brother's band was falsely accused. The stolen valuables were later found at the Dolphin Inn and the innkeeper and his wife arrested. My brother was upset that his presence on our land had brought my husband's name into disrepute. He vowed never to camp on our estate again. I have not seen him since.'

'How very noble of him, when his kind rarely miss the opportunity to thieve.'

'You attitude is exactly why he has stayed away.' She continued to stare him down and he was the first to lower his gaze.

'I am sure that you do not need me to follow you from room to room. Please respect this house as the home of a gentleman and former naval officer. I would not have your men burst in without warning upon my children in the nursery. I would reassure them.' With her head held high, she left him. She was determined now that Rhianne and Sara would not be frightened or upset.

Since Caleph's arrival she had sent word to Mr Lancros in Fowey that her daughters had developed a fever and there would be no lessons for a week or so. The little girls had not been told of Caleph's arrival in the house.

Senara's nerves were taut as a bowstring as she heard the soldiers marching through the chambers, prodding and poking in every crevice and cupboard and under the beds.

'What is all the noise, Mama? Are we being attacked?' Sara asked anxiously, as soon as her mother appeared. She was sitting on the floor with her sister with their dolls lined up in front of them, all with a bandage or a splint on their limbs. The nurserymaid Carrie was sitting by the window mending some torn lace on a gown of Rhianne's.

'No, my sweet.' Senara forced a laugh. 'Some men are searching all the houses in the district. A prisoner has escaped and they want to make sure that we are safe, since Papa is not here. Do not be alarmed. What is this game you are playing? Are your dolls sick?'

'They have all been shipwrecked and we are tending

their wounds,' piped Sara. Her daughters' active imaginations were filled with tales of adventure.

However, her warning could not stop Sara's scream when the soldiers flung open the nursery door, their muskets held in front of them. Rhianne put an arm protectively around her sister and glared at the intruders, showing no fear. Usually her nature was angelically sweet, entirely unlike her twin, the hot-headed and argumentative Joel. At eight she was also uncannily perceptive and must have sensed the tension within her mother. 'We do not need defending. Papa taught you to use a pistol, and the servants can use weapons.'

Captain Durrant glared at the girls, snapping out, 'Search every cupboard and crevice. It would not be the first time a fugitive has used children to throw us off their scent.'

Senara itched to throw her contempt for the officer in his face, but knew it would only provoke him further. Instead she folded her daughters into her arms, ready to do battle if the soldiers approached them.

There was a sudden thump from within a linen cupboard in the corner of the room.

'Arms at the ready, men,' Durrant ordered. 'Come out, you blackguard, with your hands raised. We will shoot if you try to resist arrest.'

The door slowly creaked open. The muskets were raised and the safety catches pulled back. There was another thump and a meow as Snuff, who had been given to Sara by Bridie, jumped to the floor and ran to the children. Rhianne picked him up and held him tight to her chest.

'You cannot shoot Snuff. He has not done anything,' she protested.

Captain Durrant's cheeks were crimson, his glare

murderous at being made to look a fool. He puffed out his chest and strode from the nursery, rapping out, 'Search the other rooms.'

Rhianne giggled. 'Did they think Snuff was a danger to us?'

Senara bit the inside of her mouth to stop herself laughing. She was proud of Rhianne's defiance. 'They have their duty to perform, my dear. Continue your playing, girls. You will have quite a story to tell Joel when he returns for the school holidays. He will be indignant that he missed the chance to defend his sisters against a raid on their nursery.'

For another anguished hour she had to endure the soldiers searching the house and outbuildings. Finally Captain Durrant admitted defeat.

'Your pardon, Mrs Loveday, for doubting your word.' His manner was as insolent as his tone. The high colour to his cheeks warned her that he had not forgotten the incident in the nursery, which had made him look preposterous. His leer roved over her figure, mentally stripping her of her garments. 'Your brother escaped from custody some days ago. If he comes here, it is your duty to hand him over to the authorities.'

'What was his crime, Captain?'

'He stabbed a man without provocation.'

'Without provocation?' she queried, her stare hard and accusing. 'I cannot believe that.'

His expression was malicious. 'Once a gypsy, always a gypsy. You are bound to side with them. I know he is somewhere close by. I shall hunt down and arrest the villain and any who would aid him.'

Senara hated the officer for his callous arrogance and prejudice. Yet she could not defend Caleph by saying that the death of his family, who had been made deliberately homeless, had provoked the attack, without revealing the source of her information.

She remained on tenterhooks until the soldiers rode away from Boscabel. Then she wrapped her arms across her chest, shocked at how violently she was inwardly shaking. She had tried so hard to be brave, but without Adam to protect them she had never felt so vulnerable.

Would the soldiers now leave them in peace? Would Caleph be safe? More importantly, could she allow her daughters to be placed in danger? She would risk much for Caleph, but not that. She instructed Carrie to pack a valise for the girls. They would spend a few days with Gwendolyn at Tor Farm, and the nurserymaid would go with them.

Chapter Thirty-eight

The shrill neigh of a horse and the angry shouts of two drivers arguing over a cartload of turnips that had overturned outside the house woke Tristan with a start. The room was in darkness, the shutters closed against the morning light. He sat up, easing his aching shoulder from the hardness of the floor. Someone had placed a coverlet over him in the night. The fire had burned down, with only a few embers glowing in the grate. A glance in the direction of the chaise longue showed him the outline of a figure under another blanket. He took his hunter out of his waistcoat pocket and saw that it was almost nine in the morning.

He frowned at hearing no activity from any servants within the silent house and rubbed his hand over his chin. The roughness of stubble was already darkening his jaw, and he was also aware that his evening attire of knee breeches and embroidered waistcoat would draw stares to him during the day. Fortunately, his lodgings were not far. Once he had learned the truth from Lady Alys about her extraordinary behaviour last night, he would return to his rooms and change.

He stood up, swallowing against the dryness of his throat, and crossed the room to the decanter to pour himself a drink. His hand froze over the crystal stopper as his stare, now accustomed to the gloom, noted the strangeness of the shape on the chaise longue. With a curse he flung back the cover. Four cushions had been placed along the seat to disguise the fact that Lady Alys had once more escaped him.

How had she achieved that? He was a light sleeper and no sound had disturbed him in the night. Confound the woman! She had again made a fool of him. A hasty search of the kitchen and house showed that he was completely alone. Marie had also fled with her mistress.

He returned to his lodgings thoroughly disgruntled. He had offered to help Lady Alys and she had rejected him. Last night had proved how dangerous were the circles in which she moved. As he shaved, he tried to banish her from his mind. Yet visions of her bravery and skill during the fight still amazed him. However exasperating the woman was, he admired her spirit. It matched the fierce independence that drove him. The beautiful Alys was certainly an enigma. But within that mystery, something was not quite right.

He paused in drawing his razor through the lather on his face and frowned at his reflection, analysing all he knew about her and her family. Brienne was an ardent Royalist, as had been Lady Alys's husband. She had never mentioned how he had died. Tristan's admiration for her had clouded his judgement. He should have recognised the evasion pervading her words and manner. It was after all second nature to him.

He could find no answers to the questions that puzzled him about her actions. His patience was strained to its limits. She did not want his help. She did not trust him as a friend, and she had certainly shown that she did not want him as her lover.

'She's made her own bed and can lie on it.' He wiped the last of the soap from his jaw. His hand was clenched around the handle of the razor, his feelings in turmoil. As much as he wanted to turn his back on her, how could he? Confound the woman! She had got under his skin.

He stared disconsolately at his reflection. If he was honest with himself, despite all her treachery and cold-hearted rejection, he was in love with the minx.

His pride was battered and normally he would feel only anger at another rejection. Strangely, though, she roused emotions far nobler than anything he had felt before. Chivalry was something that happened in romance legends, not real life, or so he considered. His suit might be repugnant to Lady Alys, but he could not allow her to face danger without trying to protect her. If she would not openly accept his help, he would do it secretly.

Senara could only persuade Caleph to stay at Boscabel another day. She would have preferred for him to remain for a week to give his wounds a chance to heal. She was worried that travelling and living rough would cause them to continue to bleed, risking infection that would result in his capture.

She was working in the old hall of the house. With its high-beamed ceiling and minstrels' gallery, it was only used for special occasions. There were several family portraits that had come from Trevowan, which Adam had stated should be placed here but which had not yet been hung on the walls. Senara had thought it would be a pleasant surprise for him on his return. She had selected them by size and was arranging them against each wall for the best effect. Once her decision had been made, she would summon Eli Rudge to hang them for her. She was standing by her favourite group, of Adam and St John as children sitting on the floor playing with models of the ships built in the yard, with their father at a table studying a ship's design and his father behind him. Grandfather George looked particularly stern, and as her gaze settled on his face, she gave an involuntary shudder.

'How fine you are surrounded by these ancient worthies.' Caleph made her start. She had not heard him enter the hall. His eyes had narrowed. 'The last time I was in a chamber as large as this, I was on trial for vagrancy and causing brawling in the street.'

Senara smiled, but was ill at ease that he had left the bedchamber. She trusted their servants but the visits of the soldiers had been unexpected, and he was at greater risk of discovery by the arrival of a neighbour, who would not be so understanding of his presence, or the soldiers returning.

'I know you are going to say I should be in my room, but I cannot bear to be so cooped up.'

'That is a sign that you are feeling stronger.'

Caleph stared around the hall, uncomfortable in his surroundings. He wore breeches and a shirt that were Adam's, but he had tied a coloured kerchief around his neck. He had refused to have his hair trimmed or to shave his thickening beard. It was as though he was flaunting his gypsy heritage. It saddened Senara that after so many years apart and the differences in their lifestyles, they now had little in common.

'It will be dark in a couple of hours. I shall leave then.'

'Where will you go?' she asked.

'Away from England. There is nothing for me here now.'

'You are good with horses. Japhet would find work for you in his stables.'

411

'I have no experience with racehorses.' He regarded her through his thick lashes. 'It's not that I don't appreciate what you'd do for me. But it won't work. I'm not someone who can call any man master, even if he's as lenient and understanding as Japhet Loveday.'

His gaze dropped from hers and his voice was determined. 'I've been thinking of making a new life in America or Canada. I could lose myself in the mountains and make good money trapping for pelts.'

'That is so far away,' she said softly.

'And likely for the best.' He grinned, showing two missing teeth. 'Not that I shall forget my beautiful sister.'

Senara wiped a tear from her eye. It was rare for Caleph to show emotion. 'You could have a good life in Canada. Though I hear the winters are long and it snows for many months.'

'Less people to come nosying round where they aren't wanted.'

'Then you must let me give you the passage money and enough for warm clothes and provisions to last you through the first winter.'

His expression hardened. 'I don't want your charity.'

She was about to protest when Gilly entered the hall at a run, her eyes round with fear. 'That officer be back. He's almost at the door.'

'How many men are with him?' Senara gasped.

'He be alone.'

'You have to hide.' She turned to Caleph. 'He will see you if you try to get back upstairs. Go through the arch and up the steps to the minstrels' gallery.'

As Caleph ran off, Senara ordered Gilly, 'Help me with these portraits as though I am still deciding where to put them. Another maid can admit Captain Durrant.'

'Oh Lord, is he going to arrest us all?' Gilly's voice

quivered with fear and she wrung her hands.

Senara reached for them and held them still. 'No one is going to be arrested, Gilly. As soon as Captain Durrant is announced you will bring us a pot of tea. We must act naturally and show him the normal hospitality. Now hold above your head that portrait of Arthur Loveday and his wife Joan and stand between those two windows.'

'Mrs Loveday be in the old hall.' A maid raised her voice loud enough to warn Senara of a visitor. It was followed by the sound of marching boots. 'Sir, I must ask you to wait here until I announce you.'

'I expect Mrs Loveday already knows I am here. She will have her spies in place.' Captain Durrant strutted into the vaulted room.

'The portrait will do very well there, Gilly.' Senara refused to show her anger at the officer's rudeness. 'Lean it up against the wall now and bring Captain Durrant and myself some tea.' She untied her apron, which protected the velvet of her afternoon gown, and handed it to her servant.

When the captain did not bow to her, she set her back pikestaff stiff, standing between portraits of George and Edward Loveday to remind him into whose house he had intruded. Gilly bobbed a curtsy and hurried out.

'Good day to you, Captain Durrant. Have you come to tell me that you have captured your escaped prisoner?'

'How very droll of you, Mrs Loveday, when you must be aware that your brother is still at large.' The hauteur in his voice was intended to enforce his authority.

For a moment fear coiled through her, transporting her back to her life before her marriage, where a gypsy could be arrested, thrown in the stocks or stoned out of a village for no reason other than that their presence was despised. The ancient grandeur of the old hall proclaimed her present status. She drew a calming breath. She was the wife of Adam Loveday, and her husband's honour was at stake. She refused to rise to the captain's baiting.

When she did not answer, Durrant sneered, 'There are some questions that need answering. This time I will have the truth.'

'Have a care if you would call me a liar, Captain.' Her chin tilted defiantly higher. 'That would be cause for my husband to call you out.'

'So you would encourage duelling to add to abetting a felon. Duelling is prohibited by law.' He stepped closer and she smelt brandy on his breath. 'But then what would a gypsy know of honouring the laws of our land?'

Her eyes narrowed at his insult but she kept her composure. Nevertheless an icy finger slithered down the flesh of her spine. No fires had been lit in the two hearths and the chill of the hall penetrated the velvet of her gown. She suppressed the urge to rub her hands over her arms for warmth. She hoped the lack of heat would hasten Durrant's departure.

Gilly carried in a silver tea service on a tray. 'Mr Rudge be awaiting your orders to hang the paintings, Mrs Loveday.'

'Thank you, Gilly. Captain Durrant will not be staying long.' Senara appreciated the servant's reminder to the officer that they were not without men to protect them.

Gilly retreated to sit on a coffer by the door in order to observe the proprieties so that Senara was not alone in a room with a man. Abruptly Captain Durrant grabbed the servant's arm and bodily hurled her out of the door. Then he slammed it shut and threw the inside bolt.

'How dare you treat my servant in that manner!' Senara raged.

'We will have less of your false airs and graces.' He advanced menacingly towards her. The smell of brandy was stronger and his cheeks were flaring with angry colour, and something far more dangerous.

He ran his tongue over his thin lips. 'How I despise people who rise above their station and presume to believe that they are our equals. You made a fool of me in front of my men. And my commanding officer is threatening to cashier me if I do not recapture the prisoner. I was the officer on duty the day your brother escaped.' The words were slurred. He was more intoxicated than she had first thought.

Senara swallowed painfully, her heart beating a wild tattoo. She did not know if Durrant could be cashiered for losing a prisoner, but certainly his pride was battered and he was looking for a scapegoat. His eyes had darkened with lust and the desire to humiliate her, as he had been humiliated by her brother. She cursed the slender, fashionable lines of her high-waisted gown where she had been unable to conceal a dagger. She never went outside the estate without a weapon for protection. She glanced at a suit of armour standing near the arch leading to the gallery above. A mace was grasped in one steel gauntlet, but it was too far away for her to hope to reach it. With no weapons to hand, she sought to reason with the officer.

'Captain, if you have forgotten your manners, I have not.' She moved to the tray. 'Will you partake of tea and we can discuss this matter in a more amicable manner.'

'I will not be made a fool of by a gypsy wench.' He lunged for her and she grabbed at the hot-water jug by the teapot. 'Where is he? Where is your hellbound brother?'

As her hands closed around the silver pot, his fingers hooked around the neck of her gown, ripping it to her waist. The sight of her bare flesh incensed him further as he forced her back against the wall.

'Get away from me,' she screamed and threw the hot water in his face. The thick walls and stout wooden door of this part of the house would muffle her screams from the servants.

Durrant howled with pain but did not loosen his grip. The water had cooled enough not to scald him but his cheeks had turned a fiery red. 'You'll pay for that, you strumpet.'

A fist slammed into her chin. Pain exploded along her jaw and a cascade of shooting stars erupted through her skull. Dazed, she was forced back over the table, the teapot, crockery and tray clattering on the floor as they were pushed aside. Her instincts for survival gave her the strength to fight on, and she struck out with the jug against his head. Though the soft metal dented, it did not halt what was now a frenzied attack. His hot lips were on her breasts and a hand was jerking up the hem of her petticoats. Her flesh crawled as his fingers pinched her thighs to prise her legs apart. She continued to hit him with the jug, cutting him above the eye, and a blow to his nose splashed blood across the tattered shreds of her chemise. His weight was making it difficult for her to breathe, and the corner of the table digging into her back made her spine feel it was about to snap.

She was struggling to bring her knee up to slam it into his groin when he suddenly went limp, his weight crushing her like a millstone across her body. She wriggled to push him away when suddenly he was hauled from her and slung on to the floor. It took a moment to regain her breath and lever herself off the

416

table. Caleph was kicking at the prone body on the flagstones, swearing and cursing in Romany, the steel mace from the suit of armour hanging from his hand.

'Caleph, stop!' she gasped. The pain in her bruised jaw snatched off her words.

The officer was not moving. A new fear gripped her as she screamed, 'For the love of God, Caleph, stop! He's dead.'

'Bastard deserved to die for what he did to you.' Caleph planted one further kick before flinging the mace across the hall.

Senara knelt and felt for a pulse in Captain Durrant's neck. There was none.

'You've killed him,' she sobbed.

'I've got to get away.' Caleph paced rapidly for some moments, then swung round and grabbed her arms, his eyes wild. 'The body must be hidden. A long way from here, so you're not implicated. I should never have come here. This could ruin you and Adam.'

He stopped, noticing her bruised face for the first time. Tears glittered in his eyes as he gently placed his hands on her cheeks. 'What have I done to you, Senara?'

'You saved me from a brutal monster,' she said softly, and plucked self-consciously at her ruined dress to cover her breasts.

'Mrs Loveday! Mrs Loveday!' Gilly was pounding frantically on the door. 'What's happened? Be you all right? A horse and cart has turned into the drive. It be Parson Loveday and your sister.'

'What are they doing here, of all times?' Senara stared at the corpse and was thrown into confusion.

'I can't involve them in this,' Caleph groaned. 'I'll give myself up. Parson Loveday can turn me over to the authorities.'

He strode to the door and unbolted it, throwing it open. 'Show my sister's guests in here, Gilly.'

Bridie was smiling widely as she entered the hall and threw her arms around Senara. When she felt her shaking she drew back with concern. Her gaze dropped to the torn bodice and then registered the scratches on her sister's breast and the forming bruise on her jaw.

'What on earth has happened?' She voiced her alarm. Then, noticing the other occupant in the room, she spun round, her eyes widening in even greater shock to recognise Caleph. Peter was already striding forward as though to attack their brother.

Senara was shocked by the change in Peter. His face was thinner, his eyes hooded, shielding the world from his pain. He still showed no signs of coming to terms with the death of his son. She hoped that the greater loss that Caleph had suffered would help Peter come to accept that many children did not reach adulthood.

'It was not Caleph who attacked me,' she said quickly. 'He saved me, but . . .' She gestured to the body behind the table. 'He's dead.'

Bridie was looking from her brother to her sister in astonishment, her elfin face switching between joy at their reunion and horror.

Peter had checked the soldier and he was equally stunned. A puddle of blood was forming on the flagstones beneath the officer's head. 'The man's a captain. This is extremely serious. Is that the weapon you used?' He pointed at the mace and shuddered in revulsion. 'No one could survive an attack by that. Could you not have fought him with your fists?'

'Caleph has two recent gunshot wounds. He is in no condition to fight,' Senara explained. She held the torn velvet of her gown together, her fingers trembling violently. 'That knave was intent on raping me. Caleph defended me with the only weapon he could find. Officer or not, in Durrant's eyes I was but a gypsy and therefore deserved no respect or consideration. And do not start praying or giving us a sermon, Peter. I really could not cope with that just now.'

'I intend to hand myself over to the authorities,' Caleph announced.

'They will hang you,' Bridie gasped.

'I will speak for him,' Peter said. 'Once they realise that Senara was in danger . . .'

'But you were not here to witness that,' Senara said heavily. 'They will see a gypsy, an escaped felon – and that is another story of the prejudice Caleph has faced. And a murdered officer of the crown. They will not heed the circumstances. He will be condemned before he even reaches trial.'

Bridie moved to her brother's side, threw her arms around him and burst into tears. 'I know we have seen little of each other, but you have always been my adored big brother. With Michael and Ma gone, I could not bear to lose you as well.'

'Do the servants know what has happened here?' Peter addressed Senara.

'No. Captain Durrant threw Gilly out and bolted the door before he attacked me. He wanted information about where I had hidden Caleph. Twice the house has been searched. He wanted to humiliate me and make me tell him. If only Adam had been here . . .'

'Firstly, the captain's horse needs to be put in the stables, in case anyone else visits unexpectedly.' Peter said. 'I need to think this through. The officer is not going anywhere. Bridie is tired from her journey. We will lock this door and talk elsewhere.'

An hour later, Peter and Bridie had learned all the facts, including Elspeth's rescue of Caleph from the men hunting him with dogs, and the new life Caleph had planned in Canada. Bridie had cried all through the retelling, becoming more upset and also outraged at the way her brother's family had perished.

'If anyone should be brought to trial it is the villagers who burned the wagon and condemned those innocents to freeze to death. Caleph has endured enough. Those lovely children and your wife, how can you bear it?'

Peter had listened quietly throughout, his expression haggard. 'You have more than paid the price that any man should be called upon to suffer. And Durrant was a bully and worse.' His eyes blazed with anger as he regarded Senara. 'Adam would have killed the blackguard himself. We have to dispose of the body and make it look like an accident.'

'You would agree to that?' Senara was startled. 'What of your beliefs?'

Peter's answer was a bleak glare. 'Any laws that allow the deaths of Caleph's children to be disregarded do not deserve to be honoured. Caleph is my brother-in-law and no less a Loveday by marriage than any other member of our family. The officer died because your brother defended my family's honour. I will do everything in my power to prevent a scandal that could destroy us. The only problems I foresee are from the servants. Enquiries will be made when the body is found. If it is known that Durrant was here, their evidence could be our undoing.'

'They will be outraged that I was attacked. They will not betray us.' Senara had no doubt of their loyalty.

'I leave them to you.' Peter nodded. 'It will be dark soon. I will take Durrant and his horse to the cliff path along from Fowey. If the body is rolled over the edge, it will explain his wounds. It will look either as if he was attacked by smugglers or as though his horse stumbled and he fell.'

'We will do this together,' insisted Caleph. 'We still risk running into danger. If we are discovered with the body, you must hand me over to the authorities and thus save yourself. I will say that Durrant tried to capture me and I killed him, then turned myself over to you. They will believe a man of God innocent of such a heinous crime.'

Chapter Thirty-nine

Adam searched the streets around the marketplace where they had seen Osgood. There had been further rain and the roads had turned into shallow streams, the central runnel providing little drainage. Ragged men laid boards over the water and charged pedestrians a fee to cross and save their finery. Adam was protected from the worst of the weather by his top boots and caped greatcoat. This grey and bleak Paris was very different from the one he remembered when as a youth he had visited his mother's family during early summer. His wanderings took him past the old house where his aunt, uncle and two cousins had lived. They were all dead now, his cousins killed when their incestuous relationship was discovered. They were not memories Adam wanted to dwell upon. There had been too many scandals and deaths in their family. Not least the latest one concerning Tristan. He shoved that recollection to the back of his mind. He needed to forget that Tristan was in Paris. He and Japhet were here to deal with Osgood and nothing else.

After hours of searching, there was no further sign of Osgood. Even the discreet enquiries he and Japhet had made had yielded no information. If too many questions were asked in English circles about a man with a scarred cheek, there was the chance that it would get back to Osgood, which could prompt him to leave the city. Adam was angry with himself for losing Osgood's trail earlier in the week, and that pushed him to search late into the night in both the rich and poor districts. The rain had stopped in the afternoon, but as dusk approached, a mist had arisen, obscuring the distant buildings and causing the smoke from the chimneys to thicken the air and lie like clouds over the rooftops. As the shadows lengthened and the air became colder, the crowds thinned, people returning to the warmth of their homes before preparing to attend the entertainments of the evening.

It was then that he turned a corner and almost collided with a group of men and women. Amongst them, fortunately with his back to them, Tristan held their attention as he related some audacious scandal. Having failed to locate Osgood, Adam decided that he would follow Tristan and discover what trickery he was involved in. He had no doubt that his cousin was up to no good. He watched his nemesis say farewell to his companions and stride away.

He did not risk getting too close in his pursuit. If Tristan suspected that he was being observed, he would disappear faster than Adam could ever hope to catch him.

They zigzagged through the streets for some considerable time. As it grew darker, the lamplighters were at work. The streets were poorly lit at night by a central oil lamp on a chain or rope stretched from one side of the road to the other. The lamplighter lowered the chain, trimmed the wick of the lamp and lit it before hoisting it back to swing above the height of a passing coach. Although the middle of the road was lit, the shadows closer to the houses were dark. It made it harder to follow

Tristan. Finally his cousin stepped into a blackened doorway.

Adam hid in the entrance to an unlit alleyway. As far as he could make out, Tristan was keeping watch on one of the houses further along the street. He did not take much notice when a young man in a cloak and brimmed hat stepped into the street and strolled away from them, but he was surprised when Tristan followed him. Again he set off in pursuit.

They did not walk far. The young man entered another house and both cousins drew back into the shadows, continuing their surveillance. Within minutes two other men had arrived, one from the opposite direction in a carriage, and one on foot. Moments later another carriage approached and stopped directly opposite Adam, waiting until the first vehicle pulled away.

As a precaution he drew further back into the shadows so that the lantern hanging on the front of the coach did not reveal his hiding place. The occupant leaned forward in his seat, shouting an angry command to the driver. The lantern cast a yellow light on a scarred cheek.

Adam stifled a gasp. Unmistakably it was Japhet's old adversary. Osgood also entered the house, and later one other man joined them. Tristan had kept hidden throughout the arrivals. When he made no move to enter the house, Adam wondered whom his cousin was spying upon. There would be no point in questioning him, as Tristan would tell him to go to the Devil and it could endanger Japhet's quest to expose Osgood as a French spy.

Realising that the longer he remained here, the greater chance there was that Tristan might detect his presence, Adam decided that it was time to report back to Japhet. Since the street was unusually deserted, he would need to wait until some diversion presented itself, or Tristan departed. That would be the better option, for then Adam could continue his hunt to discover his cousin's lodgings.

Without warning he suddenly found an arm locked around his neck and the cold pressure of steel against his throat.

'Why have you been following me since this afternoon?' The voice of his cousin halted Adam's first instinct to elbow his attacker in the ribs.

'Because I suspected that you were up to no good,' Adam snarled. He should have known that with Tristan's guttersnipe childhood he would have been aware that he was being followed. His freedom from arrest as a pickpocket in those days had depended on his instincts for survival.

'All the more reason why I should stop you interfering in my affairs, Cousin.' The last word was spat out with contempt.

'Then you would have to answer to me!' Adam could not believe that he was hearing Japhet's voice from immediately behind Tristan. 'What is your connection to Osgood, Tris?'

'Who?' The word was thrown out like a challenge, the blade still pressed into Adam's flesh.

Adam brought up his elbow to attack, but it was halted when Japhet demanded, 'Lower your weapon, Tris; I will remove mine from your ribs. Or we could brawl in the street like children, which is somewhat undignified at our age.'

The pressure of the dagger against Adam's throat was lessened, and with a bad-tempered shove, Tristan pushed Adam out of the shadows. He immediately spun round, his own dagger now in his hand.

The three cousins regarded each other warily. Adam

was angry that Tristan had cornered him so easily and that Japhet had witnessed the incident. It made him snap as he glared at his accomplice. 'How came you to be here?'

'I was following Osgood,' Japhet responded without his usual warmth. 'You, it seems, had other fish to fry.'

'Who *is* Osgood?' Tristan bristled.

'None of your damned business.' Adam was ready for a fight to prove that it had been a stroke of luck that Tristan had earlier managed to get the upper hand.

'It is if it has anything to do with what is occurring in that house.' Tristan ignored Adam and confronted Japhet.

'We have to talk.' Japhet shot a warning glare at Adam. They all froze when movement and several voices carried to them from further down the street. It was followed by a shout of drunken antagonism. Japhet added, 'Clearly this is not the place to loiter.'

'I am not going anywhere with you at this time.' Tristan brought up his dagger, ready to attack the first of his cousins who moved.

The door to the house opened, and the Loveday men blended back into the darkness as Osgood and a slim man stepped out.

'My coach will be here at any minute. Are you sure I cannot offer you a ride?' Osgood asked without much enthusiasm.

The answer could not be heard. Another man joined them, and while Osgood remained outside the doorway, the others walked away together. Tristan started after them but Adam put a restraining hand on his arm.

'You will reveal our hiding place,' he whispered.

'Do you think that concerns me?' Tristan twisted his arm to free it, but Adam's grip held tight.

Two more men left the house and went in the same

direction as the first two. Tristan appeared to relax, and then a carriage drew up and the cousins moved further back to avoid the light from its lantern revealing their faces. Osgood stepped inside the vehicle, the driver clicked his tongue and the horses set off.

'Shall we follow him?' Adam said.

Japhet shook his head. 'I've discovered his lair.'

Tristan had been watching the four figures walk down the street and turn a corner together. The others would give Alys the protection she needed to return to her lodgings, which were only two streets away. The drunken voices in the other direction were also now further away from them.

'So where do we talk?' he enquired. Satisfied as to Alys's safety, he was intrigued to know why his cousins were in Paris.

Adam and Tristan sat opposite each other in a tavern, their bodies as tense as bull–baiting terriers straining for an opening attack. Japhet watched them warily, ready to intercede at the first sign of trouble.

'Let us first agree to keep cool heads,' Japhet said. 'These are difficult enough circumstances without old quarrels complicating matters. Our family pride them-selves on our loyalty first and foremost to each other.'

'There was precious little of that shown to me in the past.' Tristan's antagonism whiplashed across the table.

'And we were proved to be wrong.' Japhet held up a hand in a conciliatory gesture. 'For whatever reasons, we were all interested in what happened in that house tonight. Anything concerning Osgood has to be underhand.'

'And am I allowed to know who this Osgood fellow is?' Tristan glared at his cousins.

Japhet fixed him with a forthright stare. 'Sir Pettigrew Osgood's lies and false evidence were behind my transportation. When it was apparent I was about to be pardoned, he bribed the guards to drug me and I was put on a convict ship about to sail to Australia.'

Tristan let out a harsh breath. 'Reason enough for you to hate him and want revenge, but what has that got to do with the meeting held in the house, or your interest in his movements?'

Adam reluctantly enlightened him. 'Osgood was recently at the court of Louis XVIII, and we have since learned that he sends information to Fouché.' He was watching Tristan closely and saw the tightening of his jaw at this last information. 'He is devious enough to work for both the Royalist and Republican causes to secure riches and power for himself.'

'A spy in both camps?' Tristan looked shaken. 'Do you know anything about his companions?'

'I recognised no one.' Japhet was the first to respond.

'Neither did I,' said Adam.

'However, Osgood is not to be trusted,' Japhet warned. 'Especially with Bonaparte amassing ships in the Channel ports. He plans to invade England. The truce will not last much longer. It does not bode well for any Britons remaining in France if war again breaks out.'

'What was your interest in the meeting?' Adam challenged Tristan.

'I was concerned that a friend was involved. But their sympathies have been for a return to the monarchy.'

'Which could mean that they are in danger if Osgood is Fouché's spy.' Japhet clicked his fingers and ordered tankards of wine for them all.

'Then we kill Osgood,' Tristan said in a voice just loud enough to reach his cousins. He had kept a steady gaze on the door of the inn, his sharp eyes observing any newcomers.

'If I had wanted Osgood dead, I could have killed him any time this last year.' Japhet broke off as the barmaid placed the wine in front of them.

Her glance was bold and inviting as she appraised the three handsome customers. 'Just you let me know if there is anything I can do for you. Anything at all.'

Japhet winked at her. 'We will bear that in mind, mademoiselle. But first we have business to discuss.'

Her smile faded as she regarded him. 'You are not French, monsieur. You sound like the English dogs who come to see whether the citizens of France prosper or no.'

Japhet did not allow his own smile to falter; he had been careless in that his French was not as fluent as that of Adam or Tristan. 'Mademoiselle is mistaken. I am from Alsace. Our dialect is very different from Paris. Sometimes it is not easy for me to be understood. Your pardon, mademoiselle. It wounds me deeply that a beautiful Parisienne does not understand me. I am but a country imbecile.'

'I could help you to improve your language, monsieur.' She giggled. 'Perhaps I could also teach you so much more . . . though you look very much a man of the world. I too can be a willing pupil.'

Japhet's smile was one of his most disarming. 'Such an offer is hard to refuse. Perhaps later.' He shrugged and looked regretful. 'But for now I must attend to less pleasurable business.'

An angry shout from the landlord ordered the tavern wench to attend upon another group of customers across the room. Reluctantly and with an enticing sway of her hips she left them.

'That could have ended badly,' murmured Japhet. 'I must take more care.'

'Your French is not that bad for a country imbecile.' Adam made light of the incident.

Tristan was staring into his tankard. 'If this Osgood is a traitor, he should die. Or did Newgate and our penal colony break your spirit, Cousin?'

'He will pay the price of his treachery,' Japhet returned. 'But first I would see him disgraced.'

'You have not told us the name of your friend or what you know of this meeting.' Adam pursued his own interrogation.

Tristan sat back in his chair, his expression blank and uncommunicative.

'He's not going to tell us,' Adam snapped. 'So much for trust. For all we know he's working for Osgood and was a lookout for him.'

'I am no traitor.' Tristan shot forward and made a grab for Adam's stock. Both men stood up, fists bunched ready for attack.

Japhet also rose and put a hand on their shoulders. 'It is not wise to draw attention to ourselves, even in a run-down tavern such as this. Sit down and settle your feathers. You two are worse than fighting cocks.'

Adam remained standing until Tristan was seated, then he sat with his head turned away from him.

Japhet sighed. 'If Osgood is involved with those men at the meeting, your friend could be in danger, Tristan. Any trumped-up charge could have an Englishman mouldering in the Temple prison, and if war breaks out there will no release. They could be shot as spies. Shall we not call a truce?'

'It would be betraying a confidence if I told you the identity of the one I know. I am not prepared to do that.'

Tristan stood up and nodded to Adam and Japhet. 'I do thank you for the warning, but I cannot accept your help. I wish you well in bringing Osgood to justice.'

'We could achieve more if we worked together,' Japhet reasoned.

There was a flash of anger in Tristan's eyes. 'I have no reason to trust you and I have always worked alone. I cannot betray my friend.' He inclined his head in the barest of bows and strode through the taproom and out into the street.

'I said he could not be trusted.' Adam looked ready to go after his cousin. 'We gave him more information than he gave us.'

Japhet slowly drained his tankard. 'There is more to this than Tristan is saying, but I do not think it has anything to do with treachery. Wednesday is two days away. We have our own plans to finalise.'

Chapter Forty

'Why are they taking so long? Do you think they could have been discovered and arrested?' Bridie fretted. She had chewed on her nails until one began to bleed. 'Peter and Caleph left three hours ago.'

'These things take time. The ride is a circuitous one to the coastal path, where a battered body found on the beach could look like a riding accident.' Despite her reasoning Senara kept pacing to the window, straining to hear if the men had returned. She also dreaded another visit from soldiers either still looking for Caleph or searching for Captain Durrant.

Worry was making her jump at every creak, which were so common in this old house. To calm her nerves she diverted the conversation from their fears.

'Fortune smiled on us that you arrived when you did,' she said. 'Peter was wonderful to take charge. I never thought he liked Caleph.'

'He is our brother and therefore family, is he not?' Bridie defended.

Senara bit back her comment that Peter was the most conventional of the Loveday men and a stickler for law and order. Again she changed the subject. 'How long can you stay? I suppose you have to return to Launceston before Sunday?'

'It depends upon Peter's plans.' Bridie was unusually evasive.

'When I think at how hard Ma's life was bringing us up, we have been very fortunate. It is hard to take in how cruelly Caleph has suffered.' She squeezed Bridie's hand. 'And it has not been easy this last year for you.'

Bridie sighed. 'I have a devoted husband, and many women are not so blessed.'

'Yet something seems to be troubling Peter.'

'Peter has lost his faith,' Bridie unexpectedly blurted out. 'He has resigned his living at Launceston. He came here to discuss his future with his father.'

The news shocked Senara. 'But he has always been so devout.'

'And because of that he has missed out on the adventures that he so envied his brother and cousins for.' Bridie held her sister's gaze, seeking reassurance. 'He feels his piety was in vain. That God has forsaken him.'

'But has he not always said that true faith survives the tests we have to overcome?' Senara hid her alarm, suspecting that there was something more disturbing that Bridie had yet to tell her.

Her sister looked down and pleated the folds of her sombre black gown. 'Losing Michael is not a sacrifice he can accept. That is why I need to ask you a favour.' There was a pause while she seemed to gather strength, then she continued abruptly, 'Would Adam allow me to live here with you?'

'He would welcome you with open arms. You and Peter.' Senara felt her heart grow leaden when her sister continued to evade her searching gaze.

There was another long pause that increased the sense

of fear that was now chilling Senara's body. Bridie cleared her throat, her voice quivering. 'If he is to regain his faith, Peter needs to experience the adventures that have governed his ancestors' lives. Only when he discovers his true self – not the man he has shaped himself to be – will he find peace. It is slowly choking him to curb the wilder side of his nature, especially as he seeks to come to terms with our loss.'

Senara was stunned into silence. She had thought that Peter's piety was unshakeable and that he had a true vocation to save souls.

With a brave face, Bridie continued. 'I want him to be unhindered by the responsibilities of recent years and to experience the exploration and self-discovery that the other men in his family have undergone.'

'But what of you?' Senara knew that Bridie was making a great sacrifice for her husband. 'Peter adores you, and you him.'

'It is because I love him so much that I want to give him this chance.'

'I thought you were happy in Launceston. You had plans to set up an orphanage and a school.'

'I have never liked towns,' Bridie said with feeling. 'I did not fit in. The authorities did not want another school and considered that the workhouse provided for the town's orphans.'

She absently rubbed her leg. The specially built-up boot gave her a less pronounced limp, but she was still conscious of it. As a child she had been jeered at and reviled as a freak by the crueller children. Scars like that never quite healed. 'I missed my friends from Polruggan, and seeing the family regularly.'

'I had not realised that it had been so difficult for you.' Senara felt she had let her sister down by not being more observant. She had assumed that a new beginning in Launceston would be just what the couple needed. Her intuition rarely failed her, but concern for her sister had been overshadowed by her own grief at Leah's death and worry at how difficult Adam had found it to cope with the loss of his twin and the usurpation of Trevowan by Tristan.

Bridie shrugged. 'I had hoped that Launceston would provide Peter with what he needed. I would have found a role for myself in time.'

Her sister's selflessness did not surprise Senara. 'Would you return to teaching at the shipyard school?'

'I could not take the work away from the new teacher, just because I am family.'

'He only comes two mornings a week and rides in from Fowey. He is stern and the children do not like him. They adored you. Adam would have replaced him but he was the only applicant who came forward. We would be delighted if you wished to resume your work in the school.'

Bridie nodded. Her hands gripped tightly together and a tear appeared on her lashes. 'If it is possible, I would like that very much.'

With one problem settled, there was still much that troubled Senara. 'Has Peter made any plans about his future? Do you know how long he will be away? Not that it will make any difference; you will have a home here for as long as you need.'

'He wants to go abroad. He says that if the Lord wishes him to regain his faith and return to his service, he will provide an answer.'

Senara could not stop an amused laugh. 'Then I would say that he has not lost his faith completely.' She sobered. 'From a youth he only ever wanted to serve God. Japhet survived his transportation and prospered because he had learned carpentry skills in the shipyard and often helped on Hannah's farm when his sister's husband became ill. Peter spent his time preaching to any who would listen to him.'

'He is willing to try anything,' Bridie defended. 'If Tristan managed to do so well for himself, Peter can also make his way in the world.'

The success Tristan had achieved from such impoverished beginnings must have been a further reminder of all Peter could have accomplished had he chosen a less devout path. 'I suspect Tristan's way was not always within the law.'

'Neither was Japhet's or St John's; he was involved with smugglers,' Bridie protested indignantly. 'Even Adam has resorted to privateering, and was not their great-grandfather little better than a pirate who married an heiress to secure his position and fortune?'

'I do not judge Peter.' Senara held up her hands in supplication. 'With Caleph in hiding from the authorities, I am the last person to consider that our family has always upheld the law. I am concerned for Peter's safety. He has no capital to fund a venture, and he has such high principles it will make it harder for him.'

Bridie locked stares with her sister, her tone proud and resolved. 'That is what he needs to prove to himself. His ability to succeed against the odds. It is his Loveday pride. Tonight has shown that he is willing to take on new challenges and defy convention.'

Senara could not argue with that, and she knew Adam's family would agree.

The sound of men's voices outside drew both women to the window. Caleph jumped down from the back of Peter's horse. He had ridden out on Durrant's gelding, with the officer over his legs. That horse would have been left at the site of the supposed accident. When he staggered, Senara gasped. He was clearly exhausted from their journey, his wounds not yet healed.

Rudge appeared carrying a lantern and led the horse away. When the light fell upon the two men, Senara saw Peter pat Caleph on the back, a mark of his respect and the success of their mission. Despite the seriousness of their task, he appeared in good spirits. Bridie was right. Peter was not so very different from his brother and cousins. Adventure was in his blood.

Japhet and Adam took turns standing guard outside Osgood's lodgings, hoping to find evidence that would condemn him to the British government as a spy for France. Adam was the one to follow him when he left his rooms late on Tuesday afternoon. He trailed him to the Louvre, the old palace, which displayed many great works of art. It was a popular attraction amongst the visitors to Paris. Though today, with many of the British visitors having left the capital, it was less crowded than usual. Osgood was acting extremely furtively, his nervous glances darting over the crowds. From the conversations he overheard around him, Adam also had cause for concern. Much of the talk was about a break in the treaty with Britain and speculation as to whether England was to be invaded. There was much muttering and bravado about giving the British a taste of their own medicine and destroying their fleet. It made Paris a more dangerous place to be in. If they were to get the information they needed against Osgood, they had to act quickly.

Sir Pettigrew strolled slowly through the main galleries, pausing briefly to observe a painting or sculpture. It was not long before a tall, elegantly dressed man approached him and they stepped away from the main exhibitions to a quiet corner. With a start, Adam recognised Brienne from their encounter in the ballroom, the man who had mistaken either him or Japhet for Tristan. Was therefore Tristan by association with Brienne in league with Osgood? What treachery were they planning?

He edged closer to overhear their conversation, but he was also careful not to risk discovery.

From his more commanding manner, Brienne was leading the discussion and giving Osgood instructions that did not seem to please the younger man. Brienne was not only used to giving orders; there was a set to his face and a hardness to his eyes, that would make him a formidable adversary. Although Adam was disguised by a week's growth of beard and a battered deep-brimmed hat low over his eyes, there were too few people in the gallery for him to get close enough to catch their words. It added to his frustration. He could not risk being recognised by Osgood.

He curbed his impatience, and when the two men parted, his instinct was to follow Brienne. He was certain that he was the one who was behind any plot Osgood was involved in. To bring Osgood to justice, he needed to discover all he could about the baronet's accomplices. If tomorrow was the day the conspirators would put their plan into action, he was running out of time.

Tristan was pacing the lower reception room of the house Lord Brienne had rented. Outside, he could hear a crowd cheering for Bonaparte and chanting against the British. The mood of the people was becoming more volatile by the day. He glanced out of the window and saw a crowd gathering on the next corner. His lordship had been expected to return some time ago, and Tristan grew more anxious with every passing minute. When Brienne finally entered the front room, he had been staring gloomily out into the street, his mind so locked into his fear for Alys that he had not seen her guardian enter the house.

He turned from the window, the fading afternoon light falling upon Brienne.

'Loveday.' The terse greeting held no warmth.

'It is fortunate that you are in Paris,' Tristan announced without preamble. 'Your niece is in danger. You must order her to stop whatever madness she is engaged in.'

'Lady Alys is not your concern, especially since you deserted her when I trusted you to escort her during her stay in France.' Brienne's contempt flayed him.

'There was a misunderstanding between us, but none of that is important.' Tristan swallowed his impulse to retaliate at the slur upon his honour. 'Your niece has been going to meetings dressed as a man. I believe that she is involved in some Royalist plot that is to take place tomorrow somewhere near St Cloud.' In his agitation Tristan paced back and forth across the window. 'One of her associates could well be working for Fouché.'

'You know the names of these conspirators?' Brienne challenged. 'Who are they?'

'I know only of Osgood. A man with a treacherous past. That is all I have been able to ascertain. Lady Alys will not listen to me. You have to stop her.'

'You have been poking your nose into affairs that do not concern you. If you refer to Sir Pettigrew Osgood, he has his own suspicions about your loyalty. Your family are not to be trusted.'

The ice in Brienne's voice brought Tristan to a halt. A shiver touched his spine, alerting him to danger. It was an instinct that had saved his life on many occasions in the past. When he turned, he found himself looking into the barrel of a pistol pointed at his heart.

'Lady Alys is not for you, or any man,' Brienne continued. 'Tomorrow she will clear the name of her husband, who failed in his duty. He was to assassinate Bonaparte and was shot by one of his associates when he took the coward's path and refused to act as instructed.'

'You were one of those conspirators,' Tristan recalled. The conversation he had overheard between his lordship and Veronne was now making sense. 'You killed her husband.' As the realisation dawned, a deeper dread chilled his blood. 'You intend that Lady Alys will die. Why? To inherit her estate yourself?'

'It is prize enough, and this way no implication can be laid against me.'

'Do you care nothing for her?'

'Not her. Not her husband. And not her parents. Nor anyone else who stands in my way.'

Further questions froze in Tristan's throat. Brienne's finger was tightening upon the trigger.

Every survival instinct kicked in, and he dived aside as the shot was fired. His hand sought the dagger hidden in his top boot, but he found his fingers would not work. The bullet had rendered his arm useless.

At the same moment, a pane of glass shattered in the window next to him and a large stone hit Brienne in the chest. Pain scoured through Tristan's shoulder as he fell to the floor and rolled towards his opponent, kicking upwards with his legs to catch his lordship in the groin.

Even as he doubled over, Brienne slammed the barrel of the pistol into the side of Tristan's head. He fell back, stunned, vaguely aware that the casement window was being pushed up. Then his vision was filled with the sight of the pistol butt about to slam into his head, a blow that could kill him. He had landed heavily on his wounded shoulder, and his strength failed him as he tried to roll away. Was this how it was to end?

The next he knew was the weight of Brienne's body falling across his legs, a dagger embedded in the centre of his rib cage. Expecting to be the next victim, Tristan kicked the body away and found himself staring into Adam Loveday's hostile face as he was hauled to his feet. He broke free of his cousin's hold, his mind in a chaotic spin. He could not believe Adam had saved him. It was more likely he was in league with Brienne to destroy him. Yet even that made no sense.

He shook his head to clear his wits. Brienne was groaning and clutching at the dagger. It was not a wound any man would survive. Adam calmly retrieved the weapon, his expression unreadable as it flickered over Tristan.

There was a babble of French voices outside the door from the servants drawn to the noise. Adam turned the key in the lock.

'I hope you have the strength to run,' he snapped. 'The shot will have them calling the constables.'

'You are the last person I thought to help me.'

Adam shrugged, making for the window. 'Don't flatter yourself it was for any reason other than to learn how you are connected with this man and Osgood. What treachery are they involved in?'

Tristan followed Adam as he climbed out of the window. 'You have killed the man who could tell you.'

The volume of the chanting had increased in the street, but fortunately it had masked the sounds of the gunshot and breaking glass. The crowd was still some distance from the house as the cousins fled in the opposite direction. Pain shot through Tristan at every step and he was forced to cradle his wounded arm. When he staggered, Adam grabbed his other arm, pushing him to a faster pace.

As they both laboured for breath, Adam ground out, 'You had better have some answers after all the trouble I've gone to.'

'Papa accepts that I should do whatever I think is right at this time. Mama is naturally upset at my plans,' Peter informed the sisters when he had returned from the rectory after his meeting with his father.

'Have you decided where you will go?' Bridie asked, remarkably composed at the drastic change that was about to occur in her life.

'Not exactly. It may depend upon which ship I can obtain passage on.'

'Has it really come to this, Peter?' Senara hid her own upset for the sake of her sister. 'Did speaking with Caleph not help you to accept what has happened?'

She had been surprised at how long the two men had been closeted together before Peter left for the rectory. One of Caleph's wounds had opened last night and he had lost a great deal of blood, which had left him weak. She had gone to his room with a restorative posset and heard the two of them talking. She had not entered, as her brother, who was normally reticent with others, was speaking rapidly, though the words were indistinct. When she had returned an hour later, it was Peter who appeared to be confiding in Caleph.

'Your brother is a brave man, and I respect how he copes with the burdens that life has dealt him,' Peter replied. He had spent another two hours with Caleph this morning before visiting the rectory, and now looked more relaxed than he had in months.

Senara returned to her fears that her brother was a hunted man. 'I was wondering if you would consider allowing Caleph to accompany you out of the county,' she asked. 'Mayhap he could pose as your servant. The authorities will not have given up their search for him.'

Peter studied her reflectively. 'He is impatient to be on his way. It could be a week or more before Adam and Japhet return. He will not place you in further danger.'

'I am willing to take that risk,' she said firmly. 'At least talk to him, persuade him to stay until his wounds heal. He will respect your advice.'

Peter nodded. 'I will speak with him. He is still too weak to travel for a few days.'

Senara bit her lip as Peter left them. The energy wilted from Bridie's body. After all she had recently lost, it would be hard for her to live without Peter in the months ahead, and to accept that she might never see Caleph again.

'You are the brave one, Bridie, for allowing Peter his freedom to pursue his goal.'

'I am no different from the hundreds of wives whose men are in service in the army and navy and are away for sometimes years at a time.'

'I admire your resilience.' Senara smiled.

Bridie shook her head dismissively. 'I shall not be lonely living here and will have plenty to occupy my time, especially if I can teach again.'

Another hour passed, and to their surprise Peter came down the stairs accompanied by Caleph. For a moment Senara did not recognise her brother. He had shaved and Gilly had cut his hair, and he was dressed in Adam's clothes.

'You look quite the gentleman, dear brother,' Senara laughed.

Caleph raised his callused, work-worn hands. 'Until anyone looks at these.'

'You certainly look stronger,' Bridie added, her smile wide. 'But please tell us that you will remain with us a few more days.'

'We have a great deal more to tell you than that.' Caleph shifted his weight uncomfortably.

Peter stepped forward. 'We are to journey abroad together. If Caleph is still being hunted, they will not suspect two gentleman travelling together. There is much I can learn from Caleph about surviving in the larger world.'

'And it will do me no harm to better my manners and make more of my life.'

Senara felt her throat cramp with emotion. Her eyes were bright with tears of pride when she finally managed to find her voice. 'Ma would be proud of you.'

'Just don't expect me to give up all my Romany ways. Though I will try to lead a more lawful way of life.'

Bridie clasped her hands together, her voice rich with pride. 'Ma will be smiling down on you from heaven. To have both the men I love so dearly sharing this new adventure . . . It means a great deal to me.'

As Senara watched her brother and her brother-in-law exchange a smile, she pondered silently. They might make odd companions with their diverse backgrounds – Peter and his prim reserve that had been a part of his piety, and Caleph with his lack of concern for any authority – yet it could be the making of both of them. Each had a great deal they could offer the other, and she and her sister would rest easier knowing that they were together.

Chapter Forty-one

The mood in the Paris streets was one of menace. Whilst some of the citizens were quiet, their faces grey with worry, others were eager for the war to commence.

'Death to the English dogs!'

'Vengeance upon our defeat in Egypt!'

'We will invade and conquer our enemies!'

Shouts followed Adam and Tristan's progress. They were now two streets away from where Brienne had been killed and there was no sign that they were being pursued. They slowed to a walk.

Adam's face was set in harsh lines. 'I saved your worthless hide because you have information of benefit to Japhet. No more lies, or I finish off what Brienne started.'

'You also have information that I need.' Tristan grimaced. He was breathing heavily, every step sending explosions of pain through his upper body. 'There is no time to waste.'

There was a part of Adam that did not understand why he had saved Tristan. He could not believe that the Loveday code of loyalty was so deeply ingrained in him that he would rescue the man responsible for St John's ruin.

Yet he had acted instinctively when he had seen his

cousin's life threatened after following Brienne back to his residence. His initial surprise at seeing Tristan through the window of the house had drawn him closer to the building; the raised voices within had been easy to discern. From the meeting of Osgood and Brienne in the Louvre it had been obvious that the men were plotting something. He had followed Brienne hoping to discover more evidence that Japhet could bring against Osgood. He had no idea who the Lady Alys was they had referred to. By his replies, Brienne had shown himself to be a cold-blooded killer. What game was fate playing that it should also involve Tristan, who had uncovered a link between Osgood and someone he knew?

Tristan's pace had slowed by the time they reached the inn where Adam and Japhet were staying. It would be dark within the hour. Japhet was in the taproom talking to an agitated man.

'This is Dr Davies.' Japhet introduced the man to Adam, not yet noticing Tristan, who had taken a seat at a nearby table. 'He is concerned at the mood in the city. His wife is eager to leave. Their coach was attacked this afternoon, the wheels broken and the horses run off. They barely escaped with their lives. Mrs Davies is upstairs, having taken a sedative for her nerves.'

'I would advise you to leave as soon as you can,' Adam responded. 'We were also attacked, my cousin was wounded. The French ports may no longer be safe.'

Dr Davies glanced in Tristan's direction and saw the blood seeping through his jacket, where the bullet hole was also visible. He moved closer and shifted the candle on the table. 'I am a physician, sir. Permit me, but you appear to have been shot.'

Tristan nodded. 'It may not be wise to tend me here. There are many curious glances this way.'

'There is a private room through the back.' Japhet ordered a bottle of brandy to be brought to them, his glance anxious upon Adam. 'What happened?' he whispered.

Tristan had stumbled into a chair and Dr Davies was examining the wound.

Adam dragged his fingers through his hair. 'I followed a man who had met with Osgood. Tristan was waiting for him at his house. They quarrelled; from what I heard of the conversation, the man, Brienne, was linked with Osgood's treachery. When he pulled a pistol on Tristan, intending to kill him, I acted instinctively.' Adam shook his head, unhappy at the events. 'I cannot believe it myself except that I killed the man.'

'The bullet has to be removed,' Dr Davies informed them. 'I'll fetch my bag from upstairs. I will need your assistance to hold him down.'

Tristan grabbed his arm. 'I cannot be laid low at this time. A friend's life is in danger. They must be warned.'

'If I do not remove that bullet, you will be the one to die,' Davies snapped as he left the room, frowning at Japhet as he passed. 'Mr Loveday will warn your friend.'

Tristan rose unsteadily. 'I cannot be operated on at this time.'

Japhet rounded on him. 'You heard what Davies said.'

'If we are to convict Osgood, we cannot afford to delay,' Adam stated. 'Paris is a powder keg about to explode. The ill feeling against the British is growing, being stirred up by fanatics.'

'If Osgood is a traitor, I have to save Lady Alys.' Tristan swayed, his face contorted with pain at the effort it took to stay upright.

'You're in no condition to do anything,' Japhet snapped.

Adam scowled at Tristan. 'Who is Lady Alys? Brienne also mentioned her. Is she involved in an assassination plot with Osgood?'

When Tristan hesitated to answer, Japhet gritted out, 'We have to trust each other if we are to succeed and get out of France alive.'

'Why should I trust you?'

Adam closed the gap between them, thrusting his face close to Tristan's. 'For all I know, you are involved with Osgood to destroy Japhet.'

'I have no quarrel with Japhet.' Tristan scowled. 'This has nothing to do with our family. Your suspicions prove that I would be foolish to trust you.'

'Do you have a choice?' Japhet glared at Tristan.

Their estranged cousin was deathly pale from loss of blood. For the moment he was no danger to either of them.

'Dammit, man, I just saved your life,' Adam flared. 'Though the devil knows why.'

Tristan rallied, pushing himself up from the chair as though he would attack Adam. Japhet put his hand on his shoulder and gently eased him back on to the seat. His tone was short tempered and exasperated as he counselled, 'We have to put our differences aside. Let us call a truce at least until we finish what we came here for.'

'Very well,' Tristan agreed. 'What choice have I? I am no use to Lady Alys like this. She is determined to clear her late husband's name. Brienne has tricked her.' He glared at Adam. 'He intends for her to die so that he can inherit her estate.'

'But how is Osgood mixed up with all this?' Japhet demanded. 'It seems too much of a coincidence.'

'Or it is fate,' Adam said with a shrug. 'Senara has always said that if you want something badly enough you can create your own destiny. We also have to be prepared to pay the price when what we desire has its own repercussions. I would say fate is mocking us for our pride in seeking retribution.'

Dr Davies returned and put his bag on the table. As he laid out his instruments, Tristan stared at Japhet.

'Should this operation not go well for me, do I have your word that you will do everything in your power to save Lady Alys?'

'You know who my quarrel is with.' Japhet was not prepared to say more in front of the physician. 'I would deem it my duty to save any woman who finds herself in danger from another's treachery.'

'Do I have your word also, Adam?' It cost Tristan dear to humble himself to the cousin who still hated him. 'Do we have a truce until this is over?'

'If we can save this woman, then we will.' The death of Brienne did not sit happily with Adam. Despite what he had seen and overheard, he only had Tristan's word that his lordship had been involved with Osgood's treachery. And nothing yet had convinced him that he could trust Tristan. He stepped close to his cousin, his voice too low to reach the doctor.

'I may have saved your worthless hide, but if you had been killed whilst it was known that Japhet and I were in Paris at the same time, we would have been suspected of your death. You have already caused enough scandal to our family. Any more and we will be shunned by society. I was not prepared to take that risk.'

The doctor sweated for half an hour to remove the shot. Tristan had finally passed out. Dr Davies stood back and tossed the bullet into the fire.

'It was deeper than I hoped. Your cousin will not be fit to ride tomorrow, or for some days to come. He has lost a great deal of blood.'

'Neither is it safe for him to remain in Paris, or yourself and your wife, Dr Davies,' Adam informed him.

Japhet nodded. 'There is a way you can escape.' He grinned as he looked at Adam. 'The message we have been awaiting arrived an hour ago.'

'How can I get my wife safely away?' Dr Davies interrupted impatiently.

'A friend of ours has arranged for a fishing boat to be in a cove five miles from Calais tomorrow night,' Japhet answered. 'I will give you the details later. You should leave the city tonight in a hired chaise. Take Tristan with you. We will join you tomorrow at the coast.'

'Tristan will not agree,' said Adam.

'In his state he has no choice.'

Lady Alys was too nervous to sleep. She had never believed that her husband had been capable of cowardice. The plot to kill Napoleon had been discovered. Someone had betrayed them. In her grief she had been eager to clear his name. She had adored Marcus and her life was empty and meaningless without him. She did not care if she gave her life to save his reputation. Now it was not so simple. She had become embroiled in the plot and could not in honour back down. She saw now that she had been manipulated by her uncle as Marcus had been in the past. Brienne was obsessed with his quest to regain the estate in Brienne, Normandy, from which the family had fled in the early days of the revolution. He and her father had been ardent Royalists, their lands confiscated after the death of the king. The guillotine awaited them if they returned to France during the Terror. Although

Napoleon had not been responsible for the hideous crimes against the aristocratic families, Brienne regarded him as the devil usurper who prevented their land being returned to them.

Lady Alys did not feel the same passion for the property in France. Her mother had been English and much of her childhood had been spent on their estate in Wiltshire. Even then the house had been falling into ruin, and her father had been on the point of selling it when the troubles started in France. In the following years it had become a haven from the turmoil of the unrest.

Unable to sleep, she was already dressed. Being disguised as a man gave her greater ease of movement, and she knew she was a match for most men in a fight. Her mind continued to race in turmoil. New emotions vied with the old. Nothing must set her from her course. Yet why had her heart played her so false and allowed her to believe that she could love another? That life held a better future?

She felt guilty at the lies and deceit she had used against Tristan. Especially after the attack in the alleyway when she had feigned tiredness, then, as soon as he was asleep, fled the house. It was not surprising that he had thought the worst of her in recent weeks; she had betrayed his trust. But duty had given her no choice but to turn her back on her growing affection for this dashing and complex man.

There was a tap on her door and a maid entered, bobbing a nervous curtsy. 'There is a gentleman downstairs, my lady. He said it was urgent. You are to leave at once.'

So this was it. It was too late to change her mind now. To do so would further dishonour her husband's name.

She had expected to find a messenger waiting for her.

When she discovered the identity of her visitor was Noir, she was filled with unease. This man, of all the conspirators, was the one she trusted least. It had been planned that they would meet up at an inn on the St Cloud road. Their lodgings and identities were not supposed to be known to each other, to avoid betrayal if one of them was arrested. Her every instinct screamed that this did not feel right. She should back out. She swallowed her panic. She was letting her nerves get the better of her. This was the most dangerous mission she had undertaken since she had been working secretly for the British government. Her associates trusted that she was capable of succeeding. She would not fail them. She would not fail Marcus.

'There has been a change of plan,' stated Noir.

'How did you learn where I was staying?'

'Do you really think I would not know where we all lodged in case of just such an emergency? We will meet the others on the road. This could be our only chance to bring down the tyrant. The mood of the city is dangerous. We will not return to Paris after our work is done. Nor can we risk taking ship from Calais. A vessel will be waiting for us five miles down the coast.'

When she hesitated, Noir drew his pistol. 'Would you desert us, like your husband? I will shoot you before I allow that to happen.'

'I am with you.' She pushed aside her niggling doubts. Noir had been the most scathing in his doubts of her capability. She would show him that she was no novice at espionage. She followed him to the livery stables where they had hired mounts for the day.

They rode in silence through the city and out on to the road to St Cloud. The moment had come for which she had waited for years. She was more scared than she was prepared to admit, her heart racing in time with the horses' pounding hooves. Too much was at stake for her to back down. She had been prepared to give her life to redeem Marcus's honour. How easy that had seemed six months ago, when she had felt that she had no future. Then she had thought her heart was forever dead. Fate had been cruel to give her a glimpse of the happiness that could have been hers in the years ahead. Yet how could she break her vow?

To keep her mind focused on what lay ahead, she kept running through the plans for the morning. Her word had been given. Her decision made. There was no room for regret.

They were riding along a deserted patch of road lined on either side with trees when unexpectedly Noir slowed his pace, calling out, 'Stop! My horse has pulled up lame.' He jumped to the ground and bent to examine his mount's front leg.

Alys circled her mare and came back. 'We should have met the others by now. Where are they?'

'There is plenty of time,' Noir said, his head bent over the hoof. 'I need help here.'

Tutting with frustration at the delay, Alys dismounted and looped her reins over a bush before going to assist Noir.

'There is nothing in the hoof,' she began. The words were cut off as Noir elbowed her in the throat. The impact knocked her to the ground, and as she gasped for air, her angry outburst choked in her windpipe. Before she realised what was happening, Noir had flung a looped cord around her ankles and jerked it tight, binding her feet together. Then he grabbed her thrashing arm and bent it up behind her back.

'Have you lost your mind?' she forced out from her

bruised throat, gripped by terror as she hit out with her free hand. That also was caught and wrenched backwards. As she wriggled to fight free, pain shot through her shoulders, the bite of the rope rubbing the flesh from her wrists.

Her hat had fallen off and she angrily shook her hair out of her eyes, scattering more of the pins so that curls tumbled around her shoulders. She screamed a torrent of curses at him until a neckerchief forced into her mouth and tied behind her head stifled the words. Her eyes blazed their fury at him as he propped her up, helpless now, against the base of a tree by the roadside.

Without a word of explanation Noir returned to the horses and led them out of sight of the road. She heard him return and sit down in the undergrowth some distance to the right of her. Outrage exploded through her and she squirmed and shook her body to break the ties that trussed her. All that her efforts achieved was to exhaust her. The rope held.

The cruel laugh from Noir was humiliating. 'You cannot escape. Depending on how eager your rescuers are to save you, we could be here until noon.'

What new treachery was this? Why was Noir using her as a hostage? Another laugh froze her blood. 'Neither will your band of conspirators help you. They were told that the cavalcade we were expecting from St Cloud has gone instead to rally Napoleon's troops. Our little Corsican usurper is planning his invasion to bring our country to heel. You are the bait for a very different vendetta.'

Alys glared her contempt at her captor. She should have listened to Tristan. She had been wrong about him. He had tried to protect her and she had thrown his help back in his face. Confound her stupid pride! Her muscles cramped from discomfort, her attempts to wrest the rope from her wrists searing the raw flesh. Her throat was sucked dry of saliva by the gag and her tongue felt too large for her mouth. The frantic pounding of her heart was making her light headed, and she fought to calm her breathing, dreading that she would swoon.

Noir had raised a hand and she heard movements in the undergrowth each side of her. Others had approached and he was gesturing for them to spread out. If Bonaparte was not riding to the capital, who were they lying in ambush for?

Chapter Forty-two

Alys heard horses approaching at speed from Paris. Then she saw a group of riders, their lower faces hidden by mufflers. The two leaders must have seen her, for their horses halted.

Noir stepped into the road, his pistol pointed at her head. 'Gentlemen, you are expected.' Behind them were the clicks of other guns being cocked ready to fire.

The tallest of the riders pulled down his muffler, revealing a swarthy complexion. 'Osgood, still involved in your usual treachery, I see.'

Alys scanned the riders, searching for Tristan. He was not amongst them. Disappointment swamped her. She suspected that Noir had betrayed the other conspirators, and now it was her turn. Yet why had be brought her out here? Whatever his plans, she did not expect to survive. Her only hope had been that Tristan would somehow manage to save her. That now looked impossible.

'Drop your weapons,' Noir demanded. 'Or the woman dies. Two Lovedays in one net. That is better than I expected. These men work for the Ministry of Police. You are under arrest as British spies.'

Japhet raised a dark brow, showing no fear at the

threat. 'Then Fouché will be interested in the information we have on yourself, Osgood.'

'You always think you are so clever. So superior,' Osgood sneered. The hand holding the pistol shook as his temper erupted. 'I knew you would never let matters rest between us. I have had seven years to plan my triumph. I even fooled Kilmarthen. For years he has been sniffing round, putting a man to spy on me.' He laughed maliciously. 'How well that served my purpose.'

Japhet folded his hands over the pommel of his saddle. None of his companions had made a move to relinquish their weapons. With apparent nonchalance he studied his old adversary.

'So this is the knave Osgood.' Adam eyed him with disdain. 'The man who gave you the opportunity to make your fortune, Cousin. I trust you intend to show him your appreciation.'

'Your arrogance will soon be crushed after a few weeks of questioning in the Temple.' Osgood's spittle sprayed the air in his fury, his face and neck staining red. 'Only a fool hides in fear. I knew that when you returned from Australia I would be a hunted man. In England you would always have the advantage of when and where you would strike. I was not going to wait for that to happen. I set this trap and you walked blindly into it. And you have nothing to incriminate me; only what I have chosen to give you. The pedlar was a ruse to draw you out. You fell for it so easily, it was laughable.'

Japhet grinned, incensing Osgood further. He reminded himself that his next words would wipe that smile from his enemy's face. 'I laid a trail for Kilmarthen to lure you to France. I played along with some petty Royalists and was handsomely rewarded by Fouché for the information about their plans to kill Bonaparte and claim the throne for King Louis. I have been given lands in France far exceeding my English estate. Here I shall be heralded as a hero.'

'And in England you are despised as a coward and a traitor,' Japhet spat.

Osgood pointed the pistol at the woman's head, his chuckle demonic. 'All the cards are in my hand, Loveday. You will not escape me this time. Arrest them, men! If they resist, kill them.'

Nothing happened. Japhet continued to grin at Osgood.

'Arrest them, I say,' Osgood shouted. His stare turned incredulous as he stared at his men, his jaw growing slack and the colour draining from his face. From behind a tree a short man stepped forward.

Alys's heart leapt with hope as she recognised the agent Long Tom, whom she had worked with several times in the past.

'Kilmarthen! Damn your eyes!' spluttered Osgood.

'Stand back from the woman,' the short man ordered, his pistol trained on him.

Amongst the other men who now had pistols aimed at Osgood were those Alys had known only as Vert, Blanc and Bleu.

Long Tom added, 'When you seek to deceive, beware the deceiver. These were my men you recruited. They will each give evidence that you plotted with them to rid Britain of its aggressor, intending to betray them to the French for reward. Stand aside from Lady Alys, Osgood, or I will shoot you for the traitor you are.'

He nodded to one of them to release Lady Alys.

'Throw away your weapons or she dies.' Osgood kept his pistol aimed at the woman's head, his stare darting from the Loveday cousins to Sir Gregory Kilmarthen.

'Bring my horse and we will both ride out of here. Do not follow and I will release her three miles down the road.' His finger began to twitch on the trigger.

'Kill her and how will you defend yourself?' Japhet scoffed. 'There are too many of us. You will face trial in England for your treachery.'

As he spoke, Japhet saw the woman slowly draw up her knees. Osgood licked his lips, sweating as he fixed his stare on the man he had vowed to destroy. The woman kicked out with astonishing speed, her boots slamming behind Osgood's knees. The pistol fired at the moment she rolled away. A volley of return shots from Long Tom's agents spattered Osgood's body. The bullet from Long Tom's smoking weapon had gone through his treacherous heart.

'So die all traitors. With war imminent I could not risk returning him to England for trial,' Sir Gregory declared. Drawing a dagger, he sliced through the cords around Lady Alys's wrists and ankles, then helped her to her feet and bowed. 'My lady, I commend your bravery in attempting to clear your husband's name. You were right: Brienne did kill him, and when he learned of Osgood's part in this conspiracy, he planned for him to kill you.'

'Lady Alys is one of your agents?' Adam was astounded.

'For many years. Unbeknown to Brienne, she worked closely with her husband, another British agent. She could not allow his death to go unavenged. She would have assassinated Bonaparte had it not been for Osgood's interference.'

Alys brushed the dirt from her breeches, enquiring, 'But I thought my uncle would have been involved here today?'

'He would have been had not Mr Tristan Loveday discovered his treachery. Brienne is dead.'

Her eyes widened in alarm as she regarded Japhet and Adam. 'You are Tristan's kin, are you not? The likeness is unmistakable. But where is Tristan?'

'He is on his way to the coast, recovering from being shot by Lord Brienne,' Japhet informed her. 'It was not easy to persuade him to leave. He would have risked bleeding to death to save you today. We gave him our word that we would protect you, my lady.'

'But he told me that you hated him.'

'Fate conspired that we were all in Paris at this time,' Adam replied. 'Whatever rivalry there is within the Loveday kin, we put that aside for the greater good. We stand strong through our loyalty.'

Long Tom had retrieved Lady Alys's hat and bowed as he handed it to her. 'We have a long ride, my lady, to make the coast by nightfall. Fouché's agents with whom Osgood was working have also been eliminated, but we cannot be sure that others are not also on our trail. I suggest we make all speed.'

It felt like the longest day of Tristan's life as he waited on the beach with Dr Davies and his wife. Still unconscious, he had been unaware of the first stage of the journey, when they had left the inn in the middle of the night. The rough jolting of the coach had sent arrows of pain through his body, slowly drawing him back to reality. When his eyes had finally opened, there was a glint of dawn through the window blinds and from the bitter taste in his mouth he guessed he had been given a potion to ensure that he slept.

He lifted the blinds to discover where he was. The landscape was unfamiliar and a gentle hand was laid on his arm, a man leaning forward.

'I am Dr Davies. We were at the inn with your cousins.

I took a round shot from your shoulder. It just missed your lung or you would be dead. We will rejoin your cousins at the coast. This is my wife.'

As Tristan's wits cleared, he remembered the doctor. Then the rest of yesterday's events flooded back.

'I have to return to Paris,' he groaned. 'A friend is in danger. I have to save her.'

'You are in no fit state to save anyone. Your own life still lies in the balance if you lose more blood. Your cousins said they will do as you asked them. Now rest.'

'I must go back. I have no reason to trust my cousins,' he protested. As he pushed himself upright, a wave of dizziness assaulted his senses.

'Your cousins struck me as honourable men. Did one not save your life?'

Tristan resented being reminded of the incident. 'Did they plan to have me abducted?'

Mrs Davies laughed softly. 'They had only your welfare at heart. Paris is no place for an Englishman at this time. We were lucky to escape without molestation. It seems we are again on the brink of war. Mr Loveday very generously hired this coach and gave us instructions as to where a vessel will be waiting to carry us to England. We agreed that we would tend you on the journey. There was a time after your operation when we feared you would die.'

'How far are we from Paris?' Tristan intended to stop at the first ostlery and hire a horse to return.

'We have been travelling all night,' Dr Davies curtly informed him. 'We are closer to the coast than the French capital. You will need all your strength for the crossing, which we have been warned could be perilous if we are attacked by the French. Take my advice and rest.'

Tristan closed his eyes. 'Inform me when we are at an

inn where I can hire a horse. I have to return to Paris.' He had no intention of sleeping, but his body was weaker than his resolve and the swaying of the coach lulled him into a deep sleep. When next he awoke it was past noon and too late for him to do anything to save Lady Alys. He cursed his stupidity at being taken in by Brienne and then being shot. If Lady Alys was harmed in any way, his cousins would pay dearly for their interference.

He next woke to angry shouts and the loud thud of a stone striking the coach. Mrs Davies was sobbing with terror.

'Be calm, my dear,' her husband encouraged. 'We must not let them suspect that we are English. The driver has been paid handsomely not to stop. We are nearly at the coast and it will soon be dark.'

'Where are my weapons?' Tristan demanded. 'I had a pistol and a dagger.' He reached down and found the dagger still concealed in his boot.

'The pistol was put under the seat for safety,' the doctor advised. 'I have another of my own. I pray we will not need them.'

They left the shouting behind them, and fortunately there were no more attacks upon the vehicle. An hour later the coach stopped at a small cove. When they had alighted, the driver set off back the way they had come.

'Will he alert the locals that we are here?' Tristan was suspicious.

The doctor said, 'He is English but has lived most of his life in France. He is in the pay of a friend of your cousins.'

That did not reassure Tristan as they climbed down the shallow cliffs to the beach. Out to sea were several large sailing craft. Tristan hoped that they were merchantmen and not warships. It seemed that very rapidly the clouds of war were gathering and no traveller, especially a foreigner, was safe in this land.

The doctor and his wife carried only a small carpet bag, which held few possessions. At Tristan's quizzing glance, Dr Davies explained, 'We were told to do nothing to rouse suspicion that we were fleeing the country. There is some bread, cheese and cold meat to eat if you are hungry, and a bottle of wine.'

Tristan waved aside their offerings, his stomach too tight to eat. He thought briefly of the expensive furniture stored in the Paris warehouse. He doubted that would now reach its destination. He would sacrifice it easily. It was just money, and he had won and lost more than one fortune in his lifetime. What he could not accept was the danger that Lady Alys must be facing without him there to help her. Would his cousins be true to their word? Surely no amount of hatred they felt for him would stop them rescuing a woman in danger?

He was no longer dizzy or light headed, and as he slowly paced the beach he could feel his strength returning. The sun was low on the horizon. How much longer would it be before he knew whether Lady Alys had survived?

Every bone in Lady Alys's body was aching when she finally smelt the tang of the sea in the air. The sun was slithering to sleep on the horizon when they brought their mounts to a halt. She needed all her strength to support her weary legs as she swung down from the saddle. As she strained her eyes to make out figures on the beach below them, she could discern only boulders.

Her heart contracted with fear. What if Tristan had not survived? Japhet had told her that he was severely wounded. How could she live with that? She was the one who had brought him into danger. She had witnessed the charged mood of the people as they sped through small villages and hamlets. If France was again at war with England, then word had spread faster than a summer heath fire. Although her mission here was accomplished, she had failed in her goal to complete Marcus's work and assassinate Bonaparte. The rest of her plotting, however, had been a success. Brienne had admitted that he had killed her husband and parents, and was now dead himself.

She had first met Long Tom in the early days of her marriage, when the Terror in France was at its height. Marcus had then been working to restore Louis and Marie-Antoinette to the throne. No one had thought that their king and queen would be beheaded. Brienne had become a constant companion to her father and husband, and it was only after their deaths that she had begun to suspect that he was not the loyal Royalist supporter they had believed. Long Tom had also voiced his doubts to her, and she had eagerly striven to bring the murderer of her loved ones to account. Her assignment for Long Tom was to set up a ring of conspirators, all English agents like herself, to trap the man who had been betraying her countrymen as French spies. Noir, or Sir Pettigrew Osgood, had paid the price for his treachery.

That she had been used by Long Tom to incriminate the man who had also been an enemy of Tristan's cousin was something she had not known until Adam and Japhet had rescued her. That she had fallen in love with Tristan had been another unexpected event, and the fact that the three cousins who had played such a dramatic part in her life were at odds with each other was equally puzzling. Fate had been capricious in bringing them all together. But had it smiled on Tristan now?

★

Tristan watched the sun disappear below the horizon and sank his head into his hands in despair. If Lady Alys and his cousins had survived, they would have been here long before now.

A touch on his shoulder made him start violently. He had heard no sound of approach, but suddenly he was engulfed in the scent of Alys's hair and the warm pressure of her body.

'I feared you were dead,' she sobbed. 'How you must hate me!'

He was too overwhelmed to speak as her lips locked upon his. Through a haze of swirling senses he heard Japhet's distinctive chuckle.

'We'll leave those two to become reacquainted.'

The voices became indistinct as his cousins joined the doctor and his wife and spoke of the hazards of their journey to the coast.

'I have so much to tell you, and I must ask your forgiveness.' Lady Alys broke away from his embrace. She took his hand and led him away from their companions, where their speech would not be overheard.

In the small hours of the morning, a covered lantern out to sea briefly revealed its light. The group waiting on the beach were fortunate that the sea fog had held off tonight. Dr and Mrs Davies were sitting on a boulder, Mrs Davies asleep with her head against her husband's shoulder. Tristan sat on another boulder, his arm in a sling and still weak from loss of blood, whilst Lady Alys fussed beside him. Tristan, Adam and Long Tom stood by the water's edge, listening for the splash of oars from the longboat.

'A satisfactory conclusion, was it not?' Long Tom

observed. 'Do you regret not being the one to kill Osgood, Japhet?'

'I regret he will not face trial.'

'But the government will learn of his treachery.'

'Ay,' Japhet replied. 'Perhaps it is for the best. A trial and public outcry would have brought out all his crimes, including how he treated me. That would upset Gwendolyn. She has endured enough scandal at my conduct in the past. It is time I proved to her that I have reformed.'

'And what of your vendetta, Adam?' Long Tom challenged. 'Have you buried your hatred for your cousin? You saved his life.'

'I have not forgiven him for St John's death, or ever shall. Saving his life settled my debt to him; building *Good Fortune* for him prevented the shipyard from facing ruin.'

The crackle of dried seaweed underfoot drew the three men's attention. Tristan was walking slowly towards them, Lady Alys at his side. From their set features, both had heard Adam's words.

Tristan bowed to his cousins. 'I do not expect your forgiveness, Adam. But I hope that in time we can live civilly as neighbours. If for nothing else but to preserve family honour.'

'We can choose our friends and companions, but not our kin—' Adam began.

Lady Alys cut in. 'That is true. But for tonight at least let there be harmony. I did not thank you properly for saving my life.' She smiled at Adam and Japhet. 'And having just accepted Tristan's proposal of marriage, I am proud to be part of a brave and honourable family. I hope that in time if you do not choose us as friends we shall at least be good neighbours.'

Japhet bowed to her and taking her hand raised it to

his lips. 'I cannot dispute such wisdom from so beautiful a woman.'

Adam also bowed to her. He would not argue that any family would be favoured by the grace and courage of this woman. 'Welcome to our family, Lady Alys. But do not expect too much from us. Apart from loyalty, the Lovedays also thrive on rivalry.'

'I suppose that is as near as we shall come for the time to enjoying a truce,' Tristan remarked with irony. He bowed mockingly. 'It is reassuring to learn that when adversity strikes we are united.' He led his betrothed to the water's edge, where a longboat was beaching.

'And what of your future, Japhet? Are you ready to settle down?' Long Tom taunted.

Japhet rolled his aching shoulders and moved his head from side to side to ease its stiffness. 'I am getting too old for these madcap adventures. I owe it to my wife to fulfil my promise on our marriage to put my reprobate ways behind me. And in a few months Emir Hassan's foals will be born. The racing game will be exciting enough to occupy me in my middle years.'

'And you, Adam?' Long Tom grinned up at him. 'You have more responsibilities at home since your twin's death. Will this be your last service to your country?'

'I never say never. But it will not be long before my family will be ready to spread their wings. I doubt our wild blood has been much diluted by a generation. Rowena will soon be of an age when the beaux will come flocking to court her. I have a notion my hair will turn white keeping that young madam in line. Nathan is already showing an interest in the yard, but Joel . . .' He sighed. 'There the apple has not fallen far from the tree planted by our great-grandfather. Heaven help us all trying to keep that young scapegrace out of trouble. I think he will be best served joining the navy as a midshipman in the next year. That will bring some discipline to calm his wildness.'

'And there is your ward,' Long Tom persisted. 'What of Bryn? His background is still a mystery. Will he choose the sea or a profession?'

'That will be his choice. His memory will return one day. Who knows what can of worms that could open? But whatever his background, we will be there to support him.'

Japhet laughed and slapped Adam on the back as they stepped into the longboat. He winked at Long Tom. 'I would not be too ready to turn us into decrepit grey-beards. There's an adventure or three left in this generation yet. And with a war about to break out again between England and France, when did a Loveday ever fail to heed a call to arms?'

The Loveday Revenge

Kate Tremayne

Revenge

Ne'er-do-well Tristan Loveday's return to his ancestral home in Cornwall sends shockwaves through the close-knit Loveday family. Tristan holds the key to secrets that could destroy everything the Lovedays hold dear and he's got a deadly score to settle. But with who?

Revelations

Senara Loveday, trusted wife of Adam, the family's charismatic head, would never betray her husband. But she fears a shadow from her past could bring about her downfall. Unless he overcomes his demons, Adam's brother St John risks losing all he owns. And in London, Georganna Loveday must conceal the evidence of a terrible sin.

Redemption?

As the lies unravel, so too do the Lovedays' lives. No one will escape the savage revelations, but can anyone survive them . . . ?

Acclaim for Kate Tremayne's novels:

'A fast-moving and exciting read . . . Leaves the reader breathless' *Historical Novels Review*

'This sweeping saga has the lot: colour, intensity and pace' *Northern Echo*

978 0 7553 3353 0

headline

Now you can buy any of these other bestselling
books by **Kate Tremayne** from your bookshop
or *direct from her publisher*.

FREE P&P AND UK DELIVERY
(Overseas and Ireland £3.50 per book)

Adam Loveday	£7.99
The Loveday Fortunes	£6.99
The Loveday Trials	£8.99
The Loveday Scandals	£6.99
The Loveday Honour	£5.99
The Loveday Pride	£5.99
The Loveday Loyalty	£5.99
The Loveday Revenge	£6.99
The Loveday Secrets	£6.99

TO ORDER SIMPLY CALL THIS NUMBER

01235 400 414

or visit our website: www.headline.co.uk

Prices and availability subject to change without notice.